NEVER SAW YOU COMING

S.L. SCOTT

S.L. SCOTT

ISBN: 979-8-9878634-0-4

*Visit my website for warnings. Please note this page contains spoilers.

FOLLOW ME

To keep up to date with her writing and more, visit S.L. Scott's website: **www.slscottauthor.com**

To receive the newsletter about all of her publishing adventures, free books, giveaways, steals and more:

https://geni.us/intheknow

Follow me on TikTok: https://geni.us/SLTikTok
Follow on IG: https://geni.us/IGSLS
Follow on Bookbub: https://geni.us/SLScottBB

ALSO BY S.L. SCOTT

To keep up to date with her writing and more, visit her website: www.slscottauthor.com

To receive the scoop about all of her publishing adventures, free books, giveaways, steals and more:

Visit www.slscottauthor.com

Join S.L.'s Facebook group here: S.L. Scott Books

Read the Bestselling Book that's been called **"The Most Romantic Book Ever"** by readers and have them raving. We Were Once is now available and FREE in Kindle Unlimited.

We Were Once

You do not want to miss the international sensation, **Best I Ever Had.** This book has won readers over with its emotion and soul deep love. **Best I Ever Had** is now available in ebook, audio, and paperback, and is Free in Kindle Unlimited.

Best I Ever Had

Audiobooks on Audible - CLICK HERE

The Westcott Family Series (Stand-alones)

Swear on My Life

Never Saw You Coming

Noah Westcott's Book

Marina Westcott's Book

The Everest Brothers (Stand-Alones)

Everest - Ethan Everest

Bad Reputation - Hutton Everest

Force of Nature - Bennett Everest

The Everest Brothers Box Set

Hard to Resist Series (Stand-Alones)

The Resistance

The Reckoning

The Redemption

The Revolution

The Rebellion

The Crow Brothers (Stand-Alones)

Spark

Tulsa

Rivers

Ridge

The Crow Brothers Box Set

DARE - A Rock Star Hero (Stand-Alone)

New York Love Stories (Stand-Alones)

Never Got Over You

The One I Want

Crazy in Love

Head Over Feels

It Started with a Kiss

The Kingwood Series

SAVAGE

SAVIOR

SACRED

FINDING SOLACE

The Kingwood Series Box Set

Playboy in Paradise Series

Falling for the Playboy

Redeeming the Playboy

Loving the Playboy

Playboy in Paradise Box Set

Talk to Me Duet (Stand-Alones)

Sweet Talk

Dirty Talk

Stand-Alone Books

Best I Ever Had

We Were Once

Along Came Charlie

Missing Grace

Finding Solace

Until I Met You

Drunk on Love

A Prior Engagement

Lost in Translation

Sleeping with Mr. Sexy

Morning Glory

NEVER SAW YOU COMING

1

Lochlan Westcott

I HATE TUESDAY.

More specifically, Tuesday afternoons are the worst.

We're past Monday, not quite to midweek, and nowhere close to the weekend. I've never liked Tuesdays, and today is no exception.

"I laid the facts out in black and white. A delay granted at the last minute is utterly ludicrous." As if it can relieve the frustration congested in my chest, I grip the phone tighter ready to crush it.

"It's a setback, Loch," my dad says, "not the end."

I didn't bother calling my driver, Brady, and telling him to bring the car around. I called my dad as soon as I pushed through the courthouse doors instead, choosing to walk back to the office. I had no choice since he'd been messaging me for the past hour, wanting to know the outcome of the case. Walking toward the offices with my briefcase in one hand and the phone in the other, I press it to my ear like my dad does.

Fuck.

My younger brother's right. Noah called it last Christmas; I *am* turning into our father. Who holds their phone to their ear anymore? Dad. That's who. But currently, finding an earbud is the least of my problems.

"The judge is open to an appeal, but there are stipulations—" I say.

"You know this before the case has been decided?" I tense from the suspicion infiltrating his tone, making me wonder if I've fucked up.

I'm secure in every part of my life, except when it comes to getting my dad's approval. "I know the judge . . . *well.*"

There's a distinctive pause, one that sucks the air out of the conversation entirely.

Fuck.

"How well?" my dad asks. I hear the question he's really asking without saying a word. He's one of the East Coast's most sought-after corporate litigation attorneys. I was never able to slip one by him—not as a kid or even a grown fucking man running the Manhattan branch of the family law firm.

"Well enough," I reply, hoping to move this to a different topic than the woman who threatened to rule in the plaintiff's favor simply because I forgot—*read that as on purpose*—to call her for a second date.

I had good reason.

First, showing up at my apartment unannounced and without an invite with nothing but a gavel under her robe (don't ask where she had tucked it) and trying to seduce me by repeatedly calling me bailiff didn't work in Judy's favor.

And yes, she insisted I call her Judge Judy. That was another big no from me.

As she tugged at the front of my towel to loosen it, I

thought of the woman waiting in my bed for me to return. I'm certain she wouldn't have appreciated me inviting a guest to join us. Though maybe it was a missed opportunity.

Not wanting her to fuck me over, non-sexually speaking, on my next case she's presiding over, I tried to play nice. . . As nice as I could, considering the uncomfortable and precarious situation. I told her my docket was full, but I'd slot into her next opening I had.

Judge Judy loves dirty talk.

What can I say? I'm not into role-play, but I'll do it to save my ass in court.

"What are the stipulations?" He asks exactly what I preferred he not.

"She's stringing this along to keep me front and center. The judge has . . ." I can't believe I'm discussing this with my dad. "She has fantasies I refuse to fulfill."

A grumble travels across the line and then a sigh. I'm sure he's rubbing his temples and shaking his head. "The trouble you boys cause . . ." He doesn't bother finishing. Among Harbor, Noah, and myself, we were called everything from the three musketeers to little troublemaking shits. We make our sister, the baby of the bunch, look like an angel. She's not perfect, but we don't snitch on our siblings.

In this case, though, I reply, "Can't help that we got our old man's looks."

"Nice try, kid."

"It was worth a shot."

"I have to admit," he starts with a chuckle underlying the tone he's trying so hard to hide, "that not only have I never had a case dependent on if I would go on a date but I also never found myself at the judge's mercy. I'm not getting into your sex life, but if it continues to affect the firm, we'll need to put some rules in place. That's not something I've ever had to discuss with Smith." There's a good reason he would never have to discuss that with Smith, but let's just say, at least Smith is a good attorney.

"This needs to get wrapped up," he adds.

"There's no denying the facts. My client—"

"*My* client," he corrects. "All clients of Westcott Law are ultimately mine and should be represented as such."

I stop on the sidewalk, more annoyed than before. Not wanting to get into this with him right now, I take a deep breath and continue like I wasn't interrupted, "The Reinhold Group holds the patents and copyrights, and filed everything two years before the defendant's brand existed. We shouldn't even be in court. It's a settled case already."

"The plaintiff claims they found a loophole. It holds no weight from what I've read."

"They're stalling since they have no evidence to back it up."

What a fucking mess.

"If you're not back on the docket for tomorrow, you need to find out what's going on. We shouldn't be playing games in court when the facts support our side. Wrap this disaster up, Loch. Make the Reinholds happy, and let's move on."

After realizing I'm still blocking others in the middle of the sidewalk, I start walking again. "I will."

"I know you can get a favorable outcome. You always do, but don't sleep on this, Loch. Time is money, and we have millions on the line, so close this case."

Sleep?

What's that?

Getting sleep is foreign to me these days. I should be accustomed to the endless hours at the office with the weekly rotation through the courthouse, but I'm not. I'm exhausted. That's not something I voice, not ever. I won't risk losing the trust he's placed in me.

I've done everything I can to prove my dad *can* count on me, but here I am, still working round the clock like I started yesterday. I don't consider myself a perfectionist, but I have tendencies. It comes with the territory of expectation —what I expect of myself and the weight of expectation from my family.

"I'll button up the case." Aiming for the coffee shop on the corner, I reply, "I won't let you down."

I'm about to hang up when he adds, "You never do, son."

I pause because emotions don't win cases. Evidence wins the case. Nobody forced me into the family business, but I headed straight for law school as if my path was determined long before I was born. Maybe it was.

Feels like it.

"Thanks, Dad."

Pulling the phone away from my ear, I disconnect and shove it into my pocket, knowing my plans are shot for the night. I'll be drinking caffeine instead of whiskey. Eating something delivered instead of keeping a reservation I booked more than three months ago.

The worst of it is that I'll be buried in files tonight instead of my date.

I OPEN the door to the coffee shop, discovering I'm not the only one in need of caffeine this afternoon. I take a spot at the back of the line and pull up the schedule app, once again reminded that I need to cancel my date with . . . *Christine.*

Fuck. Christine's always a good time.

I type: *My apologies, but I need to postpone dinner to another time. Court ran late, and things didn't go as planned. I have a mountain of work ahead of me. Rain check?*

I move with the line, noticing a blonde at the front of it. You'd think she was explaining the plot of a murder mystery instead of placing a coffee order by how she swung her hands around. She's definitely what I like to call a hand talker, or someone who can't carry on a conversation without looking like they're competing in a mime competition. From this vantage point, it's hard to tell if she's upset, demanding, or just expressive. All I know is the line's not moving because of her, and I don't have time to wait for Miss Handsy to get her point across.

"Is it so hard to place a coffee order?" I grumble under my breath.

My chest rises with a deep inhale. I'm working on my patience since I seemed to have been born without that trait. At least that's what my family says. I don't blame them. As the eldest of four, my shoulders bore the brunt of responsibility and leadership; typical eldest sibling syndrome, I suppose.

That's when she says, "I don't have time for this . . ." My thoughts on my growing impatience drown out the rest.

Join the damn club. If she doesn't hurry this up, I'll be forced to leave without that coffee, and I can't be held accountable for what I say or do without caffeine.

Dropping my gaze back to my phone, I start going through emails. I delegate three and reply to one before I reach the front of the line and place my order. *Finally.* Moving out of the way, I wait along with the others, who look as needy as I am for their afternoon fix.

The crowd thins as orders are called out, eventually

leaving Miss Handsy and me standing front and center at the end of the coffee bar.

Lovely . . .

Of course, that doesn't explain why I'm still standing here when my order—a basic Kona bean double espresso with the slightest hit of coconut milk—hasn't been called out.

I check the time, then look up at the counter. The line has started to build again, but the baristas have been running to fill orders, so the delay is not from a lack of effort.

"What is taking so long?" Her voice matches the cadence of her tapping foot. Both echo off the concrete floors, leading me to her impressive heels. My gaze slides up, noticing her even more impressive shapely legs. That's when I look up and see the woman who the world apparently revolves around . . . at least in her own mind.

Great face.

Sexy body.

Full lips that I could definitely keep busy.

She might be animated when she speaks, but the blonde is hot in an uptight, Upper East Side kind of way. Her hair is pulled tight to the back of her head and tucked neatly in a round knot. Not a strand is out of place. Red lips, just a hint of color to her cheeks, and eye makeup on the more subtle side make her blue eyes brighter despite the dim lighting of the coffee bar.

"Sure is taking a long time. You must have a very complex order."

"Me?" I balk from the mere suggestion that I'm the problem and move my eyes forward, mentally willing my coffee to appear on that counter in front of me. *Now.* But I'm intrigued by her enough to give her a second glance. *Naturally.*

Women have always been a weakness. My Achilles' heel. It's caused some issues in the past. Most notably, why I'm facing a scorned ex with a vendetta presiding over my trial as we speak. My tendency to love 'em and leave 'em precedes me. I've lived my life unapologetically single.

It takes a lot to get my attention, and she's managed to do it twice for different reasons—annoying and sexy.

"And why would you think that?"

"Because you're still standing here."

A camel-colored wool coat drapes over a fitted silk shirt that hangs around her slim torso. The skirt matches the coat and hugs the flow of her hips, going lower to just above her knees. It gives off high-society vibes that I'm not typically into. I have no patience or room in my life for socialites. *No matter how attractive they are.*

"I think you're confusing our orders," I reply, dipping my gaze to my phone and clicking it on while chuckling humorlessly. "I'm the least complex person—" *Fuck.* She's good with the games. I shoot her a glare. "Clever."

"You think?" She grins in pride and shrugs casually. "You said it. Not me."

I'm attempting to dedicate myself to this email I currently have open, but am stopped when I hear, "You sure are bothered for someone who tries so hard to act like you're not." Her hand swings out in front of her. "They're clearly busy. Maybe next time you shouldn't drop in during rush hour and expect to be served first. Learn how to have some patience."

"I know what you're doing." It's tempting to roll my eyes, but that's not a habit I'm getting into.

"What am I doing?"

"Fucking with my head, that's what."

Faux offense strikes her features. "*My. My.* The language. And that mouth . . ."

"My mouth can do many things, and I've heard zero complaints, especially when it comes to serving others first."

The pampered princess arches an eyebrow. "The only thing I can think of when it comes to your mouth is how foul it is. It's not just patience you're lacking."

"Listen, lady." Leaning closer, I lower my voice and say, "One thing my mouth has never been called is foul. Magical. Talented—"

She rolls her eyes. "Oh right. And here I thought you might have the moxie not to fall back on the obvious."

"The obvious being?"

"Sex." She rolls her eyes again as if the first time wasn't maddening enough. "You know what? I believe you."

"You believe what?"

Her expression sours. "That your coffee order is complex. As for you, you're a simple guy."

What the fuck?

As if I didn't deal with enough in court today, I get the displeasure of arguing with her in a freaking coffee shop. Crossing her arms over her chest, she smirks like she's getting the last laugh.

I don't think so. "Look, I'm done playing this game." I angle toward her. "It's a double espresso with a dash of milk, if you must know. Nothing is complex about it. I believe it was you who placed a 12-step coffee order and wasted more of everyone's time digging out exact change. Who pays in cash these days? No one."

"Ooh, I seemed to have hit a button. Who knew chatting about coffee would be such a sore spot for you?" Her tone drips in sarcasm as she continues, "And the part about being mad that someone paid in cash? Heaven forbid. I didn't know money had become so passé in your kingdom. My apologies, your majesty."

A barista holds up a paper cup, grabbing everyone's attention. "Kona coffee, double espresso, with a hit of coconut milk?" The guy looks at the cup as we wait with bated breath, and then he adds, "Mr. Westcott?"

Thank fuck.

But then I hear the barista call, "Macchiato with white cream, double brewed, light on the almond milk and a splash of caramel. One-sixty internal temp."

Damn, that's quite the complicated order. I stop in my tracks and look back. Her expression falls as embarrassment shapes her features. This time, I cock my brow, tasting sweet victory.

Catching my eyes on her, she says, "Go ahead. Say what you want to say and get it out of your system."

"You're three layers too deep in coffee demands and a real pain in the ass to every barista in town and mine. Have a nice day, *Mrs.*—"

"That's *Ms.* to you."

"My apologies. *Ms.* Complex."

The barista then adds, "For Tuesday."

Tuesday . . .

Go fucking figure.

I knew I hated Tuesdays.

2

Loch

WANTING to savor my victory as well as finally drink the coffee I waited for long enough to grow a five o'clock shadow before four in the afternoon, I stop a few doors down from the coffee shop.

A woman's scream catches in the wind just as I taste the hot brew. "No!" she yells louder as I search the area for the source of the sound.

Finally, I catch sight of the socialite when her coffee cup flies in the air. She swings her arm and tries to land a hit, but a man hovering over her blocks her. He then starts wrestling to free her bag from her grip.

I'm already running back toward her, glad people haven't packed the streets yet from leaving work. "Excuse me," I say, pushing past a few folks gawking nearby instead of helping.

She's shoved against the exterior of the coffee shop. The back of her head bounces off the brick, instantly silencing her as her body crumples to the ground before I have time to help. I push harder. When I reach her, I glare at the man darting between people or pushing them out of the way.

I yell to a guy pulling his phone out, "Call 911!"

A bulky guy in a hoodie seems to be debating what to do, shifting uncomfortably. When his eyes meet mine, I say, "Go after him!" As if permission was all he needed, he starts running after the guy.

I kneel beside her unresponsive body, wishing I had paid better attention in that CPR class I took as a Boy Scout. Her eyes are closed as I check for a pulse in her neck. "Fuck," I mutter under my breath, hoping she snaps back like she did earlier.

If I wouldn't have been in such a hurry to leave or . . . guilt riddles me, knowing that guy wouldn't have tried it if I'd been exiting with her. Finally, I feel a pulse. Although weak, I take it as a positive sign.

Glancing over my shoulder, I look for anyone ready to assist. The barista calling out orders earlier runs up just as I ask, "Has anyone called 911?"

"I did," he replies, kneeling next to me. "Is she dead?" I don't need flairs for the dramatic in this kind of situation.

"She needs medical attention as soon as possible." Careful not to move her, I run my hand gently along the back of her head to check for bleeding. Red scrapes across my fingertips, but fortunately, it's not enough to worry about blood loss. She'll have a concussion, though, so that concern rightfully exists in the pit of my stomach.

An officer moves people back as his partner dips to the ground, eyeing her and then me. "What happened?"

"She was mugged. The guy pushed her, and she hit her head against the bricks. Then he stole her purse."

"You her husband?"

"No."

Sirens echo down the avenue, approaching at New York City traffic speed—too slow in an emergency. The officer looks at me and then stands. "Go ahead and step back. We'll handle it from here, but stay close because you'll need to give a statement."

"Okay," I reply, moving back enough to make room for the paramedics when they arrive.

The barista taps my shoulder. "Is she going to be okay?"

He's young, no more than eighteen, but I can't give him the reassurance he seeks. "I hope so." It's the best I can do.

The ambulance can't pull close because of the cars already at the curb, but the paramedics park in the street, causing the car behind it to blare its horn in outrage. Typical New Yorkers. They're the only ones with less patience than I have.

With a stretcher in their hands, the paramedics are finally able to maneuver through the fenders and set it beside . . . Fuck, what was her name? *Tuesday*. Her name was Tuesday. I move out of the way but stand close and say, "She has a pulse, but it's faint, and there's bleeding at the back of her head."

One of the paramedics turns to look at me over her shoulder. "Did you move her?"

"No. I only checked for her pulse."

She nods and returns to the woman, checking her pulse for herself, and counting. After a pause, she nods. "Let's move her," she says to the other paramedic. In unison, they lift her onto the stretcher and start back to the ambulance.

With his arms held wide, the officer shuffles the onlookers back, including me. I owe her nothing. But seeing her—the same woman I was just bantering with—lying on the stretcher with a softness belying her earlier expression makes my chest tighten.

I'm known to be a shark in the courtroom and a total asshole to just about all the females I know, other than my mom and sister. But I have a fucking heart, even if it is frozen at its core. I can't seem to walk away from this woman, though. I need to know she'll be okay.

Fuck.

I look around, disgust settling in as I see all the people surrounding her, gawking like the attack happened for their entertainment. Acting on instinct, I follow close and approach the ambulance when the paramedics load her inside. One says, "Step back, sir."

What am I doing?

Why do I care?

She filled part of my day with irritation. Why would I sacrifice more of it to her whims?

A law professor of mine once told me I needed to forget the small-town manners I grew up with and own the life of the big-city lawyer I am now. I needed to harden up.

I've had no problem following his advice.

Until now . . .

Considering no one else has stepped up to claim a relationship of any kind with Tuesday, she's obviously alone. I contemplate how I would react if my little sister, Marina, or my mom had been mugged. I know, without a doubt, that I would never leave them alone.

But why am I making this random lady my priority? What about her makes me second-guess my ability to walk the fuck away from this situation?

I stand there like a creeper, making sure she's being taken care of when I'm shot a stern look. "I said step away from the ambulance." The paramedic's tone matches her glare.

"I'm her boyfriend." *What the—*

"Get in."

I don't have time to settle on the bench across from the paramedic before the doors are closed. I hold on as soon as the vehicle veers forward into traffic with the sirens blaring. Staring at the blonde, I note her hair has fallen from its tightly twisted knot, and the ends hang down around her shoulders, some curling around the gurney. Dragging my gaze away from her face and the peaceful expression on her face, I start to wonder if she's worse off than first suspected.

"It's not good that she hasn't woken up?" I ask, glancing across from me, needing an expert to weigh in.

"Her vitals are steady. That's good." The paramedic looks through the small back windows. "We should reach the ER in a few minutes."

I nod, noticing blood droplets on her shirt and what looks to be dirt from the street. Her coat lies on the bench next to the paramedic but appears no worse for wear from where I'm sitting. With her hands resting across her stomach, I can't help but notice the rings on her fingers, and a single diamond dangles from a necklace off to one side. Matching earrings pierce each ear, but nothing else gives me any indication of who she is. And I have a feeling any identification disappeared with the bag.

What am I going to tell them when they ask her name? Or her age? Her address or her insurance coverage? I need to snap the hell out of this. I'm trained to think on my feet.

I run my hand over my hair and lower to rub my neck. My eyes return to her face, and silently, I ask myself, "What am I doing?"

"Sir?"

My gaze trails up to the paramedic across the ambulance from me. "Yes?"

"I asked her name. What's her name?"

Without hesitation, I reply, "Tuesday."

"Last name?"

Uh . . . what do I say that won't have them shoving me out the doors of a moving ambulance? "Westcott?"

NOT THE BEST plan I've ever devised . . . *Lying never is.*

As an attorney, I can attest that lying in most cases will indict more than vindicate. Under this circumstance, though, it got me inside her room, at least for a short time. I'm standing beside her bed, unsure of what to do.

I'm also questioning whether I have a concussion myself. Because what the hell have I gotten myself into?

A nurse peeks in and then comes in when she sees me. She's pulled her hair into a ponytail that's given way throughout the day and loosened at the nape. Giving me a tight smile before turning her attention toward the e-pad at the end of the bed, she says, "I'm Nurse Belinda. How is she?"

"I was hoping you'd be able to tell me." I keep my voice low like hers. The darkened room and sleeping patient warrant it.

She starts to check her vitals on the heart machine. The steady beeps have kept me company for more than an hour. They're quite soothing in their rhythm and had me settling in as if I belong here.

The nurse replies, "I think she's doing well. The doctors expect her to wake any moment." She sticks a temperature clamp on her finger and looks up at me. "I'm sure you're anxious to talk to her, but I'd caution you to take it slow until the doctor examines her."

"I'm not going anywhere," I reply as if I'm here for the

long haul. Again, I'm not sure where this is coming from, but I won't leave her. I know it to my core.

Emails are piling up, along with text messages from my assistant. But I can't bring myself to care enough to get to them. I take a step back from the bed and sit on the vinyl sofa. The springs give way, creaking under my weight and causing the nurse to glance over at me.

"I hear you're her boyfriend."

"I'm Loch." How long do I go on with this charade? Tuesday is in good hands. That should be my cue to leave, but I sit on this sofa and nod like I have a vested interest.

Her shoulders fall, and she peeks over her shoulder at the door. "You seem like a nice guy, Loch, making sure she got to the hospital, and concerned for her well-being, so I'm going to be frank with you." Turning, she rests her hand protectively on the bedrail as she does her hip. "I'm guessing you aren't really who you say you are. You seem like a nice guy, but we have to take precautions here, so an officer is coming to escort you out of the room."

Fuck. This is not happening.

Getting arrested for falsifying information could be detrimental to my legal career. With that said, I know I could win a jury of my peers over if I risk being disbarred.

"I've given you a pocket of time by holding them off so I could speak with you first," she says.

I square my shoulders, much like I do when I enter the courtroom, but I don't speak. Only the guilty start rambling. I'm guilty of what? Being concerned about a woman who gave me a hard time and told me to have a nice day?

"Tell me the truth," she starts again. "You're not really her boyfriend, are you?"

"A friend."

"A friend who doesn't know her last name?"

Nurse Belinda hits hard. I study her unflinching gaze. She's tough and would make a great witness on the stand. Unfortunately, I'm the one she's interrogating at the moment. I've stalled about as long as I can. Like she said, she's given me a short window of opportunity. Why? I have no idea, but since I'm on borrowed time anyway, I say, "I'm not one to bend the truth—"

"Good because I'm not a contortionist. Give it to me straight." Nurse Belinda came loaded with jokes.

"We recently met, hung out a bit, and got coffee together. Nothing scandalous." Though I feel guilty for how brusque I was with Tuesday after what happened.

Her head tilts just as her brows pinch together. She's an older woman, older than my mom, and a kindness entered the room with her that has me trusting she's being level with me. But she grins as if she knows I'm stretching the truth. "Listen, Loch, stick to that story. Kelly backed you up."

"Who's Kelly?"

"The guy who works at the coffee shop. He said you two were hanging out in the corner together, and it appeared to be a date." Clearly, the kid is blind. He couldn't be further from the truth, but it's a good alibi that keeps my nose clean.

"Nice try." Leaning in, she whispers, "I'm not naive. Give me the real scoop, or I'm calling Officer Langley in to arrest you."

"The truth?"

"The whole truth."

Feeling like I'm on the witness stand, I ask, "Has anyone ever told you that you should be a lawyer?"

"Yes," she replies straight-faced.

She's very good.

I glance at Tuesday on the bed, still sleeping. "We made

small talk about the complexity of coffee, and then we parted ways. It was that simple."

It's never that simple, and she knows it.

"If you'd parted ways, why were you the first on the scene?"

"I wasn't the first on the scene. I was just the only one who helped her."

Belinda's shoulders fall as does the pointed glare. Her whole being softens, and she exhales. "I knew you were a good guy. I'm a great judge of character."

I've been honest both times I answered, but tackling the question using two different tactics buys me a little time. "What are you going to tell the police?"

"The truth."

Saved by a sigh.

Tuesday takes a breath and releases a quiet hum that attracts our attention. The nurse jots something on the e-pad while I move to the opposite side of the bed from her.

A small smile embeds into Belinda's cheeks. She glances at the door and then to me again. "You did the right thing by helping her. Timing is critical with a head injury."

"What will happen to her from here?"

She sets the e-pad on the rolling station, then heads for the door. "As I mentioned, the doctor will examine her once she wakes up. We'll keep her overnight for observation for the concussion, though. If all is good, she'll be released tomorrow morning."

"That seems fast."

"We have a shortage of beds." She shrugs, opening the door. "If all is good, there's no reason to keep her here longer."

When the door closes and we're left alone with the sound of her beating heart, I peer down at Tuesday. Her lipstick has been wiped away, and her hair hangs loose in gentle waves around her shoulders. Otherwise, she appears to be sleeping. My mom always said we do three things when we sleep: grow, recover, and renew. I'm sure Tuesday will be as good as new when she wakes up.

I take one last look at her, reaching through the bedrail to brush my fingertips against the top of her hand. "Guess this is goodbye."

Walking away, I have no regrets. From choosing her over chasing down the mugger and saying what I needed to make sure she was taken care of. Even my confession to the nurse felt right when I did it, and it sits right in my conscience.

So I don't understand why my chest grows heavier and each step pulls at me to stay. I push through the hesitation and hail a cab outside, leaving the hospital *and Tuesday* in the rearview mirror.

3

Loch

"Evening, Mr. Westcott." The door hasn't even closed behind me. Our building's nighttime security guard monitoring the lobby desk always beats me to the greeting.

"Evening, Joe." I ordered food as soon as I left the hospital. Picking up the bag from reception, I head for the elevators.

"Another late night?"

Turning back, I manage a half grin. "You're stuck with me again."

"I'll be here all night."

"I hope I'm not."

He chuckles. I step into an elevator and punch the button for the twenty-third floor. It's not a big office, but with four attorneys, two litigating specialists along with assistants, paralegals, HR, and accounting, we've grown a lot in the past two years and now occupy half the floor.

Everyone's gone for the day when I step off the elevator. At least, I thought they were. As soon as I round the corner,

Leisa pushes back from her desk and stands. "I haven't received anything about time or date for court and—"

"Although I appreciate you staying late, you shouldn't be here, Leisa. It's almost eight."

"If you're here, I'm here."

My assistant is dedicated beyond her pay. I need to make sure her bonus makes up for it, and she gets a raise. "Unlike me, you have a life. You should be out living it."

She laughs. "So should you, but here we are." She follows me into my office and sits across the desk from me.

Placing the bag in front of her, I say, "If you're staying, let me offer you dinner. Eat something."

The crinkling of the bag makes my stomach growl as I take off my jacket and hang it behind the door. When I sit in the black leather chair that matches the one my father uses at his office in my hometown of Beacon, I lean my head back and exhale as if the day has gotten the better of me. I hate to admit, this Tuesday has . . .

Tuesday. I can't stop thinking about her and wondering if she's awake.

Leisa says, "Boss?" I look up to find her staring at me expectantly. Being in her early thirties shouldn't have her sporting dark circles under her eyes. She's knotted her hair on her head, which is more her style once our coworkers have gone home than during business hours. She's too much like me, letting each day become longer without time to live life anymore.

"I'm not going to eat your dinner. But more importantly, what happened after court?" she asks.

What happened? It's a loaded question. I'm still not sure what the hell happened. I scrub my hands over my face, then drop them to the wooden desktop. "I bought coffee, but I have no fucking idea what happened to it."

Her forehead wrinkles. "What do you mean? That doesn't make sense."

"A lot doesn't make sense, starting with why the judge delayed the ruling."

She puts the plastic dish full of pasta in front of me along with the included plasticware. "I'm not sure we can do much else tonight other than wait since you presented the evidence in our client's favor, so eat."

"You should eat it."

"I'm taking your advice and going home to eat. Maybe one day, you'll take mine and take care of yourself." Standing back up, she slips out toward the door. "If you need anything—"

"I won't need anything tonight. I'll see you tomorrow morning."

With a nod and an empathetic smile that always makes me think she feels sorry for me, she then replies, "Good night, Loch."

She learned years ago that she couldn't coax me into going home when I feel the need to be in the office. "Night, Leisa."

After she's left, I roll up my sleeves, log in to my computer, and start reviewing the Reinhold case file.

I rub my temple. A fine-tooth comb couldn't find a discrepancy. The research and evidence are solid. Feeling confident in the case I've laid out, I rock back in the chair and stare out the window. A few lights scatter across the business district of dark skyscrapers, but otherwise, the city that never sleeps has gone to bed.

Glancing at the clock on my computer, I realize more time has passed than I thought. The pasta that I forgot to eat sits in its covered dish nearby. No wonder I have no energy. No food. *No caffeine* . . . What did happen to my coffee? I must have dropped it when running to help Tuesday.

Tuesday.

Tuesday is the last thing that should be on my mind.

That damn gleam of victory that shone in her eyes at the coffee shop still lingers. I should be annoyed that she got the better of me then, but I chuckle instead, her words no longer burning my ego like they did before.

But it was when she was in the ambulance and later lying in the hospital bed that I got to see the other side of the frustrating woman. The softer side of her lost in the tranquility of sleep. It didn't matter that chaos surrounded us, which disappeared under the unrelenting connection we had now formed. Whether we liked it or not, we were entangled together because of one act of violence.

Sitting by her side, I felt a pull from outside myself to take care of her. That's when I knew I was right where I was supposed to be.

I pick up my phone, indulging my own need to know, and track down the number for the hospital.

NINE A.M. SHARP.

Just as instructed by Nurse Belinda when I called for an update last night, which she only begrudgingly gave me because no one else had shown up for Tuesday.

I'm sitting in the back of the SUV now, waiting when I don't even know what her caution of "releasing her into the wilds of the city at nine a.m. sharp" meant, but her words still rumble around my head this morning. *Is it code for something?*

Apparently, it was all she could say and more than she

should have. I'm trusting the process. From the driver's seat, Brady offers, "I can move closer."

"No. This is fine. I don't want to block other cars."

He seems curious as to why we're parked in the hospital driveway and sitting here. I wish I had a better explanation for him, but I'm at a loss as well.

My phone buzzes on the seat. Leisa's name flashes on the screen. I answer on speakerphone. "Don't tell me."

"Yep," she replies, sighing. "She called court to order for nine thirty. Can you make it in time?"

Hospital personnel walk inside just as an older couple exits, but there's no sign of Belinda. I check my watch. 9:03. Even if there was no traffic, I wouldn't make it. "I'm across town. There's no way."

"How late will you be?"

The hospital doors slide open, and my gaze lengthens, locking onto blond hair that lifts in the wind and blue eyes searching as if she's looking for me.

Tuesday.

I've been looking for the wrong woman.

My heart starts thumping in my chest in unwarranted anticipation now realizing that Belinda set me up.

"Loch?" Leisa's voice returns as I open the door to the SUV. "Mr. Allendale is at the courthouse to meet his clients for a ten o'clock appearance. Would you like me to have him step in for you?"

"Yes. I need to go." I hang up, get out, and shut the door.

Tuesday stands in stark contrast to her appearance at the coffee shop. Although she's bundled up in her coat, the skirt dipping out the bottom, and the same heels I last saw her wearing, everything about her is softer, from the lines on the sides of her mouth to her stance and the gentle waves that run through her hair and over her shoulders.

She's *fucking stunning.*

But when I catch her gaze, it's like she's lost—stormy clouds full of fear settling in. It's a look that should never cross her face.

I start for her. "What the fuck am I doing?" I mutter to myself, tempted to run my hand through my hair. I don't. I have court later, and I pride myself on always being put together, even under pressure. "Hi," I say. "Not sure if you remember me from the coffee shop?"

She's staring at me, and for a split second, I detect a hint of recognition spark in her eyes. "I, um . . ." She starts but is already shaking her head in doubt.

"Of course, not." I'm shaking my head to let her off the hook. Stopping a few feet away from her, I continue, "It was a brief encounter. Before—"

"Before?" she asks, her eyes traveling from mine to my mouth, lower to my chest, where her gaze lingers, and then back up. Tilting her head, she studies me like I'll give her the secrets to the universe if she searches long enough. "Before what?"

"Before you were mugged." Touching the back of my head, I add, "And hit your head," as if she needed the reminder. I shake my head for acting a fool. *Why am I like this with her?*

"Ah." Disappointment is seen in the curve of her shoulders as she takes a breath and then lets them fall. Rubbing just above her eyebrow, she asks, "You were at the coffee shop?"

Holding out my hand, I reply, "As you know, I didn't make my best first impression." Not that she did either, but the impression stuck enough for me to be here today, behaving like an idiot. "I'm Loch Westcott."

As she slips her hand in mine, our gazes fix together, and

her smile encourages mine. "It's nice to *officially* meet you, Loch. I'm Tuesday." She smiles as genuine as I've seen on her. "You rode with me to the hospital?"

"It was the right thing to do."

"Thank you."

A flush of embarrassment floods her cheeks as her gaze lowers between us. "One of the nurses said you also stayed to make sure I was taken care of. Is that true?"

Despite how wrong she rubbed me, she was still beautiful the first time I saw her, but now, she knocks the breath from me. I look down at our hands still latched together and take a breath, finally easing in her presence. Her hand falls away from mine too soon and then she tucks both of hers into her coat pockets.

"How are you?" I ask.

A gentle shrug pops her shoulders before a weary smile hangs on her face. "Maybe you can help me."

"I'd be happy to."

Pulling a piece of paper from her pocket, she says, "I need to go to this address, but I don't know where it is."

Before I resort to another episode of the boyhood awkwardness she keeps bringing out in me, I offer, "I have a car." I glance at the Escalade. "And driver. Brady. We can give you a ride?"

She glances at the vehicle parked ahead at the curb and back to me. "Are you sure?"

"Yes." She hands me the paper, and I walk with her. Opening the door, I say, "Brady, this is Tuesday." I offer her a hand up. "Tuesday, this is Brady. He's been with me since—"

"Since he arrived in Manhattan," Brady adds, nodding.

"Yes, five years now." After giving him the address, I add, "He knows this city inside and out."

I climb in after she's settled on the far side of the back

seat. "I appreciate it. I didn't know how I would get there since my purse was stolen. I'll repay you as soon as I can."

"No need."

Brady pulls into traffic, and says, "It's not far from here."

Because stress had my mind muddled, I hadn't thought about who would look for her. I hadn't made the connection that Nurse Belinda hinted to the need for me to be here. *Until now.*

Why did she tell me?

I hold out my phone. "Do you need to call anyone?"

"No." Although the phone is within her reach, she seems determined to pretend it doesn't exist and shifts her body toward the door, angling her knees away.

I'm known for my skill in analyzing my opponents and getting them to confess their secrets inside the courtroom. My talent extends outside of work as well. Women don't stand a chance at withholding much from me. I can usually see it coming by their obvious tells—a lick of their lips as they stare at mine, desire darkening their pupils, and getting handsy with me.

But I'm struggling to read this woman. With Tuesday, I'm wading in unfamiliar waters. She's got my attention in a tight grip, so I struggle to focus on the details of the situation.

There's nothing for her to admit or confess. The bottom line is I'll be dropping her off soon, and we'll never see each other again. So maybe she's playing this right, and I'm doing this all wrong.

Keep it casual. Stop acting like a kid with a crush. Remember how she owned me with her sharp tongue in the coffee shop. She knows how to stand on her own. That puts things back in perspective. "Glad you're okay."

That brings the bright coloring of her eyes back to me. "Thank you."

"Are you sure this is the right address?" Brady asks.

Her head jerks back toward the window, her gaze rising to the top of the building. I expected to see a high-rise with a uniformed doorman decked out with epaulets crowning his shoulders. Or at the very least, a skyscraper leading to a company befitting her designer attire—high-powered meetings, even something creative like advertising. This place is neither of those.

We're not even in a particularly great part of the city.

The run-down building has cracks through the bricks, and the steps of the stoop have chips on the right side where the handrail has gone missing.

Brady hops out as soon as she confirms the address and opens her door to the sidewalk. Not sure what to do, I scramble to pull a card out of my briefcase and lean toward the opening. "Here's my number."

When she turns back to take it, I add, "If you need anything, anything at all, just call or text."

"Thanks." A half-hearted smile peters out before it has a chance to bloom. She tucks the card in her pocket and takes a deep, stuttering breath as if she struggles to keep herself together.

That's when I catch her eyes beginning to water. "Are you okay?"

"I'm fine. Thank you again." The door closes, and she walks away, leaving me no option to say more.

The whole situation is fucked up, so I shouldn't be bothered by this goodbye. She doesn't owe me anything. I'm just the stranger who stepped in, not her knight in shining armor, for fuck's sake.

Yet when Brady shifts the Escalade into drive, the sound

of the tires grinding against the rubble in the streets, I realize the universe is conspiring against me regarding the Reinhold case.

I should be heading to court or, at the very least, checking in with Leisa to see where the date stands or if the judge granted us another hearing time. Yet that's not what I do. I slide across the seat and look at the letters hung above the door. All Welcome Shelter of New York.

I pop open the door just before Brady drives forward.

"What are you doing?" he asks, slamming on his brakes.

Without a bag or money, a phone or a friend, Tuesday stands on the sidewalk looking up at the building before her. Nothing about this feels right. And if I gauge my future actions by my past with her, I refuse to leave her here to fend for herself. "Tuesday?"

Her expensive and sky-high heels plant among broken glass on the dirty sidewalk, and her coat doesn't look like she's worn it before yesterday.

The wind catches her coat, the front flapped open. Instead of the silk top she was wearing yesterday, she's in a faded hospital gown tucked into her skirt. What's really going on? "Why did you want to be dropped off here?"

Glass scrapes against concrete under her designer heels when she turns to find me standing here. "This is where the hospital coordinator told me to come since I have nowhere else to go."

"I don't understand. Why don't you go home?" I thumb toward the SUV now parked at the curb. "I can take you anywhere you want. I can take you home."

The water in her eyes from earlier has formed tears in the corners that fall down her cheeks. "I don't know where I live, Loch."

I narrow my eyes, more confused than ever. "What do you mean?"

"I can't remember anything."

My mouth falls open, but I close it to ask, "Nothing?"

"Nothing."

. . . I didn't see that coming.

4

***

Tuesday

FEAR HAD JUST SETTLED in along with a heavy dose of reality when someone said, "Tuesday."

Tuesday.

Tuesday . . .

Not a fiber of my being reacts when someone calls that name in my direction. Worrisome, but something about it must fit since that's what everyone calls me. Apparently, that's what I also used for my coffee order before I was attacked. But that name doesn't feel like mine, and that's a problem. More than not knowing my own name though, I have bigger and more pressing concerns at the moment.

I have no money.

No credit cards.

No phone.

No identification.

No address.

Nothing but this designer coat, a skirt too tight to be comfortable wearing for long, and pencil-style four-inch heels that not only are a perfect nude shade but also designer. *Fancy.* But impossible to wear if I'm walking far.

Although my blouse had blood along with some black stains, it was ripped yesterday and replaced by a hospital gown, which I fashioned into a top to wear today. *Not so fancy.*

At my urging, Nurse Belinda researched the brands to see if anything would bring back a memory. The designers themselves didn't, but I've been stuck in shock by the sticker prices. How did I afford an outfit that cost the equivalent of a mortgage?

Who am I?

"You don't know who you are?" Loch asks, standing close but also giving me space.

I stare at him, noting how the sun chose his eyes to set in. Who can blame the sun? Not me. I'm just as drawn to the golden coloring that sparks like fire in the chestnut centers. I move slightly closer to steal some of the heat radiating off this ridiculously handsome man.

Whoever I was yesterday, I knew exactly what I was doing by choosing to talk to him. A rogue section of hair has escaped what looks to be a style he tried to control, yet it only adds to his attractiveness. Now, finding myself staring purely for pleasure, I can only imagine how stunning his parents must be to have produced a modern-day Greek god straight out of mythology.

I can't deny the man also knows how to fill out a suit. A tailored midnight-blue suit with a crisp white shirt and black tie only adds to his appeal. I'd like to think I'm above leveling another person to nothing more than some sexy savior, but clearly, I'm not. Loch Westcott is the kind of hero I wouldn't kick out of bed for eating crackers. The crumbs would totally be worth it.

Wonder if he's the type to eat crackers for a late-night snack...

"Tuesday?"

There's that name again... "Sorry, I got lost in thought." He has my mind tumbling into the gutter when I need to focus on what I'm supposed to do with my life while I try to figure out who I am and where I belong.

Loch's expression contorts as if I'm a *New York Times* crossword puzzle he can't figure out. I get it. I feel just as confused.

Clearing my throat, I use the distraction to stop myself from staring at him, and reply, "I guess I'm Tuesday."

The corners of his eyes soften though I don't mind the whiskers that have started digging into his skin there. It's really unfair that men age so handsomely.

"At least that's the name you told the barista, and what everyone has been calling you."

My bones stiffen in defense, and I shift my weight to my right foot, unsure what to say or do, and still wondering why he's here. It seems like I don't have anyone else, but why is this stranger so interested in me? "Why are you here, Loch?"

"Because I can't leave you—"

"Leave me? I thought we just met yesterday?"

"We did."

I swing my hand in front of me and then flip it over. "A chance encounter at a coffee shop doesn't make me your responsibility. You don't know me much less owe me anything. You've already done so much, too much."

"Just because we don't know each other doesn't mean I can leave you to fend for yourself. Your bag was stolen, and you don't remember anything. You have a concussion and amnesia."

He's said the word I've been avoiding. At some point, it

had become unavoidable. That point is now. "I do have amnesia." I feel nauseous. I wrap my arm over my stomach, realizing saying it makes it reality.

"My mother would kill me if I left someone stranded instead of helping."

He's living up to the knight in shining armor the nurses made him out to be. But why is he? "Other than bonus points with your mom, what do you gain from helping me?"

"Gain?" he asks as if the word itself is offensive. Shoving his hands in the pockets of his pants, he looks down at his feet, and then his lips tighten. "I don't gain anything that I'm aware of. I'm here because I think you need someone. Do you have anyone?"

I don't know what he'd be gaining either, so I understand the lack of an easy answer. Despite his attractiveness, something about his stance with me is unguarded—shoulders straight but with an ease within his body, the eyes, and even the lack of contrived answers give me comfort. Wouldn't someone wanting something be ready for the task in the moment that counts most?

This seems like a prime moment to take what he wants. I probably wouldn't even know better. But he doesn't. He just owns the answer he's given and leaves me the stage to ask more questions. I don't have more, though. I don't have much of anything.

Biting my lip, I'm still trying to read between the lines, worried I'm missing something obvious when he says, "I don't know what I'm doing here. I guess I just needed to see you with my own eyes. I needed to know you were okay." His hand falls out of his pockets, and he glances back at the SUV.

A lump has formed in my throat at seeing him slip away from me—his gaze, his kindness, his proximity. He takes a step back and checks his watch. "I should be in court."

"Court? What did you do?"

He chuckles, and it's the most relaxed I've seen him. "Fortunately, nothing. I'm an attorney."

"Ah. That makes sense." I cover my mouth, realizing a second too late that could be construed as rude.

"My brother jokes the first word I spoke was objection, so yes, you're not the first to say I fit the job."

"It's the suit," I add, hoping to keep it light, "and maybe the formality of how you carry yourself." It's too late to worry if he has ulterior motives. He's the only one who knows me from before the mugging and the only one who has shown he cares. Well, other than Belinda, but she can't take home every victim that comes through the hospital doors. "Loch?"

His full attention weighs in his eyes as he looks into mine. I continue, "You're the only person who knows anything about me."

"It was only a brief conversation." I hate the feeling that I'm interrogating him, that any morsel he gives matters so much.

"It's all I have."

"The police should have the missing persons reports—"

"It hasn't been twenty-four hours. I'm hoping . . ." Fear squeezes my chest, and I take a sobering breath. "There's a chance no one files a report."

"Someone, if not many, are looking for you, Tuesday," he says with such confidence. "I promise you. You are a woman who is being missed. There's no way anyone would forget you."

I nod, clinging to his words. "I'm not so sure that's true. And right now, it's all I have." Closing my eyes, I clench my eyelids tight. When I reopen them, sadness intervenes when the reality of my situation returns. "I'm told availability is based on a first come basis, so I should probably go inside to check in for the night."

Silence between us allows the honk of a horn down the street, a group of teens chattering as they walk around us, and the backfiring of a nearby truck to infiltrate the space that felt gentler minutes prior. Uncertainty begins to race through my veins knowing that when he leaves, I'll be alone, all alone in a city where nothing feels like a place I know, much less like home.

Loch comes closer again, not so close to whisper, but close enough for me to feel a familiarity with him. "What if . . ." He starts, but pauses to run the pad of his thumb over his bottom lip.

"What if?" Attaching myself to the hope that those two simple words offer me.

"What if I give you a place to stay until the police receive the missing persons report, today or however long it takes?" Before I have a chance to reply, he adds, "You'll be safe and not have to worry about a place to sleep every night. I know of a great hotel."

"A hotel . . ." I roll the words around in my mind as if I have all the options in the world. I don't. I have one other—the shelter. "You'd do that for me?"

"Of course."

Loch was there for me yesterday.

He's here for me today.

I have no reason to doubt his intentions. If he were a bad guy, he could have done away with me yesterday. He didn't. He made sure I got the medical care I needed. Now he's offering more than I have a right to ask for—a place to stay.

Loch Westcott is all I have, but curiosity is killing me,

and the same question still burns. "Why are you helping me?"

"Because everyone needs help every now and then."

I look back at the shelter just as a woman exits. She grips the railing to help herself down the steps but stops to look my way, our eyes meeting. She's much older than I am, a poor guess at forty or more years, judging by how life has dug into her forehead, the streets matting her hair as hunger hollows her cheeks. The whites of her clothes have yellowed as the dress that can't be much heavier than my hospital gown hangs loosely off her shoulders.

The sun shines, but the temperature drops as fall becomes winter. When a shiver runs through her body, I go to her. Taking off my coat, I offer it to her. My heart pounds in my chest when I approach. She wears her pain openly on her face and a lost look in her eyes.

"Here. I think you need this more than me."

Guilt tangles with the fear I already had growing inside my gut of what will become of me. I may have left the hospital with the bare minimum, but I'll have a warm place to stay tonight when she may not.

There's no great reward in response or even a grateful smile. No, she mutters something I don't catch and carries on like I don't exist. That doesn't bother me. I didn't offer it for accolades.

I take a breath and wrap my arms around myself as I return to Loch. "If the offer still stands . . ."

He moves to the vehicle and opens the door without hesitation. "It does."

I follow, stopping just shy of getting in. "I don't know how I'll repay you, but I will. I promise."

"Don't worry about it. Let's just get you back where you belong."

Where I belong? My heart kicks up in panic. "What if . . .?" No. Stop.

Hope.

"LOTTE NEW YORK PALACE HOTEL," Loch directs Brady to our destination.

"Yes, sir," Brady replies. When our eyes meet in the rearview mirror, he smiles and then pulls into the lane and starts driving.

The warm SUV protects us from the cold outside, and I'm glad I accepted his offer. "The sun's out," I say with my arms still wrapped around myself. "But it doesn't look like it will shine for long." Keeping my eyes trained out the window, I search for anything I might recognize—landmarks, restaurants, street names.

"Winter looms." Loch pulls his phone from his pocket and starts texting. "You're going to need clothes." Not looking at me, he continues to text. "I'll have some sent over unless you have a store preference." His gaze slides over the leather seat and higher to meet my eyes.

"I don't remember." I shake my head, already feeling annoyed with the answer. Will I ever remember, or am I stuck learning to live my life all over again? He doesn't say anything and starts typing again. Swallowing my pride, I whisper, "I appreciate it, but nothing expensive. You're already doing so much for me."

Although nothing rings any bells, so to speak, as we travel through the city, I smile because of the relief I feel tucked inside this vehicle. "I bet I live in Manhattan."

"Yeah?" My comment piques Loch's interest, and he rests the phone on the seat next to him.

I nod. "Based on what I'm wearing, the officer thinks the mugger targeted me for the brand of bag I was carrying. They've requested footage from the buildings, but I'm sure he's right."

"That makes sense." Unlike the world outside, in the back of this SUV, he appears unhurried, which surprises me, considering he said he was supposed to be in court. Not sure if I'm reading him or the situation well, but a sense of peace washes through me.

Is that what I'm doing?

Trusting Loch?

Since I have nothing left to lose, I settle in for the ride and glance out the window again. "I could live anywhere, and I wouldn't know it." Taking a staggering breath, I confess, "Amnesia is strange. I go from feeling nothing to a tidal wave of emotion all at once." I hold in the oncoming wave the best I can before it crashes down on me again. I don't want to break down in front of him.

"Nothing looks familiar?" A question within a question is heard from the intonation of his dulcet tone.

"In my heart, everything feels familiar as if I've been here before, but in my head, nothing feels like my own." Looking at him in the shadows, I add, "The truth is, I'm at a loss for more than my memory." I'm in so deep that there's no point in hiding anything anymore, even the one thing I've kept closest to my chest since I woke up. "I've lost myself."

It's quiet for only a second, and then he lowers his head and his voice between us. "I'm sorry."

I don't know why he's apologizing, but his sincerity makes me feel less alone. Or maybe it's *him* that makes me feel better.

5

Tuesday

THIS IS IT.

Loch called the hotel a palace earlier, and it lives up to the name. It's grand, and if I wasn't dressed in a hospital gown, I might be inclined to feel more like a princess. But the nerves making my hands shake and my breath quicken bury that fantasy.

Even though it's inevitable Loch will be leaving, once he does, I'm truly on my own. It's going to be okay. I try to reassure myself to calm my racing thoughts. I know I shouldn't worry so much. As soon as a missing persons report hits the system, I'll be notified and reconnected with my old life.

What if no one files a report?

What if no one misses me?

What if—

"This is where my family used to stay when they came to the city." Loch stands next to me in the lobby. He glances in my direction, seemingly doing a double take. "Is everything all right?"

I swallow hard, feeling the heaviness in my throat. He can't be responsible for me forever. *Be brave, Tuesday.* The name still feels wrong. "Fine," I snap with irritation not intended for him. Licking my lips, I take a breath and face him. Loch Westcott is all I have. "I'm sorry," I reply, exhaling a deep breath. "Everything is fine. Thank you for asking."

He angles toward me, and leans in to whisper, "Are you sure?"

Is it wrong to want him to stay?

Is it unwise to invite him up?

I already know the answer . . . That doesn't stop me from dragging our time out just a little longer. "Where does your family stay now when they visit?"

"They have an apartment on the Upper East Side."

"Ah." I grin, a sudden realization hitting me like a ton of bricks. Appearances can be deceiving, but I know how to piece a puzzle together. The private car and driver, the suit, his profession, and the wealthy family who lives in an upscale Manhattan neighborhood. The details all add up to one big picture. *Loch is rich.*

Even tucked in, my raggedy hospital gown makes me feel underdressed in the luxury of this place and around him. I only have to suck up my pride a little longer. I'm so close to a hot bath, a comfy bathrobe, and a good night's sleep that I can taste it. That is if I can manage to fall asleep. How can there be so much on my mind while it's blank of anything that matters?

I stand straighter, walking beside Loch as we're led to a private desk to check in. Circling the room, I run my fingers along the backs of overstuffed velvet chairs and a bookcase full of dusty spines. The old books with worn covers tempt me. I want to take them down and smell the musty pages. Is anything so soothing as an old book full of adventures?

The transaction is fast. As deals probably are when you have money of Loch's magnitude. He comes to me and gives me the keys. The attendant moves back to the main lobby and then turns back to us. "I'll have your bags placed in the room." Then he looks around. "Do you have luggage?"

"Some packages will be delivered shortly," Loch says. I catch his gaze on me, but as if he's being forced to look away, he pulls his attention back to the manager.

"Very well. I'll have them delivered to Ms. Westcott's room as soon as they arrive." *Westcott?*

"Thank you," he adds, his voice as stiff as his shoulders.

I grin ruthlessly, taking pleasure in this. "Care to explain?"

It's hard to be upset when I look into his eyes, but then he says, "He thought you were a call girl."

That'll do it.

"What?" My head jerks back. I glance back over my shoulder at the hotel clerk. Speaking of jerks . . . But for real, I'm in a hospital gown that ties at the back. When I turn back to Loch, I ask, "What in Hades would make him think that?"

He runs his hand over his hair, looking down briefly. "He asked me your last name. When I hesitated, I saw the look on his face. I was caught in the heat of the moment, so I went with Westcott."

"Your last name? Because that makes sense," I snark and roll my eyes.

"Would you have preferred Smith or Dawson? Maybe Johnson or Johnston?" Annoyance has his gaze hardening as he stares across the palatial lobby. When he eyes me, he adds, "Or maybe her highness suits you better."

I try it on for size, but I get nothing, not a vibe or any

inkling from it. "Okay. Okay. I get it. Trust me, I get it. West-cott isn't so bad."

"Wow, thanks." I almost get an eye roll out of him, but he stops himself.

"No, I didn't mean it that way. I know he put you on the spot, but please understand how embarrassing it is not to know your own name."

"I should go." He says his words clipped as if he's already wasted too much time.

I'm not sure what happened when I wasn't listening, but his whole demeanor has changed.

Checking his watch, I can tell he's ready to leave. Not just from that gesture but the air has even altered under his commanding presence.

It takes me a hot second, but then I realize what's different about him compared to the man who showed up for me. He's back to business. I don't know how I know this, but he's the first thing that's felt familiar to me.

The shirt buttoned up to his neck with his tie twisted into a perfect Windsor knot.

The glare as he covers the distance of the room.

The stern tone heard just seconds prior.

Even the aura he's now projecting makes me wonder if the nice knight in shining armor was just an illusion.

When he hands me the key card, I'm starting to feel more like the transaction he spoke of earlier in a wrong assumption. I say, "Okay." Is there anything else to say?

Taking me in as if he'll never have another chance to see me again, he turns abruptly and walks away with such purpose that hurt has the nerve to seep into my chest.

"Loch?" Stopping, he turns back, his gaze meeting mine. "This is goodbye?"

The hard lines embroiling themselves into his brow

loosen the grip, and a kinder expression reshapes his face. "You have my number if you need it." He turns back, not in such a hurry this time.

"Hey!" I rush to him before he reaches the door.

He stops and looks at me. "What is it?" The shortness of his words from earlier is absent.

"What made you stop when you could have carried on with your day, lived your life no differently than you normally do?" I ask as if the third time is a charm.

His gaze lengthens over my head. He exhales as if I've asked too much of him. Maybe I finally have. Then he says, "You were unfinished business, and I don't like loose ends. Good day."

Unfinished business . . . Bottom line: *This is not a fairy tale.*

This is nothing more than the current predicament I'm stuck in. I'm sure I'll be cozy at home by tonight with . . . I glance at my ringless finger.

No tan lines.

No indention.

No precious metal.

No serious relationships or entanglements. I attempt but fail to reassure myself after being called Loch's "unfinished business." I'm not sure which switch I hit, but I prefer the nice guy from the hospital this morning over this version.

"Guess I got my goodbye." I turn my back on him and start walking toward the elevators.

The sound of shoes echoing off the floors reaches me just before he does. "I have a favor to ask."

"And there it is . . ." I knew he was too good to be true.

"There is what?"

"No one does anything out of the kindness of their heart." He's like every other guy out there. I roll my eyes. Here we go . .

. "What's the favor?" I ask too short to hide my annoyance. Left in suspense, I look away from him and cross my arms over my chest. I finally turn back to him with a cocked eyebrow. "Well?"

"I've upset you."

"Nothing ever comes without strings attached." It's interesting that this is my natural response. Was I a cynic or someone who understood the way the world works?

"There are no strings. You can refuse the favor, and you'll owe me nothing in return." Taking a step back, he says, "You know what? I was out of line for even thinking this was appropriate. Best of luck, Tuesday."

Loch leaves me stunned when he walks away so fast that I don't have a chance to say anything. He pushes through the door to the outside. This goodbye feels final.

I hate it.

I might hate myself more for letting it happen, so I rush to the door and land on the sidewalk just as he climbs into the back of the SUV. Why do I now feel like I owe him an apology? "Loch? Wait."

He looks at me before the momentum of the door forces it closed. The window rolls down, and he doesn't give me the courtesy of saying a word.

With nothing to lose, I ask, "What's the favor?"

A victorious smirk slides into place, and I already regret asking. The man knows how to own every inch of his body and sports it confidently by resting his elbow on the door. "The hotel will close the bill, but they won't know the ending to the story."

"Is that what I am to you, Loch Westcott? A cliffhanger in your book? Unfinished business." At least he has the inclination to look a little ashamed when he looks down, and I spy the minutest of headshakes.

His eyes find mine, and he says, "I shouldn't have said that. My apologies."

I have a feeling he isn't one to make apologies, so I take it for what it's worth. "Okay." With everything going on in my life, finding him attractive isn't at the top of my to-dos. Good or bad, I do. "But what are you asking?"

"Let me know what happens."

I stand there steady on my feet for the first time since I got out of that hospital bed this morning and nod. He's given me a lot. This is the least I can do for him. "I will."

I step back from the curb, ready for that hot bath upstairs. "Take care."

"You too, *Ms.* Westcott."

My brow rises as I stare at this stupidly handsome and moody man. "Why do I suddenly feel like I just sold my soul to the devil?"

"Maybe you did."

He smirks.

I roll my eyes, then turn around before he can see me smile.

The doorman opens it wide, but before I step through, I hear, "Hey, Tuesday?"

I give in and turn back. "Yes?" My voice lilts in hope. Hope for what? Ugh. *Damn him.*

"It suits you."

Angling back, I cross my arms over my chest again, knowing he can't be talking about the hospital gown. "What suits me?"

"The name."

"Tuesday?" I shrug. "It will have to do."

He chuckles lightly. I hate that I enjoy the sound of his laughter. "Westcott." He winks and then rolls up the window, and the SUV pulls away from the hotel, giving him the last word.

Do I feel cheated out of a comeback or flattered by the compliment?

With him? *Both.*

The nurse told me to be careful and to trust my instincts, but with Loch, he left me more uncertain than I was at the shelter. Do I think he intends to harm me? *No.* There's still a strong possibility of getting hurt anyway.

I shouldn't rely on him because I'm taking the risk of losing more than I've already lost by placing my trust in the one person who's helped me the most.

Loch Westcott.

6

Tuesday

SLIPPING my arms into the hotel robe, I tighten the belt as I hurry from the bathroom to answer the door. I peek through the hole first. "Who is it?"

"Delivery for Ms. Westcott."

Nervousness claws at my chest as I'm unsure of what to expect. I know what Loch sent, but I'm still uncertain of what to take from this situation. I unlock the chain and turn the bolt. When I open the door, a uniformed valet has Nordstrom bags draped on his arms. He asks, "Would you like me to bring them inside?"

I open the door wider. "Yes. Thank you." He sets the four shopping bags on the dresser, lining them up in presentation. When he returns to the door, I realize I don't have any tip to give him. I hate the feeling of shame that I succumb to. "I'm sorry. I don't have any money to give you."

Bowing his head briefly, he says, "Not necessary. Mr. Westcott already took care of it. Have a good day."

Mr. Westcott did, did he?

I close the door and lean my back against it, not sure what to make of Loch. His moods are as mercurial as Edward Cullen's. How do I remember trivial things like *Twilight* but not my own life? Shouldn't my life have left a more significant impact than a fictional character from a book? That says a lot about it, right?

Pushing off, I walk to the bags. Loch practically had me eating out of his hand, happily accepting any help he offered. He's generous to a fault to a stranger with whom he only chatted briefly at a coffee shop. Or maybe he just likes flashing his wealth around.

But the change in his demeanor toward me still sticks in my mind. I know he was joking about the manager thinking I was a call girl, but the distraction seemed to work well for him to get me off the scent of the last name debacle. Was he truly bothered by choosing his own last name for me?

I huff, knowing I'm not cracking that nut anytime soon. As for the packages . . . I cheer up, feeling like it's Christmas morning. I probably shouldn't be this excited about clothes, but I'll be thrilled not to have to put on that skirt again.

Based on the style of the outfit I wore to the hospital, I assume I enjoyed nice things. I add that tidbit to my growing list of clues that I hope can lead me to who I am.

Pulling the tissue from the bag, I drop it to the floor and discover a pair of black pants. I pull them out and hold them against my body. The flowy material hits just above my ankles when I hold them to my body. I raise an eyebrow, impressed. *Very nice, Mr. Westcott.* I'll give him a point for choosing something that will go with pretty much any top I choose.

Next out of the bag is a white, silk, long-sleeve button-up blouse similar to the ruined one. It's pretty. Another solid staple for a wardrobe, so great first pieces to add to mine.

With the pants, a classic look. Both are from the same designer. Judging from the material and cut, I'm thinking these weren't inexpensive like I asked.

I hang those in the small closet by the door, then open the next bag. Black leather flats tucked into a shoebox tied with a ribbon. Cute and a nice reprieve from the heels I already own.

Having other clothes than the ones I've been wearing is already a treat, but having nice things delivered that seem to be made for you feels indulgent. Such luxury. I'm wondering if this is something I was used to in my previous life.

I'm still curious as to how he got my sizes right when I don't even know what they are.

The third bag has a cozy black coat that hits at my hips. I hadn't even thought about needing a coat since I gave mine away. Being whisked from a warm Escalade to inside a hotel and then straight into a hot bath, I haven't thought about the weather outside. I haven't had to so far. Not sure how I feel about that.

If he hadn't shown up when he did, would I have been able to stand on my own two feet?

I flip the tissue paper over my shoulder and then rummage through the last bag. There are packages of underwear and a few bras. When I hold them up, I can tell they're not cheap—and when I see the price tag, I gasp in shock. And there are a few accessories added—like a beautiful YSL bag and a pair of gold earrings.

He spared no expense and was meticulous to ensure that I had literally everything I needed. Does he know what a woman truly needs?

Does he have a sister?

A girlfriend?

Or a wife?

Oh God, I hope he doesn't have a wife.

My mind starts to wonder to my own life and who is in it. *Wonder if I have any siblings?*

I place the items in the closet. These luxuries remind me of the little bag of my jewelry the nurse gave me before I left —diamond earrings and a pendant necklace. I go to the skirt in the laundry bag where I've put it and dig the bag out of the pocket. *Thank God.*

I can't afford to lose these.

When I fold the bags, I realize there's one more small box tucked inside the last bag. *A phone.*

Nope, he doesn't miss a thing.

But this is too much. How can I possibly thank him for what he's done? Besides the beautiful clothes and accessories, he's given me a way to stay connected to the world.

Wait . . . will I be able to connect with him again?

My focus doesn't need to be on him when I have so much other stuff, like my life, to worry about, but he makes it impossible to deter my thoughts. A note with the phone number is taped to the bottom of the box. I stare at it. A flash of something I can't interpret comes to mind. But it's gone too fast.

I rub my temple to ease the onslaught of an ache and close my eyes. I was given instructions to take it easy since I hit my head. I wouldn't describe my morning as easy based on how twisted in knots with worry my stomach has been, but when it growls in demand, I decide that might be the best course of action.

Sustenance will do me good.

I flip through the menu and call room service. When I hang up, I take the phone and turn it on. As soon as it's activated, I retrieve Loch's number and enter it into my contacts.

He may be a little Billy goat gruff on the surface, but his generosity is unparalleled. For this gift, he deserves the honor of being my first contact.

Thinking of phones, I'm reminded that I haven't heard from the police since I left the hospital. Glancing at the hotel phone, I didn't miss any calls while in the bath. Oh God, they don't know I'm here.

I remember the business card from the detective assigned to my case and call to check in and give him my new number. He's not available, so I leave a message and lie on the bed with the phone next to me. I hope he calls me back because the waiting is torture.

Exhausted, my body is weak, my head hurts, and my hair feels like straw and is a complete mess. I could look in the mirror, but what's the point? I'm already mortified that Loch saw me like this. Squeezing my eyes closed even tighter, I cringe.

Does it matter if he saw me looking horrific? No. I was attacked. He knows that. So why do I care what he thinks of my appearance?

I know why.

The man is gorgeous, and I can't say for certain what my type was before, but visually, I feel like he would fit it . . . *since he does now.*

The food arrives, and I settle on the bed with the tray, dipping the fries in ketchup, then devouring half before I tackle the burger. When my mouth is full, my phone rings. I recognize the number and chew faster before I answer. "Hello?" I ask just after swallowing too fast.

The detective replies, "Hi, Tuesday?"

"This is she."

"I only have a minute, but I wanted to return your call."

"I appreciate that. Have you heard anything from my family? I bet they're worried."

"Unfortunately, there's no new news. It hasn't been twenty-four hours, so no reports of your disappearance have been filed. As much as you hate to hear it, it's a waiting game. We did receive some footage from across the street from where you were mugged, confirming the details already filed. The footage is grainy. From that distance, it will be hard to identify anyone facially. We'll be able to build out a profile, though. I should tell you that a lot of times, bags turn up in alleys or trash bins. Most of the time, the muggers just want cash or something they can resell. So time is not our friend in cases like yours, so we need to rely on the missing persons report to come in to get you home."

"What about the fingerprints you took at the hospital?"

"They didn't pull anything. That's not a bad thing. Just means you haven't been booked before. Ran your photo but nothing popped up. Those are the initial steps. We're digging deeper, don't you worry."

I had hoped that would lead me home. I mean, I'm glad I'm not a criminal, but how is there no trace of me using photos or fingerprints?

"I'll contact you when I have more to share."

"Thank you, Detective Langley." I can't hide my disappointment. I've seen enough movies and crime shows to know twenty-four hours is standard procedure, but when your life hangs in the balance, that period might as well be a mountain I have to climb to get to the other side.

I've lost the rest of my appetite. I lie back on the bed, wishing for the hours to pass. When I check the time on the phone again, it's been two minutes. "Ugh!" I slam my hands down beside me. I want to scream, to kick my feet in protest, to get the answers I so desperately need to the questions plaguing me.

Who am I?

Where do I live?

Where am I from?

Is anyone searching for me?

When my anger causes my body to heat, I stand and strip off my robe. Ah, a detail Loch overlooked. *Pajamas.*

I climb under the covers, thinking he's probably the type who sleeps naked. It's not a bad image since he sure has the body for it. But then his mood kind of ruins it. That won't stop me from texting him, though. I grab the phone to type: *Thank you. You did more than necessary, but I truly appreciate the gifts. Hope you were able to finish some business.*

I hope he can find the humor in the last part like I did. I stare at the screen, but when nothing happens, I set it down next to me, closing my eyes again. Maybe he's thinking of something clever to say . . . The phone buzzes on the bed, and I roll to my side to read the message: *You're welcome.*

Huh. Or maybe not.

Polite but abrupt. Maybe I should have expected as much. He's an attorney, of all things, and based on how we parted ways, I'm not surprised that he doesn't placate me and fall into the opening I left for him with my text.

I can't fault him entirely. He tried to turn it around at the end, but it was too late. I'd already raised my defenses.

MY BODY ACHES in places that don't make sense. My head pounds, and my mouth feels like I ate cotton. I wedge open my eyes like I'm coming out of a long winter's hibernation but slam them shut when I see the light from outside flooding the room. I roll onto my back and try again.

This time, more slowly, I open my eyes and raise my head. I reach for the glass of water, lifting just enough to take a few sips to wet my throat and clear it. I fight through my heavy head and foggy mind, and force myself to get up. With my legs draped over the side of the mattress, I glance at the phone on the bed and tap the screen. My heart sinks when I see the time—four hours later—and no notifications.

No calls.

No messages.

Nothing.

Twenty-four hours have officially come and gone. A yawn catches me off guard before I force myself up, grabbing the robe and wrapping up again. I use the bathroom and splash my face with cool water to help wake up. It's a slow process, something Belinda told me not to rush. By how fast my heart beats, she's probably right. I shouldn't push myself.

Once I feel steady on my feet and in my thoughts, I walk to the window, pushing the sheers aside, and stare out. I feel lost and so alone.

Knocking on the door pulls me away from my troubled emotions. When I open the door, the earlier valet hands me a Bergdorf Goodman bag. "Delivery, Ms. Westcott."

"Thank you." Maybe these contain pajamas. That would be a wonderful surprise.

I let the door close automatically and set the bag on the bed. Taking hold of two spaghetti straps, I slowly pull the ruched black material out until I hold it in front of me. It's stunning, but it's not pajamas.

Peeking back in the bag, I find a shoebox. I think these

heels go with this beautiful dress. I'm just confused as to why he had this sent over. Where on earth am I going to wear this?

The phone buzzes on the bed, drawing my attention back to it. When I pick it up, only two words are on the screen: *Dinner tonight?*

7

Loch

I'D SENT the car for Tuesday and chose to walk. The restaurant isn't far from the office, maybe nine or ten blocks. It's not a restaurant I visit often, but they know the Wescott name, so it wasn't too hard to secure a reservation. Doesn't matter. I had plenty on my mind to keep me company.

Between the Reinhold case and being sidetracked by Tuesday, it's not been a great week. The judge rescheduled their court date for Monday. As for Tuesday, she seems set for the time being. I'm hoping to hear how things went today. Though, I was surprised she accepted my invitation.

I thought she would be at the police station to deal with details or even headed home. I didn't expect to receive her text: *When and where?*

The simple response was the lighter moment I needed in my day, but I quickly wiped away the silly grin when Leisa came into my office to drop off a file. I cleared my throat and got back to business.

I've been looking forward to tonight ever since.

The transition between the happy hour crowd and the dinner guests keeps the noise level elevated inside the restaurant, so I choose to wait at the far side of the bar for Tuesday. Hoping we get some reprieve from the chatter of the main dining area.

Bourbon won't do me any favors, but it should get me over the hump of midweek.

I take a sip, letting the amber liquid flow. It tricks my mind, making me relax before it hits the system. It's been a week, and it's only Wednesday.

Leisa's orders were to take the rest of the night off. I chose to do the same, to unclutter my brain and not think about work. That left my mind to wander to the only other thing keeping me busy.

Holy shit.

Tuesday.

I stand the moment I see her. The Bergdorf shopper promised she wouldn't be disappointed with the dress. When she strips off her coat, revealing the black dress that hugs her waist, heels that not only advertise her five-five, five-six height but also show off those incredible legs leading to her curvy hips, I'm not disappointed either. Not that I could be with her.

The host takes her coat and hands her a check before pointing at the back of the restaurant where I'm standing, gawking like a fourteen-year-old boy. *Jesus.* Pull yourself together, Westcott.

You'd think I'd never seen a beautiful woman before.

Is that what Tuesday is?

Dumb question. *Of course, she is.*

But am I going to use that as a baseline like she's nothing more than a pretty face?

So far, she's so much more.

I can't go there, though. I won't twist this relationship. Although I've always had a deep appreciation and weakness for beautiful women, Tuesday and I are platonic, and I intend to keep it that way.

With her hair hanging over one shoulder when she approaches, her smile grows when she sees me. "Platonic," I mutter, gulping from my glass in a feeble attempt to remind myself, but I think it might be too late.

"Hello," I say, then clear my throat from the frog that seems to have settled in it. Puberty was a bitch the first time around. I don't intend to repeat it.

With a sweet laugh, she leans in as if she's going to kiss my cheek. Is that what we're doing? Air-kissing when we see each other?

She backs away with a look of mortification, sucking in her breath and her gaze away. Her hand flies out as if she can shoo the air of awkwardness away. "I don't know why I did that. I'm—"

I catch her hand, stopping her words. "Don't worry about it. Maybe it's a memory reflex, something you did before."

"I feel like that's all my life is now—something I did *before*, a life I'm not privy to anymore."

"Well, if it gives you any comfort, you haven't forgotten how to rhyme." Damn, I probably shouldn't have said—

"Very funny, Westcott." I also win a grin from her, even if just a little one.

With a shrug, I chuckle dryly, still holding her hand. "I try."

She's a paradox of a woman, as complicated as her coffee order. She changed from the demanding woman at the coffee shop to smiling after being attacked and injured.

When her eyes go to our bonded hands, I let go of her

and tuck mine into my pocket, glad for the bustle in the restaurant. It keeps her from hearing me gulp nervously. You know, like I'm that kid back in school.

Her scent travels the small space between us, and I take a deep breath. Floral mixed with vanilla. She's making me rethink my stance on our relationship and keeping it platonic. Platonic doesn't begin to describe my thoughts while looking at her in that dress.

Trying to be subtle is fruitless, so I defer my attention. "Drink?" I offer, forcing my eyes to the bar and taking my glass in hand.

"I'm thinking I shouldn't just yet." Touching her head, she says, "Still healing."

"Right. I almost forgot." Why am I acting like this? *Fucking hell.* It's not a date.

"And interestingly enough, I guess I do drink since I don't seem opposed to the idea in the general sense."

"I suppose you do." I hold up my glass. "Do you mind—"

"No, not at all. Go ahead. If I thought I could drink, I'd order a glass of champagne." Her eyes go wide, and her smile cracks her expression. "I like champagne," she confesses as if she's won an Olympic medal. "I've been keeping mental notes when I recognize a piece of my puzzle, hoping it helps me figure out who I am just in case my memory never returns."

"The doctor said you might not get your memory back?"

"No," she says, shaking her head. "I think it's more of a backup plan to help me cope while I'm recovering."

She's so easy in her words, so sure of herself for someone who claims to be the opposite. Tuesday may not remember her past, but she knows who she is in the moment. That's more than most people can say.

"Ah. That makes sense."

The host comes up behind her. Holding menus at her side, she says, "Your table's ready, Mr. Westcott." She tilts her head away from the bar. "Follow me."

"Are you ready?" I ask Tuesday.

She nods, then turns to follow the host as she guides us to our table. It's one I've sat at before on a date—a cozy corner where interruptions are fewer. I'm not sure how she'll feel about the intimacy of it, but we're about to find out.

I move behind her when she sits and tuck her in before moving to the other side of the table for two and taking my seat. When we're alone, Tuesday leans forward with a genuine smile that makes me wish this were a date. The women I date don't typically have stars in their eyes. It's been a long time since someone looked at me as more than a means to an end, a layover in the city for one night, or like someone they might want to have a conversation with that doesn't involve intercourse as the dessert course.

Tuesday is a breath of refresh in her enthusiasm. I won't wax poetic about it since she's suffering from amnesia. Everything is new to her and, by extension, more exciting. *Even me.*

She lays her napkin across her lap, and says, "I'm happy you texted."

"You are?"

"I don't know, but being alone all day wasn't that fun."

"I thought you'd be resting."

"It was nice to be out of the hospital. I took a bath and ordered room service. I have to warn you. Don't look at the bill." She winks, the woman captivating me.

"Oh yeah? What will I find?" I glance around to make sure no one is listening and then lower my voice. "Porn?"

"What?" She draws attention from neighboring tables

and recoils. "For the record, I don't watch porn," she adds, not worried about everyone in the restaurant overhearing. Struggling to maintain her composure, she starts laughing. "I was referring to the double order of fries. Wow, you slipped and rolled right into the gutter with that suggestion."

"Apparently, it's one of the top charges at hotels. Go figure."

"I have nothing against it, but . . ." She scrunches her face. "Why are we talking about this again?"

"You mentioned the bill."

"Ah. Right. *Annnyway*," she says, her smile still shining under the restaurant's dim lighting. "I'm excited because I have no idea when I last ate pasta, but I'm so hungry for it right now."

That was an impressive journey, detours and all. I chuckle. "I'm glad you're here, and I can fulfill your pasta fantasies."

"Pasta fantasies? You're naughty, Mr. Westcott." If she keeps calling me Mr. Westcott, she just might find out how naughty I can be. She goes on to say, "But truer words have never been spoken." Sitting back in her chair, she gazes at the menu. "Now, what do I want?"

Although I'd chat aimlessly with her all night, I glance down, pretending to scan the menu because this is not a date. I already know what I'm ordering. It's the same thing I order every time I'm here. "What looks good?" I ask.

When I look up, I find her eyes on me. Not even bothering to hide it, she asks, "What do you recommend?"

"The classics are always a safe bet at Italian restaurants."

"Like you?" There are those stars again, shining bright. She's trying to do me in, one sweet smile at a time. "A handsomely tailored suit, knows about etiquette, and oozes charm."

"I didn't know oozing could be charming."

"Yet here you are, proving my point." She laughs. "Tell me something, Loch."

"Australia is wider than the moon."

"Huh?" She giggles with a slight roll of her eyes. "No, I meant something else."

"A hashtag is actually an octothorpe for the eight points."

A pointed look doesn't hold under her laughter. "Other than wanting to be on your team for trivia, why do you know that?"

"I enjoy reading."

Her jaw slacks open, and her brows shoot toward the ceiling. "So do I."

I love that she makes it sound like we're the only two people in the world who like to read. It's another connection to her that I won't take for granted. "We should hit the book-store together sometime."

Relaxing her features, she replies, "I'd like that."

I rest back, then ask, "What would you like to know?"

"What do you mean?"

"You said you'd like to ask me something when we were talking about classic dishes—"

"Right. That was before you derailed the whole conver-sation," she jokes. "Actually, teasing aside, I wanted to ask if you ever lose hope when the pressure feels like it's too much to handle?" Her intense eyes make it seem as if she needs a lifeline right now. Her eyes dip closed, and she adds, "I'm not sure if anyone's going to show up for me."

"You don't need to worry, Tuesday. I'll be here for you as long as you need." *What am I doing? What am I saying?* I'm not in a position to make her that promise, much less keep it.

"How can you say that, Loch? We just met."

Exactly. She understands I spoke in the moment. "I don't want to see you sad." *The truth.*

"Why?" *Why?*

Her eyes water, doing exactly what I hoped to avoid. I work in corporate law because I don't have the skill set to deal with raw emotions. She needs someone in her corner, someone on her team. Am I ready to be that for her? To commit to see her story through?

A tear falls as she looks at me. "Got any advice for me, counselor? I can't pay you now but send me a bill, and I'll add it to the pile," she says, trying so hard to sound like she's not broken, but I hear the crack in her voice.

"I never charge the people who are important to me."

A smile escapes her sadness, and she sweeps strands of loose hair in with the others over her shoulder. "Oh dear, Mr. Westcott, did you just admit I might be important to you?"

Despite the teasing in her tone, I scrub a hand over my face, my own grin cracking through the conversation. "Eh, we all have our weaknesses."

"I'm glad we finally found one of yours."

She's most definitely mine.

8

Tuesday

LOCH IS SO MUCH MORE than he lets on.

Savoring the full meaning of his words, they've penetrated my heart, and all I can do is stare at him in disbelief. He tried to fool me, but he didn't succeed. The man behind the attorney has a heart of gold.

But I'm starting to realize he wants people to think emotions have no place in his life. That benefits him at work, but in his personal life, it makes him vulnerable to the prosecution, a.k.a. me. That's why he's left me in the cold absence of the warmth of his gaze. He's been looking everywhere but at me since his confession, probably thinking it makes him weak. It doesn't. I see his strength more than ever.

I reach across the table and lay my palm flat beside his silverware. "Loch?" His eyes slide back to mine, the laughter we shared dying down. "I appreciate you opening up to me, especially since I realize that's not a place of comfort for you."

"You appreciate it, but I shouldn't have said anything at all. It's . . ." He looks at my hand and raises his from his lap, but then he stops and lowers back down. "It's not something I usually offer up easily."

"That's why it means so much to me." I'm careful as I paddle through his choppy waters of emotions. "I took it as intended. You're under no obligation to me." My heart starts racing and I look away, almost wishing I had a story or distraction to detour us back on track. With nothing but darkness in place of memories, I slide my gaze back to him and offer him one of my secrets instead. "I don't know how old I am." A humorless laugh escapes without permission. "How crazy is that?" I ask with a half-hearted eye roll.

He's angled in his chair, his build too large for the wooden frame. "I'm sorry."

"Pfft. Don't be." I reach over and take his glass. I know I shouldn't drink but feeling like this has to be worse than any side effects from the concussion. "What is it?"

"Bourbon."

"Wonder if I like it." I take a sip, letting the flames of alcohol scorch my throat. I scrunch my face when my chest can't take it and end up coughing and scrambling for water to douse the fire. I take a long pull of the cool water, reveling in the relief it brings. Inhaling through my nose, I slowly exhale a tinged breath.

The crack of a smile splits his face, and he says, "I don't think you like bourbon."

I rub my throat as if I can soothe it. "I don't know why you do."

"Sometimes the burn is worth the respite."

"And here I thought the relief came after with the water."

He chuckles. "It's both."

After taking another sip of water, I ask, "What in your life deserves that kind of respite?"

"Everything."

The last thing he'd want is for me to feel bad or sorry for him. Doesn't he have it all?

Money.

Looks.

A successful career.

A private car and driver.

I'm sure some fancy apartment on 5th Avenue.

But the sorrow in his eyes has me reevaluating my stance. Maybe he's lost communication with the most important part of life—*his heart.* I ask, "How can I—"

"Here's your soup and the salads," the server says with perfectly bad timing as I was about to see if Loch would open up even more to me. He sets the dishes down on the table, bursting the bubble Loch and I shared.

I move out of his way as he fills our table and refills our glasses. I can feel the weight of Loch's eyes fixed on mine, but I don't look up. I don't even breathe, much less move. I wait until we're alone again, then bravely drag my eyes from the vegetable soup in front of me to meet his searing gaze.

Under the intensity of his stare, I go blank as if amnesia strikes twice. His mood has shifted, and the masterful attorney has arrived. I don't stand a chance against him, so I stop prying, *for now*, and eat my soup.

I only get a few hearty bites in before he says, "I've been thinking."

"About?"

"Because you haven't received the call doesn't mean someone hasn't filed a report. There are procedures and processes in place that take time."

"I understand, but . . ." Holding my spoon above the

bowl, I stop and look around the bustling restaurant, needing to gather my thoughts. When I feel better prepared with my own clear thoughts, I say, "If I loved someone, I'd find them. I'd be searching day and night, have photos plastered everywhere, and file a report the minute legally allowed."

"Maybe they have, Tuesday. You may wake up tomorrow to your old life. So much can change in an instant."

"I know that better than anyone." I hate how harsh my tone has become and how desperate I feel not just for answers but for someone to come out of the woodwork to show me an ounce of the care that the man across from me has.

"I know you do. I didn't mean to insinuate that you're naive."

I roll my head. "Might as well. Everyone else does." My breath stops hard in my chest, and my spine straightens.

"What did you say?" he asks, leaning in.

I shift my gaze to the wall, hoping to find the void that will allow me to see my thoughts, but there's nothing. "Why *did* I say that?"

With his mouth open, Loch stares at me. "Why *did* you say that?"

"I don't know." I search the nooks and crannies of my mind for any clue as to where that came from but come up empty . . . *technically blank*. "Nothing comes to mind."

"Maybe your memory is returning because that was definitely something."

"You think?"

He nods. "We can hope."

I'll hold on to that hope as tight as I can.

I'm not sure if we're stunned or uncertain about what to

say after that, but the silence doesn't make me feel alone. It bonds us, not needing to be filled.

We eat, enjoying our food and the company of each other.

When the server returns to take my soup bowl and his salad plate away, I ask, "Can I ask you a favor, Loch?"

"Seems I owe you after I put my foot in my mouth."

"You didn't. You owe me nothing. Instead, you have spoiled me rotten, which I'm not sure I'll ever be able to pay you back for. Like this dress—"

"I'm happy to help. What favor do you need?"

I don't know why this feels important, but I need to do it. I'd just rather not do it alone. "Will you take me to the coffee shop tomorrow?"

A million things roll around this man's mind, and when he shuffles his knife to the other side of his plate, I'm not sure if it's a stall tactic or if he can't bring himself to say no to me.

Sitting in the shadow of his discomfort, I'm quick to add, "I shouldn't have asked. I know you're busy."

"I was working through my schedule. What time are you available?"

"Anytime you can squeeze me in."

"I'll send Brady to pick you up at seven forty-five. I'm locked in meetings starting at nine for the rest of the day."

"I'll be ready." I reach across the table and brush the tips of my fingers across his knuckles before retreating as if he suddenly had second thoughts. "I sound like a broken record but thank you."

He nods once and then starts on his spaghetti. The way he maneuvers the noodles around the fork playing off the spoon is truly a thing of beauty.

Does this man have any faults?

I'm not sure it's right to feel this safe with someone I don't truly know. But that's how he makes me feel.

Is it smart to trust him after barely spending any time with him? *Who knows?* But I'm going to. He's given me no reason not to.

———

"I'M IMPRESSED." Loch's eyeing the remains of my dinner.

Setting my elbow on the table, I rest my chin on my hand. "I did a solid job. I really have no idea why I'm so hungry today."

"You probably didn't eat for a while after waking up, so that's a long time to go without a meal." Maybe I'm too in my head, but I think Loch likes to look at me. He does it enough that I've come to accept the intensity of his eyes on me. He makes it tempting to do the same. Although we're both strong-willed, I don't. Instead, I drink in the heaviness of his gaze and let it smolder inside. Whether it's a temporary yearning or a true desire, I feel we'll catch fire one day.

Thinking of him alone on that bed causes my heart to squeeze. Sadness is the last thing I want to feel around him. I ask, "Dessert?"

"I'm good, but order what you'd like."

"I don't think I should. I'm stuffed. I'm going to sleep like a baby tonight."

The server drops the check on the table, and our eyes both land on it. We look up to meet each other's eyes. Popping my shoulders, I slink down in my chair a bit. "Thank you," I whisper again, annoyed with hearing myself repeat it another time, feeling like I'm once again at his mercy.

He deposits his card inside the folder, and it's swept away. "You're welcome," he says, picking up his glass of water to drain it. He checks the time on his watch, something I notice he does quite a lot. Maybe a bad side effect of being in a profession that bills for his time, or perhaps someone who's too busy to enjoy his life. For Loch, I think it's a combination of both.

"So—"

Tony returns and says, "Thank you, and we look forward to having you return soon."

I take it as a sign and stand as soon as Loch closes the booklet. He looks up at me, then stands, tucking his wallet inside his jacket pocket. "You look ready to go."

I'm not sure how to reply. I wouldn't mind spending more time with him, but I'm not sure if he has more time to spare for me. "We have an early morning coffee date."

"We do," he says, smiling at me.

The heat of his hand embraces my lower back as we weave through the tables toward the front. I hand my ticket to the host, who quickly retrieves my coat from a large walk-in closet.

Loch and I move to the door, but he stops and takes the coat from me. Holding it open, I slip my arms inside, then pull it tight around me. "How do you feel about red?"

"It's not my favorite color."

"Blue?" I ask when he opens the door for me.

We walk outside, hit with a chill of gusting wind. He lifts the collar of his jacket and flips his lapels up for more protection before tucking his hands in his pockets. "Brr. I like blue," he says, just barely nudging me. "You have beautiful blue eyes."

I hate that I'm fluttering my eyelashes in response. I really have no couth, especially comparing myself to his manners. He's still watching me, which makes me giggle, and then he asks, "What's your favorite color?"

"Since I don't know, let me think." I tap my chin, hoping something comes to mind to give me a clue.

"If you had to pick one color right now, what would it be?"

"The warmth of brown."

"Brown? I don't think I've ever heard of anyone choosing brown as their favorite color."

I could go into some deep description of all the colors of his eyes, from the golden centers to the caramel layer to the heat of the amber and the comfort of the chestnut. I won't, though, to save myself the embarrassment.

He adds, "Then again, you were dressed almost entirely in brown yesterday."

"I consider that more camel-toned."

We walk a little distance to get out from the entrance of the popular restaurant. "I'm not getting into the weeds on shades of brown, but let's just say it was a flattering shade on you."

"You're too kind, Mr. Westcott." I stop and turn back to him. The man has a way of seducing me with only a look in his eyes. *That* look currently on his face, to be specific. My knees weaken, but somehow, I manage to remain upright. "Do you mind giving me a ride home?"

"No."

One single syllable word voiced in that sexy, dulcet tone has my stomach tying itself in knots. With his deep voice and that ridiculously handsome face, I'm fairly certain this man never goes home alone after a dinner date.

Will I be his first?

I take the honor and get in the back of the SUV parked ahead at the curb. "Evening, Brady."

"Good evening, Tuesday."

The vehicle's cab feels like a haven from the wind and crowds outside. I put my seat belt on and relax against the soft leather. We ride in relative silence most of the way. I point out something of interest, and then he does. Nothing triggers any memories, though.

When we pull up to the hotel, Loch hops out before the doorman has a chance to open the door. He escorts me inside the luxurious lobby decorated in burgundy velvet and rich gold trimming with marble floors and a grand staircase.

We stop in the middle. One step more feels like an invitation upstairs. I'd be cheated of my time with him if we'd taken one step less. "So . . ." I say, rocking back on my heels.

"So . . ." He picks right up, then finishes with, "I'll see you in the morning."

"Seven forty-five." I slow my breathing, hoping to tame my thumping heart. The lobby is so quiet he might hear otherwise.

"I had—" we both say in unison, stop, then start laughing.

"I don't know why this is weird."

"Awkward."

"It's not like it was a date?" I look up as if he'll save me from embarrassing myself. He doesn't. He just watches me shovel myself deeper. "Thanks for the pity party. I needed it."

Nodding slowly, he studies me before saying, "Have a good night, Tuesday."

"Good night."

He covers about five feet, but then stops and turns back. With his thumb rubbing over his lower lip, he eyes me like I'm the dessert he's having tonight. "I didn't take pity on you.

I invited you because I wanted your company. You didn't disappoint." A smirk lifts the left side of his face, and I think I even catch a waggle of his eyebrows before he turns away. "See you tomorrow."

Damn, that man knows how to make a woman swoon. I steady myself on these heels and try to drag myself upstairs. If I've learned one thing about him, it's that the devil has another name.

Loch Westcott.

9

Loch

YOU DIDN'T DISAPPOINT?

I drop my head in my hands, embarrassed for me. *What the fuck am I doing?*

I was right to leave, though. If I hadn't, I would have kissed her right there in the hotel lobby. Who does that to someone in her situation?

She has a fucking concussion. *And amnesia.* Apparently, I think that's a great time to hit on her. *Fucking hell . . .* I'm such an asshole.

Such a mind fuck.

Yesterday, she showed me a glimpse of her old self. She was difficult and didn't take any shit. She dished it out in droves. Today, she's pleasant to be around—sweet, almost naive—but it feels genuine. How do I know which version of Tuesday is real? Is it the woman I met in the coffee shop or the woman now?

If I give it time, I'm sure things will resolve naturally. Although selfishly, I'd rather keep the version of her that I'm getting to know. That's not fair. She deserves her life back, even at the expense of our newfound relationship.

Relationship? No, I don't do relationships. I need to get that out of my fucking head. It's a friendship.

"You okay there, boss?"

"Just great, Brady," I lie between my teeth, slumping back in the seat. Today will be hard to beat—good and bad. I stare out the window, wondering how badly I'll fuck things up tomorrow.

I fill Brady in on the plan for the morning, then get out, dragging myself through the lobby of my building and into a waiting elevator.

Once I'm home, I toss my keys in the small bowl on the console just inside the front door, feeling victorious when they don't slide over the edge like they do most days.

The solitary sound from the hard soles of my shoes fills the short entry feeding into the living room. I don't expect to hear anything when I come home at night, but the barren echoing still bothers me two years after moving in.

It's early, just past eleven.

I'm finally home. I don't think I've been home at this hour in some time. This is where I should feel most relaxed, easing under the covers and getting some rest. Instead, I'm changing into workout clothes and then heading upstairs to the building's gym to burn through another hour or two, and hopefully some of this stress.

But running can't stop my thoughts from spinning faster than the treadmill. Weights can't exhaust my muscles enough to dull my mind. Focus. Stay in the moment.

I give it a solid twelve reps before I sit down on a bench and drop the dumbbells on the mat beside me. Is it normal to be this stressed, to work so hard that you not only miss sunrises but also sunsets? That I account for every daylight hour in billing minutes to clients, including not being able to enjoy my personal life even when it's dark?

Every other attorney at Westcott Law was already married when they joined the firm. Two had kids, and one is seven years older, while the others are decades ahead of me. I don't have time to see my friends or family enough. I can't imagine having enough time for a wife, much less a family right now.

Setting the weight bar on the rack, I droop forward on the bench and let my head hang down. Sweat drips from my forehead, hitting my leg, and I take it as a sign. I could stay longer but decide to push up and grab my towel. Dragging it over my face and down my neck before wrapping it over my shoulders, I clean the equipment, grab my water, and head to the elevators.

Since it's somewhere just past midnight, the building is quiet, and the elevator is empty, which is how I like it. Back in my apartment, I crank the shower faucet on, strip my clothes off, and toss them in the hamper. Stepping under the hot water equally heats my skin and soothes my muscles.

Planting my hand on the tile above my head, I close my eyes and let the water pummel the back of my neck. I know what I need . . . a release

Blue eyes.

Full hips.

"You're too kind, Mr. Westcott," she purred.

She's been driving me crazy, but desire wins the war I've been waging with guilt. I didn't help her to get laid. Fuck, I'm such a bastard. Right now, I don't even fucking care. I give in to my carnal side, taking hold of my erection and sliding my fist down and slowly back up, easing into pleasure.

I see how she looks at me when she thinks I don't notice. And the brazen exchange of stares we challenge each other with has me holding on tighter and pumping faster. When Tuesday licks those lips, I'm convinced she'll be my undoing if I ever get the chance to have them wrapped around me.

I imagine her kneeling before me, her body soaked from the shower, her pussy wet for me, and the image has me close to the edge of a release. Picturing that sexy mouth of hers sucking me off instead of my hand pumping hits just right, my release hitting harder. "Oh fuck," I groan just as I finish coming.

I stay like that until I catch my breath, only to open my eyes and find I'm alone. *Fuck.* I shake my head and swallow. She was so good, too. At least in my dreams.

Grinning as I wash up, I have no doubt the real thing will be even better.

I crash into bed just shy of one, finally ready to fall asleep.

Buzz...

Buzz...

Buzz...

Wait...what?

I open my eyes just enough to realize the buzzing isn't part of a dream but real. "Oh shit!" I reach over to turn off the alarm on my phone before lunging out of bed. 7:10. "Fuck."

Charcoal-gray suit anchored on a hook.

White shirt—crisp and clean pulled from a row of others.

Black tie will complete the look.

I told Tuesday seven forty-five, but here I am, the one running late. I never run behind, but I've been late to just about everything this week. Still shaking my head in disbelief, I rush into the bathroom to get ready.

Ten minutes later, I grab my keys and head for the elevators. I already know I'll be stuck in traffic, but I still don't want to add to it.

When the doors open, 16B stands straighter and smiles. The brunette is attractive, but the last thing I intend to do is put a neighbor into the rotation. That would get messy and fast. I don't want to be forced to avoid my building or, worse, have to move because she's catching feelings I have no intention of returning.

I don't have time to think these days, much less get involved in a relationship. Though my stupid grin might reflect otherwise. But thinking about brown being Tuesday's favorite color is so different. *She's different.*

I shouldn't be giving any more of my time away. I have clients who pay me a lot of money for every minute of my day.

Call me a sap for this woman, but she made it impossible to say no last night. *Impossible by existing?* Yeah, pretty much.

She's been through hell and still going through it. I'm not going to pile on more problems. If she wants me there to make her day a little easier, I'll be there.

The doors open, and I pivot my gaze to a man in a light-gray suit. I believe he lives on the twelfth floor. We exchange a gentlemanly nod, and then I stare blankly at the doors, keeping my eyes forward and on anything other than the pair of eyes burning a hole into my back.

16B is relentless in her efforts to get my attention, but

ironically, we've never spoken beyond a basic greeting. Not a word.

Thankfully, the elevator makes no more stops, and as soon as we land on the first floor, the doors open. I rush across the lobby and push through the door but then come to a standstill on the sidewalk.

My car is usually at the curb. What the—I look left and then right. Brady's nowhere to be found. What the—*shit!* I sent him to get Tuesday, which means I have ten minutes and six blocks to cover. Better get to running.

My thoughts race as fast as I am, and I hope I don't break out in a sweat. It's too late to worry about that. I'll have to shower and change at the office. But I'm glad I didn't drink much last night, or this run would be going differently.

It's funny because I ordered the bourbon to relax. I didn't need a stiff drink to help with the rough week. I just needed to spend a little time with Tuesday again to brighten my day.

I know how selfish it sounds, and I would never voice this aloud, but I judged her all wrong. I'm not discounting the unprovoked attack, but I'm just as guilty for responding. I should have ignored her, especially considering her mood matched mine. I never intended for that conversation to end differently than it did—poorly. But even then, something about her made it really fucking hard to resist.

There still is . . .

I'm in so much trouble.

10

Loch

I WANTED to be the first one here, to be here when she arrived. You never know what this place may trigger, and it wouldn't be good for her to go through that alone.

I finally reach the block and slow down to catch my breath but pick up my pace again when the SUV pulls to the curb up ahead. I reach the shop just as she steps out of the vehicle.

She may think the "classics" are boring, but she looks beautiful in the black pants and shirt. The wind catches, and the fabric flutters against her skin. Even in flats, she's sophisticated and just as beautiful as last night.

Focus on why we're here and not the woman.

Unfortunately, they're one and the same as her demeanor takes a downturn when she looks at the building ahead. It's written all over her body language from the lip she's biting to the way she's clasping her hands so tightly together as if she'll fall apart if she doesn't.

As soon as she sees me, a smile that could light up the

skyline breaks through her worries. "Hi," she says as I approach her.

I give Brady a wave, but I think he's laughing too hard to notice, making it obvious that he knows I ran to get here. Whatever. Turning to Tuesday, I say, "Good morning. How are you doing?"

"I'm good." Her eyes leave our surroundings and meet mine briefly. "I think."

"You sure you're ready to do this?"

She shrugs as she scans the coffee shop. Then her eyes go to the wall near the window, and she asks, "That's where I was attacked?" When her gaze pivots to me for an answer, I decide right then not to lie to her. She deserves the truth about the memory she carries forward instead of trying to protect her by creating a prettier picture.

"Yes. You'd just come from inside and took a right. I don't know if you stopped, or he grabbed you hard enough to make you stop."

Glancing back over at the brick wall, she says, "He came up behind me."

As much as I want to fill in the blanks in hopes of bringing back her old life, I don't know what happened once we parted ways. "Would you like to go inside?"

"Yes," she says, steeling herself and taking a quick breath before moving forward. She walks with intention toward the door.

I grab the door and hold it. Others bustle in after her, unaware of the pain she's dealing with. I only get pissed when a guy bumps her from behind and startles her. He turns back to say, "Sorry," but then jumps into the line to cut her off.

Yeah, real fucking sorry. *Asshole.*

Tuesday steps back out of the busyness of the line and

looks around. Her eyes widen like she's seeing the wizard behind the curtain for the first time, but then her shoulders slack as she takes in the space. "It's not that big."

"No," I reply. "When I walked in, you were at the register. I was back here at the end of the line. I remember you paid cash because the line wasn't moving while you dug out change from the bottom of your bag."

Covering her eyes with her hand, she drops her head. "Oh God. I held up everyone?" Straightening her neck, she says, "Sorry."

"None needed." I leave out how I mentally called her Miss Handsy for the demonstrative display she put on at the register. *Maybe I'm not ready to be one-hundred percent honest . . .*

"How did we end up talking?" she asks so innocently.

Now I'm questioning why I ever thought I could be honest with her at all. *Fuck.*

I shift and look at the line forming a few feet from us. "We just happened to be the last two left."

A small smile comes into play as she rocks with soft laughter. "Did you speak to me first?"

"Actually—"

"I spoke to you first? *Oh no.*" Her head falls into her hands. Lifting up, she peeks through her fingers. "What'd I say?"

I'd like to forget that part. "Um . . . Nothing much. We just talked about our coffee orders."

"Coffee, huh." Her gaze lands on me, and she licks her lips. Another image to save for later.

"Well, if you want the truth . . ."

"I want the truth." The words rush from her mouth.

"I think you were hot for me."

Leaning back, her lips purse. "Really?"

"You didn't come off like the subtle type."

Her sigh has me waiting for the rest of her reaction. "Do you think I'm still the subtle type?" You'd think I'd just accused her of stealing Christmas by how she pulls her brows together in confusion.

"I think you're cautious, which is wise in your circumstance."

"I agree with that analysis. Thank you, Dr. Westcott."

"My pleasure."

She nudges me playfully with her elbow just before turning her attention toward the front counter. "All of the employees working that day have been questioned as possible witnesses. Does anyone look familiar?"

I recognize the kid manning the steam machine. "The guy in the corner, red hair. He was the first one to call 911. He also came outside to check on you."

Tuesday moves between the few tables that fit inside the shop, heading for the barista. I follow, giving her the time and space she needs to maneuver not only through the small shop but also through her emotions.

I pull out my phone to make use of the time but decide that's not why I'm here.

Then I realize what I'm missing.

Fuck. Fuck. Fuck.

I sigh, letting anger boil in my blood.

"Everything all right?" she asks, sneaking up on me. I guess it's not really sneaking just because I wasn't paying attention since she walked right up.

"I forgot my briefcase at my apartment this morning." I run my fingers through my hair. "I was running late, and I have a meeting as soon as I walk in the office." Glancing at the barista, I then look at her. "How'd it go?"

"He shared what I ordered. No wonder it took so long."

It's cute the way she scrunches her nose. "It doesn't even sound good." She nods toward the door, so we make our way to the exit. Outside, she continues, "He doesn't know anything else other than their corporate office has to approve the release of the footage. That seems to be the holdup."

Horns blare, the sidewalks are packed, and the sun finally appears. She shakes her head, and says, "I don't think their footage will be any better. So this crime might just go unsolved."

Moving us out of the foot traffic of the shop, I ask, "Is anything familiar or—"

"No. I could be anywhere, and I'd feel just as lost." She exhales, her body deflating. Her eyes are still so brilliant, but I can see the clouds moving in. "I appreciate you being here, Loch, but I know you need to go. It's okay. I'll find my way back."

"No, the SUV is yours to use." Leaning in conspiratorially, I chuckle. "I think Brady prefers you anyway."

"Let me do something for you."

"What's that?"

"You go to work, and I'll retrieve your briefcase. I have nothing, *literally*, nothing else to do today and the waiting is killing me. This will keep me busy just for a bit, and it will help you out. What do you say?"

I'll need to shower and change at the office, which I won't have time to do if I go home for the briefcase. But I can't make her run an errand for me. "I can't ask—"

"Right. You don't even have to ask. I'm volunteering for the job."

Hm . . . "It would be a huge help."

She smacks her palms to my chest. "It's decided then."

I suppose it is. "Thanks."

"Least I can do." We walk toward the Escalade.

"The office is a few blocks away. It will be quicker if I head there while Brady drives you to my place. The doorman will give you a key. You can run up, grab it, and Brady will get you to my office."

"Sounds like a plan. Where is the briefcase?"

"Right by the door." I walk her to the SUV and help her inside. "You won't miss it."

Saluting me, she laughs. "I've got my orders, and I'm off."

"I'll call the doorman to let you in." When I close the door, she rolls down the window. I back up from the curb and stand there.

She rests her elbow out the window, enjoying this a little too much by the grin on her face. "This has nothing to do with anything, but I like your hair a little messier. You should wear it like that more often."

Not having time to style it in place, I only ran my fingers through it before leaving. I try to catch my reflection in the shiny exterior of the vehicle, but it starts moving before I do.

"Hey, Westcott?" she calls back to me.

I smirk. "Yeah?"

"You didn't disappoint."

I burst out laughing. She plays a solid word game.

But I already know when it comes to this woman, I'm definitely in trouble.

11

Tuesday

As if the building itself isn't mind-blowing with its high-end modern design, I can practically smell the scent of money filling the elevator. It also might have been the woman who looks like a model giving me a dirty look like I just snuck in off the streets. Little does she know, I did.

I restrain the cackle I want to free and put on an air of disdain until she flips her hair as she exits on the sixteenth floor. As soon as the doors close again, I flip my hair just to do it. I may not be as sophisticated as her, but I like what I see when I look at my reflection in the mirrored doors.

I may not have memories, but as I get to know myself again, I like who I am.

The elevator dings, and the doors slide open on the eighteenth floor. There are two ways to go. I take a chance and go left. With only three doors, his is easy to find at the end.

I stick the key in and turn to open the door. I'm hit with

a view that steals my breath and am quick to grab the frame for support. I exhale and smile. "Oh my, Mr. Westcott. You've got quite the apartment."

Glancing down at the briefcase, I let the door close behind me and stroll toward the picturesque view. I should grab the case and go . . . I really should, but I look around like the snoop I am, still smiling like a dork.

His apartment is exactly like Loch—classic and styled with everything in its place. I wish I could stay longer, but I know he needs his briefcase. I peek out the windows, getting a stunning city view and a glimpse of water in the other direction.

Other than a few photos hung on one side of the living room, he has art on the other walls. It's so tempting to see who fills the frames, but I've already stayed too long. I hurry back, grab the case, and lock up.

I squeeze into the elevator with a guy with a dogwalker tag on his shirt and a trio of corgis. Bending down, I rub their little licky faces. "They're cute."

"They're a handful too," he says, laughing.

The dogs barge into the lobby as soon as the doors open, dragging their walker behind them. "Have a good day," I say with a wave.

Brady stands by the door and opens it as soon as he sees me. "Nice place," I say, hopping in the back.

When he gets into the driver's seat, he says, "It's not too shabby. Did you see the water?"

"Not long enough. I didn't want to keep him waiting." I cuddle the briefcase like it will explode if it jostles. When I realize what I'm doing, I set it beside me and keep myself from running my fingers over the black leather.

Brady says, "Loch has had me over for meals and meetings. It's a nice view, but I don't think he enjoys it."

"What do you mean?"

"He works all the time, so he's not home enough to appreciate that apartment."

I'm nodding like I know this firsthand. I've known him a few days, and although I have a strong sense of his life from the hints he's dropped, I'm starting to think that Loch doesn't have much of a life at all. Of course that's easy for me to say since I don't know how I filled my days or made money.

Wonder what I did for a living?

"We're here. Twenty-third floor."

I peek out the window and look high into the sky to see an impressively mirrored skyscraper disappear into the clouds. "Thanks."

Stepping onto the sidewalk, I need to steady myself. Maybe I've been running around too much this morning, but I feel a bit woozy. I walk inside, and after checking in with the front desk, they find my name, give me a pass, and direct me to the elevators.

I'm front and center in an elevator packed full of men in suits. I might have seen a woman in the back, but she's not tall enough to see now with the doors closed. When I step off and see the Westcott Law Firm sign, I walk toward the reception.

"Hello?" A man, maybe early twenties and covered in freckles that give him a youthful look, greets me.

"I'm here to see Mr. Westcott." I never thought to ask if this is his company or a family-run business. What if he's not the only Westcott around? "Loch."

The man grins. "Yes. He's expecting you." When he glances down to read the log in front of him, his brow furrows. His eyes lift slowly. "Ms. Westcott?"

"It's a long story," I reply with a chuckle.

His eyebrows shoot up. "I bet. Enter right there, take a left, and follow it around until you reach the corner office. His name plaque hangs outside the door, so you can't miss it."

"Thanks."

I push through the door to reach a good-sized room with cubicles. I follow the path along the windows and keep walking past the offices on the left until I come to Loch's office. A desk sits outside it with a large area full of cabinets and a purse on the floor near the trash bin. Looking both ways, I don't see anyone, so I check the doorknob. It's unlocked.

"Hello? Loch?" I walk in, but he's nowhere to be found either. The spacious office has a sitting area, a large desk, and a captain's chair-type wingback. I feel a little weird being in here without him. What if someone finds me here?

I close the door, then set the briefcase on his desk. He did say he had meetings all day. I'm sure he's stuck in a conference room in another part of the office. Dragging my finger across the top of the wood and metal desk, I walk to the windows and peer out. Another incredible view. Probably one he doesn't get to enjoy, either.

My head spins.

I step back and sit in the closest chair with my hand cupping my head. Should I be concerned? Is this normal for having a concussion?

I feel nauseous.

Desperate, I look around, not feeling able to stand just yet. Spying a door that blends in with the wall, I know there's a strong chance it's a closet, but what if it's a private bathroom? Wouldn't a big-time attorney in Manhattan have one of those?

I carefully lift from the chair and make my way over to the wall. Pushing on it, I hear a click, and it releases. Score!

When I open it, steam billows toward the opening and engulfs me. I hear faint humming, and when my vision clears, I see Loch in the shower. *Completely naked.*

I cover my mouth, afraid to make a sound or move an inch, yet it doesn't once occur to me to look away. He's tilted his head back, eyes closed, as the water rains on his chest and travels down his body. *Like my gaze.*

The Greek gods hold nothing on this man—sculpted from steel muscles that flex when he turns, letting the water pummel his shoulders to that glorious indention in the sides of his ass to that cut V that digs deep into his sides and veers down in the front to his— "Tuesday?"

Our eyes meet through the glass just as a wave of nausea rolls through me. *Oh no!*

I run for the toilet, dropping to my knees, and lift the lid just in time.

Behind me, the water cuts off, and the faint sound of his voice reaches me through the convulsions. Tears fill my eyes while my body revolts and my head pounds.

He scoops my hair up off my neck with one hand while his other strokes my back. "Try to breathe." His voice soothes as he continues, "Breathe through it."

I focus on the direction, closing my eyes and slowing my breath until my panic subsides and my stomach settles. Mortification might get the best of me when I have to look into his eyes again, but I can only tackle one thing at a time. Right now, the vomiting takes precedence.

He says, "Breathe in and slowly release."

I grab toilet paper and wipe my mouth. The heat of embarrassment floods my face, causing my head to pound again. But I feel steady enough to look behind me.

Oh God!

My breathing picks up again when I see him in nothing but a towel wrapped around his lower half. I turn away just as quickly and use my hand as a shield.

He says, "I think it's a little late for that, don't you think?"

I toss the paper in the toilet and flush. Turning back, still feeling my face on fire, I sigh. "I'm so sorry. I didn't know it was a bathroom."

"What were you looking for?"

"A bathroom, just not one you were showering in," I reply, giggling a little. I finally meet his gaze again. "I felt ill waiting in your office."

"So it's not the sight of me that made you sick?"

"Oh God no. You're incredible." As if throwing up wasn't bad enough, now I'm vomiting my words as well? Raising my hand, I say, "Ignore me. I'm not thinking clearly."

"So you don't think I'm incredible?"

I whip back to catch his eyes set on me already. "No, that's not what I mean at all—"

"I know. I'm teasing, Tuesday." *He's teasing?* Loch Westcott bantering with me? That has to be a feat I've accomplished. Too bad I don't feel so great, or I'd be celebrating.

I push off him—his wet, hard, and hot body—instead, this just feels like a punishment for me. "Listen, you, don't give me a hard time."

"You ruin all the fun."

Standing up, he tightens the towel to my disappointment and then offers me a hand. When I slip mine into his, he pulls me up carefully until water droplets soak into my blouse. "You're getting me wet."

"About time."

"Loch," I say, my eyes widening on his face because I'm

trying so desperately hard not to lower them to ogle his body again. "What the heck has gotten into you?"

"You're right." He runs his hand through his hair and waggles it, sending drops flying, including spackling my shirt. Soon I'll look like I've entered a wet T-shirt contest.

"I should get dressed." I start backing out, but he asks, "Would you like to brush your teeth?"

That's an offer I can't refuse. "I'd love to."

He squats down and digs through the cabinet under the sink. I use the time to brazenly look at him again. Out of all the people in New York City, how did I end up with this man being my hero?

Luckiest damsel in distress ever.

He sets a toothbrush and paste on the counter, then moves to the door, and says, "I'm going to get dressed in my office if you can give me a few minutes."

"Of course."

As soon as he shuts the door, I look around. There's no closet in here, so I guess I just got lucky again in choosing door number one. I brush my teeth and rinse. I'm not sure how I did it, but I kept my shirt clean. The wet spots have already faded. Though the steam in here has made my hair a bit frizzier.

I hang out for a few extra minutes, then knock on the door. It's pushed open, and he greets me with a smile that makes me feel like I just made his day. The golds of his eyes brighten, and the shadow of stubble dusting his jaw tempts me to jump him. *What?* Not jump. *Kiss?*

God, I'm hopeless. "I brought your briefcase." I walk into the office, swinging my hands about.

"I see that. Thank you."

I stop in the middle of the room. "You have meetings."

"I do."

The door opens, and a woman says, "The Bakers—" Her eyes land on me, and the questions that fill her expression are on display. "I didn't know you had a guest."

After closing the bathroom door, Loch moves behind his desk. "Yes, well. Ms. Wes—Tuesday brought me my briefcase." He doesn't sit. "Tuesday, this is Leisa. Leisa, this is my. . ." He hits another stumbling block. The pause seems to make us all uncomfortable by how we all shift.

She says, "It's nice to meet you, Tuesday." Her gaze returns to Loch. "Mr. Baker and his attorneys have been shown to conference room two."

"Thank you," he replies, looking down.

As soon as the door closes, he says, "I'm sorry. I'm usually quicker on my feet. I didn't want to—"

"No explanation needed. I don't know what we are to each other either."

The lightness his lips held straightens into a flat line. "I was going to say I didn't want to overstep a line by calling you my date or disregard how much I enjoyed last night by calling you a friend."

"Oh, um . . . yes, I understand. I guess we left her to fill in the blanks." I laugh behind my hand. "I'm sure that will go over well."

His grin returns. "I'm sure I'll hear all about it later."

I enjoy his company too much to leave, but I know I should. "Mr. Baker and his attorneys . . ."

"Yes, they're waiting."

I walk to the door. With the knob in hand, I turn to look at him over my shoulder. "Would you like to go out tonight?" I rock my head back and forth, feeling much better, and wave my hand. "And when I say that, it means you also have to pay for everything."

A chuckle rips through him. "In that case, how can I say no?"

I pull the door open, but before I go, I add, "You have my number."

Smirking, he watches me with those eyes that could seduce the panties right off me, and then replies, "I sure do."

12

Tuesday

I DON'T KNOW what's come over me.

Correction. I know exactly what's come over me. Loch Westcott. *Naked.*

Yep. That will do it.

I should be mature about this. I've never been jealous of water before, but ever since I saw him in that shower, I am. I mean, what the hell? How does he look like that? Who knew he was hiding that body under that suit? Well, I think anyone can tell he's fit. But built like *that*? What I saw in the shower, *that* was unexpected.

I thought he was working all the time? I think, in fact, he's working *out* instead. He has to be. There's no way he can look that good without putting in some serious effort. I'll give him credit where credit is due. He *is* incredible.

Ugh. This is all wrong. He's more than a wet, so very hard, and lickable body.

He's also incredibly generous and kind, supportive, and so interesting.

There. That should cover the bases and hopefully save me from going to hell for thinking about his body in the most sinful of ways.

I cover my face with my hands. Oh goodness. I'm definitely going to hell for these dirty thoughts.

"You doing okay back there?" Brady asks.

Getting caught up in my thoughts had me forgetting where I was. My face flushes as humiliation runs rampant through my veins. "Fine," I reply with a squeak to my voice.

We catch each other's eyes in the reflection of the rearview mirror. I know he sees right through me by how his shoulders shake with laughter. He's kind enough not to say anything about it, though. Instead, he asks, "You sure you want to return to the hotel? Loch won't need me until this evening, so I can drive you anywhere you want to go. The city is at your fingertips."

We pass a clothing store, and that gives me an idea. "Hey, Brady? Will you take me to Bergdorf's?"

"You got it, Tues."

"I'M SO SORRY." A lady dressed in a bright-fuchsia pantsuit and her red hair pinned in curls on her head rushes into the personal shopping area where I've been waiting. "I had a mother of the bride melting down in the dressing room in ladies' underwear. Crisis averted, and she's off to the wedding."

"That's good."

"Very good. Sixteen months of demands, and she's finally satisfied." She sits in the chair next to mine and says, "I'm Kelly. I hear you're looking for a dress for dinner tonight?"

"Yes. Nothing over the top."

"Too bad. Over the top is my specialty." She laughs at her joke and stands. "I'm kidding. Come on, let's get to shopping."

We walk to the sales floor, and she leads me straight to the floor-length gowns. "I'm thinking this is the over the top you're referring to. So let's cut through to another special section, and you can tell me about your date."

"Actually, you may know him." That pulls her eyes back to me. "Loch Westcott. He ordered something for me yester—"

"Ah, yes. Mr. Wescott. We've never met, but he's ordered a few things over the years." She whispers, "I once googled him. He's very handsome."

"He is."

She stops to look me up and down over a rack where the dresses use less material than a handkerchief. "I knew I recognized the name. You're Tuesday. Tuesday Westcott. I didn't know he was married."

"Oh, we're not... Well, he's not." I don't know why I say this. I know I'm not married. I would surely feel differently —like I was missing half my soul—but I don't feel that at all. "What I mean is we happen to have the same last name, but we're not married."

She stares at me as if I lost her somewhere in that conversation but then picks up right where we left off. "There's a new selection of dresses on the back wall. They're perfect for your figure, and from what I know from Mr. Westcott, something he would like."

Something he would like?

This might not have been a great idea. This was supposed to be fun. I didn't count on feeling jealous. I wonder if I was jealous in my former life since I seem to be in this one. "Has he sent gifts to a lot of women?"

"Only a few over the years." She casually flips through the hangers as if I'm not hanging on her every word. *Only a few women . . .*

My heart sinks, though I have no right to be jealous. As I think about how he stumbled over the introduction to his assistant, a seed of doubt is planted right next to where my heart buried itself in the pit of my stomach.

I can be jealous, or I can be proactive. I choose the latter because two can play this game. "What do you have in blue?"

HIS PERSONAL SHOPPER had no problem charging Loch's card on file for all the things we picked out, especially considering her commission. But I hesitated. It may have been a grand plan when I concocted it, but I don't want to be beholden to someone else for anything, much less financially.

But I have no other options.

Brady offers to help me carry the bags, but I load my arms so he doesn't have to park the SUV. I dragged him around town with me, and we even grabbed lunch in the Escalade. After being sick earlier, that hoagie hit the spot.

But he's sacrificed enough of his day. The bags aren't heavy. They are just awkward. I still manage to make it to my room with only one incident. I hear the valet will heal just fine now that he's been bandaged. Who knew they made the corners of the bags so pointy sharp?

Well, Craig knows now. *Lesson learned.*

In the room, I unload my goodies and run a bath. Stripping off my outfit, I put it in the bag with my skirt for laundry pickup tomorrow. Every action is a calculated attempt not to check my phone. I've been successful most of the day, but it's just past four, and I've not had one call or text from the detective. *How is that possible?*

It's been forty-eight hours since I went missing, and I'm starting to think this might be it. *What the hell?* Why is no one looking for me? Is the universe being for real right now? Not one person in the world cares about me?

The detective told me he would contact me with new information. And although the blank phone tells me there's nothing new to report, I have a deep-seated need to hear him tell me otherwise.

Distract.

I have to keep myself together here and not completely lose it.

After I tie my hair up high on my head, I wash my face free from the makeup I tried on at the store. Then I run a bath, sinking until my shoulders are underwater, and rest my head back on the towel I'm using as a pillow.

The more I relax, the more thoughts of Loch creep into my head. I don't think I really processed what was happening at that exact moment, too stunned to move, too intrigued to walk away. From the water sheen highlighting his athletic muscles to the sound of him mixing with the pouring water. I thought he was humming, but now I think he was moaning.

There was more going on in that shower than getting clean. *Loch was getting dirty.*

Should I feel bad for interrupting? *Probably.*

Do I? *Not really.*

Images of Loch gliding his hands over his body have been running on replay in my mind all day. I close my eyes, wishing those hands were sliding over me. My chest gets heavy with each breath as sparks run through my veins like a live wire caught on fire.

His hand slipping between my legs, his mouth pressed to my neck. Hot whispers asking me how I like it—*Oh God.* Yes. Water splashes against the sides of the tub, my finger grabbing hold of the edges. "Tell me how you like it."

Overheating, I force my eyes open, realizing I don't know how to answer. You know, if he was asking me in real life instead of in a fantasy, what would I say? I have no idea.

I don't even know if I've had sex. *Have I?*

Maybe . . .

Maybe not . . .

What if I get to experience it for the first time all over again?

I grin as I rest back again. A giggle erupts, and my cheeks start to hurt from smiling. It's a ridiculous theory, and it doesn't matter if I'm a virgin, but I could really have fun with it.

Speaking of fun, I reach for my phone and text: *Hope your meetings have gone well today. I've been thinking about you.*

Three dots roll across my screen, and then a message pops up: *You've been thinking about me? Interesting. I'd love to hear your thoughts.*

Loch can be uptight. And I know we're still figuring out what this is between us.

Would it be appropriate to tell him what was really on my mind? *No.*

Do I want to throw caution to the wind and do what feels good? *Absolutely!*

But I think it might be too soon to share my real thoughts or what I just imagined him doing to me in the tub. Though I'd love to see his face if I ever have the chance to tell him the truth. I'd be hit with those eyes and that look that wavers between tearing my clothes off and spanking me.

Huh . . . *do I like that?*

I don't think so, but how do I know for sure? This is too much to deal with right now. I decide to tease him a bit and dance around the truth instead: *I'm sorry I interrupted your shower.*

I don't feel bad in the least, but I think he already knows that. There's a long pause before the next message pops up: *I'm not.*

He's not?

My mouth drops open, but my fingers fly across the screen: *Naughty, Mr. Westcott.* Maybe I'm not ready for this. I might be in hot water, but I'm starting to get overheated. Before this gets out of hand, I add: *Where are you taking me tonight?*

Loch: *A little place in the West Village. Be ready at 8. I'll meet you in the lobby.*

Me: *It's a date!*

Me: *Hey, Loch?*

Loch: *Yes?*

Me: *I'm still thinking about today.*

. . .

Me: *See you later.*

I quickly exit out of messages and toss my phone on the rug just out of my reach. I'm not sure I want to see how he'll respond to that.

I finish in the bath and dry off. I grab my phone and set it on the nightstand, deciding to lie down. Seeing Loch in the nude is enough to drive any woman to swoon, but I've also spent every minute of my day searching for clues to my identity.

With a slight headache, I've pushed myself too hard. And if resting gives me a better chance of getting some memories back, then I'm all in.

———

WHEN I COME DOWNSTAIRS, I look around for Loch, but I'm early enough to be here before him. I drape my coat over a nearby chair and wait, wanting him to see me in the full glory of this dress and the sparkling shoes.

"Miss Westcott? Miss Westcott?" A hotel clerk waves from across the grand lobby, then starts walking toward me with an older man at his side. I look behind me, but they're coming toward me and whispering when they approach. I don't catch what they say, but it sounded like they were speaking another language.

"Yes?" I ask, still in the dark.

The older man looks at me, letting his gaze travel, then settle on my chest before smiling at the clerk and giving him a nod. I have no idea what he wants, but I don't think I want to find out. Creeped out, I glance back over my shoulder in hopes of seeing Loch come through the door before reaching for my coat.

"Good evening, Miss Westcott."

Before I turn to go, the clerk says, "I'd like you to meet Benedettu Serra. He's visiting us from Sardinia this week."

The other man takes my hand and brings it to his mouth. "It's nice to meet you."

Before he has a chance to go any further, I remove my

hand from his grasp and take a step back. Holding my coat in front of me, I shift to drape it over my arm. "Mr. Wescott will be here any minute. I'm going to wait for him near the entrance."

The clerk's gaze shifts over my shoulder and the color drains from his face. "My apologies for keeping you. I'll make this quick."

"Make what quick?"

"Mr. Serra would like your company this weekend and was wondering if you have an opening in your schedule?"

I look back and forth between them several times, feeling like I'm missing something obvious. "I'm not following."

"He'd like to pay for your services."

"My services?" My head jerks back when it dawns on me. *Oh. My. God.* "Do you think I'm an escort?"

"I've been operating under the assumption. It's not something we normally allow in the hotel, but the Westcott's have been clients of ours for a long—"

"Let me be very clear for both of you. I'm not, nor have I ever been an escort." Feeling my anxiety rising, I swing my hands wildly in front of me. "I'm not a call girl. I'm not a hooker." Noticing the band around the man's left finger, I feel my anger surge. "So get it out of your head and tell your friend here to go home to his wife and appreciate her instead." I spin on my rhinestone-encrusted heels and head for the door. My heart pounds in my chest when I rush outside and straight into strong arms that embrace me.

The scent of the ocean with a hint of musk.

The perfectly cut suit.

Hard muscles wrapped around my soft frame.

Loch.

"Hey, there," he says, holding me tightly to him. "Everything okay?"

I close my eyes a few seconds more just to appreciate the compassion and concern of this man.

Stroking my hair, he bends down to catch my eyes when I open them, and whispers, "Tuesday?"

Pull yourself together. I take a breath. "Yes. I'm hungry." What else can I possibly tell him? That everyone thinks I'm his personal call girl?

"What's really going on?"

I take a moment to think about what I want to say. *Am I making something out of nothing? Is it really that big of a deal?* I'm sure I'll be laughing about it in a few minutes. "Do you remember how you told me the hotel clerk thought I was a call girl when you checked me in?"

I'm hit with a harder glare than before. No gold can be found in the centers of his eyes at all. *Only fire.* "Yes," he replies with a sharp edge to his tone. "Go on."

"I thought you were joking, but I think he meant it."

"Why do you say that?" While I try to figure out how to soften the offense, his temper sparks to life. "Are you going to make me drag it out of you, Tuesday, or will you tell me?"

"I was just offered a job." By the way he's fisting his hands by his sides, I can tell he's failing to see the humor. I get it. I failed as well at first. "There was a man from Sardinia. The hotel clerk introduced me as someone he could hire to keep him company while he's in town."

"What the fuck? Stay here."

My hands start shaking, panic making my heart beat faster as I watch Loch storm toward the hotel entrance. "What are you doing?"

"Handling it."

"There's nothing to handle, Loch. It's done. Over with."

He stops and turns back, then comes toward me. Opening the car door, he guides me into the cavernous back seat. "Wait here for me, okay?" Shooting his eyes to Brady, he adds, "I'll be right back."

"And then what?" I ask.

"And then you're going home with me."

13

Loch

THAT ASSHOLE DOESN'T EVEN SEE me coming. I could get in a punch, or a few, knock him the fuck out before he knew what hit him.

The tall counter between us can't save him, but I'm not looking to be arrested tonight for assault.

Pressing my hands against the marble in front of him, I lean in really fucking close.

He looks up with a grin I'm tempted to knock the fuck off his face. "Welcome to—Mr. Westcott?" Fear consumes him, causing his teeth to chatter like an animated skeleton. "How may . . ." His words stagger out of his mouth, and then he gulps heavily. "I, um, help you?"

"You ever talk to her again, and I'll ruin your fucking life."

Straightening his bow tie, he has the nerve to keep talking. "I tried to apologize, but she left."

"So it's her fault that you're a skeevy little fucker?"

"No, sir. I just—"

"How about this? You want to keep your job?"

"Yes, sir?" he replies, lowering his voice as he looks behind him to make sure the coast is clear.

"You want to keep your teeth?" When his eyes practically bug out of his face, I continue, "Have her belongings packed and delivered to my address before I return from dinner. Better not be you. Don't dare step one foot in that direction or near her stuff. You understand me?"

"Absolutely, sir. I'll have concierge take care of it. And I'll be comping her stay as well. With my deepest regret, my apologies." When I keep glaring, he gulps again. "Sir."

"That's what I fucking thought."

I turn and head for the Escalade. The flames continue to stoke my anger just thinking about how Tuesday was treated. *A fucking call girl?* She was attacked only a few days ago, and now she has to deal with this bullshit? Is she not safe anywhere?

I push through the door and see Brady standing with his arms crossed over his chest. "Anything I need to handle?" he asks like he's ready to torch the earth if I ask him to.

The guy's built like a tank, but I don't need his help. "I appreciate the offer, but I can't let you fight my battles."

He shrugs, a grin sneaking onto his face. "Always here if you need me."

We give a quick fist bump before I open the back door and climb in, sliding into the fog of tension that's built up while I was gone. By the time I buckle in, Brady is pulling away from the hotel. He glances back, and asks, "West Village?"

"Yes," Tuesday is quick to reply when I say, "No."

"You still want to go?" I ask, dropping my chin. Her gaze

never wavers from mine despite what little light drifts in from the signs we pass outside.

"I thought you did?"

"I'm in no mood to deal with crowds on a Thursday night." Unlike usual, I'm struggling to shake off this confrontation. *Why?*

"Then we shouldn't go." She shrugs, turning her gaze out her window, but nothing about her response—from her casual body language to her tone—backs what she's saying.

Giving in isn't a familiar trait of hers—either before or after she lost her memory. She has opinions and shares them freely. Something I respect, but I also appreciate the honesty. *So what has changed?*

Silence builds, shifting the air between us as I stare at her, waiting for anything other than her sacrificing her night for me. When she doesn't elaborate, I look out my window, uncertain how to proceed. *Call her out, or let her be?*

My knee begins to bounce from the waning adrenaline still coursing through my veins. I'll be the first to admit that losing my temper is not good for my reputation. It's not good for the firm, and if my dad gets wind of tonight, I'll soon be dealing with a tense phone call. But I'm not in the wrong. *I didn't hit the fucker, after all.*

That's progress from back in high school when my brother, Harbor, and I got caught in a few scuffles. We never started it, but it was hard to walk away without finishing it. Not so unlike how I just behaved.

Anyway, the guy looked scared enough. I don't see the weasel causing a commotion for fear of losing his job, so I should be in the clear.

I'm sure Tuesday would find it hard to believe I wasn't always so buttoned up. "Classic" as she likes to call it. Or maybe she would after the display I just put on.

She glances over, her eyes lingering on my knee that's still bouncing, and then raises an eyebrow before turning away. "Are you okay?"

"You were mugged, attacked, got a concussion, offered sex for money, and you're asking if *I'm* okay?"

"Yes." Angling her knees toward me, she rests her hand between us on the seat. "How are you, Loch?"

"I'm . . ." I start but then let the question sink in. How am I? How the fuck *am* I?

She finally says, "Maybe we shouldn't go to dinner."

When I look at her, my left hand still fisted by my side, I reply, "I'm angry."

"Why? He didn't call you a hooker." A smile cracks through the gloom of the car.

I chuckle. "No, he didn't."

Sliding just a little closer, she says, "I appreciate you fighting for me, standing up for my honor, and all those amazing chivalrous things. But you don't have to be my protector. It's not your job or your responsibility."

"I—"

"I know you want to help." I'm captivated by the way the tips of her fingers tap against her chest and then slide over her delicate neck. She reaches for me, gently prying my fist open and then pressing her palm to mine. "I'm not something you can continue to check off your daily agenda. If you want to spend time with me . . ." Even in the shadows of the SUV, I spy the sweetest pink creeping onto her cheeks. She looks down, but when she gathers herself together again, she looks me in the eyes. "I'd very much like that, but your duty is done, Loch."

"So what you're saying is that you do want to go to dinner?"

She bursts out laughing, resting her head back with a

smile that lights up my night. I don't even think she realizes her fingers have curled around my hand when she asks, "How do you feel about staying in tonight?"

"Staying in with you sounds like a better plan."

Just my luck.

16B would happen to be walking into the building behind us. I hold my arm in front of the elevator doors while they walk on, then join them. She drags her tongue over her full upper lip. "Thank you," she whispers to me when she passes.

I keep my eyes on Tuesday or the shiny metal walls of this box. I will purposely avoid her at all costs. Tuesday has been a real sweetheart, but I have a feeling she'll get some of her bite back if pushed too far.

The other woman doesn't even try to hide the fact that she's staring at me. Desperate for my attention, she shifts, aligning herself with me. My eyes flick to Tuesday in the reflection, who appears to be stuck in an eye roll.

I restrain a smirk, but barely.

16B glides off the elevator like she's walking the runway but makes sure to say, "Good niiight," to me as she exits.

Fuck, this won't go over well.

The doors close, and Tuesday comes behind me. From behind my ear, she whispers, "Good *niiight*."

"Yeah. Yeah."

She's laughing, walking around the elevator like she finally has the run of the place. I turn around. "Who's the model?" Her voice dances between teasing and genuine.

I don't blame her for being curious. I'd be asking all

about some dude if he acted like that with her. I reply, "Long story."

The doors open, and she walks into the hall but stops to wait for me. "You know . . ."

Here it comes. Fortunately, she's turned my mood around, and I can enjoy a little playful banter with her. "I do know. I know a lot."

"And so humble, too, Mr. Westcott." Her tone stays light, bordering on a giggle.

"I try to remember my roots."

"Why do I have a feeling your roots were never humble?"

Money never meant bragging or above others in my family. She'll see that when she meets my mother . . . *Wait. My feet stop ten feet shy of my front door. Why would she meet my mom?*

She keeps walking like she's been here a million times before instead of once. Stopping in front of the door, she turns back, her brows cinching together as she waits for me.

I don't know what's gotten into me, but I need to get her out of my head and realign my goals. As I unlock the door and she walks into my apartment, I realize there's one fatal flaw to my plan.

I just told her she's staying with me.

Does telling her she's coming home with me equal a temporary situation, transitional, or moving in? Running my hand through my hair, I grumble, "Ah, fuck." We probably should have put rules into place before making a drastic decision like this.

Too late . . .

She rushes to the windows, pressing her hands against the glass to look at the skyline. Glancing back at me, she says, "It's more stunning at night."

I close the door, locking it. "It is," I say, making my way to see the view as if I don't have the option every day. The thing I don't do is leave fingerprints or, worse, handprints on the glass.

But it's hard to be bothered when seeing the pure joy in her eyes. I add, "I'm rarely home during the day, so this is my view most of the time."

She turns around, her back pressed against the glass. "It's magical."

I hold out my hand. When she takes it, I pull her closer. "Magical indeed." Now that she's safe, though, I move toward the kitchen. "Water? Soda? Wine?"

"Water, please." She comes to the bar, resting her arms on it, watching me.

"Bubbles or flat?"

"I don't even know what that means?" She shrugs and touches the faucet. "Tap works."

I've never felt more pretentious in my life than I do right now. How did I acclimate to this life so quickly? I grab a pitcher from the fridge and pour a glass. "Filtered okay?"

"That works." She takes a sip as I pour myself a glass. Resting her elbows on the bar, she has her back to me as she takes in the view again. "It's weird what I remember and what I don't."

I come around and pull out a chair at the table. "Like what?" I ask, then take a drink of my water. Unable to keep my eyes off her, I watch as her expression flickers through a myriad of emotions. "Like the age thing, or . . ." She stops herself and takes a deep breath. Moving to the windows again, she smiles as she looks out, but it doesn't counteract the sadness seen in her eyes.

Glancing at me, she says, "I don't know if I can drive a car or what I do for a living. What's my favorite fruit? Do I have allergies? I don't know my own last name, but I know who the president is, and something in my gut tells me I love the ocean and going to the beach. Do I like tuna casserole? How do I even know what tuna casserole is?" Her face pinches, but she laughs, though the humor is lost. "See what I'm saying?"

"It must be hard."

We haven't turned on a single lamp or light in the apartment but seeing the soft glow from the skyline against her skin has me thinking. "I speak of my life in past tense like I've been reincarnated instead of what existed in this universe. I was living an entirely different life earlier this week."

"Maybe this is your second chance to get it right."

"That's just it. Get *what* right? On the same line of thinking, maybe that's why no one is looking for me. Maybe I was awful."

"You weren't awful, Tuesday."

"How do you know? I'm tired of waiting to find out just so I can start living again."

"I just know," I say with conviction.

"What do you know about me?"

"That you were a great person. A strong woman. You don't have to wait on anything or anyone. Just live."

Massaging her temple, she drops her head down. "It's a lot to process."

I set my glass down and go to her. "It is, but you don't have to do it alone."

A half-hearted smile creases the corners of her mouth. "When are you going to stop trying to save me?"

I don't know what makes me do it—her attempt at smiling to make me think she's all right, the lights that shine like stars in her eyes when she's looking up at me, or I'm just a sap when it comes to this woman—but I bring her into my arms and hold her tight. "When you no longer need me."

She feels so right, and when her arms wrap around me, her cheek resting on my chest, I realize I was wrong. Asking her to be here isn't my fatal flaw.

The thought of her leaving is.

14

Tuesday

THIS MIGHT JUST BE my life moving forward.

I can think of worse ways to spend my day than with this man. I'll probably never fully understand why, but he'd move heaven and earth for me if he could. He's shown me in ways that I'll never be able to thank him properly.

My throat thickens, and the tears threaten to fall under his sweet words and an embrace warmer than the comfort of seeing his eyes. I've never felt safer than I do right now.

When my stomach growls, we both start laughing, the levity of the interruption welcome after the heavier conversation we just had. I push him away under the guise of being playful when all I really want to do is stay in his arms forever.

Rubbing his stomach, he says, "We have two choices."

Although I'm dressed up, I flop onto the couch and kick my feet up. "What are they?"

I see the way his eyes travel my body, lingering on my shoes. He squares his shoulders and cuts across the room to flip on a switch, breathing soft light into the room. "We salvage the night and go out, or we—"

"Salvage the night and stay in?" I shoot my hand into the air. "I vote for staying in."

He's chuckling. "Staying in it is, then."

Pushing up on my elbows, I peer at him over the back of the couch. "I'm starved, so let's get to ordering."

With his phone in hand, he asks, "What are you craving?"

Now that's opening a can of worms. As if he can read my mind, he says, "Let me rephrase that. What are you hungry for?"

"Not much better." I wink and lie back. "Italian."

"We just had Italian last night."

"I had pizza. Now I want pasta."

When I don't hear any pushback, I push up again. Sitting on a barstool, he's staring at his phone. I ask, "Can you eat Italian twice?"

Holding the screen so I can see, he already has the restaurant app up. "What can I get you?" After he places the order, he walks past me, and says, "I'm going to change clothes. Make yourself at home."

As I drink the rest of my water, I look around the space, trying to bridge the gap between the workaholic and the man I know. Loch isn't so much in the design of the apartment, but I see his taste in individual pieces, like the straight lines of the leather couch and the buttons that give a sense of family passing it down through the generations.

Not a coffee mug left out from the morning or a half-read newspaper lying on the table. Loch seems like the kind of guy who likes to get that ink on his fingers. The floors have a soft shine to them, and until I touched the windows, they gleamed. Everywhere I look, it's clean, so clean that I'm certain of two things: He has help, and I won't find any dust bunnies in the corners of the room.

"Wow."

"Wow what?"

Startled, I turn around with a jump just as Loch strides from the hallway back into the living room and cuts across to the kitchen. *Shirtless.*

I thought he was drop-dead gorgeous in a suit, but holy mackerel! This man knows how to wear, *or not wear*, anything. Seeing him in a pair of low-hanging lounge pants is a whole other level of hotness. I try to stand, but my ankles wobble at the sight of him as he pulls a T-shirt over his head, so I shamelessly stay put. "I, uh . . ."

He anchors his hands on the V hidden beneath the fabric I remember so vividly. "Tuesday?" He points at his face. "Eyes up here."

"Um, yeah. Sorry." Needing to distract myself, I decide confessing a sin is a good way to go. "I forgot to tell you that I charged a few things on your credit card this afternoon at Bergdorf. I intend to pay you back with interest—"

"It's fine." His eyes search mine, and then he walks into the kitchen like he's seen everything he needs to. "I know you need things. You really don't need to worry about paying me back." Our eyes connect once more from across the room. "By the way, you look beautiful in that dress."

He dips down, but his voice travels. "I know you're not drinking, but do you mind if I have a beer?"

"Not at all," I reply with a smile as my back finds the support of the nearest wall. He peeks up at me, and I swear to God he's trying to do me in with that wink and the smirk resting on his face.

Testing to see if my knees work after the way he tried to kill me with his good looks, I push off. The sound of my heels against his hardwoods makes me pause and bend down to remove them.

That's when I hear the release of a bottlecap and the sound of him swallowing. Stepping out of my shoes, I look up to catch his eyes locked on me. My breath stills, and I lick the corner of my lips. "My feet were hurting," I tell him in a moment when my mind went blank of anything else that would make sense.

He sets the bottle on the counter and comes around the bar. I don't move a muscle as he walks right for me, other than the embarrassingly loud gulp I can't stop from swallowing.

Tapping my wrists when he passes in front of me, he nods toward the bedroom. "Come on."

I should be running, but my feet don't take a step. Is he . . . is this Loch Westcott seducing me? A wink? A hot look shared across the room? A come-on and walking into the bedroom? Is that all it takes for him to get a woman into bed?

Damn right.

Like a moth to a flame, I quick step toward the bedroom light only to find the room empty. "Loch?"

"In here?"

I follow his voice and find him in the closet.

Maneuvering inside, I take note of the padded, black leather bench centered in the room. My eyebrows quirk. "Kinky."

"What?"

With plenty of room between the counter that flanks the wall under the windows and the other wall of cabinets and drawers, I start to wonder how to begin. "Where do you want me?" I sit on the bench, crossing my legs, and then rest back on my hands. "How's this?"

"There's fine, I guess." I'm not loving the wrinkle of his brow, but maybe I'll get the look that makes me squirm when he's warmed up. "I think you might be more comfortable over here, though."

I pop to my feet and scurry the short distance to him. Resting my shoulders against the closed storage doors beside him, I spread my arms, pushing my hands against the custom cabinetry. "Like this?"

There's a blankness to his stare that I recognize from my own amnesia when I look in the mirror. That can't be right, though. He invited me into his little love closet. "Sure," he says, not taking advantage of me offering myself against his built-in storage. "Whatever's comfortable."

Worried about my head hitting the cabinet, I nod. "You're right. This might not be wise. At least not yet, maybe down the road."

"What road are we talking about?" Bending down, he slips his hand behind my leg, and he pulls open a drawer.

A subtle bump against the back of my thigh has me shifting out of the way. "My healing journey."

With the drawer full of T-shirts pulled open, he stands back up and scratches the back of his neck. "What are we talking about?"

"We're talking about se—wait a minute. Why'd you invite me into your room?"

He pulls a T-shirt from the drawer. "So you could find something more comfortable to wear than that dress." He holds up the burgundy tee.

Beacon University is printed across the front, though it's worn and faded. It looks soft, so I touch it. It's as soft as I suspected. I take it from him and then look up. "So it wasn't to—oh God. I'm mortified."

"Why?" As if the obvious hits him square in the eyes, his

bulge. "You, uh. Um. Huh." He drags his hand across his forehead. "You thought I invited you back here to have sex?"

Fanning my face, I rush through the door. "We don't have to say it out loud."

He follows me out of the bedroom. Walking behind me down the corridor, he says, "Dammit, I'm sorry. I didn't mean it like that."

I turn back, fisting the shirt in front of me. "Why are you sorry? And what didn't you mean?"

"I'm sorry you think I'm the guy to just ask you to come to my room to fuck, rather than me romancing you and making love to you. Properly. Like you deserve." He comes even closer, cupping my face. Lowering enough to look deep into my eyes, he says, "Trust me, Tuesday, there will be no doubt in your mind when I do ask you to come to my bed for that purpose."

Dead.

Just bury me now. I'm dead right here in his apartment.

Sliding his hands down, he gently pinches my chin between his thumb and forefinger. "Got it?" A cute smirk lifts one side of his mouth.

Words are my enemy, escaping me under the intensity of his gaze, so I nod.

He walks back to the bedroom but stops in the doorway and looks back. "Good girl." He signals for me to join him again.

If he can kill me twice, he just did. Am I a "good girl" kind of lady? Do I like this? I'm not sure about "before" me, but "now" me definitely likes this, especially with Loch.

Since my body melted into a puddle of mush, I glide across the floors. By the time I enter the room again, he's entering the room from the closet. "Shorts or boxers?"

I look between the choices, trying to pretend I didn't assume we were about to have sex. "Shorts."

He tosses them to me and says, "You can change here or the bathroom over there." When he walks out, he turns and closes the door behind him. I look around, not taking the time earlier. Painted slate-blue walls surround creamy bedding and a large rug that's super soft under my feet. I wiggle my toes and notice the wood headboard and night-stands in the same stain but different in style.

"Good girl" begins playing on a loop, a wave of goose bumps ripples across my body, and my nipples pert to the memory. Since I don't have many, that will be one I'll regularly play on repeat.

Running the tips of my fingers over my chest, I take a deep breath, relaxing into the mattress.

"You okay in there?"

I jump like he just heard my naughty thoughts. "Good. Fine." I rub the back of my head, knowing I should be more careful. A rush of blood to my head doesn't help with the pain. "Be right out."

"You sure you're okay?"

"Yep. All is good."

I hear him chuckling as he walks away.

"Food should be here soon."

"Thanks."

It's fun to pretend, but I undress and slip the shorts and T-shirt on. The shorts instantly fall to the ground. I walk into his closet and find the boxers he had pulled lying on the bench. I try those on for size. If I roll the stretchy band down twice, it tightens them enough to fit around my hips.

I take my dress and return to the living room setting it across the arm of the chair and settle on one of the barstools tucked under the counter.

"Perfect timing," he says. "The food is on its way up." A knock punctuates his words. He retrieves the bag. A friendly conversation ensues before he tips and returns to start unpacking the food on the counter in front of me. "I hope you're hungry."

"Starving."

"I'm surprised you wanted Italian food again." The lids are removed, and he sets plates beside the dishes.

"Last night was pizza. Tonight is pasta. I love Italian."

"You just said you love Italian."

I gasp, covering my mouth. But I start smiling too big. "I did say that. Wow, I love Italian food. Of course, who doesn't?"

A smile that puts me at ease spreads slowly across his mouth. "I think you're recalling memories."

"You think?"

"Seemed like it to me."

I catalog the tidbit along with the few others. I notice how his smile lingers as he looks at me. "What is it?"

"Earlier, I wasn't just talking about the dress."

"What do you mean?"

"When I said you look beautiful in the dress, I was talking about you. You're an incredibly beautiful woman. No matter what you're wearing."

This man saw me at my worst. He saw me without makeup for two days, in a ragged hospital gown, dressed up last night and tonight as well as casually. He's seen every version of me, including before everything changed, and he stands there looking at me like I'm the sunshine who broke his rainy-day streak.

I slip off the stool and walk around the counter until I'm standing next to him. I whisper, "Thank you."

He angles to face me, reaching across the small space I

left between us and wraps his large hand around the side of my neck. The pad of his thumb rubs along the underside of my jaw, and he moves closer. With a tilt of his head, he's closer to me than ever before.

His breath kisses my skin, sending a shiver up my spine. I close my eyes just as my breathing picks up, matching the beat of my heart. With his lips so close to the shell of my ear, I can feel his lips when he whispers, "How hungry are you?"

I tug him close, fisting his shirt, and whisper, "What's food?"

Our mouths crash together in a frenzy of hands groping for purchase against each other and heavy breathing.

Buzz...

Buzz...

His mouth slows, his fingers stilling in my hair.

Buzz...

I steal a breath and slowly pull away when he does. Licking my lips, I look up at him. If he was to ever fall apart, this is how I imagine he would look—messy hair, a wild look in his eyes, his shirt askew. Loch kisses me gently, and then says, "I need to answer it. It's the front desk."

"Okay," I reply, pushing my hair back from my face.

He puts the phone to his ear. "Yes?" Glancing at me, he says, "Tell them to come up. Thank you."

When he sets the phone down again, disappointment comes in the form of his lack of eye contact. "Your belongings from the hotel are here."

Now I understand why his mood changed. It was fun while it lasted, but that call was all it took for his disappointment to become contagious.

15

_____

Tuesday

EVERYTHING IS PERFECT.

Or should *feel* that way, but it doesn't.

I need nothing . . . other than my own pajamas, though I've become partial to his clothes.

My clothes hang on the hangers.

My shoes line up at the bottom of the closet.

The hotel bags are in the trash bin, though I debated if I should hold on to them for my next move.

Even my accessories and make-up are organized on the dresser.

The bed and pillows, the lamp and nice furniture, nothing is less than luxurious. Like a checklist at the end of the night where I've ticked each box, we ate dinner while I uselessly searched for the heat we shared before that call. I've said good night, brushed my teeth, and washed my face.

I'm not sure what my expectations were when Loch went sexy protective over me back at the hotel. I can't say I had any next-step thoughts of what would happen next, but it wasn't lying in Loch's guest room at two seventeen in the morning all alone.

Since I forgot to buy myself pajamas, I'm still wearing his clothes. It makes me feel closer to him, which is odd since he feels farther away than ever.

I reach for the glass on the nightstand before remembering I've already drunk the water. Holding on to it, I slip out of bed and tiptoe to the door. I pull the door open as quietly as I can and pad down the hall through the living room and into the kitchen.

I'm stunned every time I see that view. I don't think it's possible to ever get used to it. After refilling my glass of water, I return to the windows and take a sip. With my arms tucked over my chest, I hold the glass close and admire the inky-blue buildings and sky. The lights have no pattern but shine like stars against the dark night.

"It's quite the sight." His voice is low like the hour deems.

I glance back to see Loch walking toward me. "It is. I can't stop staring at its beauty."

"Neither can I, but I'm not talking about the cityscape." When he's standing by my side, staring ahead, he asks, "Why are you up at this hour?"

"Couldn't sleep and needed water," I say, holding the glass up.

He looks down out of the corner of his eye and nods. "Ah. I'm not a very good host."

"You're perfect at everything you do."

"No, I work hard at everything to be perfect."

Leaving no room for anything less, he outlines his tone with melancholy, which begs the question, "What happens if you're not?"

"I don't know." A genuine answer.

Too fascinated to look away from him, I turn so I can blatantly stare. "You've never failed? Not at anything?"

"Not that I remember."

"I have a feeling you don't forget much."

The pregnant pause has me anxious to hear what comes next. "You're right," he finally confesses. "I don't fail."

I expected no less, but I still hoped for a different answer. Though I think he does just fine. I mean, look at the view. That perfectionism has paid off. But still . . . "That's quite the burden to carry."

"What about you?" A smile falters on his lips. "Sorry, I forgot."

"So did I." I smirk, failing to keep my smile contained. "*Ba dum dump.*"

He gives me a lighthearted nudge. "The girl's got jokes."

Turning back to face the window, I add, "I try." I sip my water, only able to wrap around one consistent idea. "My thoughts? I have a feeling I failed others more than myself."

"Why do you think that?"

"Because I'm here instead of at home."

Without hesitating, he moves in front of me, takes me by the upper arms, and bends to look into my eyes. "Let me tell you something, Tuesday. You need to get that out of your head. Cases take time to solve. You aren't the first person to go through this, and you never hear of people not getting their reunion."

"Because we don't hear about them at all."

"You think you have all the answers, but there's an ocean of discovery waiting to happen. You could wake up tomorrow and be off to your old life." An enemy occupies his eyes, an unfamiliar emotion. Fighting against it, he gulps and closes his eyelids, clenching them tight. They lift in milliseconds, but it was enough to stave off the unknown invader. *But I saw it.*

His hold has strength, intention that feels more than proving a point. More like he doesn't want me to go. Dread wiggles in the pit of my stomach, reminding me that our ending is looming whether I want to accept it or not. I can't live here forever. I can't add to the burden of being unchecked boxes he needs to tick to feel good about his day.

"What do we do in the meantime?" I ask, desperate for guidance toward the light he sees at the end of my story.

He slides his hand up to my face, and the warmth of his gaze reaches my chest. I hate that a wave of emotion threatens my eyes with tears. How can a moment that doesn't have an ounce of sadness manage to bring tears to my eyes still?

His smile is gentle like the world at this time of night. He rests his head against mine, his lips caress my forehead, a breath is sucked in, and then he whispers, "Make the most of it."

Angling, he kisses my cheek and then lower to the corner of my mouth, causing my breath to hitch. But when his lips reach mine, there's no frenzy like before. No, he kisses me with calculation—one hand woven into the back of my hair, the other cupping my cheek, a gentle pressure steadily increasing until our lips part and our tongues meet, tangling together and deepening the connection.

I wrap my arms around his neck, and tighten, his body a lifeline to the life I'm living. If I return to my other life, my real life, what will I do without him? He's right. We're given no choice but to make the most of the present.

Pressing myself against him, I kiss him with the same intensity as he usually stares into my eyes.

His arms slide around my waist and under the hem of

the shirt, our heat welcomed as our skin sends currents of electricity through my body, making me feel alive for the first time since I woke up in that hospital bed.

Ever so slightly, he pulls back. In protest, the sound of our lips releasing echoes in the quiet room.

With his head against mine again, his eyes are closed as he tries to regain control of his breathing. His fingers clench in the sides of my hair, tugging enough to pull my attention to him. But the only pain is what's battling in the lines of his face. He says, "You make me lose control. You make me forget who I am."

I cup this strong man's face, knowing he's so much more than a hotshot attorney. I want to show him that the advice he gives me to just live can be a new start for him. "Maybe that's just what you need in life. Just a moment to forget who you are."

Kissing him, I want his hands on more than my face and in my hair. I want to feel one with him, even if only for a night, to make me forget the pain of losing my identity and fill the hole not just in my mind but also in my heart. Together, we'll create new memories.

This time when he pulls back, he takes me by the hand and starts leading me down the hall. We pass the spare room and walk into his. I silently climb under the covers, settling in the middle.

Amusement dances in his eyes as he smiles at me. "Are you a bed hog?"

"I have no idea. Let's find out."

He climbs into bed and pulls the covers over his lower half. Unlike when life and responsibility rudely chilled the heat between us, it's radiating under these sheets. Rolling on his side to face me, he runs his hand under my shirt and around my middle to hold my side. "Now what was that about not being able to sleep?"

"I was thirsty, too," I say, thinking it's not possible to sound thirstier for him than I do now.

He chuckles. "Well, let's make sure you're well taken care of." He leans down and kisses me. I loop my arms around him, holding him to me, our kisses intensifying as our bodies find purchase against each other.

When his hand slides under the waistband of the boxers, I press against it, craving not only his heat but his touch lower, between my legs. He doesn't disappoint, though I knew he wouldn't. He takes over my body as if it belongs to him.

Keeping pressure on me, he slips his fingers between my thighs, pushing slowly over my pulsing center. His tongue claims every corner of my mouth, and then a finger slips between my lower lips. "Aah," I breathe into him and then turn just enough to catch my breath again and kiss him.

I thought his kiss brought me to life. *It's this.* With his mouth on mine and his hand taking full possession of my body, the moment this man sinks a finger inside me, I'm living again. My body moves as if summoned by the devil himself, and I meet his hand as he starts to thrust.

Moans escape without permission, filling my ears as the sound of his mingles with mine. I grab his shoulders, pushing, tugging him back up, and then grappling to hold on to how incredible he feels. But it will be short-lived. The one thing I can't hold on to is the coil in my core threatening to spring apart.

This feels too good, so when he pulls out and begins rubbing my clit, I stop fighting to hold on and start allowing my release to come. Rocking my hips, I find the pressure so pleasurable and too much to know which way is up or down. "Feels so good," I breathe against his neck as he drives deeper into me with another finger. His thumb encircles my neediest spot as his other fingers take control of my every breath and moan, sending me into the darkness.

Tremoring under his hand, no fear is found as I fall deeper into this beautiful abyss. My breath finally catches as I float back to him, his hand holding onto my hip and sweet kisses sprinkled across my forehead.

My breathing is still jagged when I open my eyes. So many emotions he'd never claim are seen in his admiring gaze. It makes no sense to fall so soon, the reasons easily dismissed to anyone other than us two. But I am falling . . . I wonder if he is, too.

A yawn sneaks up on me before I can restrain it.

Falling back on his side of the bed, he says, "We should get some sleep. I have work early in the morning, and you . . ." He turns, his eyes finding mine through the dark room. "You have so many things ahead of you. You should rest up."

"What about you?" I roll to my side, gliding my hand over those hard abs I only had access to ogle earlier.

He covers my hand when I start sneaking south, effectively stopping me. "Tonight was about you."

I do worry, though. He sees it. I know he does because he reaches over and rubs my cheek with the pad of his thumb. He leans over to kiss my head once more, then whispers, "Get some sleep."

Worrying about tomorrow won't do me any good tonight. So I decide to take his advice. But first, I slide closer, snuggle to his side, and then leave a kiss on his chest. "Good night, Loch."

"Good night."

16

Loch

"You ready?"

I look up to see the door to my office open, and Leisa tipping her head inside. I shrug. "Sure." *Did I just fucking shrug?* I never shrug. Attorneys don't shrug. I don't waffle like I don't know the answer. I always know, then do my research to fill in the gaps.

"Sure?" she asks, raising an eyebrow. "Rough night." Not really. It might have had a rocky beginning, but it had a rewarding ending. "Are you going to tell me what has you smiling like you know a secret?"

Standing up, I tuck my phone into my pocket. "Was I smiling?" I ask, still grinning like I have a secret. I tuck my arms into my jacket and yank on the front to align it properly on my shoulders.

Nothing like a well-fitted suit to make you feel unstoppable. Kissing Tuesday this morning also helped. When she woke up, I was already out of bed, which she took as a challenge.

Her sultry eyes lured me back in and rolling in the covers with her had me feeling carefree. She had me so turned on that I was ready to call in sick for the first time in my career.

But it was her lips, those sweet lips tasted of pure contentment. It's a heady aphrodisiac at seven thirty in the morning, and something I've never felt before with anyone.

I've won the lottery, and it's all because I was the one lucky enough to have her not only in my bed but now in my life.

I wonder for how long . . .

Sitting here now, I'm filled with regret for not canceling my morning, staying in bed with her, and making up for the hours we lost sleep.

No fucking shame.

How many times do I need to be reminded she has a concussion and amnesia, for fuck's sake? Even when I remember, I still can't keep my deviant hands off her. Did I take advantage of her and her situation? Am I still doing that? It feels reciprocal, but maybe it's not fair to put her in this kind of situation at all while she's recovering.

I make a mental reminder to research how long someone with a concussion should wait before having sex.

"You're smiling like a man who had a good night. I don't want details—"

"Good, because you're not getting any. And," I say and give a nod. "I did have a good night."

"Huh," she hums with her laptop held close and following me. When she catches up to me at the corner, she starts doing roll call of the attorneys waiting for me in the conference room. By the time we reach the door, she cuts me off by spreading her free arm out and planting her hand on the frame to block me. As if she could.

I chuckle. "Something you need?"

"You look good happy. Whatever caused it, keep doing that."

"Isn't that against company policy? HR might have something—" I chuckle, unable to hold on to a straight face. It's freeing to feel this light. This must be how other people feel about Fridays. I feel it about Tuesday.

This time, she's the one shrugging once she lowers her arm. "If seeing you happy is against policy, I'm guilty. Can I still get a recommendation?"

"Absolutely." I step off to the side and spy on the enemy. They're fine for the time being. Shifting back, I say, "In all seriousness, I appreciate you."

Her expression melts as does her shoulders. "That means so much to me. Not my work performance, just—"

"I appreciate you."

Hugging her laptop to her, she replies, "Thank you. I appreciate you, Loch."

This is a lot of . . . *feelings* for one day. I'm starting not to recognize myself. Good or bad is to be determined. "Enough of the chitchat. We need to get in there."

"Yes, sir."

Leaving the sappier side of myself in the hallway, I open the door and walk in. "Counselors."

. . . *concussion wait to have sex?*

I finish typing, hit go, and wait for the result to populate on my phone. Choosing reputable medical sites, I read a few of the search returns before determining results vary and it's up to how the person feels.

Based on last night and then this morning, a safe bet is that Tuesday feels pretty damn good.

Pushing the remains of my lunch off to the side, I kick my feet up on my desk and lean back in my chair to text her: *How's your day?*

I look out the window at the city, finding a new appreciation today for the view I have. When I'm at the office, I don't typically have time to enjoy such simple pleasures. Makes it almost pointless to pay this much a month when one of the highlights goes unnoticed.

My phone buzzes. *I heard from the detective. There's nothing to report.*

I type: *No news is good news?*

Tuesday: *We'll go with that.*

She's trying her best to stay positive, but it doesn't surprise me that his update, or lack of one, feels more like a punch to the gut. I can't imagine my family, or even Leisa, not searching until they found me.

I plant my feet back on the ground, remembering when I was told to get to the hospital back in Beacon because my brother was near death. I chose to bury my head in my studies at university and ignore what was really happening while he was running around with a cousin that only wanted to bring him down. We didn't know if he'd survive. I didn't know what I would have done without him in my life. We grew up close, and I would do anything for my siblings and parents.

I rub my hands over my face. Every family has its battles. I'm just glad his death isn't one of ours.

Nothing she's shown me would cause a rift in her family. I feel the same as I did the other day. Not getting off on the right foot can be chalked up to a bad day. If she were mine, I would be searching heaven and earth for her.

I don't know why I didn't think of this sooner. With my unlimited financial resources, I can do what the police can't on their limited budget.

Sending another text, I type: *I should be home around 7. Do you have plans?*

Tuesday: *I do. At 7. See you then.*

Knowing she'll be in my apartment waiting for me inspires me to shift gears and get out of here.

My energy drops, and I hit a wall just after four. I need to stretch my legs and get some caffeine to wake up if I'm going to be ready for my next meeting. I tap Leisa's desk as I pass her. "Going for fresh air."

"Who are you?" she asks with a laugh as she spins in her chair.

Throwing my arms out wide, I shrug because I guess I'm now a shrugger. I start walking backward. "Guess it's true. It's never too late to change."

That sends her into laughter. "I approve of said changes."

Determined to steal some of the energy of the city, I turn around and push through the door. As soon as I reach to punch the button to call the elevator, one of them lands on the floor and the doors slide open. I step forward but stop. "Dad?"

My dad steps off and grabs my shoulder, squeezing it. "Loch. Just the man I came to see." He turns back. "You heading out?"

I watch the doors close again, noting my good mood descending with it. "No."

"Good. Let's set up in your office."

Leisa hears us before we reach my office and stands. "Good to see you, Mr. Westcott."

"You too, Leisa. All good in your life?"

Her warm smile welcomes him. "Peachy."

"Excellent."

When my dad enters my office, she whispers, "Did you know he was coming?"

"I was about to ask you the same." I keep my voice just as low as hers.

She nods, shrinking her shoulders. "Sorry."

"All good things must come to an end." I follow him inside and close the door behind me. My dad is a good guy. I shouldn't feel this way about seeing him. But wind and sails come to mind regarding his timing.

"Why didn't you tell me you were coming to the city?"

He sits on the couch with his briefcase beside him, grinning as proud as a peacock. "Thought I'd surprise you. I have plenty of work to do and figured I could do it in Manhattan as easily as in Beacon. Harbor's back from his trip. We can have a boys weekend."

I know Port Westcott better than he thinks. Work is just an excuse to visit. As I sit at my desk, it's hard to be bothered by a father who just wants to spend time with his kids. Normally, I'd be all for it. We always have a good time, but his unexpected arrival puts a wrench in my plans with Tuesday. Not that I thought getting laid was guaranteed, but it's on the table based on how eager she was to proceed last night.

Fuck.

Just thinking about her last night and the feel of her coming undone has me scheming to get out of this predicament and into her instead.

"Noah's not here," I point out like a desperate idiot. I know he's at school and probably has a game this weekend. I don't get home to Beacon enough. I need to make more of an effort.

"He's covered." He stands and faces the windows. Crossing his arms over his chest. "He has the best cheering section around. Mom and Marina traveled to Pennsylvania to watch his baseball game." He looks back over his shoulder. "It's an off-season fundraiser, but we heard he's being scouted for the minors."

"What about grad school?"

"It will always be there. Opportunities might not." He sits on the couch and opens his briefcase. This is not the strict hard-ass I grew up with. He used to be all business, rarely home, sometimes even missing vacations because of a trial. He had made his fortune, enough for him to retire and for his kids to never work again, but he continued, longer hours than ever. But when Harbor almost died, something clicked for him.

He's been present and available, a good dad. Noah and Marina have it easy. If I'd had the same version of him, I wonder if I would have become a lawyer. "That's great," I reply. Everything my youngest brother touches or tries turns to gold. He's the luckiest little shit I've ever known. He's also lucky to have awesome big brothers to keep him out of trouble, and there's been some over the years that my parents don't know about.

He asks, "When's the last time you saw Harbor?"

"A few weeks ago. I didn't know he was back from Italy." I click open the file on my computer for a last review of the case before my meeting.

"I'm sure Lark's keeping him busy."

Glancing at him, I laugh. "She's a doctor, Dad. I'm pretty sure she's busy herself."

"True." He asks, "What does the rest of your day look like?"

"I have a five o'clock."

He rubs his hands together and says, "Excellent. Let's get to it."

Oh great. I get my dad watching me perform like I'm a kid in grade school. Okay . . . "Let's get to it."

The meeting drags past when I told Tuesday I'd be home. She doesn't text, and I haven't had a chance to. As soon as I walk the clients to the elevator, I hurry back to my office, hoping to give Tuesday a heads-up about my father and the meeting.

Unfortunately, he's on my heels, clapping me on the back. "Impressive, son."

I set my phone on the desk and start on my post-meeting notes. "Thanks. Is there anything you know that might benefit future cases?"

"No. I think you've covered the bases and outcomes. Besides their comfort level with you being evident, winning the case seals this relationship. I think you're really making a name for yourself." He takes his briefcase from the couch, and then says, "Should we celebrate over dinner?"

This is it.

I don't know what he's going to think about my involvement not only with Tuesday's attack but also this new relationship with her happening so quickly. I need to rip off the bandage and tell him before this blows up in my face, and he finds out some other way.

"I need to talk to you about something."

"Let's talk on the way. I'm starving."

Other than Brady silently laughing at me the entire way home, I feel like I do a solid job of explaining Tuesday's circumstance.

I'm about to put the key in the front door when my dad's troubled expression reaches me. "Just terrible. It's really a tremendous thing you're doing for her. Her recovery won't be easy, so I'm sure she's grateful to have your help." He pats my shoulder again just as I insert the key. "She's lucky to have you, Loch."

Though I wouldn't change a thing, I might have failed to mention how beautiful she is. Not that it's relevant to why I helped in the first place, but it hasn't hurt since. "I wouldn't go that far."

"Such a traumatic event. This poor woman."

I open the door only to hear a scream in front of us.

Tuesday. And she's wearing nothing but a Westcott Law T-shirt.

Fuck.

17

Loch

I SLAM the door closed and turn to face my dad. "I—"

"I take it that's Tuesday?" He's not really asking, considering there's no confusion whatsoever on his face. There is, however, a very pointed glare aimed in my direction.

Looking down, I don't know what to think. My thoughts race through a hundred different scenarios and how I'll explain this away. I take a deep, exasperated breath, and then reply, "Yes."

"You made her sound . . . *different*." He's still studying my face, so I'm careful not to crack under the scrutiny. "I was expecting someone a little older, more my age."

"A little?"

"One day, you'll be my age—"

"And it will be a fucking honor."

He chuckles. "I don't know what's going on here, but you do have, from what I could tell, a lovely young woman in there who is probably mortified that your dad just saw her in a Westcott Law T-shirt and what appeared to be nothing else. Go check on her, Loch."

He's right. I failed to mention how incredibly sexy and beautiful she is. The half-naked welcome home greeting didn't help my case. So I shrug. "I never claimed to be noble."

I knock and then open the door again, closing it behind me. "Tuesday?" I walk into the living room and then down to the bedroom. "I'm alone." When I enter the bedroom, I notice the closet door open. Before I start for the bathroom, I check the closet. "Hey there."

She's draped over the long bench with her arm across her forehead, and says, "I didn't know you'd have company."

"Neither did I, if that matters."

Lifting onto her elbows, she looks at me through a lens of distress that's pinching the features of her pretty face. "What do you mean?"

"That's my dad. He showed up at the office unannounced. He's never done that before."

"You couldn't send a warning text?"

"I can't text in meetings, and he was practically looking over my shoulder the rest of the time. I thought telling him the truth about you would settle it. Except . . ."

"Except you didn't count on me greeting you like this." Pointing at herself, she says, "Oh my God." She drops her head into her hands as she sits up. "I will never be able to look at him without knowing that he knows what I was doing to his son."

"What were you doing to his son?"

She shoots me a look that pins me to the spot. "You know what I was doing." She sighs and leans her head back. "I'm never going to live this down." I kneel in front of her, resting my hands on her thighs. "I'm so humiliated, Loch."

Cupping her face, I lift enough to give her a quick kiss. "I want to tell you not to be because we've all done things that we find embarrassing after the fact, but I know you won't listen to me. So tell me how I can make things better instead."

"Well, for one, it's not *after the fact* embarrassment. I was mortified in the moment as well, hence the surprise and scream. I'm going to die of humiliation."

I stand, taking her by the hands and pulling her onto her feet. "Okay, that's fair. What's number two?"

"The thought of going out there and meeting your dad after that disaster." She drops her forehead against my chest, toying with a button on my shirt.

"Listen, Tuesday," I start, lifting her chin until our eyes meet again. "Does it help to know that his only concern was how you were doing?"

She nods gently, but her hands fist my shirt until it's wrinkled. "Kind of." I start to smile, and hers follows suit. "That's very thoughtful, like his son."

"So I know this is a lot to ask, but I'm going to ask anyway. Will you come out of the closet and meet my dad?"

Her laughter is sweet relief to my ears. "Should I get dressed first?"

"Probably best." She turns, but I catch her arm and bring her back to me. "Not so fast." Tilting my head, I kiss her neck, then her cheek, and finally that soft spot behind her ear that covers her skin in goose bumps. Her eyes dip closed, and I press my lips to the shell of her ear, and just barely whisper, "You look so fucking sexy in my shirt that I have one more request."

"What's that?"

"You wear it, exactly like that, again for me tonight."

I feel her shiver under my hands. With her head tilted

back, our eyes meet again. Wordlessly, she nods. I give her a kiss, then whisper once more, "Such a good girl. I'll make sure to reward you later."

It's hard to walk away, but I do it, giving her time to change into something that makes her more comfortable—physically and emotionally. And because my dad is still standing in the hallway, I open the door.

He asks, "All clear?"

I check behind me again just in case. "Come on in."

Taking each step with caution, he stops just inside the door. "How is she?"

"She'll be fine."

He sets his briefcase down and walks into the living room at the same time as Tuesday arrives dressed in black pants with the same shirt still on. "Well, this is embarrassing," he says. He's great about taking the spotlight off others when they don't want it.

She smiles, reaching out her hand. "You're telling me," she replies with a laugh as they greet each other.

"The Westcott Law logo is a nice touch." I grew up going to court and watching him interrogate the prosecutors' witnesses and his opponents on the stand. He reads people well. It's a skill I inherited from him. He knows how to read a room as well. Nothing he does goes without careful consideration, so seeing him being lighthearted and approachable with her reminds me again how lucky I am to have him as my dad.

It takes the edge off the previous introduction, which I know she'll appreciate as much as I do.

"I can't take credit for it," she replies, "but thanks." By her calm voice and her steady disposition, you'd never know she was in the closet about to "die of humiliation" minutes prior.

"Loch's mom designed it. She took graphic arts classes as part of her degree back in college and took on this project for the firm."

Tuesday pulls the shirt away from her and looks down. I know what she's thinking . . . classic. It's a law firm, so it's hard to go wild with a logo representing attorneys. "I like the details. What was her degree?"

"Art History. People have given her a hard time about it since we're from a small town with no museums. She used to spend days in the city visiting museums to fill her cup, as she phrased it, but she really sees the beauty in everything, even in Beacon." With his hands in his pockets, he chuckles. "She also had to do her best to balance against me. No one would ever call me creative."

"I'm sure she'd say differently. I'm like her. I love going to museums."

The words catch my attention. "You love museums?"

She nods, but then I see when it dawns in her eyes, and tears spring to her eyes. God, I hope they're from joy. "I love museums?" Her giddiness erupts in the tiniest of squeals. "I love museums, Loch."

"You *love* museums," I say, sharing her excitement.

My dad says, "That's really, um . . ." His lips tense under a furrowed brow.

I start to laugh, realizing we must sound outrageous. "She loves museums, Dad." I give him a nudge, hoping he catches on. "That means she *remembers* she loves museums."

It takes a second, but then he looks at her, and I can tell her joy is contagious when it reaches him. "You remember you love museums?"

"I do. Not sure which ones, but I know I loved going."

Running the tips of my fingers along the inside of her

wrist, I say, "I'm glad we've found another piece of the puzzle."

She moves without thinking, her hand rubbing my back, but then stops shy of snuggling to my side. Taking a step back, I see that sweet pink creeping from under her collar.

I'm not sure if my dad notices or not, but he takes a few steps away and says, "I called Harbor while I was waiting in the corridor." His attention shifts to Tuesday. "He invited me to stay with him and my daughter-in-law. I agreed it was probably best since Loch already has a guest."

"We can make room, Dad."

"No." His hands go up. "I didn't come into the city to be a burden."

"You're not a burden."

"You know what I mean. You two have a lot going on. I don't want to disrupt your routine."

Routine? Do Tuesday and I have a routine? It's only been a few days and less that she's been in my apartment. The assumption doesn't bother me.

I have concerns that we're moving too fast. We'll need to talk about it when we're alone again. "Dad, you can stay."

"My mind is already made up. You kids have fun, and I'll catch a cab." He starts down the hall toward the door. "Anyway, they just made dinner and are saving a plate for me." When he picks up his briefcase, he says, "How about we celebrate tomorrow night? The five of us?"

Honestly, he's right. If he took over the guest bedroom, that would force Tuesday to sleep in my room whether she liked it or not. I'd rather her always have a choice and choose to be with me than out of obligation.

I walk him to the door, and mouth, "Thanks."

His subtle thumbs-up makes me laugh. Being the worst

actor ever, with a raised voice, he says, "You two have a good night. Nice meeting you, Tuesday."

"Bye, Mr. Westcott. Nice meeting you, too."

As soon as the door closes behind him, Tuesday asks, "What do you want to do?"

I move into her space, taking hold of her hips and wiggling them. "Pick up where we left off this morning?"

"Race you to the bedroom."

"You better be naked under there."

"What are you going to do if I'm not?" She tightens her grip on the covers, holding them under her chin.

I take a long deep breath keeping it locked inside my chest until I figure out what I want to do with my bad girl. A good start is tossing my jacket to a chair by the window and rolling up my shirtsleeves, my eyes never leaving hers. I maneuver to the end of the bed and dip my hands under the covers.

Finding her ankles, I yank her down. Her hands fly above her head and a squeak are the last signs of her before she's buried under the blanket. Flipping the covers off, I stand before her and take her in. I sigh. "Very disappointing." The match is lit in her eyes, the fire already burning. "I thought we had an understanding."

"Which is?"

"In your bed, you can wear whatever you like. Here, in *my* bed, you've broken policy."

"I forgot the rules," she says, playing along like the good girl she is. A restrained smile is too much to control so she bites her lip in a feeble attempt. Fully dressed, she gets to her knees and starts toying with the buttons of my shirt.

They slowly loosen as she peers up at me. "Are you going to punish me?"

"Sex isn't a punishment. It's a reward."

"Damn," she gasps, worry streaking through her expression. "How can I make this right?"

I smirk, stroking her hair and then caressing her face. "How do you feel about tacos?"

She smacks me on the hip. "You tease."

Laughing, I catch her flailing hands. "What? I'm not really into the whole roleplay thing."

"Well, you could have fooled me."

Helping her to her feet, I bring her in for a kiss and cup her face. "How about this? I take care of you, and then we eat dinner because there's no way I can go all night if I don't get some sustenance in me."

"Go on, I'm listening." Her smirk is adorable despite how sexy it is when she's rubbing against me. I don't even know if she's aware she's doing it, but I am.

Fully. Aware.

I can't resist her any longer. "Ah, fuck it."

18

Loch

OUR HANDS BREAK free into a frenzy of clothes flying over our heads.

I barely get my shirt and undershirt off before she's standing in nothing but her bra and lace underwear. She doesn't hide her body, but that doesn't mean I can't detect a note of vulnerability hazing her eyes. I kiss her, whispering against her lips, "You're so goddamn amazing."

When I see her smile, my whole world shifts in that instant. She's not just the woman I met a few days ago or someone who could change my whole world. She's quickly *becoming* my world. How did that happen? When did we go from officially meeting outside an ER to not being able to keep our hands off each other?

As she rubs her hand over my stomach, the sweetness is gone and replaced by a siren. She kisses my chest, then takes my hand, leading me to the side of the bed.

Turning, she says, "Unclasp me."

I could snap this bra off with one hand, but I take my

time with her and brush my knuckles against her soft skin. Freeing her from the material, I slide it down her arms and drop it beside me. Quick to return my hands, I rub her shoulders, causing her head to loll back, and then sweep her hair off to one side so that I can take full advantage of her delicate neck.

Reaching around, I squeeze a breast in each of my hands while kissing down the curve where her neck meets her shoulder and licking back up. Her little moan has me hardening in my pants. I blow across her wet skin, sending a shiver down her spine. "Be a good girl and take your panties off, then get on the bed."

She does but doesn't hurry. She's slow in her movements. Keeping her eyes on me. She owns the space and takes control of the things that matter to her. These moments remind me of the woman I met in the coffee shop and how she controlled the room.

Moving to the center of the mattress, she watches as I work on my belt and then lower my pants and boxer briefs. Licking her lips, she returns her eyes to mine. "My. My. Mr. Westcott. I'm definitely in trouble."

I'm beginning to dig this little thing we're doing. Usually, sex is about a need, a craving to satiate. Yet it's that and so much more with Tuesday. It's a need to protect her from the world mixed with my carnal desire to mark every part of her inside and out.

Possession *is* nine-tenths of the law.

Does that make her mine?

Like her, I can own a room, but she's at the center of it. *Center of everything I know.* I hover over her, dipping my hand between her legs and sliding right up between the soft of her lower lips. I rub her clit, then dip down to her entrance, but she's so wet for me already. When I look into her eyes, she asks, "I love when you touch me, but I want to feel you inside me, Loch."

I could ask just to make sure, but she's already made herself clear. Who am I to argue with her desires?

It's moving fast, and I'm not prepared. Keeping one hand on her pussy, I keep circling while I reach into the nightstand drawer and pull out a foil packet. I bite the corner and tear it open. When I drop the condom on her chest, I say, "I want you to put it on me."

She's more than willing and reaches forward to grab the condom from me. I lift enough to help her get closer. To say she's ready is an understatement. . . She sighs in discontent when my hand leaves her body as I position myself above her.

I use my knee to spread her legs and settle against her, pressing my dick to her entrance. Foreplay wasn't needed to get us to this point. We've been building toward this for days. That doesn't take away the fact that looking down at her fantastic fucking tits and that dip from her waist to her hips, I know I'm not going to last.

She's a goddess in need of a good fucking, and I'm just the mortal tasked with the job. Like work, I take this very seriously. "You better hold on, sweetheart. This isn't going to be gentle."

Raising her hand over her head, she presses them to the headboard. "I think I can handle you."

With my elbows planted on either side of her head, I kiss her sweetly one last time. "Famous last words." I thrust in, filling her to the hilt in one hard push.

Her eyes are closed when she cries out, "Oh God." But when her nails dig into my shoulders, she looks at me and encourages. "You feel amazing."

Dropping her arms around me, she holds on as I pull

back out and push in again. Who needs clear thinking when ecstasy has consumed your body?

I wrap my body over hers, thrusting and kissing. The sound of fucking . . . no, it's love-making. She meets me push for pull and pull for push until we're each chasing our own release and thrusting against each other.

Sliding my hands under her ass, I take a firm grasp and angle her up just as I get to my knees and start fucking like we won't get another chance.

"Loch," she breathes, her arms wide by her sides as she fists the sheet beneath her. I thrust, tasting what heaven feels like, and then give her a reprieve before pushing in again and again. Her breathing is erratic, her body moving just as freely as I push harder and faster when she demands.

Her chin tilts to the ceiling, and she finally catches her release, tremoring around me and causing mine to entangle with hers. I push, still pushing even when I'm buried as deep as I can be inside her until her body eases and I've given everything I can to her.

I lower her back down but stay buried inside her, collapsing until my head is beside her, and I can lick the sweat from her neck. "You are fucking spectacular."

She abandons her laughter when she sucks in a harsh breath and pushes me off her. "I can't breathe, Loch." I'm still given a smile, this one more languid, less about happiness and filled more with satisfaction.

"Sorry." I place a kiss on her shoulder and roll onto my back. Trying to catch my breath, I close my eyes and just lie in my contentment. This is the life—good, pure, exhaustingly profound between the sheets. I'm starting to believe that magic exists. How else could the connection between us be explained if not through supernatural forces?

Our hands touch, but it's not enough. I turn hers over

and hold it, wrapping my fingers around her, and then we weave them together in an embrace.

The room never had the lights on, the city providing enough light from the outside, but when I look at her now, her eyes shine as if I put the stars and moon in them. "Hey."

"Hey," she replies.

"How are you doing?"

"So good. You?"

I look back at the ceiling, trying to find the words to explain how I feel inside because there's too much all at once. She runs the tip of her finger over my chest and then doodles a heart. Holding that hand just where it is, I finally know how I feel about her. It's too soon for three words, but I remember one. "Apricity."

"What does that mean?" she whispers.

"The warmth of the sun in winter. That's what you are to me."

"That's beautiful."

"Like you."

My whole body relaxes, and my mind follows quickly behind. I could sleep, but then she says, "Guess I don't need to worry anymore about being a virgin or not."

I bolt upright and stare down at her. "What?"

Curling onto her side, she acts innocent. *She's not.* "What?" She grins like the cat who ate the canary.

"You're a virgin?"

"Not anymore."

"Fuck." I drop back on the pillow as another blow of guilt sideswipes me. "I wasn't even thinking about that. I fucked up."

"And down, if we're getting technical."

I shoot her a glare, but it's hard to be mad at her for making light of her own situation. "You're not upset?"

"Upset?" As if the idea is unfathomable, she laughs. "First of all, I don't even know. How messed up is that? Second, why would I be upset? You just made love to me."

Now I'm the one surprised. I lean over and run my finger over her bottom lip before kissing it. "That's the only way you deserve." Settling between her legs again, I caress her pretty face. Her blue eyes waver between the light of hope and a darkness ready to take over.

My heart aches. I can do so much, almost everything in the here and now, for her, from taking care of her emotionally, physically, and financially. But I don't know if I can give her the reassurance she truly needs. "I'll be here for you, but the rest . . ."

I lift just enough to see the emotions waging war in her eyes. I don't know how we got here, or how I did. Love has never held intrigue for me. It's not something I go near. But with her, and because of Tuesday, it pains me to give voice to it, unlocking a fear of losing her. But with that deep-seated admission to myself, I remind myself that honesty is also equally valued, and say, "The rest is up to you and what you choose to do."

19

Tuesday

SATURDAY MORNINGS ARE for sleeping in, coffee and books, and lazing the day away. Or is that Sunday?

I wish I knew what I liked to do on the weekends, but nothing Loch has suggested could coax me out of this bed right now. I don't seem to be able to summon the same energy he has in the morning. He returned more than an hour ago, has showered, made breakfast, and then showed me an app of "Top Things to Do in New York City."

I had drifted back to sleep at one point until he busted me and dove onto the bed, effectively waking me up again. I've been scrolling the app ever since. Frustrated by the lack of any recollection of these places, I ask, "Wonder what the bottom things to do are? Oh wait. I know. Getting mugged and having amnesia."

"I can't tell if you're joking or not."

Keeping his funny bone in suspense makes me laugh. "Why would I joke about getting mugged and having amnesia?"

"That's what I thought, but the way you laid the ground-work for a punchline was top-notch."

"It's a joke that would never land."

His brows squish together in the middle. A few days ago, that appeared to be his resting face, but something has changed in that time, and the lines have eased along with his demeanor. "See? I have no idea if you're being funny."

I toss the phone to the bed and roll over to face him. Still feeling too far, I decide I need to touch him all over or have him over me. I need his comfort and heat. Getting to my knees, I straddle him and then lay my body with the length of his. Loch's arms come around me. He even kisses the top of my head while continuing to scroll.

"What do you like to do on the weekends?" I ask, closing my eyes while using his chest as a pillow.

"I have no idea anymore. My brother and I used to find a court and play basketball or head back to Beacon and spend the weekend with my family. Now, I work."

"Mm. That's why you never fail. It's work, work, work all the time."

"I'm thirty, Tuesday. What I do now is the biggest predictor of how my career will turn out. Working hard is not a bad thing."

"Not bad. Perfect. *Too* perfect." I thought I wanted to sleep right here, but that seems less likely by the second. I lift my head and rest my chin on him. With his head resting on a pillow, he gives me his gaze, which makes me smile. "You are so much more than you realize. You're funny and . . ." I want to blush from how fast he made me come. "Incredible in bed—"

"This is how rumors get started."

"See? Funny. But you don't show it to the world very often."

"I don't show them how incredible in bed, your words not mine, I am either." His hand covers my left shoulder blade, wrapping half of me in a hug. "Law isn't generally a lighthearted profession. Have I become a dud?"

"I don't know what a dud is, but you're not one of them. That's my point." I lay my head back down, listening to his heartbeat.

"I'm not everyone's cup of tea. I work ridiculously long hours, I spend little time at home, I've been known to sleep at my office, and I end up canceling ninety percent of my dates due to my caseload. So yeah, I don't have much time to give people, and even fewer deserve it. I'm selective, and some might think that callous. That's not how I see it. Driven to the point of exhaustion, I don't have many opportunities to have a good time and crack jokes. If you're in my life, it's because I want to spend time with you."

Not rushing in with a response, I lie there quietly enjoying our time together, but then I realize that his words are different from his actions. "But you've cleared your schedule and opened your life up to me."

He places the phone on the nightstand and rolls us over until he settles on me. I wrap my legs around the back of his legs and rub the back of his neck, going higher into his typically perfectly styled hair. It's not today. It's sex-messed, and he's never been hotter. I love that he gets a little messier for me and lets me see his carefree side.

"You gave me a good reason. I knew what I would miss if I let you slip away."

"Which is?"

"A chance to have a life."

I kiss him, wanting to give him everything he needs, and it quickly deepens. But when our lips part before we get a chance to tangle beneath the sheets, I stare into those eyes that have quickly gone from stranger to safety. "What if I was brought into your life to help you remember who you really are, just like you were brought into mine?"

Loch is still, so still that I worry I said something wrong. He places a kiss on my neck and then higher until our gazes catch again. "Maybe we both needed saving."

A hurricane of emotions storms through his irises before he reaches into the nightstand. There's something about how rough he is when his knee spreads my legs farther apart, his hand pins my hip to the bed, and his eyes roam my body that tells me I need to hold on—to him, to this bubble we've created, to this moment before it slips away.

When he pushes into me, my eyes close, and I allow myself a moment to feel not only our physical connection but also the emotional one that's been blooming all along. The fullness inside me makes me realize that it's not only my body that's complete but my heart doesn't ache anymore.

Loch is a part of all my existing memories. He's been with me since before I woke up. Standing steady by my side, he's a pillar I can cling to day or night, and now the only one who knows me inside and out. I memorize this moment with him, wanting his fingerprints to mark me as a reminder of how much he's become my life.

It's too late to save myself. Despite how people warn about not rushing into relationships, I'm already so invested in him. Nothing else matters anymore.

Driving me wild, Loch pushes my body to the brink of ecstasy before pulling me back to reality and sending me soaring again. I come before he does but give myself wholly to this man, eagerly riding him until he can no longer hold on. The tips of his fingers dig into my hips. I want to be marked, to be owned in this way by him. If I need to leave tomorrow, I want to feel where Loch left his fingerprints.

Breathless and tired, I lie on top of him. His hands stroke my back, and he kisses on my head. Life in the present has suddenly become precious, now knowing that everything could change in an instant.

"ARE YOU NERVOUS?"

Loch looks down at me, our hands clasped tightly between us. "Not nervous, just . . . I'm not sure. It's my brother and Dad, Lark. They're great and good fun. We get together all the time."

"Not with a woman on your arm." I'm not naive enough to think he's an altar boy. As a matter of fact, I know he's not by how talented his mouth is, and yes, he didn't lie when he told me his mouth was magical. My body still vibrates in the aftermath of what he did to me on his kitchen bar. The stone counter may have been cold, but his mouth, *ohhhh my* . . . I fan my face, not wanting to be beet red meeting his brother and sister-in-law. Much less embarrassing myself in front of his father again.

Just outside the entrance to the restaurant, he pulls me around and holds my hand between us. "You're not arm candy, Tuesday."

I rock forward, trapping the heat we're creating between us on this wintry night. Smiling up at him, I ask, "What am I, Loch?"

"Not one rational thought comes to mind."

"Then tell me what does."

"Girlfriend . . ." He looks away and takes a deep breath as if he's tempering what he really wants to say.

I understand too well. I've been feeling much the same. I press against him. "Nothing about us or this circumstance makes any sense to me either, but I can't imagine anyone else I would rather be with." When I falter, not afraid of him in any way but of acknowledging my true feelings out loud, he brings his arm around me and holds me closer, giving me the confidence to share my heart. "I've been going along for the ride to see where I end up. But maybe it's not about being a passenger on this journey, but instead the driver, directing it where we want to see it go."

"What does that mean to you?"

"That as much as I love hearing you speak so openly of dating and having an official title, this feels, *we* feel like so much more."

"I agree."

Most people need three words to make them feel complete. I only need two from him—I agree. I lift, and he leans down, our mouths meeting in the middle. The sweet aftertaste of our admission coats our kiss, but the fire always burns within for when we're alone again.

A throat is cleared . . . *technically, three*. We jump apart as if caught breaking the rules. As soon as I see our three dinner companions staring at us, my face flames like a bad sunburn after a long day at the beach. One day I can only dream that I don't wear every emotion on my face.

It's easy to see the resemblance between the three men —all mythological gods in their own right. And then his sister-in-law, stunning with her brown hair that reflects the lights, kind smile, and green eyes that shine despite it being night. How can a family be so beautiful?

This is actually getting a little ridiculous. I probably stand out like a sore thumb with my light hair to their dark, exempting his dad's salt-and-pepper mix. My sky-blue eyes are the opposite of the comfort of their earthier hues.

I'm not usually one to pick apart my looks. I'm confident, even after waking up in a hospital bed with no recollection of who I am. I've grown to love my body even more because of what it went through. But I will say, being in the land of mythical creatures—Loch's family—definitely makes you question who got the golden ticket in the gene pool lottery.

"Hi, I'm Lark." She holds out her hand. I don't know why, but I lean in and hug her. As if she was holding back before, she embraces me.

When we pull back, I say, "It's so nice to meet you. I'm Tuesday."

She takes hold of the sleeve of her husband's coat, and says, "This is my husband, Harbor."

"Hello." His eyes are similar to Loch's—warm and inviting.

We shake hands. "It's nice to meet you. I've heard a lot about you." My gaze darts to Loch. "Not from him. I barely get him out of the office these days." Nodding beside him, he adds, "But my dad said you two had quite the meeting."

I laugh. "I know how to make a first impression."

His dad leans forward, taking my hands in his. "Good to see you again."

"You too, Mr. Westcott."

"Call me Port."

Huh. I tilt my head, unsure if I should mention it, but curiosity gets the best of me. "I'm noticing a trend with your names. Loch. Harbor. Port. They're all associated with water."

Loch starts to laugh. "My parents thought they'd throw all reason out the window and give us this insufferable connection for life."

Maneuvering Lark in front of him, Harbor locks her in his arms, and says, "Or as our parents would tell the story, they already had a head start with theirs. My mom's name is Delta." Tipping his head in concession, he adds, "Loch, Harbor, Noah, and Marina. The teasing at school was brutal."

Lark starts laughing and then gives him a little elbow to the stomach. Looking up at him over her shoulder, she says, "Why do I find it hard to believe you were ever teased?"

"I'm a work in progress. I wasn't always the man you see now."

"Yeah, okay, let's not do this. I like Tuesday too much to risk revealing our weirdness just yet," Loch says, chuckling with a shake of his head. He slides his arm around the small of my back and brings me to his side.

With my hand resting on the front of his coat, his words sink in. I freeze, not moving an inch, except for my eyes that jump from his brother's widening eyes to Lark's that look like she's in on a secret to his dad beaming with a smile.

I think it takes those same expressions staring back at Loch for him to realize what he just said. The moment it dawns in his eyes, his hold on me tightens, and he turns us around. "Our table should be ready." All signs of the fun he was having disappear as we start for the entrance. He mutters, "Fuck," under his breath before he opens the door to the restaurant.

The others follow, soft laughter trailing, but we all caught what he said. That's when I realize he was telling me the truth the best he could. I'm not just arm candy or a woman simply joining the family for dinner. *I'm heart candy to him.*

20

Tuesday

Iᴛ's a round table of Westcotts, and I'm happy to be a part of this dinner. With Loch's hand resting on my thigh, and the laughs we've shared, I don't think I've stopped smiling once. Their teasing is always underlined in respect, good humor, and love. They seem to naturally know where to draw a line and not cross it. If only my family knew the same.

My heart clenches, and I suck in a harsh breath the moment the thought crosses my mind. My family didn't understand boundaries, were hurtful, or worse, both?

I wrap my arm over my stomach and reach for my glass of water. I drink it down, hoping to swallow the ache that's formed inside me.

"Are you all right, Tuesday?" Lark's fingers just barely touch the table's edge, hanging on after pushing her empty dessert plate away.

Setting my glass down, I look at her and nod. "Amnesia is tricky. It's a gatekeeper to all my memories that I can't get past most days. Then one just sneaks up on me out of nowhere. Sometimes it's clear, and sometimes I have to guess what it means. Either way, it strikes, leaving me feeling vulnerable, like my happiness in the now is at risk."

Her hand returns to her lap, but her attention is fully on me. It would be easy to say it's her polished bedside manner, but I really think she's genuinely this caring all the time. "How are you feeling? Any dizziness or headaches?"

"Occasionally, I get a pain in my head, but it's not so much a headache, more of a temporary reminder that I'm pushing myself too hard."

"Port shared that you have a concussion. When is your follow-up appointment?"

It's not something I've discussed with Loch because the last thing he needs is more reason to drop his life, or more money, to help me. But I can't lie to her. "I don't actually have one. I was told there are free clinics if I had concerns."

"Why would you need a free clinic? Your doctor should have scheduled the follow-up before you checked out of the hospital." I appreciate her keeping her voice low and our conversation private.

Leaning closer, I whisper, "I have no money. No insurance. No way to pay. So the follow-up was not approved by the hospital. The nurse told me to come by this week, and she'd be able to help me find a clinic that can fit me in, but that's not necessary—"

"It is necessary, especially at this point in the healing process. Would you like me to do your checkup? I'm limited to the tools I have at my disposal, meaning no X-rays or CT scans, but I don't think you need those. But if the need arises, we'll figure out how to get those done."

I don't know what to say. Sure, she's my . . . she's *Loch's* sister-in-law, but this is more than I could ask for. "Honestly, I'm sort of speechless. Thank you. I do have a few minor concerns I'd like to discuss. I promise I won't take up too much of your time."

"You're welcome. The guys were discussing a potential basketball game tomorrow before Port leaves town, so I could come over then." A thought has her bolting straight and grinning. "I can bring lunch, and we can go shopping after. Depending on how your appointment goes, of course."

"There's just a tiny issue. *Money.* I hate to even mention it because it's a little embarrassing. But since I don't know who I am, I can't figure out if I even had a job or a savings—"

"I understand." She laughs lightly. Her eyes are sincere, with her smile reaching the outer corners. "Don't worry about a thing. If the guys get to play, so do the girls." Her gaze fixes on Loch. When he turns from his conversation with his brother and father, she says, "Loch, we're going to need your credit card to go shopping tomorrow."

A mischievous look raises his eyebrow and quirks the right side of his mouth. Glancing at me out of the corners of his eyes, he says, "Shopping, huh?" He reaches for his wallet, pulls a card from it, and then hands it to me.

I take the card and waggle my eyebrows. "What's my spending limit, Daddy Loch?"

Ohhhh, damn.

Why.

Did.

I.

Say.

That?

The table is silent, but that's better than the mortification I feel. Loch starts tugging at his collar, and I hear him gulp. "I, uh—"

"I was only joking." Meeting his dad's eyes across the table, I pray he doesn't think less of me. "I don't call him

Daddy. *Oh no.* I'm making this worse." I turn my gaze to Loch and plead, "Please save me."

Taking hold of the arm of my chair, he scoots me closer, the legs grinding against the floor, causing others at tables around us to stare. Not helpful. Then he kisses my temple and says, "Spend as much as you want. You've been a very good girl."

Oh.

My.

God.

The man could take me right here on this table, and I would let him.

"What?" Harbor asks, drawing our attention. He's staring at Lark like she just did some damage to his ribs. "Hint taken, babe. If you want me to talk dirty, I'll do it."

"I'm not making the same promise to limit my spending like Tuesday did," Lark adds. "I only get to shop when Delta or Marina are in the city." And being the thick as thieves friends we've become, she starts a story to get the heat off me. She reaches over to touch my forearm. "So I'm happy to have a shopping friend. I'm sure Harbor is as well."

"I like being your baggage handler. Instead of tips, Lark goes—"

"Okay," she says, riddled with laughter. "That's enough." We all join in, causing her to drop her head forward in embarrassment. I can empathize. But also, I recognize how I put them on pedestals because of the shallow reason of their looks. Each of them is so much more than their physical appearance. They wear their hearts right in the open for everyone to see.

I thought Loch was the pot of gold at the end of the rainbow, but I don't know how I got so lucky to be here with all of them. My memories may lack, but my heart is over-flowing.

Harbor wraps his arm around her shoulders, and though he's still laughing, he brings her head to the crook of his neck and kisses her.

My presence feels invasive to the intimacy. I look away, feeling overwhelmed and teary, though I'm not sure why. Loch's head comes to mine, just barely touching, as he rubs my thigh under the table. "What's wrong?"

I shake my head at first, unable to speak without my emotions overflowing. I swallow and then whisper, "I'm just so happy."

With his finger curled under my chin, he lifts until our eyes meet, and whispers, "So am I." He kisses my forehead, then sits up while taking my hand to hold and resting the bond on his leg. "Are we ready?" he asks, the bill already paid and the server clearing our plates.

After a round of hugs and goodbyes outside, we take a taxi home since Brady is off on the weekends. I lean my head against his shoulder, still smiling, as we travel through the city. "I love them."

He chuckles. "You're telling me you love my family before you say it to me?" The words cut through the air, causing me to sit up.

Nothing in his tone was heavy. It was the opposite, in fact. Playful even. Reading between the lines has me wondering if he's ready for such declarations, though. "Loch . . ." I don't even know what I'm saying or if I should bring this up, but I can't stop myself from finally finding the opening I need. "You don't think it's too soon to say that to each other?"

His hand runs under the hem of my dress, stopping to hold me just above my knee. "Do you?"

I take a breath, letting the shock wear off. Angling toward him when I lean back, I giggle. "I asked you first."

"Well . . ." He starts, his gaze dashing out the window briefly before returning to me. "Ask me that a week ago and I would have had a different answer."

"I wish I'd known you then."

"No, you don't." His response comes so fast that I do a double take.

"Why not?"

"Because I'm only who I am right now because of you." He takes my hand, our fingers folding together, and kisses the top.

Bringing our hands to my mouth, I turn my wrist and kiss his hand the same way he kissed mine. "You've always been this person, Loch. You just needed a nudge in the right direction."

His arm comes around me, and he places another kiss on the side of my head. "You were right before. You've reminded me who I used to be before I got caught up selling every minute of my life away."

"What if you billed yourself for a few hours each day and bought your time back?"

A single laugh escapes, and he shifts, finding my eyes in the dark of the cab. "That's actually quite brilliant."

"Thank you." I do a little faux curtsy that would get me kicked out of the palace. I poke him in the chest. "All you have to do is buy back your time."

"And how do you suggest I spend it instead?"

"I have a few ideas." I catch the cabbie watching us in the rearview mirror. "That I can't wait to show you at home."

The word slips out without permission. We both catch it. I can tell he does by the slow-spreading smile on his face. Kissing my hand once more, he whispers, "Home."

HE UNLOCKS the door and then turns around. I'm not sure what lit the fire in his eyes, but he's smoking hot. "Ack!" I scream in a fit of laughter as I'm scooped into his arms and then tossed over his shoulder as he pushes the door open and then kicks it closed behind us.

"Not very Prince Charming of you." I smack his hard ass, but with his coat on, I don't get in a good whack.

Cruising down the hall, he smacks my ass because my coat sucks and is currently riding up my back. "It's not the title I'm going for."

"What title are you after then?"

Slipping into the bedroom, he stands bedside, gets a good grab of my ass in, and then gently lays me down on the mattress. "Boyfriend." My heart swoons, and I fall back. But when he sits next to me with his hand on my stomach, he replies, "What do you say? Do I fit the bill?"

I reach out to the side and take his hand, and he comes without me having to ask, hovering over me with our eyes staring into each other's. I love that we have a silent language the other knows how to read. I take a breath, not because I need courage but because he always steals it, and say, "I love you."

21

Tuesday

"I LOVE YOU, TOO," Loch says as if the words have been on the tip of his tongue all night.

Looping my arms around his neck, I lift to kiss him, then fall back on the pillow again. "Well, look at us being all in love. Who would've guessed?"

"Not me," he deadpans.

I laugh, but then I second-guess his tone and the delivery of that response. It rolled off almost as easily as the "I love you" did, so I ask, "What do you mean by 'not me'?" He shifts, but I hold tighter so he can't escape. "Why not you?"

He pauses, his eyes searching mine, then he looks away. Confused by the change in his mood, I cup his face, silently begging him to look at me. When he doesn't, I start to feel sick in my stomach. "Talk to me, Loch."

I'm finally given his gaze when he says, "Now is not the time."

The moment my arms slack, he breaks free, not just

moving off me but getting off the bed completely. I watch him walk to the window, that pit in my stomach feeling hollower. The blinds remain open when he stops to stare at the city like I often do. I do it to admire the grandness of it all, or I'm trying to make sense of the world. I wonder which one he's doing.

When he rubs one of his shoulders and bends his neck to relieve his obvious tension, I sit up and rest my back against the headboard.

"You know," I say, the distance between us feeling its greatest since he came into my life. "Nothing good ever starts by putting off a conversation."

"I know. I'm sorry."

Crossing my legs in front of me, I hunch over my fidgeting hands. "You're sorry for what, Loch? I'm confused about what's happening. We've had an amazing night. We just shared some of the deepest feelings you can have for another person. So now I'm wondering what's changed?"

When he turns, I can see the bad news coming like a train down the tracks. "It's no big deal."

"Then tell me." When he doesn't make an effort, I spring out of bed and start for the door.

I barely get two steps into the hall when he says, "You weren't very polite."

Stopping in my tracks, I walk back but stay in the doorway and cock my head to the side. "What do you mean by that?"

"You wanted to know why I said I wouldn't have guessed we'd be together. I'm telling you." He rests against the windowsill and tempers his expression by shifting it into neutral, making it impossible to decipher what he's thinking. Where's the man who's been so open, whose walls are down when it's the two of us? Where's the man I just proclaimed my love to? He says, "You weren't having a good day."

Every bone in my body goes on defense. Throwing my arms over my chest, I cross them. We're plagued by the silence growing between us. I start tapping my foot, trying to process my irrational anger and what he's really saying. And because it's better than the silence that's exacerbating my worries of fighting with him. This is new for us. It could ruin everything, but I still need to know the truth. "Are you talking about when we met at the coffee shop?"

"Yes."

"I wasn't having a good day, or I was being rude? Because you've said both."

He shrugs. "Probably both."

"Both?" I'm struggling to wrap my head around the accusation. Or is it fact? "You thought I was rude?"

"I think you were someone who wanted things in a very specific way—"

"There's nothing wrong with that."

"I agree. Clearly, you've met me." He pushes off the sill and comes to me. I hate that I move out of his reach, but I'm not sure what to think. Or worse, what he thinks about me. "I didn't tell you to upset you. It just came out—"

"That's just it. You didn't tell me. You didn't tell me information about who I used to be—Oh God, am I like that now?"

"No, you're an entirely different person. I mean, you're you, still, but now I get to see the kind and witty side of you, and your generosity." His arm goes out toward the window. "You gave that woman your coat without even thinking about yourself. You're a paradox between then and now, an anomaly, which I find fascinating."

Despite the nice things he's saying, my heart has already sunk. "I was awful, and you think it's fascinating?"

"You're not listening to me, Tuesday." I finally lower my guard and let him get close. Selfishly, I want him to hold me and make me feel better about being a bad person in the past.

His arms wrap around me, and he kisses my head. "I'm not fascinated by you because of who you were. I'm captivated by who you are." Leaning back to find my eyes, he says, "I love you. All of you. Your past and you in the present. But I really look forward to loving you through our future."

"Really?" I crack a smile that is, at best, minuscule.

"Really."

I roll my eyes. "Fine. I love you and love all that too." He chuckles. "I can't believe I was rude."

"Like I said, I think you were having a bad day. I was having one, too."

I've asked him before, multiple times, why he helped a stranger. His answer has ranged from his mom raising him to help those in need to how could he not? All great responses that you would want to hear when asking this question.

Maybe it's me who's broken since I can't seem to take someone at their word and keep asking, wondering if I'm going to get the same answers. What was my life like before that makes me so suspicious of everyone? "If I was so awful, why'd you save me?"

He rests back on the doorframe, his hands holding me by the waist. "I could have caught the guy who mugged you, but I thought you were more important than a handbag. So when faced with a split-second decision . . ." He pauses, but his eyes never leave mine. "I'll never regret choosing you."

My knees weaken under his words, his grasp of me firming, and his gaze gentle as he stares into my eyes. My heart clenches as my breath wraps around how he loves me. "You chose me," I whisper just to savor the words.

"Yes." His tone is low, kept so quiet, but something still seems to bother him. "I forced my way into your life on some whim that makes no sense on any level to any rational person." Oh wow, he's not holding back. "And fell madly in love with you."

He's exactly who he was when I met him, but now, instead of his heart being closed to the world, he's living again. I fist the front of his shirt, pressing myself to him. "Is it so awful being in love?" I give him a teasing grin.

"There's nothing better."

Spinning us into the room, he walks me backward with his lips attached to mine. The back of my legs hit the bed, and I sit, falling with my arms wide to embrace this giant-hearted man.

We share I love you through kisses and moans, licks across our bodies and glistening sweat. But it's when he says it with his body buried inside mine—a brush of my hair stuck to my cheek, eyes wild with ecstasy staring at me, and both of us still, so still that we can feel each other's heartbeat—that's when I know. He's my soul mate.

"It must be so exciting to be around the fast cars," I say with a pen light shining bright in my eyes.

"As a doctor," Lark starts, "I can't say I'm fond of fast cars. I'm nervous every time Harbor gets behind the wheel." She lowers the light, but spots still fill my vision. After blinking a few times, her smile comes into view and then her eyes. Both are comforting. "Not so much in the city since there's too much traffic to let the engine loose, but he meets his clients at a racetrack to hand off the keys."

Dressed in dark-fitted jeans, muted gold flats, and a black blouse with full, long sleeves, she sits on the dining chair next to me with her hair twisted on top of her head. The messy knot complements the refined style of her outfit. She's beautiful and approachable. She fits right in with the Westcotts I've met so far.

"Loch said Harbor's custom cars cost a million and up, but I didn't think about how fast they can go."

"I try not to because it's his dream and makes him happy. Happy is something I fully support." She packs her pen in a pouch next to the Oxometer she used earlier on me. She says, "The company is only a few years old but already has a six-year waitlist." From anyone else, that could come off as bragging, but with her, you can see the pride in her eyes and hear the love in her voice when she speaks of Harbor.

"Amazing."

She turns back to me. "You know what's amazing? The body's ability to heal itself. Your eyes look good. They're clear and focused. Your blood pressure was within the recommended range. No fever." She sits back. "I'm comfortable telling you to continue to take it easy regarding your healing from the concussion, but I'm not giving an all clear just yet. The back of your head looked good as well. You mentioned you had a few concerns?"

She unpacks her salad from the bag, then takes a sip of tea. I've eaten half of mine already because I was starving, so I try to give her time to enjoy hers as well. "The amnesia. I've spent so much time researching, but it seems like it's a case-by-case basis when and even if the memory returns."

"There have been some good studies, including fairly recent ones, that have provided insight on what to expect and not expect with amnesia." Setting her tea down, she seems to get caught in her thoughts as she bites her bottom lip. Her gaze darts to mine again, and she says, "A traumatic event caused the injury, leading to the loss. One of the focused treatments is to keep the trauma from returning. Another is to find people from your past or items and spend time with them. The point is to find the underlying cause beyond the physical damage you suffered."

Picking up my fork, I toy with a diced tomato, trying to understand. "You had me until the end." I smile, kind of cringing because I really don't want her to think I'm dumb.

She smiles, stabbing a piece of lettuce, but glances at me. "Basically, the physical injury of hitting your head might not have caused the amnesia." She waves the fork around in a circle. "Your brain just used that opportunity to protect you from something else in your life." She takes a bite of lettuce, the crunching disappearing under my mind being blown.

"You're saying my brain wants me to forget my past?"

"I'm not entirely sure, Tuesday. No one can truly answer that but you."

"Will *I* get my memory back?"

Dipping a carrot into the little container of dressing, she replies, "They're there. You just need a key to unlock them."

"Please tell me we can buy one when we're out shopping today," I say, giggling and taking a bite of my salad.

With a devious gleam in her eyes, she says, "I say we check Fifth Avenue first."

"I think we're going to be fast friends, Lark."

Her knee bumps mine as she smiles. "We already are."

I enjoy my day with her. It's been one of my favorites. I just wish this storm cloud of a question hadn't been hanging over my head all day. What is my brain protecting me from?

22

Loch

"THAT'S the third fucking dunk you've scored off me, asshole." Out of breath, I pace the half-court. I used to kick my brother's ass at almost everything, but now he's getting his revenge. I'm only thirty, but I feel fucking old. "How're you hanging in there, Dad?"

My dad has downed two bottles of water and sat out more than he's played. "I'm done." He waves me off. "You guys play without me." He heads off to the bench by the gym bags while Harbor dribbles the basketball around and then shoots from the foul line.

And makes it. *Asshole.*

Passing the ball to me, he asks, "Best two out of three?"

"I think I'm done like Dad."

Harbor starts chuckling. "You need more cardio in your life."

"I run five miles on the treadmill at least three times a week, and I'm walking all over this city the rest of the time. You'd think I could keep up with a scrawny kid like you."

Harbor's built, taking after his big brother, but I can't let him think I noticed. I jack the ball at him.

Catching it against his gut, he's chuckling too hard to hold a conversation. He finally manages to say, "Okay, gramps."

Fucker.

I grab a towel from my gym bag and start to dry off the sweat. "I want to see you take on Noah, then we'll see who the gramps is."

"I did. Last week. He plays baseball, not basketball. I kicked his ass, too."

I toss in the towel, literally and figuratively. "I'm thinking a beer might do me a solid."

Harbor is there and ready to go. "I'm in."

My dad stands with a towel wrapped over his shoulders, and says, "That's more my speed."

WE SHOWERED at the club and put on fresh clothes. It's been a while since I've been out of the house in anything other than a suit. It feels good to be relaxed, to get some exercise, and spend time with my brother and dad.

"When are you heading back to Beacon, Dad?" I ask over the second round of beers.

The crowded sports bar has TVs playing everything from pro football to college basketball. There's a lot to be distracted by, but Dad's been content listening to us ramble on about my work and Harbor's travels. Lark comes up a few times with casual mentions of starting a family. I'm not sure how he can stay so calm about it. But after I think more about it, I know he's calm because he has Lark. Will I ever be that way when it comes to starting a family?

He takes a gulp, his gaze shifting to a TV hanging on the far side of the room. "She's busy with her career. I'm busy with mine. Nannies are fine, but she's mentioned wanting to be more hands-on than her current job would allow."

"What does that mean?" I ask, setting my empty glass down on the table.

"She says she wants to be home, at least while the kids are little." He rubs his forehead, unease showing in the lines of his face. "I can't believe she and I are even discussing having kids."

My dad asks, "Do you want kids?"

I appreciate his judgement-free tone with my brother. I've been put under the interrogation light a few times over the years by guys who tell me it's time for me to settle down, the same people who prefer working late at the office to going home to their families. *Go figure* . . .

My parents have never pressured us. I know they want grandkids, but I firmly believe that people should have kids for their own reasons and on their own timelines, not others. But maybe that's because I've never been in a relationship that inspired different feelings on the topic.

Tuesday.

I'm not sure if I should be concerned or happy that Tuesday is the first thing that comes to mind. That's a big step, and it's too soon to be taking it, much less thinking about it.

Harbor relaxes, and says, "I want kids. I'm not committed to a number or a certain timeframe, or anything like that. Our lives and careers will need to adjust to have the family life we want. My business is growing so fast . . ." He looks back and forth between us. "I love it, but there are offers on the table that I need to seriously consider."

"You're living your dream," I say. "You'd sell?"

"I've also achieved that dream. We change. Dreams change. I'd do something else with cars, but it would be because I want to instead of needing to. You know finances aren't an issue now. The offers I've received mean doing what we want for the rest of our lives. With Lark, my life looks a little different these days. My priorities have shifted. Nothing is changing anytime soon." Spinning his glass around, he lifts his eyebrows and smirks. "And we're having a good time right now. Perks of the honeymoon stage."

"Too much, kid." My dad laughs and shifts his attention and his shoulders toward me. "Tuesday is good for you, Loch."

"Where did that come from?"

"It's been on my mind since I met her. Not trying to criticize, but you're not usually in that great of a mood. With her, I see the difference, and you're happier."

Twisting on his barstool, Harbor says, "Lark and I really liked her, and since we don't usually meet the women you date, if date is what the kids call it these days—Wait." He turns to my dad. "Not counting high school, has Loch ever brought a woman to meet us?"

My dad chuckles. "I believe last night was a first. Your mom and I used to think he was too embarrassed to bring around his big city 'dates.'"

"Fucking hell," I reply, not giving in to the teasing that has me on the verge of laughter. "Really? We're doing this?" I shake my head and glare out of the corners of my eyes, basically sulking, which is unlike me. But the fun is too good to take it all seriously. "My 'dates' are just that . . . ah, fuck it." I anchor my elbows on the high-top table. "The ladies love me, but our arrangements don't usually involve meeting the family."

"Until Tuesday," my dad says.

I can't lie. "Until Tuesday."

My brother asks, "You bringing her to the house for Thanksgiving? The four of us can ride together."

"Why are we talking about Thanksgiving in . . . shit." I massage my temple. "The days are running into one another. Other than Tuesday, I haven't thought beyond the Reinhold case lately."

"You have several cases on the docket for December, Lochlan. If you're spread too thin, then we need to—"

"We don't need to do anything, Dad. I'm handling my cases, and financially speaking, the office is having its best year yet."

"I'm not adding pressure. I can just tell your—"

"Priorities are shifting," my brother says. "Welcome to the club."

"My priorities aren't shifting, Harbor," I snap, slipping off the stool. "And what the fuck club are you talking about?"

"Settle down, brother." He stands. "There are worse clubs you can be a part of than the love club."

"There's no love club."

My dad says, "You did use we the other day."

I stop from bolting out the door and redirect my glare on him. "What are you talking about?"

"At your apartment, Tuesday had a memory, and you said we found another piece of the puzzle. Not just her, but we, as in the two of you—"

"I understand what 'we' means."

"Okay, both of you were a team at that moment. That's my point. It may be too late for you. You may already be a permanent member. Welcome to the roster, brother."

"Pfft. Permanent . . ." I grumble. "You two are absurd, so I'm going to leave you to it."

Harbor sits back down and laughs. "You know we're only giving you a hard time, right, Loch? You're allowed to have a life outside the law firm. You haven't had one in years. Right, Dad?"

Throwing his hands up in surrender, my dad chimes in, "If you can speak some sense into him, you're doing better than I am."

"No one needs to speak anything into me. You guys entertain each other. I'm taking off."

I can hear Harbor chuckling as I walk away. "See you at Thanksgiving."

Flipping him the bird while leaving, I say, "See you then." We don't hold grudges. I'm not even upset, but that was getting out of hand. Mainly because I'm not sure what Tuesday and I are other than new to this whole boyfriend-girlfriend thing.

We've moved at the speed of light so far, but I'm not in a hurry to rush this along. I have a feeling she feels the same. Taking it day by day is the best way to approach it.

I decide to walk home. I'm in sneakers, and the time could help clear my head. Cutting through a park, I take another route that allows me to shoot across to my street.

"Dreams change."

Harbor's words repeat like a broken record in my mind.

There wasn't an ounce of regret in his tone when he confessed. Is it priorities or dreams that are changing, adapting to who we are at that moment? Or do we just lose sight of what we once strived toward?

Did something better come along?

WORK IS A DISTRACTION. Nothing more than a way to bide my time until she comes home.

I've gotten dressed and am sitting here ready for dinner plans we never made, thinking she'll want to go out. But as the hours tick by with no texts, calls, and nothing that gives me a sense that Tuesday is safe, I find myself rereading the same thing. I can't concentrate any longer, needing to know where she is. But I can't control what she does.

I can't control her.

I would never want to.

But the more time passes, the more I wonder what she's really doing. Worrying won't make her come back any faster. All I'm doing is creating a distraction for myself. And distracted people make mistakes.

Have I ever been this worried about a woman?

I know the answer. No, because I love her. She's the best distraction I could ever have.

"Loch?" *I hear as if she heard my worries.*

I look up from the desk.

Her silhouette fills the doorway to my office, and she asks, "Why are you sitting in the dark?"

"I didn't realize it had gotten dark." I'm in the smallest room in my apartment, with a lackluster view, caught between missing her, the concern of not knowing if she was okay or even returning, and unwarranted anger. I look out the window to temper my mood.

When she comes around the desk, she swivels the chair and positions herself on my lap. Cupping my face, she leans her head against mine. "What's wrong?"

"I . . ." I sound like a possessive idiot.

Leaning to the side, she kisses my cheek and again near my ear before whispering, "Talk to me, Loch. Tell me what's wrong."

The words that explain the battle in my brain don't come. Even if they did, it wouldn't be fair to put that on her to make me feel better. So I kiss her, burying my fear of losing her to an unknown life that could claim her any day.

Kissing is sweet, but that's not enough to satisfy the hunger I didn't know I had until I tasted her again. I grab her hips and angle her my way. "Hey," she starts, but then she feels my hands sliding under her waistband and dipping into the front of her jeans. "Oh."

The denim is tight around her waist, so tight that I can't fit my hand in easily. "New clothes?" I growl.

"Just a few." She unbuttons the top and lifts just barely to unzip.

"I don't like them."

She laughs. "You don't like them because you don't have easy access to me?"

"Exactly."

She lifts again, this time taking her jeans down. "Better?" she asks, her voice lowering to fit the mood.

"Not yet." I move her hair to the side, but everything is too bulky, covering too much of her body. "Stand up and take the sweater off." She stays seated on me for a few seconds before she stands, pulling her sweater over her head and setting it on the desk in front of her.

I push her jeans lower on her thighs and then sit back to admire her. Her bare ass has a slip of lace daring to cover her and then slip between her full cheeks. She eyes me over her shoulder. "What are you—"

"Shhh." I hold my finger to my mouth. Reaching forward, I run my finger under the white lace, gliding it a few inches and then returning to the top again. "I'm going to ask you questions, and I want you to tell me the truth. Okay, Tuesday."

"Okay," she says, turning around.

"Keep your eyes forward and rest your hands on the desk. Can you do that for me?"

There's a pause, and I hear her tongue dip out to lick her lips in that emptiness. But then she leans forward, doing as I ask. Her shoulders rise and fall with deepened breaths.

I graze over her hips with the palms of my hands. "That's a good girl."

Her breath hitches, but she doesn't say a word. She releases a held exhale as her gaze falls to the desk. With her hands planted firmly, I could do anything to her, and she'd let me. Rubbing the mounds of her ass, I say, "You trust me."

"I trust you with my life."

"I'm not sure you should."

Standing behind her, I run my hand the length of her spine, leaving goose bumps to flourish across her skin. When I press my erection against the crease of her ass, I lean over and whisper against the back of her neck. "Feel what you did to me, what you caused."

She lowers to her forearms and pushes against me, then wiggles. I take her hips and hold her still so she can't. "Did I say you could move?"

Except for the sound of breathing, anticipation heats the room. "No."

"No?"

... "No, Mr. Westcott, you didn't."

A grin formed from control spreads across my face. I don't want to control her. I don't want to own her. I want the chance I know I'll never be given. To truly love her.

Anger surges inside me, and my belt flies open, the ends of the leather slapping against her skin. I yank my pants open and drag my clothes down. I'm close to fucking her so hard she'll never forget me until I realize I don't have protection.

"Motherfuck," I grit through my teeth, digging my fingers into her hips again as I lean over her. "Don't move a muscle. You understand?"

"Yes." My hands leave her body when she adds, "No condom needed."

I stop.

Turning back, I look at my beautiful girl bent over my desk and waiting for me. My heart thumps in my chest as I wage a debate in my head. I know the right thing to do, but she makes me want to be so bad.

Why'd she have to be so goddamn tempting?

Fuck me.

"It's not time." I retrieve a condom from the bedroom and return before she has a chance to miss me. As I roll it down my dick, it doesn't take much to get me back to where I was. Hard as steel for her. The anger hasn't tempered. I feel drunk with the power.

Taking the white lace, I shred it like I'm about to do to her innocence and toss it onto the desk beside her. My sweet girl's about to get a fresh taste of the man I really am. Reaching between her legs, I slide my fingers through her lips and into her opening.

"Ah," she groans. She's needed this as much as I have.

When her hips start to gyrate, I pull back. "I didn't give you permission."

Her body stills despite her ragged breathing. "Loch," she pleads, resting her head and chest on the desk. Her light hair falls over her face, hiding her eyes from me. "I need you."

When I move the strands, her eyes are closed, and her palms are flat as she waits for me to take her. Moving my hand from the heat between us, I position myself at her entrance, then lean against her and kiss her back. "I need you, baby. So much."

I thrust, forcing her forward and then back when I pull myself almost all the way out of her. When her mouth opens, I fill it with the fingers that just left her body. Her lips close around them as her pussy clenches around me.

When she moans again, I move to her shoulder and start fucking her. *No texts.* I fuck. *No calls.* I fuck. Angry with the world because I know I can't have her forever. *I fuck.*

And then I fuck harder, losing myself in her like it might be the last fucking time. Looping my wrist around the front of her thigh, I find her clit and stroke in desperate circles. "Loch," comes out of her mouth in a frantic whisper, and she repeats, causing me to drive harder as sweat drips from my forehead.

My orgasm creeps at first, climbing steady, so I move faster—my mind, my body, my heart trying to capture hers.

"Oh." Her cry of ecstasy brings me back to the moment we're sharing. "Keep going." I keep thrusting, losing sight of myself again. And then her body contracts and squeezes, tremoring around me as I reach my peak and start coming. Our bodies move against the tide of each other, seeking completion. And then stillness as she lays beneath me. "God, yes," she says, her pleasure driving a smile across her face.

A few erratic jerks of my cock force me forward until I have nothing left. My breath comes in heavy, and as worn as I am, I kiss her shoulder and the sweat on the side of her neck. Opening her eyes, she reaches around and holds me to her.

Brushing her hair back from her face, I kiss her red-hot

cheek, then her temple. I scoop her into my arms and sit in the chair with her across my lap. "Dreams change."

She smiles, sweeping my hair from my eyes and resting her head on my shoulder. "They do."

I love her . . . more than I ever thought possible to love another, and all because of six words. Words that changed my life tonight. *"I trust you with my life."* Those six words just changed *me* forever.

23

Loch

THE SUN HAS BARELY TOUCHED the morning sky, but it provides enough light to see Tuesday sleeping. I used to dread this hour—already drained by what was ahead, knowing every hour had already been scheduled weeks in advance. But with Tuesday, it's become one of my favorite times of day.

I don't even need an alarm to wake me.

My body stirs instinctively, but I lie here and hold her, soaking in every minute I have with her. I might be taking advantage of the situation, but I kiss her twice on the cheek and then on her forehead, selfishly wanting her to wake with me so I can have more of her.

She has her arm draped over my middle, her head resting as her body curls around me. A smile graces her face, but her closed lids hide her blue eyes. She whispers, "Is it already morning?"

"It is." I grin when her arm tightens around me, followed by a soft sigh.

"I want you to stay in bed with me."

"I wish I could. I have court."

Finally leaning back to look up at me, she says, "And there's nothing I have that you might be interested in more than court?" I know she's teasing, but my brain is fully awake now.

"I'm interested in so much about you that I almost don't know where to start." Holding her under the chin, I kiss her lips but then reluctantly slip out of her embrace. "And unfortunately, I wasted too much time watching you sleep. I won't make that mistake again."

She laughs but then pushes up as I walk away. "Two things, Mr. Westcott."

When I turn back, I catch her eyes lifting to meet mine. *So busted.*

"First, the weekend went by too fast." I couldn't agree more. "Second, nice ass." She waggles her eyebrows unabashedly.

"First, it always does." I chuckle and walk into the bathroom. "Second," I call out, "Those five a.m. workouts are paying off." I start the shower.

A few minutes pass while I'm waiting for hot water when I hear, "Loch?" panic striking her voice.

Dipping my head back into the bedroom, I ask, "What?"

She holds up my phone. "Leisa just called, but it only rang once. I didn't answer it."

I walk back out to grab my phone and text: *Good morning. You called?*

As if she had it loaded and ready to go, I receive her reply text: *Update listed for the Reinhold case. 8:30. I'll go by the office, get the team to bring the boxes, and meet you at the court-house. 8:15.*

What is Judge Judy up to this time? This has got to end.

I'm putting a stop to it today. I know the plaintiff is as fed up as I am. As for the earlier time, I'm lucky to have an assistant who's always on the ball. I respond to her text: *Thank you.*

Tuesday lies back on the bed, her brow furrowed. "Everything okay?"

"My case got bumped up on the docket." The good to the start of our day has vanished. I set my phone down on the nightstand, feeling the day already getting away from me. It's been different with Tuesday, but this, *me* . . . feels a lot like I used to—cranky. "Happy Monday."

I walk through the courthouse doors, stopping to check the large brass clock hanging on a marble column. 8:10 a.m. Time to spare. I grin, getting a taste of the victory I intend to claim.

Turning to look behind me, I see Leisa pushing the boxes through the security scanner and two assistants she's directing to carry them once they reach the other side. I start toward her, ready to help.

She puts her hand up. "We're good."

The guys stack the boxes and are lifting them by the time I reach them with my briefcase in hand. They greet me and then head toward the doors to the courtroom.

As soon as Leisa makes it through the checkpoint, she shakes her head. "She's out of hand."

"I agree."

"Besides the sneak change for the trial this morning," she says as we walk together. Her heels clack against the stone floor, her own crankiness revealed through her voice and the heavy steps she's taking. "You ready for this?"

"Am I?"

"No," she says, "trust me, you're not."

"Hit me with it anyway." We stop, and she holds up her phone to show me an email.

I read the first two lines, which is enough. "You're fucking kidding me."

"I wish I were. Sorry to be the bearer of bad news."

"It's Monday fucking morning, and she wants to pull this shit?"

"I honestly didn't know if I should laugh or cry for you. Judge Judy is persistent. I'll give her that."

"I can handle her." Though I thought I had already made my personal views on dating her clear. I raise my hand to run it through my hair, but I gelled it today, so I shove it in my pocket out of frustration. "This is not only highly irregular and disruptive to my client, but this is the last stand. We can't get a fair trial with her acting like a loose cannon."

Leisa laughs. "You're more polite than I am about this sexual harassment. I was about to call her a lot worse than a loose cannon."

We start walking toward the courtroom. "Just another reason we work so well together."

After getting our boxes settled beside the table, the bailiff leads me out of the courtroom and down a short hall. Judge Wexham is on the plaque next to the door. I'm given a dirty look when I laugh. If he only knew she was using her appointed position as a dating service for herself.

He knocks and then turns the knob.

"Your honor," I say, sick of this shit but smart enough to handle the situation with kid gloves. "What's the meaning of this?"

She's tucked behind her desk, looking like she might want to actually conduct business. *Oh.* This is unexpected, but I'm relieved to see her acting like a professional. "Sit down, Mr. Westcott."

I remain standing.

She appears ready for a standoff with her arms firmly

planted in front of her on the desk and not a hint of smile on her face. "How are you?" Leaning forward, she adds, "Friend to friend."

"Better than ever."

"Good." Sitting back, she lets her hair flow from the elastic she had it tied back with and shakes it free. "I've been thinking that you and I got off track somehow."

Track? I jumped from the train traveling that track and heading for a disaster the night she showed up at my apartment. But I keep my mouth shut.

She continues, unzipping her robe, "Have you reconsidered my offer? We could make such a powerful legal team." She better have on some fucking clothes underneath.

A royal-blue suit covers her to the neck. *Thank God.* "I haven't, your honor."

"Please, call me Judge Judy in my private quarters."

I stare at her, not sitting but rocking back on my heels with my hands in my pockets to keep myself from filing at least four ethics and code of conduct violations against her. "You know all the evidence supports my clients, but you continue with this onslaught of indecency in the courtroom, making a mockery of this courthouse. Let's end this now and wrap up this trial."

"And what are you going to do for me?"

Pressing my hands firmly to the desktop, I say, "Let you continue to sit in that chair and preside over cases."

"Are you threatening me, Mr. Westcott?"

"No," I reply, shaking my head and standing back up. "There's enough evidence to convict yourself. So you tell me how we end this amicably and get this done."

She huffs, her eyes sliding to the window and staring out. There's no tension between us, which surprises me. I don't feel impatient with anger or even the layers of annoyance I was suffering from earlier.

I'm calm.

I'm not sure I've ever felt this content before. It's the Tuesday effect. My body's makeup is rearranging all because of her.

As for Judy, I just feel sorry for her now. But I'll work with her to find a solution that will satisfy both parties.

"It's lonely at the top, Loch." It's good to hear her tone based on trust instead of being on the hunt. "I thought I'd be married by now, but here I am, taking the little bit of attention you gave me during our date and turning it into a circus."

There's an inclination to reassure her or make her feel better regarding her actions. But I do understand her craving to be loved. Until I met the right person, I didn't realize I needed the same. Now, I've changed for the better. Even Harbor, Lark, and my dad see it, so I can sympathize.

"You're looking in the wrong places."

"What do you mean?"

Signaling behind me with my head, I say, "You're not going to find something real in your courtroom. There's no real opportunity to get to know someone. And this, summoning attorneys to your office, won't make them stick it out in the long term."

"What do you suggest?" Preying on her courtroom doesn't seem to cross her mind as unethical.

I sigh.

He will kill me, but I feel like they might get along. "I know someone you might find interesting. Great guy. Steady job. Up for a good time."

Sitting forward, she smiles, revealing her intrigue. "Do tell."

I'm not an idiot. I'm willing to win this trial fair and square, but I have to get her to announce the verdict. "First, there's a matter of this trial."

"Right." She stands and starts on the zipper of the robe, tugging it up. "Let's get this case closed."

Forty-five minutes later, I push out the courthouse doors and start walking back to the office. With the phone to my ear, I hear my dad answer, "Hello?"

"We won."

"Way to get it done, son. How did it wrap?"

"The other side offered a settlement behind closed doors to cut the losses and not spend the next year battling over money they know they'll lose anyway. The Reinhold Group accepted."

"Fantastic news. A hard-fought battle you can be proud of winning. But promise me something."

"What?" I stop off to the side in the doorway of a building to hear him better.

"When the competition comes around to offer some ludicrous amount of money at another firm, stick with family."

"Guess it depends on the offer." I'm joking. I have more money than I know how to spend now. It stopped being about that a few years ago. I'm building a firm and a legacy of my own. I can do that with Westcott Law. "Joking, Dad. Why go anywhere else when the firm already bears my name."

"My name," he corrects with a lot less humor than seconds earlier. "But maybe it's time to talk about your future when you're here for Thanksgiving. You're still coming to Beacon, right?"

"Wouldn't miss it."

"And you're bringing Tuesday?"

"I'll ask her tonight."

"Good, and job well done on this case, Lochlan."

"Thanks, Dad. Talk soon."

When we hang up, I start walking again. I've traveled this way a million times, but it feels different this time. I stop when I near the coffee shop where the attack on Tuesday happened, seeing the wall and the concrete with a stained blood spot. And I know what needs to happen. It's time to get Tuesday some answers.

———

I CALL Leisa and have her contact a few private investigators our law firm uses on occasion while I stop into a local restaurant to place a catering order for our office party. And as I make my way back into my workplace, moods are high and victory evident.

I stand in the corner of the conference room and stare out at this incredible view, a view that I took for granted before Tuesday taught me to take a minute to appreciate our surroundings, when I hear Leisa call me. "You have a call, Loch." Turning to her tapping her phone, she adds, "Line one in your office."

"Thanks." *Here we go.*

"Loch Westcott."

After a productive call that lasted more than twenty minutes, I hang up the phone, justified in my actions. I had to do it.

For Tuesday.

The call with the investigator doesn't make me feel better even though it should. She deserves answers. But what will happen to us once she finds out who she is? My gut fills with dread that any moment she could be taken away from me or, worse, willingly leave me.

I set my selfish needs aside and look at it through the long-range lens. She needs to know. She deserves to know who she is and make decisions based on what is best for her in life.

Her happiness is all that matters.

"I OWE YOU ONE, BRADY."

"You owe me more than one and a raise for this." He straightens his tie, then asks, "How did I get talked into this?" The shaking of his head counters the amusement in his voice.

"Because I distinctly remember you asking me if I knew any women to set you up on a date with. Voilà."

"That was like three years ago."

"Better late than never."

"She better be hot."

Hot. *Check.* Also slightly stalkerish. *Check.* But equally sexually explorative. *Check.*

"The Kitty Kat Club over on Staten Island."

"Nice place. High end."

Resting against the back of the couch, I say, "Leave it for the Yelp review. Remember, she's wearing a mask so no one will recognize her." I try to hide my laughter behind my hand but fail miserably and burst out.

"Sounds like the judge has a wild side."

"She does, and a penchant for the gavel."

He looks at me; his eyes set harder than usual. "What does she do with the gavel?"

"You'll find out." I pat him on the back. "Just go with it."

He laughs. "What have I gotten myself into?"

I hand him cash. Flipping through the bills, he says, "Two K?"

"She loves a big spender." I pat his shoulder. "You clean up good, Brady."

"Wish me luck."

"Trust me, you don't need any with Judge Judy. Go get 'em, tiger."

He opens the door but glances back. "Thanks for the cash." He shuts the door, leaving me just enough time to pull plates from the cabinet before Tuesday walks in.

"Where's Brady going all spiffed up like that?"

"He has a date." I'm still chuckling under my breath. He's definitely getting a raise. "How'd it go down at the station?"

She hangs her coat by the door. "I filled out more paperwork and listed your address as a way to reach me. Hope you don't mind."

"Of course, I don't mind."

For someone who's spent time in a police station most of the day, you wouldn't know it by looking at her. She comes around to kiss me, a glow penetrating her smile and eyes just as bright as when she rolls on top of me in the morning and wants to have sex. *Fucking gorgeous.*

"How can they not have any leads?" she asks.

"Seems impossible." *Frustrating, actually.*

"I don't think they're in a rush to solve my case."

"By the way, I'm so proud of you." Though I called my dad after we won the case since I knew he was waiting for it, she was the person I most wanted to share the news with. Her genuine joy for me extended through the connection.

"Thank you." I kiss her, my body pressing to hers. "I'm glad you're home."

Home.

This is her home.

I still don't understand how she came into my life and flipped it around so fast. Maybe it's the suddenness of us having to adapt quickly after what happened. Or perhaps she lit a match, shining light into the parts of my heart that had never been revealed before. Either way, it's impossible to explain the change she's caused in me, this alternate version of who I used to be, but I welcome it, *like her*, whole-heartedly.

I need her.

I want her to be a part of my life, every part I have to offer. "Will you spend Thanksgiving with my family and me?"

Sinking against me, she says, "I'd love to."

24

Tuesday

<small>THANKSGIVING</small>

"YOU'RE VERY GOOD AT DRIVING," I say, struggling to keep a straight face. "You haven't driven outside the lines once."

Loch chuckles. "Funny girl."

Making him laugh is one of my favorite things to do. Hearing him laugh is one of my others.

We're about halfway to Beacon, the town where he grew up. I can't wait to see where this amazing man came from and to meet the rest of his family. I've been giddy all morning.

Since Brady is with his family, Loch drives the Escalade. Sitting in the front seat gives a different perspective.

I thought I'd be content munching on a bag of popcorn and taking in the scenery ever since we stopped for snacks an hour ago, but nope. Something about our close confines has me needing to fill the silence, so I've been peppering him with questions and anecdotal observations ever since.

The goat we saw on the roof of a barn.

Pineapple on pizza? *Firm no from him.* Me, I don't know. I'd have to try it.

A cloud over a grouping of trees miles from where we were driving that looked like a wolf howling.

Passing a couple in a RX-7 having sex. I don't know how they managed it, cruising at what appeared to be eighty since they sped past us, but they seemed to be doing just fine.

Resting my heels on the seat, I wrap my arms around my bent legs. "Tell me about your hometown?" If he wanted to share his whole life since birth, I'd happily listen. I've been captivated by him—his generosity, his kindness, his open arms. God, I could go on about how brilliant he is, and this man's good looks cannot be discounted. His answers are quick yet informative, and you can see his lawyer brain working to keep up with my interrogation.

How has he not been snatched up yet?

Maybe the anecdotes were a means to get him to open up. There's one specific topic I had in mind. We've been trapped in this vehicle, and now seems like the perfect time, so I ask, "Can we talk about the sex on the desk?"

"What the . . ." His head jerks to look at me. "You don't just sideswipe someone like that."

I laugh. "Sorry, guess it seems out of the blue, but it's been on my mind."

"Okay. We can talk about it. What's on your mind?" His eyes return to the road, his fingers flexing.

I don't want to upset him, but beating around the bush won't clear the air. "Let me preface this by saying it felt amazing. You always feel amazing." I reach over, tenderly running my fingertips along his arm to temper the words I'm about to say. "But you weren't making love to me, Loch. You were taking your anger out on me."

His knuckles whiten when his grip tightens around the steering wheel. He glances at me. "That wasn't my intention. Was I too rough?"

"No, you weren't, but you had something going on in your head, and instead of talking to me, you got your message across another way. I know you would never hurt me. It just worried me a little because I want to be able to communicate."

"I'm sorry."

"I don't need an apology. That's not why I'm bringing it up. I need to know you're okay."

His gaze remains focused dead ahead, and that silence I've been anxiously filling returns with a vengeance. But then he takes a breath and says, "No one asks me that."

"I know. You're used to isolating, and here I came along and invaded your space. If I've upset you—"

"No," he starts, reaching over and rubbing the top of my knee. When his eyes return to the road, he says, "The truth is, I was worried about you. Logically, I shouldn't have been. You were with Lark. Safe—"

"But we were later than we expected, and that caused you to worry. Am I correct? I was having such a good time with her that I lost track of time. But I should have sent you a text to let you know we decided to go to a few more stores." I rest my hand on his leg.

His hand covers mine—large, warm, comforting. "You don't have to check in with me."

"I know I don't, but it's important for you to know I'm safe. I'm sorry for taking so long to realize how this affected you as well."

"Don't apologize for having fun, Tues. That's not what I want, and it's not what I'm asking of you. I need to manage the reality that not every moment of your life will include me . . . and it shouldn't." Giving my hand a squeeze, he says, "I'm sorry if you felt anything other than pleasure when we're together, especially in bed. That will never be my intention."

"I know, babe. That's not why I brought it up. I just wanted to make sure that you're doing okay."

A slow grin spreads on his face. "I am. Thank you for asking."

I feel so much better, and I hope he does, too. I just feel it in my core that relationships should have open communication built on a foundation of honesty. I'm glad to have that with him.

"Babe?"

I look at his quirked brow and start laughing again. Shrugging, I say, "It just felt right to call you that."

"I like it."

I'M NOT sure when I dozed off, but Loch rocks me gently awake. "Hey there."

It takes me a few seconds to get my bearings. Loch. Escalade. Beacon. "We're here?"

"Shortly. My parents live in Beacon Pointe, just outside of town. I thought you might want to see the downtown area."

I sit straighter, reaching for my water bottle. "This is it?" I take a few sips because I'm feeling dehydrated.

"This is Beacon. It's about as small as they come, but like the rest of us, it's starting to grow up." He points toward a grouping of buildings up on a hill. "The university has brought in a lot of new businesses over the years along with a few high-rises. But the high-rises there don't extend much above a low-rise in Manhattan."

"It's picturesque, like from a movie."

"It's actually been used in a few movies."

Taking the main road through town, we keep going until fences that extend for miles start lining the landscape. When Loch slows down, he pulls up to a gate and stops to punch in a code. The large iron gates swing open, and he pulls through the entrance to the property.

I sit up, taking notice. "This is your parents' property?"

Reaching over, he takes my hand, our fingers entwining. Is he preparing me, comforting me, or I don't know, but the house is huge. Beautiful in its classic architecture with a white exterior and green shutters.

"This is where I grew up."

"Wow." I'm not sure what else to say since my jaw drops on my lap.

He parks on the side. I'm quick to swipe on some lipstick before we hop out. Instead of taking me to the front door, he grabs my hand again and leads me to the back. "Don't be nervous."

"Easy for you to say."

Chuckling lightly, he brings our joined hands to his mouth and kisses the back of mine. "I get it, but really, they're going to love you. Not only because of how amazing you are but also because I do."

He's so free with expressing his love to me that my anxiety begins to wane. Opening the door, he says, "We're here." I step into the kitchen with him behind me and stop in the middle of a bustling family.

They stop, too, and stare.

His mom takes off her apron and tosses it on the island as she comes toward us. "Loch," she says, seeming to break the ice for the others who follow her lead. Embracing him, she says, "Welcome home, love."

He releases me to hug her. I can't stop my heart from swelling seeing them together.

She's stylishly put together in a flattering evergreen sweater and fitted blue jeans that hit above the ankle. Shorter wedge shoes give her a tad of height, but she doesn't need them. She's beautiful—blond hair but darker than mine hitting above her shoulders, vibrant blue eyes that hold her joy of seeing him inside. I expected nothing less from Loch's family.

She angles toward me with a smile. "You must be Tuesday. It's nice to meet you. I've heard so many wonderful things about you."

"Thank you." I shake her hand, but something about her offers such comfort that I lean in, and we hug. "It's so nice to meet you as well."

I'm tempted to apologize for hugging her like she's my mother, but her kind smile tells me I don't need to. She angles toward the living room, and says, "This is my daughter Marina, Loch's younger sister."

"Hello," I say. We shake hands as she moves in closer. She's a pretty girl with the same matching hair as her brother's, though her lighter strands add a goldenness to it. Her eyes match her mom's as if a decision was made the boys follow their father's genes and the daughter her mother's.

The kitchen door opens behind us, and we step out of the way. "Hello and Happy Thanksgiving," Lark says, entering with a pie in her hands. Harbor follows her in with several bags on his arms. Loch mentioned her dad joining us, so I assume he's the last to enter.

AFTER DINNER, the guys make their way outside for what Loch's youngest brother called "a pickup game," so I settle in on the couch, mindlessly watching the football game on the big screen.

"How are you doing?" Delta comes from the kitchen to sit in a nearby chair. It's been bustling here, so we haven't had a chance to chat except for a moment here or there over a few appetizers on the island.

"Starting to feel stuffed from all the food. Everything is so delicious I've had a hard time saving room for dinner."

She laughs. "I'd love to throw the formality of the meal out the window and just graze on appetizers all day." She leans in as if she's sharing a secret, and says, "My husband loves turkey. Loch loves the mashed potatoes. Harbor the green bean casserole. Noah the stuffing, and Marina adores cranberry sauce. Lark loves deviled eggs, and her dad, John, always requests my queso no matter the event. So here we are with an island of appetizers to tide them over until dinner is served."

"I don't know how you keep up with all that. What's your favorite?"

"Pumpkin pie." Her smile holds a hint of mischievous-ness. "How are you feeling?" The concern in her tone that reaches her eyes is noted and appreciated.

"I'm good." Now sharing my own secret, I add, "As good as can be, considering I don't know who I am."

Reaching over, she takes my hand and covers it with her other. "The circumstances are awful, but I'm so glad you and Loch have each other through this."

My first thought jumps back to Loch on the drive here and what he went through, checking on him after no one had, including me. "I wouldn't have made it without him. I'm so grateful, but I don't know how I'll ever return his generosity."

"There's no favor to return. Even though Port had mentioned how close you two had become, I can see how much he cares about you just by how he looks at you. My son is not a frivolous man, so call me sentimental, but it means everything to me to see him this happy. Thank you."

There's no hiding the tears in my eyes. She's thanking me for what I've done for her son when I owe everything to him for what he's done for me. "I'm so grateful for him . . ." The words clog in my throat when my emotions get the better of me. I refuse to cry, to be this silly with his mother.

"I understand." She gives my hand a little squeeze, then pulls her top hand back. "That's a beautiful ring you're wearing. I love rose gold."

I smile, happiness overtaking the rest and leaving the tears to fall another time. I didn't want to mess up my makeup either, so I appreciate the detour in topics.

She studies the ring wrapped around my finger, admiring it. "Thank you. I bought it when I was shopping with Lark."

"Tiffany's?" she asks. I nod as she continues, "They have such delicate and feminine designs. The leaves are lovely and how it wraps around your finger, but the branches don't meet, is such a beautiful detail."

"I heard you studied art."

"I did. I didn't end up using it in a professional capacity, but I still appreciate the exposure it gave me to the world of art."

"What are we talking about?" Loch's voice draws our attention toward the back door when he walks in.

I touch the ring, turning it slightly and admiring it. "Your mom's degree in art and . . ." Holding up my hand, I waggle my fingers. "And the new ring I bought when shopping with Lark." He comes around, slides down next to me on the couch, and touches it. "It's an olive branch and just spoke to me."

"It's pretty, like you." He kisses me.

"I think that's my cue to check on the turkey."

We laugh, but I turn enough to say, "It was nice talking to you, Delta."

"You, too." Tying her apron around her waist, she asks, "You never told me your favorite part of Thanksgiving. I want to make sure we have it."

I want to say this family. *How can I not?* They've opened their hearts and home and treated me like one of their own. I stuff those emotions down because it's too soon to wish I was a part of this family, to wish it were my own. Instead, I say, "I love warm rolls with lots of butter."

She smiles. "A woman after my own heart. Warm rolls are coming right up."

25

Tuesday

PORT AND DELTA have gone to bed, Marina had a friend come to sleep over and disappeared to her room hours ago, but Noah is holding court like the king of the castle. It's quite entertaining since he's probably a drink past what he should have consumed.

"So I say to her," he says, "you got one Westcott. You're not getting two."

"Noah," Harbor warns. "Enough. Lark and Tuesday don't want to hear about this."

Loch rocks forward on the couch next to me and sets his beer on the table. "None of us do." He scrubs a hand over his face, then looks at me. "You ready for bed?"

I nod.

The Westcotts have their hands full with Loch's youngest brother. He comes off as a lot of fun to hang out with, but he's also a heartbreaker. We've laughed a lot tonight, with everyone sharing stories from when they were teenagers and in college.

Not once am I made to feel excluded because I have nothing to share. I just like watching Loch with his family.

Noah groans. "I was getting to the good part. No one cares to know who I'm talking about?"

Standing, Loch offers me both hands and pulls me to my feet. He says, "I don't."

"Good because it was a girl Harbor hooked up with."

"Fucking hell, Noah. Shut the fuck up." Harbor stands. "My wife is right here."

Lark is laughing, though. She stands and straightens her shirt before patting her husband on the chest. "Don't forget, I grew up here. Rumors spread like wildfire up and down the grapevine from Beacon to the Pointe." She rolls her attention my way and laughs again. "He acts so innocent." Taking his hand, she pulls him toward the front of the house. "Come on. You can show me what a bad boy you are upstairs." She sing-songs, "Good night."

"Good night," I say. "Happy Thanksgiving."

Loch stops in the kitchen and fills two glasses with water while I wait on the other side of the island.

Noah's still riding his alcohol high when he holds up his phone. "Guess I'll have to find someone else to entertain tonight. The old folks are all going to bed."

Loch starts laughing. "Nice try, but we're going to bed."

"Poor sports."

"Eh, I'm sure you'll find a better way to pass the time than spending it with us 'old folks.' Just keep it down. We don't want to listen to you 'entertaining' yourself all night."

"That's a lot of air quotes, bro."

My guy shrugs. He's adorably tipsy and spills water over the lip of the glass as he hands it to me. Coming around the marble island, he cups my face and kisses me.

Noah says, "Get this guy to bed. He can't hold his beer. Night."

I caress Loch's hands on my cheeks. "Don't worry, I'll take care of him," I reply with laughter. "Night." Hugging him to me, I whisper, "I'll make sure he gets the best care ever."

His erection catches on fast . . . and hard. I grin from the pun. "I definitely think it's time for bed."

There's no fight to be had. Loch leads me upstairs to his room in the kid's wing of this mansion. Although I saw it when I freshened up when we arrived, I spent the day downstairs enjoying his family's company.

Now, in this bedroom that could rival most Manhattan apartments in size, I take a moment to really look around. Besides the normal bedroom furniture, this room is so all-American—trophies, books, photos, flags from his university, degrees hung on the wall, a letterman's jacket on a hook by the door. I walk the perimeter as Loch opens his suitcase. "You were being honest when you said you never failed at anything."

I catch his eyes on me across the room. He doesn't say anything, but what could he? He digs out pajama pants and a T-shirt. "Wow, I didn't know we were trying to prove Noah right, Gramps."

He chuckles. "We don't have to sleep in pajamas but figured we should have them near just in case."

"Just in case of what? A fire? If they barge in? Fill me in so I'm prepared."

"I don't know." He stands, leaving the nighttime attire on the suitcase, and sits on the end of the bed. "Come here, baby."

"Baby?"

Another shrug is released before he says, "It just felt right."

I hurry to sit on his lap and wrap my arms around him. "I like it."

"I like you." His eyes fixate on my lips until his gaze lifts to mine. "I love you so much, Tuesday."

"It's the beer and tryptophan talking."

I win another chuckle. "No, it's me talking to you." He kisses me, caressing my jaw and holding me to him. When our lips part, he says, "You fit right in."

Love blooms inside and spreads, making my heart race to grasp this acceptance and hold on for dear life. I've felt his love every day since before we uttered the words, but to know he feels this way about me with his family . . . I soak it in and try to keep myself from crying.

I tuck my head to the crook of his neck, still holding him. "You have an amazing family. They express their love in humor and support. The happiness you all share . . ." What started in a revelry of praise twists inside me as my reality sets in again. The tears fall first, and then the sob I can't contain. My hands fall to my lap when the pain tidal waves over me.

I'm wrapped in his stronghold, an embrace that won't allow me to fall apart. Words of love whispered in my ear slow the downpour of my tears, but no amount of tenderness seems able to keep my heart from aching. He asks, "Tell me what's wrong, baby, and I'll fix it. I promise you. I'll do whatever I can to make this right."

"That's just it. It's not about you or money." I finally have the strength to look into his eyes and meet the sorrow I've caused. "I know you would do anything for me if you could, but being here with your family reminds me that I don't matter to anyone."

"You matter to me. You matter more than anything else in this world to me, Tuesday." His sweet words coat my heart like armor, making me feel stronger at the moment, but can it last? With each passing day of no new information, no missing person reports filed, the little hope I have left is replaced by this world that I've fallen in love with and this man who will do anything for me.

Why does it all still feel so fleeting? Like one day, I'll wake up and lose everything that matters to me?

"I don't want to lose you, Loch, but I have nothing to offer, not even a family."

"You don't need those things. You have me. I'll be your family."

Our gazes latch onto each other's as the moon shines on us, *for us*. I kiss him until his lips part, and our tongues begin an erotic dance. I kiss him until he pulls me into his arms, and we tumble into bed.

I don't know if I could love him more, but I plan to do my damnedest.

We make love, slow and steady with adoration, and then fast with passion before we know what hit us. It's the way we fell in love and how our story will always be told.

"Let me know if you need anything," Delta says as we walk to the car the next morning. "Port said you love art as much as I do. I'd love to visit a museum with you the next time I'm in the city."

We've already said goodbye several times, but like her, I'm sad our trip is already ending. "I'd love that. Just let me know when."

We hug once more, then she gives Loch a big hug. "Take care of each other."

He says, "We will. I love you, Mom."

"I love you, too."

We climb into the Escalade, getting a later start than we wanted. Harbor and Lark left just after sunrise because she has a shift today, but we're racing a storm headed toward the city by midday. The meeting with his dad ran longer than expected this morning. Loch says we need to hurry to get home.

Home.

I love that we have a home together. I decided I wouldn't live in the unknown anymore and brushed the negative thoughts away. Living this life with Loch is all I need to be happy. So I'm choosing him instead.

26

Tuesday

"You're not going to let us celebrate?" I sigh, my excitement deflating from my chest. I want to do this for him. It's small compared to what he's done for me, but I'll take any opportunity to celebrate this man, and this accomplishment is a doozy.

"No. We don't need to. It's no big deal." He barely glances up after he sets the bottle of bourbon down on the counter in the kitchen.

We got home hours ago and settled in just as the storm blew through the city. Snow falls outside the windows, but we're cozy in here. But I'll tell you, he makes it hard to concentrate standing there shirtless.

I decide the only way to convince him to let me throw a party is to plead my case. "I think we do. You're now a partner at the law firm. That's a very big deal. Every letterhead, the sign on the building, the gold sign when you exit the elevator, the business cards . . ." I throw my arms in the air. "It all has to be updated to Westcott & Westcott Law Firm. That is huge, Loch."

Setting the glass down after sipping it with more enthusiasm for the bourbon than my argument, he leans against the counter, and says, "People will say my dad gave me the partnership because I'm his son."

"Fuck those people."

"I'd rather fuck you, and since when did you start swearing?"

"It's your favorite word. I figured my swearing puts us one step closer to becoming one and the same person. Eventually, we'll wear matching Hawaiian shirts in Waikiki and finish each other's sentences without even noticing."

"Couple goals."

I laugh. "I tried really hard to make that sound unappealing, too. Who knew you were so into retirement leisurewear."

"Your first problem is that nothing about you is unappealing." I come around the bar and latch onto his sexy body. His black sleep pants hang low enough for me to appreciate that deep V on display.

"You're so sweet. What's my second problem?" I ask, hoping he's saved the best for last after that goodness.

His hands, cold from the glass, slip under my T-shirt in the back, making me jump. He holds me tight, and the heat between us overpowers the cold. Sliding even lower under the hem of the boxer shorts, he gets two good handfuls of my ass and presses me against his hardness. "Your second problem is that you're irresistible."

He leans down to kiss me, but I shove my hands against him. "Wait. Tell me I can plan a party to celebrate. Please, Loch. Not only will it make me so happy to do this for you but I need something to do. I need to use my brain constructively."

Eyeing, I see the moment he gives in—the corners of his eyes softening to me. His grip holds firm, though. "You can plan a party. But I get you in the bedroom in five minutes."

"I'll accept these terms, counselor, but on one condition."

"Which is?"

"I get to choose the first position."

A wry grin twitches on the right side of his mouth, and he replies, "You've got yourself a deal." We seal the deal with a kiss.

With his hands still holding my ass, I say, "You drive a hard bargain."

"Get your ass in that bedroom so I can show you just how hard I drive."

I start for the bedroom, not needing to be told twice, but stop at the far side of the living room and turn back. "Hey, Loch?"

Despite the naughty talk, his love for me shines in his eyes even across the dimly lit room. "Yes?"

"Congratulations. I'm proud of you."

His smile goes from bad boy businessman to the hot guy who lives next door, causing my stomach to flutter. "Thank you."

This is what utter and complete happiness feels like. With a grin that refuses to be wiped away, I go into the bedroom, ready to show him a few skills of my own.

I leave the blinds open but light a candle I bought for my nightstand. The candlelight gives such a dreamy glow to the room. But this is not where I want to begin our night. It's where I want to end it.

Moving into the bathroom, I turn on the hot water in the tub and then light three candles I found in his hall closet last week. They're probably gifts from another woman, judging by the orange and pomegranate scent. I hate that my chest aches in jealousy. Loch had a life I have no knowledge of as much as we aren't privy to mine. Who are these women buying candles for him, or are they just trying to leave their mark on the place? I'm just going to literally burn those thoughts away.

I'm not surprised Loch doesn't own bubble bath, so I squeeze shampoo into the tub instead, which foams up quickly. I strip off my clothes and try to figure out where to wait for him—on the counter, in the tub, across the floor?

"Hey," he says, his dulcet tone wrapping around me like a warm blanket. Stepping just inside the bathroom, he leans against the wall and lets his gaze travel my body, lingering on some parts of me without remorse. Then he glances at the tub. "Are we taking a bath?"

"Yes." I grapple for the counter but almost miss it as I try to act as nonchalantly as I can while standing naked in front of him. I'm just relieved that the heat is on in the apartment.

"Come here, Tuesday." The demand in his voice sends delicious shivers up my spine.

I walk to him, taking a deep breath and stopping with only a few inches to spare between us. "Yes, Mr. Westcott?"

"Sir works."

"Sir."

Eyeing me, he reaches to touch my neck, his thumb running down the middle of my throat before sliding his palm over my shoulder, inspiring me to go down. "I want you on your knees."

I hold his stare while silently counting in my head. I'm not sure how I feel about dominance and submission since none of the games we play feel like either. I could take control just as he has, so it's nothing more than just a thing we do from time to time. When I reach five, I blink, then lower per his request.

"Good girl." My body purrs as it awakens, and I see the devilish grin settling on his face. He knows that's my kryptonite. "Stay exactly how you are." He walks behind me and shuts off the faucet in the tub. When he returns, he caresses my cheek and then slides his fingers into my hair. "Do you know what's wrong with this picture, Tuesday?"

"No, sir."

"I'm still dressed."

I want to giggle like a schoolgirl, but I hold my composure and reach forward to pull down his pants, freeing his erection. He steps out of them and asks, "What do you want to do, Tuesday?"

I look up, knowing exactly what the right answer is. "Taste you."

"Go on then. Taste me." He moves closer.

Taking hold of the back of his legs, I lean forward and lick him from base to tip. It's not until I wrap my hand around his penis that I can take back some control and swirl my tongue around his tip. Dipping his head back, Loch groans, reaching forward to hold me by my hair.

I slowly take him into my mouth as he prods deeper toward my throat. I swallow to relax and then slide back again, using my tongue to trace along the underneath of his length. I hum as he strokes my head, another "good girl" given in appreciation.

The sound of my mouth working him until he loses control has me squeezing my thighs together. I could come from giving *him* pleasure.

My hair is pulled on end, motivating me to please him. Sucking, I drag my tongue around him and take him deeper.

My hand bridges the distances to his base when I pick up speed. "Feels so good," he says.

I drink in his praise with every hollow of my cheeks, knowing I'm about to bring this man to his knees. His body begins to move erratically, so I hold on to the back of his leg and moan in my own ecstasy.

He holds my head as his body fucks my mouth, every thrust he serves becoming a new challenge I'm determined to win, and when he comes, I swallow everything he gives. My name rolls off his tongue in repeated gratitude while he loses himself to the hedonism until the moans fade and the fist in my hair loosens.

As his release winds down, he's left unsteady until he stills and then drops to his knees before me. "I'm going to take such good care of you, baby."

My insides tighten in anticipation as he kisses me. Standing, he then helps me to my feet and walks me to the tub. "You're incredible, so good."

My breathing begins to settle, but my heart's on fire in lust with this man. "I need you."

"I know," he says, dipping his forehead to mine. Caressing me, he closes his eyes and breathes me in. "I've never . . . it's never been this good, raw . . . real before."

I may not have the reference, but the way I crave to be with him tells me what he says is the truth. I grapple for him, needing to hold on to everything we have, not just now but always. "I love you." The words escape in a heated breath against his neck. "So much, babe."

"I love you." He kisses me. "I love you," he says, reaching my neck. "I need you so much." But through the desperate utterance of the words, it's not sex he needs—it's me.

"I'm here, right here for you. Always."

He nods so gently as if the reassurance is all he needs.

Pulling back, he meets my gaze, and languorous grins reflect on our faces. I don't know why a giggle bubbles up, but he chuckles as well. "We're a fine mess," he says, dipping to kiss my cheek once more.

"A mess I'm more than happy to make with you."

Stepping back, he tests the water with his hand. "Still warm. Want to take a bath?" He runs the pad of his thumb over his bottom lip. "We can do a lot of dirty stuff in there while getting clean."

"That's an offer I can't pass up, counselor." I step into the tub, glad he's right. The warm water feels like a hug as I slide my body under it.

"You relax because when I get back, I'm going to make you c—Did you hear that?" He looks toward the door.

"Hear what?"

He's already grabbing a towel from the rack and wrapping it around his lower half. "How is someone knocking on my door in a secured fucking building?" And there goes his good mood . . .

"Brady?" I offer, wondering if I should get out of the bath.

"Maybe," he says. "Stay in the bath. Relax. I won't be gone long. Wine?"

He's already left the bathroom, so I yell, "Please."

"You got it."

I lie back, but something doesn't sit right. He's right. No one has access to this floor without being given prior permission. I get out of the tub to investigate. *Is someone here, or is he just hearing things?*

27

Loch

"Fuck," I grit through my teeth.

Closing the peephole, I debate what to do. If I open the door, I can end it, tell her I'm a goner for another woman. If I don't open it, she'll start calling. *Fuck.*

"Loch?" Christine calls from the other side of the door and knocks again. "Open up."

"Loch?" Tuesday says from the bathroom. *Fuck. Fuck. Fuck. Fuck. Fuck.*

I jog to the corner of the living room and yell down the hall. "Coming." I'm so not coming until Christine is long gone.

Rushing back to the door, I know I need to end this and not let it drag on. I learned the hard way with Judge Judy. Lesson learned. I open the door, but her hand is on it, and she pushes in. "Why'd you keep me waiting so long?" she asks, dragging her fingertips across my bare chest. "*Oooh*, I see you're ready for me." *Shit.*

I fast-walk backward, trying to barricade the apartment

from her breaching the living room. "What are you doing here?"

Instead of walking back to the door, she stands her ground. "The last text you sent asked for a rain check. I'm cashing in." She glances at the door. "Do you mind grabbing my suitcase?"

"You never returned that text to claim the offer, and unfortunately, I need you to leave." I try my best not to sound callous, but there's no time for niceties. I need her gone before Tuesday gets wind of this visitor.

"What do you mean, Loch? I'm here now. Anyway, I just traveled from the airport in a snowstorm." She sidles up to me with that look she used to give that meant I wouldn't get any sleep. "Plus, everything's closed."

"I am too."

She straightens, eyeing me with half-mast lids. "What does that mean?"

Walking around her, I open the door and wave her toward the upright suitcase still in the hall. "A lot has changed since I sent that text. I have a girl—"

"Loch?"

Fuck me . . .

I turn back to see Tuesday wrapped in a towel, standing at the end of the hallway. She's twisted her hair up on her head with wet strands stuck to her neck. She tightens the towel at her chest, staring at us—no smile or comfort in her expression. Not even anger creeps up her neck. Her gaze volleys between us before she takes a deep breath and plants her hand on her hip. "Who's this?"

Christine might get her way on her transatlantic business class routes where she calls the shots as a flight attendant, but in her personal life, she's not one for competition.

She crosses her arms over her chest and cocks an eyebrow at Tuesday. "Who are you?"

Tuesday glances at me first, then replies, "I'm his girlfriend."

Fuck me . . .

How do I make this nightmare stop?

"Is that true, Loch?" The tapping of Christine's foot punctuates each word from her mouth, especially my name.

Here we go. This is definitely not what she'll want to hear. I owe her nothing, but I owe Tuesday everything. "This is my girlfriend, Tuesday."

The statement catches her off guard, causing her neck to jerk. She looks over my shoulder to the woman I know is still standing there, probably like a deer in headlights, and then back to me. "I . . ." She steals one more look at Tuesday, and then the strangest thing happens. She smiles. It's not like the killer one she gave me the night she pursued me at a charity event in Brooklyn. No, it's almost . . . *happy*.

She angles toward Tuesday and says, "So you're the woman who caught the uncatchable." Looking at me, she adds, "She's very pretty."

Tuesday says, "What's happening?"

I can't answer that, so instead, I say, "Christine was in town and stopped by." I move to where Christine stands and hold the door open with my back, so there's no misunderstanding about what should be happening next—*her leaving*.

And then Christine adds, "Have we met before?"

I see it, the moment hope fills Tuesday's eyes, and I hear the little gasp. "Have we?"

Like a pin to a balloon, Christine says, "Never mind. I wouldn't be able to place a face if I tried." She laughs at what I guess was supposed to be a joke. We don't. "So I stopped trying years ago."

I say, "I'll call you a cab."

Tuesday steps closer, her bare feet leaving the lightest trail of water. "There's a snowstorm outside?"

Unsure of the question she's asking, I look toward the windows that span the length of the living room. Snow has begun to collect in the corners, falling so heavily that it looks like a sheet of white floating outside the glass. *Fuck.*

I run my hand through my hair and look at Tuesday. Silently, our eyes speak to each other. Her nod is so minute, but the shake of my head isn't. Is she really telling me to do this? *What the fuck is happening?*

Turning back to Christine, I begrudgingly ask, "Would you like to wait here until we can find you other accommodations?"

Her mouth opens and then closes again while the forehead that's usually frozen cinches her brows together. "Really?"

With a loud sigh, Tuesday comes closer. "The weather's awful, so you're welcome to stay."

To stay? That's not the fucking offer I had on the table.

What universe did I teleport to?

How is the woman I'm in love with asking my former regular fuck to stay the night?

What madness is this?

I take Tuesday's hand and turn to Christine. "Excuse us. We need to talk in private."

Closing the bedroom behind me, I lead her into the bathroom just in case our voices carry. As soon as the door closes, I turn on the shower for soundproofing and then turn back, and she pops me in the bicep. "It's a friggin' snowstorm out there, Loch. We can't just send her packing."

I'm still lost on her train of thought. She crosses her arms over her chest. "Loch, you know I'm right."

"Okay. Okay. I know you're right, but what? We're supposed to be roomies with her for the next three days?"

Her head tilts, her gaze lengthening toward the window. Even though the shade is drawn, the shadow of bad weather still haunts us. When she turns back, she says, "I hear what you're saying. I'm not looking to feel uncomfortable in my home for days. It's late, and the worst of the weather is expected tonight. She'll stay the night, but then we'll find her a hotel tomorrow."

"So what do we do in the meantime? Play Monopoly?" I ask sarcastically.

I get poked in the chest. "I'm the one missing out, mister. You got yours, and now mine seems to be on permanent pause."

"Loch?" Christine calls. *"I need you."*

We freeze, and then both of us look at the door at the same time. Tuesday's eyes bulge, and she mouths, "What the hell?" and then whispers, "Is she in our bedroom?"

I say, "Be right out," loud enough for Christine to hear.

Tuesday wraps around me as if her life depends on it. "I made a mistake, babe. I don't want her here. You need to take care of it."

Okay, I shouldn't laugh, but she's fucking adorable. I rub her back and kiss her head. "I'll take care of it." I release her to leave the bathroom, cut through my bedroom, and head straight for Christine. "We need to . . ."

"I have another friend in the city who thought he'd be out of town. Turns out," she says, grinning like she won the grand prize. "His flight was cancelled, too." Grabbing her suitcase by the handle, she heads for the door. And I don't stop her.

"That's some luck."

"Yeah." She pulls open the door like piranhas nip at her heels.

I hold it open as she wheels her luggage through and starts for the elevator. "He's sending his car."

Standing in the doorway, I reply, "Fantastic."

Then she stops and looks back. "I'll miss you, Loch, but I'm also happy for you. She seems like a great girl. And so familiar."

Oh shit. I'd almost forgotten she'd said that.

"You recognized Tuesday?"

She shrugs. "I don't know if we've met. She kind of has a generic face."

And just like that, I realize I'd made a mistake with her. I always claimed it was about sex, but even that wasn't *that* good. Seconds pass, and she gets my disdain because even though I haven't said another word, she starts to back away. "Have a good life. Maybe our paths will cross again one day."

I hope not. I don't bother replying for her. I'm already done. I return to my apartment without looking back and shut the door, realizing this moment represents more than closing a chapter with Christine.

Tuesday is there with her beautiful smile and bright eyes that light up when she sees me. I go to her, scooping her into my arms and carrying her back to bed to have my wicked way with this angel. Tuesday isn't just another chapter. She's the whole damn book.

Like a present I wished for, I unwrap the towel from her body and spread her knees apart. She falls back under the weight of seduction, her breaths coming heavy in her chest and her eyes closing as she takes me in.

I kiss her inner thigh, then go lower, ready to devour her sweet little p—*knock. Knock. Knock.*

I bolt up and start getting out of bed. "What the fuck?"

Lifting on her elbows, Tuesday says, "Tell me about it."

Now that makes me laugh. When she falls on the mattress with her arms spread wide, I say, "I'm sorry. I promise I'll make it up to you."

"Swear?"

"Swear on my life." I give her a wink and grab a towel from the floor again.

Just before I leave the room, she says, "It better not be another ex-girlfriend."

"No worries then because I didn't have girlfriends until you."

"You're not charming your way out of this, sir."

Fuuuuucccckkk . . .

I'm about to turn around, but another rap on my door has me answering it. I look through the peephole—relieved that it's not Christine again but also wondering who this guy thinks he is. "Who is it?"

"Delivery for Mr. Westcott from Private Eyes of New York."

My heart drops into the pit of my stomach.

Is this the moment I lose the woman I love?

Before she has a chance to surprise me again, I open the door. The guy says, "Sign here."

I sign on the electronic pad. Then he hands me an envelope. The printed label reads *Westcott Case: Tuesday.*

"Thanks."

I close the door, sickness contaminating the happiness I felt not two minutes prior. There might not be anything in this file. It's only been a few weeks. Logically though, I know that the PI wouldn't have an envelope delivered in the middle of a snowstorm if he had nothing to report.

"Who is it?" she asks, her voice the sound of angels to my ears. Her eyes dip to the large envelope. "Wow, someone delivered that during the storm?"

"Yes, it's important." I run my hand through my hair and avert my eyes so she can't see the lie I'm about to tell her. "Work stuff."

"Oh. Okay. Do you need to work tonight?"

I walk down the hall, fully aware I'm an asshole for what I'm about to do. "No. Just putting this in my office." I look back, and the trusting smile that sits so pretty on her face just about does me in. "I'll meet you in the bedroom."

She nods, and when she passes me, her gaze locks on mine. In that exchange, I know she sees right through me. I still close the door behind me and go straight to the closet. I shift an old box of yearbooks and photos to the floor and open a container filled with mementos my mom brought for me last year. Tucking the envelope inside, I put the lid on, then add the other box back to the pile.

My legs feel filled with concrete, making every step harder to take. I can't lose her. *I won't.* I just need a little more time to think before our world crashes down.

Just before I enter the bedroom, I put on a face of indifference. She sees me, and asks, "Everything all right?"

Diving onto the bed, I pull her into my arms under her fits of giggles and memorize the sound. I kiss her until her lips are swollen and her body begs for more. I want to make her feel so good. Make love to her. Create more love with her. Please her until she collapses from the pleasure.

That envelope ticks like a fucking time bomb in my head.

I love her too much. And I can't lose her. *Not ever.*

28

Loch

Three weeks Later ...

It would be wrong to ruin Christmas.

"The other one, please."

The jewelry attendant closes one case and unlocks another. She pulls out a velvet tray of rings and places them before me. I stare at them—all brilliantly beautiful under the spotlight.

Is that how Tuesday and I are as well? Remove us from the light, and the dark reveals the cracks in our foundation?

I know I shouldn't be looking at rings. Nothing about rushing into a marriage to convince her to stay is rational.

"Would you like to see any in particular?" the attendant asks. "These are our exclusive designs, and the diamonds are exquisite. She'd be lucky—"

"I'm the lucky one."

She smiles as if I'm making small talk. I'm not. She gets the hint and stands quietly on the other side of the case.

"Nothing stands out to me. Thank you." I head for the door with my phone buzzing in my pocket. As soon as I'm outside, I answer, "I'm heading back to the office now, Leisa."

"Are you okay? I wasn't sure if I should cancel your afternoon meetings when you left for lunch earlier."

Leaving for lunch is cause for concern since I never do it. I need a fucking life . . . I have one, actually, but it's about to be taken away from me.

I trudge back toward the office building, holding the lapels of my coat tighter at my neck to block the frigid air from slipping under the wool. "I have a lot going on. I shouldn't have left."

"We all have bad days, Loch. Sometimes fresh air does you good."

She's right. Also, clearing one's conscience can alleviate the guilt. "Hey, go ahead and clear my schedule. I need to take care of some things."

"Done. I'll see you tomorrow?"

"You know it."

I call Brady and wait for him under the awning of a candy shop. As soon as he pulls up to the curb, I dash for the back door and climb in. He says, "Sweet tooth?"

"Huh?" He points at the shop. "Ah. No. Just waiting for you."

"You say such sweet nothings to me."

I laugh, though I shouldn't encourage the jokes. He'll continue to make me suffer through them if he thinks I enjoy them. "Did I ever tell you that you're not funny?"

He chuckles. "All the time. Where are we headed?"

"Home."

"You got it, boss."

Normally, I'd love to surprise her and spend the rest of the day in bed with her or take her out to wherever her heart desired. Not today.

Today, I walk in, hoping Tuesday is out.

"Hello?" I call as soon as I open the door. I'm glad silence greets me, but how long will I be alone?

I hurry to my office and into the closet, moving the box out of the way. My stomach churns when I think about what I'll find in the envelope as I lift the lid to the container. Not knowing has been torture, but the truth, which could lead to her leaving me, will do me in.

Taking the envelope, I sit at my desk and unclasp the brads holding it closed. Breathing in through my nose, I pull the file out and release a long exhale. This is it.

It sits before me. All I need to do is open it.

I flip over the cover and am instantly hit with a photo of her from another life, the life when I first met her at the coffee shop—hair pulled back and polished in every detail from makeup to her outfit.

She's so opposite of that now. With me, she's carefree, as carefree as she can be under the circumstances. Her hair hangs down most of the time in waves that look like the sea air shaped them, and though she's put together, there's such a breeziness about her style, like she doesn't take herself too seriously, preferring jeans to a well . . . what she used to wear.

It's the name below the photo that I can't stop staring at, though—Céline Schroder.

Céline is Tuesday.

But Tuesday is the name she gave for her coffee order. This makes no sense.

Now, I'm more confused than ever and have to live with this information. I can't hide it from her. No matter how much I don't want her to return to Rhode Island . . . fucking hell, she's from Rhode Island? That's not Manhattan, which means if she goes home . . . if she goes to wherever she's from, she won't be with me. Fear officially unlocks.

"What are you doing?"

"Shit." I scramble to my feet, hitting the folder closed in my hurry. The envelope flies off the front of the desk just out of my reach from stopping it.

"I didn't mean to scare you," Tuesday says, striding into the office to help with the mess.

"I got it!" I don't mean to yell as I practically hurdle the desk to grab the envelope.

Startled, she stops, holding her hand over her heart. "My God, Loch. What has gotten into you?"

"I, uh—"

"Does that say Tuesday on the front?" she asks, pointing at the label I'm trying to hide.

Fuck.

"It, um, huh . . ." I look at the front again like I don't already know what it says.

"What is that?" Her curiosity will do more damage than good.

I've not always been forthcoming, but I've always been honest with her. I can't lie to her. The truth would come out eventually. Better from me than the police or some stranger on the street who happens to recognize her.

I just wish I had more time to think, to figure out the next step and ease her into the truth.

Handing her the envelope, I then sit down and wait.

With a scrub of my face, I know I've done the right thing, but the anticipation of what happens next is going to kill me.

Her eyes go from the front to me and then back again. "Why does it have your name and mine?"

"The police weren't making any headway, so I hired a private investigator to uncover your identity."

Her gaze drops to the folder on the desk. "And that's what that is?"

I nod, suddenly unable to speak.

She steps forward but then appears reluctant, stopping after only one more as if she's just as afraid of what it contains. I push the papers inside and then tap it against the desk before handing it to her.

Taking it, she cradles it to her body, and then asks, "Do you know who I am?"

"Yes." I swallow down the lump in my throat. "Since the moment I saw you at the hospital when you walked out. I know your heart, Tuesday. I know your soul." My throat feels dry when I add, "I know who you are. You're the woman I love."

I'm not sure what I expected from my confession, but it wasn't ice. "You got this weeks ago. I remember when it was delivered during the snowstorm." She searches my eyes for anything that will make this make sense.

I'm failing to comfort her, which is why I need more time, but I still can't hide from responding to questions she didn't ask. "I was afraid to open it."

"It wasn't yours to decide. It was mine. Why did you hold on to it this long?"

"I was going to give it to you. I just needed time to figure out a plan—"

"When?" she snaps. "Tomorrow? In ten years? On my

deathbed?" She takes a breath. "Or never? Were you going to let me live my life without ever knowing who I really am?"

"No, I was going to tell you. I just—"

"You just thought you should have the final say as to when and where?" She's still holding the file like it's a life preserver. Maybe it is for her.

For me, it's a bomb that's been detonated.

"That's not true, Tuesday."

"Is Tuesday even my name?" Flipping through the file, she says, "It's not felt like it until the past couple of weeks." Just as she opens it, she closes it again even faster. Taking a breath, I can see the fight in her shoulders subsiding, dragging them down. "I love you, Loch. I love you more than words can say, but this feels like a betrayal."

"I hired him for you, to help give you answers that no one else will."

"And then you withheld the file from me."

I'd been hesitant to approach her, thinking she wanted space to work through this. I was wrong. If I let an inch come between us, it could end up with her being in Rhode Island and me stuck here without her. I go to her. "Listen to me—"

"No, I won't." She backs toward the door. She's fighting against the tears in her eyes but finally gives in and swipes at them. "You had the chance to tell me, to help, to take the journey *with* me, but you chose to hide the truth. Why?"

"I chose to hire the investigator because the police were hitting dead ends. How is that possible when you're from Rhode Island?"

She's staring at me, her expression wavering between hope and desperation. "I'm from Rhode Island?"

I walk to her, ready to comfort her in any way she'll let

me, but as her chest reddens, I think I'm the last person she wants touching her. "Please, let's take a breath, and I'll explain everything."

Closing her eyes, she rubs the middle of her forehead. When she reopens her eyes, she says, "I trusted you."

"I know you did, and you still can."

Taking another deep breath, she says, "But can I?"

My temper flares, but I hold it in. "I did everything for you—"

"And I never asked for any of it."

"That's not what I meant." I fist my hand, frustrated that I can't get her out of her head.

"I know what you meant, Loch. I do."

"Please know that I only had your best interest in mind."

"I know I should have been a part of the decision-making regarding *my* life." She turns and leaves the office.

"Where are you going?"

"The bedroom. I need to be alone."

I give her the time away from my presence, the time I hope she'll use to understand that I never meant to upset her. I don't approach the bedroom. I won't until she's ready to see me again.

Lying on the couch, I stare out the windows on a clear night until I can no longer keep my eyes open.

"Babe." A shake of my shoulders follows the whispered word. I open my eyes to find the blue eyes I dream about. "Come to bed," she whispers, taking my hand.

My mind hasn't caught up to the fact that I'm in the living room, much less why. I sit up and then stand to my feet when I'm finally coherent enough to understand. Tuesday clings to me, her arms holding me so tight that I don't think pliers could pry us apart.

When her tears start to fall, I embrace her, kissing her head and telling her, "We'll be okay. It will be all right."

"Promise me." She looks up, resting her chin on my chest. "Promise me that nothing will come between us, Loch."

I caress her cheek, then kiss it. "I promise you." I mean it and will keep that promise every day I'm given a chance—to protect her, be with her, and love her long into the future. Together always.

I hope.

29

Tuesday

LOCH HAS NOT SAID a word about the file since he gave it to me three days ago.

He's caught between worrying about me leaving and hoping I'll stay. *Me too.* I wish I could reassure him either way.

I hate that I can't tell him I won't go, but that would be a lie. I have another life out there waiting for me to discover, people I knew from a former identity in Rhode Island.

Rhode Island...

How can I be from somewhere only a few hours away, yet no one recognizes me, or misses me, or bothers to file a report? Nothing makes sense, and I'm tired of living in the dark.

I walk into the bedroom and pull the file from the nightstand drawer. Sitting on the edge of the bed, I flip it over a few times as the gravity of what's inside starts weighing heavy on my heart.

Shouldn't I be thrilled and over-the-moon elated that

I'm finally getting the answers that no one else could find? That is, no one else but Loch.

Bracing myself, I take a breath and flip open the file. My gaze darts from the photo to the name to the address, and this is only page one. I close it, now well aware of the implications of what I hold in my hands.

Céline . . .

I stand and walk to the window. The snow isn't pretty anymore. It's turned to slush after the wavering temperatures couldn't decide if they wanted to go up or down. I'm just as confused, so I understand.

Céline. *Not Tuesday.*

Schroder. *Not Westcott.*

Nothing about the former feels familiar, but I do find myself smiling over the latter because it's who I've become. It's come to feel like safety to me, including his family. And of course, Loch. I love the tie to the man who's given me everything from a roof to his heart, and now my identity.

Céline. Céline. Céline. It's not an entirely foreign feeling if I were going off vibes.

"Céline." I say it out loud to see if it feels right.

"It's a beautiful name." The warmth of his voice coats me like the first time we met. He didn't have to show up that morning at the hospital, but he did. Like he is now, knowing the consequences might not be in his favor.

I turn back to see him in the doorway. "I thought you were at work?"

"I'm supposed to be." But he's here for me. As always.

"I didn't mean to punish you."

"The situation is punishing, not you. We're just caught up in it."

I go to him, dropping the file on the bed and embracing this man who loves me for who I am. When his arms come around me, I melt against him, needing this more than I thought. The past few days have tortured my soul, but now I see how much it's affected his soul as well. "I'm sorry."

"You don't need to be. I do. I messed up when I hid that file from you." He kisses the top of my head, then says, "I'm sorry, Tues . . . I mean Céline." His body tenses when he realizes what he just said.

I look up and wait to catch his gaze. "It's okay to call me by my name. Tuesday. That's who I am with you."

"You're Céline without me, though, and it crushes my soul that you're forced to choose between two lives."

"I don't have to choose. Not yet." I sigh and release him before returning to the file. Sitting on the bed, I'm drained of the enthusiasm I once had for this part of the healing process. Here I thought the concussion was a concern. No, it's the amnesia that's winning. "Do you want to open it with me?"

"Do you want me to?" he asks, crossing the room to sit by my side.

"You deserve to know, too." I look into those caramel eyes. "You've been my support up to this moment, and I'm not letting that go now."

Rubbing my leg, he nods. "You got it."

The file is easier to open this time. Maybe because I know there's no use in pretending it doesn't exist, or perhaps because I already know my name, which felt like the biggest reveal. But really, his being by my side gives me strength.

I flip it open and smile at the photo. "It's weird to know that's me but not, like I'm looking at a twin that's not quite identical."

He traces along the arm of the woman in the photo. "That's who I met in the coffee shop. Everything perfectly in place." He glances at me with a small smile on his face. "She used her hands a lot." Tapping me on the nose, he adds, "But you use yours more."

"It's so strange how I'm two different people living separate lives in two worlds." I look back at the photo. "Maybe that's why I'm not missed. Maybe she's still out there living her life. Best life judging by the fancy clothes and jewelry." I laugh, though it's light.

"I think I got the best version."

I know he's giving me a sweet compliment, but tilting my head, I rest it on his shoulder. "I'd have to agree." But to me, this side is the best because he's a part of me. Lifting back up, I flip the page to see a copy of my birth certificate. "Céline Vivienne Schroder. French and . . .?" I glance at Loch again like he's my personal Wikipedia.

"German?"

"Huh. French mother and German father. Fascinating." When I see my birthday, I say, "April first," and can't stop myself from laughing. "Joke's on me."

"You're twenty-seven."

"I am." I grin as I double-check the year on the paper and purse my lips. "That's so weird. I didn't feel a day over twenty-five." I laugh because, at this point, it's only information. None of these details feel like who I am these days.

I flip through a few more documents, including a bank statement. "Oh my God! Is that my money?"

He picks up the paper and studies it. "Holy shit. You're rich."

I should feel happy, and maybe in a way, I am, but this is too surreal to comprehend. "Guess I can pay you back, after all."

Chuckling, he says, "It's not your money I'm after."

"What are you after?" *Please say my body*. Though if he says my heart, I'm okay with that as well.

"I'll show you later." *Hubba. Hubba.*

Before we get sidetracked, I say, "For some reason, I don't feel like Céline did much of anything other than maybe shop?" I look down at my body. "She also did some intensive working out for this body. I can't seem to find the same motivation."

He bumps me. "Don't be so hard on Céline. She was probably doing the best she could."

"I keep going back to what Lark said during my checkup. About my brain trying to protect me from my past."

"What do you think that's about?"

"That would be the million-dollar question or, should I say, the multimillion-dollar question if I'm referring to that bank account. Either way, I wish I knew the answer."

The last page contains a photo of what I assume is the house where I lived. "It's big." Thinking back to how I thought the Westcotts' Beacon home was a mansion, this home would shadow it. I say, "Really rich."

I close the file and angle it toward Loch. "You know what I've been dying to know?"

That brings the smile I was hoping to see back to his face. "What?"

"At home, you drink your coffee black, but how do you like your coffee at a coffee shop?"

He stands. "Not as complicated as yours."

"Oh." I perk up even more. "How do I like *my* coffee?" I add only a dash of creamer here, but he's got me curious about what I ordered the day we met.

"Hate to disappoint you, but I can't remember. It was a lot of this, some of that, and more who knows what. Complicated."

That's something else I've been thinking about a lot lately. Loch left. I even saw it on the video, but he returned to help when he saw me get attacked. I stand and press the palm of my hand to his chest. "There were so many bystanders that day who did nothing, but you did. You came back for me."

"I always will." He kisses my forehead. "What happens next?"

"I guess I'm going to Rhode Island to visit my past."

30

Tuesday

TWO DAYS LATER ...

I DON'T HAVE A LOT, but there's now enough to fill a suitcase.

None of this stuff matters to me, though. It's clothes, shoes, and accessories. Superficial stuff that came into my life as nothing more than necessities.

Necessity?

Loch is the only thing I need, but he won't fit in my luggage. If only there were a way to bring him into the life I used to know, to convince him to stay with me and continue to be my strength when I need him most. But he insists I do this alone.

Deep down, I agree.

He's so much of my life, though, that I'm not sure I need time and space to welcome any potential memories back. Knowing he's right doesn't wash away my fear of the unknown, but I find comfort in having him to come home to when I return.

As much as I'm anxious to discover my old life, I'm also excited. *Céline Schroder.* It explains why Tuesday didn't sound like me when I first heard it. Tuesday has become my identity, though, and represents this new life I'm living. It's the one I *want* to live.

I put his T-shirt on top of the pile of clothes in the case, claiming it as mine.

"How's it going? Anything I can take to the door?"

I quickly shut it so he doesn't see the shirt because I need it more than he does. "No," I reply, glancing over my shoulder. "Everything will fit in one case." I zip it closed and am about to pull it from the bench but stop and stare at it as reality dawns. "One case. My entire life fits in one suitcase. It's not even the largest suitcase you had either."

Strong arms that make me feel safe wrap around me from behind. His warmth permeates between our bodies, and I lean back, melting into him and wishing I could always be this person. *I like me with him.*

I grin because I really like him with me, too. Yet, somehow, the next step in my journey doesn't include him. Everything about that feels wrong, because the way he's holding me feels so right. He makes it hard to walk away. Walk away for now. *Only for now.*

He lowers his chin to rest it on my shoulder. "You're braver than you realize. Don't be scared, baby," he whispers, then rubs his hand over my heart. "I may not be with you, but I'm always in here."

Tears spring to my eyes, and instead of fighting against the pain and loss I'm already experiencing, I give in and let them fall. Curling forward as sobs wrack my frame, I'm scooped into his arms and carried to bed. He settles on the mattress with his back against the headboard, cradling me on his lap. My name, the one he calls me, whispered in prayers of gratitude. "My life is better because I met you, Tuesday . . . lost without you . . . find your way and come home to me again . . ."

I take his words, soaking them into my soul to keep me warm when he's not around. "I will." Looking up into his eyes that gleam for me, my breath catches, but I finally manage to say, "It's not over."

"We're not over, baby. We never will be."

I DON'T THINK for one moment I've felt like the wealthy woman the bank statement claims I am. It's too surreal, but it begins to sink in when we pull up outside the mansion listed in the file. We opted to drive with the logic that it would take less time than dealing with the airport.

It was time we needed.

Hands clasped for hours.

Kisses to my neck.

Whispers in our ears.

Promises to keep.

Commitment.

It's all so much that my heart broke a few times. Loch held me, making me feel better, but like at the apartment, I worry it might only be a temporary reprieve from the pain ahead. *What's ahead for me to discover?*

Through the window, the home looks magical, with snow falling gently, like one you'd find in a snow globe or a picture-perfect Christmas movie set. "Do you think it's mine?" I ask. "Or my family's?" Nothing seems far-fetched anymore or out of the realm of possibility. Every day, I receive new information in some form that gets me closer to solving the mystery of me.

Today, the house.

But what else is waiting for me?

Birchwood wreaths with red bows adorn each window, and candles anchor the sills. It's so inviting, but none of it makes any sense. Curiosity has questions running wild in my mind. Where are the people who live here? Tucked inside by a roaring fire? At work? We've sat in the car for a good five minutes, and no one has come out to see who might be here. Who decorated?

Odd.

Loch's leaning over to see out my window when the smallest of shrugs pops his shoulders. "Guess we're about to find out. Do you want me to knock?"

I glance at him as if he has all the answers. "Maybe no one is home? Then what?"

"Then we come back later." He rubs my leg. "Do you want me to stay until you feel more comfortable? Safe."

When I glance back at the house, I see nothing but a welcoming image before me. How bad can it be? "No, I can do this alone. It's my home, after all."

"It's not your home." An injured tone is laced through his words, his concern for me, his love, causing my heart to constrict.

I don't know that he's looking for reassurance. He knows how much I love him, but I reach for his hand anyway, and hold it to my heart. "It's a house. Nothing more."

Sitting up, he squeezes my knee and gives me the smile I've come to rely on. "You are the most courageous woman I know. Look how you've navigated this transition in life." His eyes dart past me to the house and then to me again. "This part will be easy."

"I appreciate the faith in me, but I'm not sure how brave I'm feeling right now."

"Take the time you need to recover and find your memories. I'll miss you so much, but I'm only a phone call away."

"I—"

Brady clears his throat.

Loch shakes his head with a wry grin on his face. "Brady *and I* will both be here to pick you up the moment you need us."

"Thanks," I tell Brady. Knowing I have them in my corner, that I can leave any time I want, makes this so much easier. Staring into the eyes of the person I trust most in the world, I slide across the seat and into his arms. "Thank you." I close my eyes to kiss him like it might be the last time. It won't be, but everything feels dramatic in the shadow of the unknown. "Thank you will never be enough, but it's all I have."

He caresses my face like I'm the most precious jewel in the world. "*You* are enough." With the immensity of our emotions starting to weigh us down, he slips out of my hold and gets out of the Escalade.

I get it. We were unexpected and not what he had in his plans. And I know the time has come to walk away. *For now.* But I'll be complete when I return to him with no loose ends left to tie up so we can start our life with no lingering unanswered questions.

Taking my suitcase from the back, he closes the trunk and then comes to my door and opens it. Ready or not, it's time for the dreaded goodbye. I'll do as he said and be brave. It's all I have to carry me through the next few days. "Bye, Brady."

"Take care of yourself, Tuesday, and if you need anything—"

"Don't worry about me. I'm a survivor."

Giving me a nod of approval, he adds, "That you are."

With one deep breath, I turn and land on my feet in the driveway that's been cleared of snow. I look up at the house again. It feels even bigger from this angle, and although it's beautiful, it's also intimidating.

Who lives here with me?

Who's clearing the snow?

Do I walk in or knock on the door?

My head spins, so I focus on what I know and what's right in front of me—Loch. *My love.*

He's set my case on the top step but stands before me now, his eyes seeming to struggle to lock on mine. Such new territory for the both of us—hopelessly falling in love so fast and then forced to part because of my memory loss makes me feel bad. I'd apologize again, but I know he'll never accept it when he doesn't feel it's owed.

I embrace him again, loving him through a tight hold. He leans down to rest his forehead on mine. I say, "I love you."

"I love you more than you'll ever know."

"That's not true. I've felt your love since the moment I saw you."

He kisses my head and my lips. "I never saw you coming, and then you flipped my world upside down." My eyes water again as he kisses the corner of my mouth. "Upside down and right side up. I need you to know that I'm letting you go but only for a few days," he says with a wry grin and a little wink, "hoping when you return to me, you won't long for the unknown anymore. You'll be whole again. So this isn't the end, Tuesday. It's only our beginning."

Tears roll down my cheeks until he catches them with the pads of his thumbs, leaving only the pink I know has streaked my cheeks. "I'll only be gone a few days." Forcing myself to leave the safety of his arms, I walk backward, and add, "I love you, Loch."

He shoves his hands in his pockets. "I love you, too."

I turn and jog up the steps before I can back down from this challenge. I can still feel his presence tethering me to him. I look back, my breath stolen like the first time I saw him at the hospital. His hair darker in contrast to the falling snow, the embers in his eyes always burning inside when he looks at me, and his frame—broad shoulders and that sexy athletic build. Gah! I'll never get enough of him.

But here, during winter in the middle of what feels like nowhere, he wears his heart on his sleeve in a fervent tribute to me.

"You go first," I say, unable to walk away from this amazing man.

He still has his hands tucked in his pockets when he rocks on his heels. "You sure?"

"I'll be okay. I promise to call if I need you."

"Need me, huh? Baby, I hope you find that need because I'll always need you."

My heart leaps to my throat, and I struggle to stand on my own. I swallow it down, and reply, "Always."

He nods as if the one word was all he needed and then gets in the SUV. Rolling down his window, he says, "Come back to me. Do you understand?"

The right side of my mouth slides up my cheek despite the cold trying to freeze me. "Yes, sir."

He winks. "Good girl."

I grin like the woman in love that I am.

Sitting back, he rolls up the window as the vehicle pulls away. It's a long drive through the property to return to the entrance, but they soon disappear over the hill in the distance.

Since I had no number to call ahead and warn anyone of my arrival, showing up will either be my best idea ever or the worst plan ever devised. I knock. And then again. Eventually, I look around, wondering if I'm the only one who lives . . . lived here. Maybe no one is here to answer.

It's too big of a place to live alone. I ring the doorbell twice in a last effort before calling Loch to come back to pick me up. *Or help me break in . . .*

The door swings open. "Do I have to do everything around here?" a man yells from inside the house. When he turns around, his ice-blue eyes pin me to the spot as the color drains from his face. "Céline?"

31

Tuesday

"Hello."

As I stare at him, I stand here stupidly, any scrap of a plan I had already out the window. Did I really think I could show up and everything I wanted to know would be answered the moment the door opened? What do I do? I don't even know who he is, much less how he'll react.

Is this safe?

Am I?

Is he?

Blond hair. Light eyes. Around my age. I have no clue who he is—brother, cousin, someone who works here, boyfriend, or . . . I don't give voice to the last guess. I can't imagine he'd be my husband since I wasn't wearing a ring when I was found, and I don't want to put that out into the universe anyway.

I glance back over my shoulder as if I'll be able to silently plead for Loch to come back. As if the thread that harnessed our love can stretch the miles between us, and he'll return to get me. Secretly, I'd hoped to be home with Loch before tomorrow with my memories intact. I realize now that I was foolish.

"You're back." The man glances at the suitcase and then at me again, but something is missing that I thought would come naturally—a smile that he's happy to see me and that I was missed. "Back for good?" He looks behind me, but then asks, "Where's the rest of your luggage?"

Despite using the strength Loch gave me to dive into the unknown and reclaim my life, this man feels more like a speed bump than an ally. Shouldn't something, even just a feeling in my gut, be revived by him? Not one memory is triggered, though. He's no different than a stranger on the streets of New York. "This is all I have. Did I leave with more?"

I hadn't spent energy on my time in Manhattan prior to the attack, but now I can't stop from wondering where I was living and where's my stuff if I took it with me?

Ignoring my questions, he contorts his face, furrowing his brow. "Why did you knock?"

"I . . . I made a mistake." I grip the handles of my hand-bag, so tempted to run away from my past—literally and figuratively. It would only take a week or so on foot if I start now. I know I can't, but the thought makes me grin just a little.

I need to know who I am . . . *was.*

Brave face, Tuesday.

He's handsome in a way that speaks of old money—polo player, life of privilege from a day's labor. It's easy to imagine him smoking cigars at a men's-only club and patting servers on the ass as they deliver his next drink.

I don't like him. But more so, I don't trust him because

his eyes fail to meet the half-hearted smile sitting awkwardly on his mouth.

HE TAKES a step as if he's going to embrace me but stops just shy of doing it. I'm cold from standing outside for so long, but mostly from this stranger who must be familiar enough to think he could touch me. He steps back. "Thank God you're home in time for the holidays. Now I don't have to spend it alone."

"Holidays here?" My gaze travels the roofline before looking at him again.

"Of course. Where else?" He laughs, but no humor is heard. "So much has changed. I've been staying here while you were away."

"Staying here? Where I live?"

He chuckles again. "Yeah, where else? Figured since I've been working so many late nights that it only made sense to start staying here. Cuts the commute. And since you weren't here to take care of the place, I stepped in." His hands go out in front of him as if that will put me at ease. It does the opposite. "Only while you were gone, though. We can talk about it, though. You might like having me here full time. I should hope, considering . . ."

I'm afraid to ask for fear it might mean exactly what I think it does. I'm not ready for relationship confirmations, not yet anyway.

I'd planned to hold my amnesia close to my chest. But I still have no idea who he is, and this will get awkward if I don't reveal the truth soon. I ask, "Who are you?"

With a wide grin, he laughs, but it favors mockery this time. "Who am I? What are you talking about, Céline?" I catch a slight annoyance flicker in his eyes before the grin is adjusted in place again.

Hrm. Not good. And since I don't have a reasonable explanation other than the truth, I detour, and ask, "Do I get to come inside, or do I have to stand in the cold all day?"

The most authentic expression finally settles on his face, one that tells me he recognizes this version of me. One corner of his mouth rolls higher, and the blue in his eyes brightens, finally making me feel welcome. Grabbing my case, he opens the door wider and steps inside because I guess he goes first in this world. *Noted.* "Can't keep you out of your own home."

This is my home? My heart could argue otherwise.

Taking a deep breath, I stomp my shoes on the mat and enter, hoping to have answers the moment I step inside. Though I'm greeted with a huge staircase in an expansive foyer where light floods in from the windows above the door, colorful landscape paintings line the walls while beige carpet trails the stairs themselves, that doesn't happen.

The interior is not as traditional as I first suspected when I saw the outside and the architecture. Surprisingly bright and airy, the decor has a modern beach house vibe due to the soft palette, despite the massive size of the entrance.

Céline has very good taste.

With each step echoing, it must be hard to sneak around on these marble floors. He closes the door and sets my case down near the stairs. I bend to the side to take in the grand room ahead, where a Christmas tree twinkles next to a fire crackling in the white stone fireplace. The house is cozy despite its size and even smells of cookies.

Although the creature comforts of an old-fashioned

holiday decorate the home, making it pretty enough to be on a greeting card, I feel out of sorts.

He says, "I can't believe you're home." I turn back to him, gripping the handles of my purse even tighter. His palm hugs his forehead as he stares at me.

Home . . . Why does he keep saying that? Each time feels like the twist of a knife. "Me either." *The absolute truth.*

"I hoped you wouldn't be gone long."

"How long has it been?" I slowly ponder out loud, willing him to fill in the blanks.

His gaze hardens as he looks at me twice. "Well, since September. You've already forgotten? It was a pretty eventful exit. One I'll never forget."

"Just slipped my mind." *If he only knew . . .*

He leans on the railing and gives me a once-over. "You look tired . . . and different. Long journey?"

Tired and different? I look down at my jeans and sweater. The photo of Céline comes to mind. I should have considered how I used to dress before arriving, but I wanted to be comfortable for the drive. *Now I have regrets.*

"Yes." Be brave . . .

Besides the memories of my past, I'd almost forgotten how Loch told me, very nicely, that I wasn't having a good day—aka being rude—before the mugging. That's who Céline is. I need to play that part. I hold my chin up and look around nonchalantly as if this isn't the most beautiful house I've ever been in.

Grabbing my free hand from behind, he spins me around abruptly and brings me into his arms. "I missed you."

Petrified, I lean back, but I swear my heartbeats echo off the walls like my footsteps did. I pull myself together and fix my eyes on him. "Why did you miss me?"

"What do you mean why? I care about you. I love you, Céline."

Love?

I think my jaw just hit the floor. Metaphorically scooping it up, I stare at him, unable to fathom what he means by that. The calm I carried under my defiance of letting him in disappears with those four words, knowing my fear is being realized. How can he love me? He doesn't even know me. He didn't even know where I was or care that I was gone. He didn't come for me, and more importantly, he didn't file a report wanting to find me.

The most alarming thing is that he appears to believe that he genuinely loves me. It's the most welcoming he's been.

My heart starts to race as I question what I'm doing here. Is this worth it? Letting this man believe we have a chance? God, is that what he thinks? That I'm back to rekindle this relationship?

Will remembering who I am be worth the sacrifice of who I've become?

Getting the answers takes precedence over the temporary fear. "You say you love me, but you had no idea where I was or how long I'd be gone. Where did you think I was?" Asking questions that I should already know the answer to makes me sound ludicrous, but so is living with amnesia.

"What is going on with you?" he snaps. His disconcerting tone causes me to still. I push through my emotions, intent on getting what I came for—my past back. "Don't do that."

"Don't do what?"

"Look at me like I'm your enemy. You know how that makes me feel."

Guess this is a regular occurrence. And if I routinely do

that, it begs the question of why I do it in the first place. The picture is filling out. Much to my dismay, it's not in a positive light for him.

He signals to the door. "The time away was supposed to help—"

"Help what?"

"Help *us.*" *Not the response I wanted.* He rubs his hand over his face and sighs in frustration. "What were you doing all this time if you weren't figuring out your damn life?"

Another surge of concerns clogs my chest. Is he violent? Or angry I left? Why *did* I leave? My own frustration sets in, but I know one thing for sure. The knowledge of my amnesia is not safe in his hands. Make that two things. I now know why no one was looking for me. I willingly left on my own.

"Why are you acting so strange?" he asks, his hair falling over the severity of his eyes. Despite telling me he loves me, nothing is comforting about him. Since I've arrived, his body language and tone have been anything but loving or welcoming. It's as if I've interrupted his day.

"Traveling," I blurt, needing a reprieve from him to collect my thoughts and make a new plan. "I'm tired. Do you mind carrying my suitcase for me?"

"I had really hoped three months away would have helped your head."

Uh-oh. Does he know? "What's wrong with my head?"

He shoots me a glare that would end a weaker person. That's not me. I'm not going to run, spiting my alarm. Not only do I have the love of my soul mate as armor, but I've been to war these past seven weeks and have a strong shield. A hard stare won't deter me from getting my life back.

"If you're tired, you should rest. We have a lot to discuss."

"We sure do," I say as my own personal power play.

His brow pinches again before he starts up the stairs. Stopping a few steps ahead, he turns back. "I know the fight we had was bad, and the timing terrible, but the way you left . . . left *me* to deal with the guests, I questioned if you were ever coming back."

There's that smile again, the one that adds no warmth to his face. I'm shocked he doesn't realize he's completely transparent. Instead, he marvels in his stance as if his words should have greater meaning. "I should have known better."

"Why is that?"

"Because that's the agreement we made."

"Well, maybe one day I'll stay gone for good."

He stops at the top and looks back, our gazes fixing in a way I can't read. His indifference mars the love he claimed for me only a few minutes prior. "Sometimes I wonder if it would be easier."

A shiver runs up my spine as a breath escapes, sinking my chest. I'm lost to the deeper meaning, and I hate it. "I don't know."

He looks up at the ceiling as sadness shrouds his face. "Yeah, me neither." He leads me upstairs and to the right down the hallway. Opening a door on the right, he walks in like this is his room, causing my stomach to churn from the implication of what that really means.

I steady my voice as I enter the room, holding my head higher like I know where I am. "I don't remember what we fought about now." *God, give me something to go off from here.*

"Good. No point in rehashing the past." He sets the case down and then leans against one of the four posters on the bed frame.

"Actually, I'd like to sit down with you and do exactly that."

"What good will that do?"

"For me, the closure I'm seeking."

He blinks several times, burning time. "Why get upset again? It's in the past. Everything was handled, Céline."

"Everything?"

"Everything." Our eyes search each other's, and I wonder what he's looking for in mine. Do I hold secrets he wants to uncover as much as he holds them for me? He shifts and moves to the windows, opening the curtains. Particles of dust fill the air as if the room has been closed off for years. *Not months.* "I know I was wrong, so we can put that behind us and aim for March."

"What happens in March?"

"Are you wanting to do it sooner?"

I feel like I'm stuck in a mental roundabout of questions. "Do what?"

"Get married."

"Married?" I squeal, my voice trembling around the word.

"We can skip the wedding, if you don't want to go through that again, and elope. Then we'll host a party when we return. You love parties."

I also love Loch. I don't even know what to say to him. I need to get my thoughts straight.

"Tourist season picks up in April. You know this." He seems to be waiting for a reaction, but what can I say? No way am I marrying this guy. "I finished work earlier. I can get the ball rolling."

"Rolling?" I'm shaking my head. "No. This is too much. Too fast."

His eyes narrow on me like prey. "Too much, too fast for you?" he asks, the gall of it hitting his tone and expression at the same time. "I'm the one who had to handle the crowd. Me. But it's too much, too fast for *you*? Do you know how humiliating it was for me to stand and announce I had a runaway bride?"

Oh my God. So many questions are fighting to be asked, but only one comes out. "Why'd I leave?"

"Because I fucked up. We had a deal, and although I abided by the rules, I used poor judgment that day and disrespected you."

Naturally, I'm tempted to make him feel better and accept the apology hidden between his words, but then I realize what he means. "You cheated on me."

"I'm not proud of myself, but I was told you were busy getting ready."

Not sure why this feels like such a gut punch when I have zero feelings for this man, not an ounce of understanding that I loved him comes to mind or is felt toward him. "You cheated on our wedding day?"

I sigh and look toward the window where the curtains remain closed, keeping the sunshine out of my life. I have a hunch that was par for the course in my former life.

As tempting as it is to probe him for more details, his fidgeting with the pocket of his pants extends, making me anxious as well. "What did you—"

"You left me no choice, Céline." I'm not sure if it's the question or my presence that sets him off, but he begins pacing. I stay out of his way, setting my purse on the dresser and pressing my hip against the large piece of furniture. I'm reminded that I don't even know his name. He's just a big blank in my memory, and we were engaged, for crying out loud. That really tells me everything about why we didn't marry.

I have one life, so I'll only marry someone who shares the same soul. *Like Loch.*

I'm still lost on the type of relationship we had where he

felt he could cheat and still marry me on the same freaking day. Tempering my reaction, I say, "Maybe we should talk when we're not as heated."

He replies, "I warned you that this is where we'd end up. Arguing." He stops and looks at me like he's seen me a million times and not just returned home. "So we're on the same page. I told our guests you were seeking treatment. That ended speculation. It also made sense under the circumstances since you ran out during our ceremony."

"And I have no doubt you made yourself out to be the supportive fiancé."

"Every story needs a hero." *He's not mine.* Tapping his watch, he says, "I didn't know you'd be coming home. I already made plans for the evening."

"As I said, I'm tired." I grip the dresser's wood edge behind my back. "I think it's a good idea for you to stay the night at your place now that I'm back. I'll be turning in early anyway."

As if I've kicked him when he's down, his gaze drops to the rug. "Fine."

Not learning from the first time, he comes toward me again. I reflexively stiffen. "Get some rest." He tries to kiss me, but I turn my cheek, which is where he lands. My skin is coated with his heavy breath, and then he walks to the door.

Squeezing the hem of my sweater, I don't feel anything but repulsed by him.

"I was hoping things had changed," he says, shooting his eyes to mine. "To be clear, I was hoping *you* had changed. Guess you were right. You can't make someone love you." Before he closes the door, he adds, "Your parents won't be back for Christmas. They're in Nice through the new year." His smile is kinder in nature this time, but I still don't trust him. "But I'm glad I won't be celebrating alone. I even put a gift under the tree in hopes you'd be back. I'll see you later."

He leaves me with little more information than when I showed up at the door. This won't be as easy as I expected.

I push off and start to snoop around the room. The first point of business is to discover who he is and why I'm marrying a man I clearly don't love. It's fun to solve a mystery, but not when it's *my* life that's locked in secrecy.

32

Loch

WHAT HAS BECOME of my life?

I don't even recognize it anymore. That doesn't upset me in the least. We haven't even made it back to the city, and I already miss Tuesday.

The Escalade veers into the exit lane and off the highway. "Where are you going, Brady?"

"I'm hungry. Time for a pit stop."

You have to love when the boss is told what's happening after the decision is already made. This time, I'm good with it. I'm not one to indulge . . . at least, I wasn't until I met Tuesday, but I could fucking devour a hoagie right now. He parks at the pump to get some gas. I detour inside the large convenience store attached to the gas station. "What can I get you?"

He pulls the gas pump from the holder. "I'll be inside in a sec."

I go ahead and take a piss. By the time I walk out, I find

Brady eyeing the corn dogs. "Anything fresh, like a sandwich or a salad?"

Side-eyeing me, he scoffs. "You're kidding, right?" I'm not sure what part of that seemed like a joke, but he turns to me with his arms crossed over his chest. "Do you ever let loose, Loch?"

"Of course, I do. You've witnessed it for the past two months."

"Ah, the Tuesday effect. I already miss it."

"Gee, thanks," I reply with sarcasm embedded in it. I move a few feet, checking out the cold section of the counter display. "The Tuesday effect," I mumble, not going near their shrimp salad sandwich. Skipping over the roast beef, I'm still bothered by what he said. He's just gotten a corn dog when I return. "What do you mean by that?"

"It's a corn dog, boss."

"No. What do you mean by the Tuesday effect?" I have an inkling, but I need this defined for me.

Brady chuckles, then takes a bite off the top of the dog. I admit by how he hums and the steam wafting off it that I'm tempted to try one. "It's when . . ." He starts talking with his mouth full but then stops to finish chewing. "It's the effect she has on you. It's been, what?" He references his watch. "Two hours tops, and you're already back to the stiff lawyer with no life. You're back to pre-Tuesday."

Fuck it. I hold my finger up when the guy looks my way. "I'll take one."

He reacts with another hardier chuckle as he hits my chest with the back of his hand. "I'm talking about not living, eating salads and healthy all the fucking time, not veering from your regimen."

I'm handed the corn dog and take a bite, and it's actually

pretty damn good. "Look, I'm breaking from my regimen right now. Happy?"

"How long will you spend in the gym to work that off tonight?"

"It shouldn't take long—*fuck*, I see what you did there."

He's almost finished his corn dog and shaking his head when I realize I walked right into his trap. "It's not a trick, Loch. It's living in the present, no schedule dictating your day, not being able to enjoy the simpler pleasures like a gas station corn dog or a forty-four ouncer of soda." He starts for the back of the store.

"You understand I'm here during a workday. I canceled billable meetings to ride to Rhode Island with her, knowing I'd be working this weekend to catch up."

"You'd be working anyway, but I'm glad you gave her the time she deserves." Grabbing a cup, he starts filling it with ice.

Fuck. I really don't want forty-four ounces of sugar coursing through my body, but he'll shame me with every slurp he takes if I don't. I grab the damn cup. "I can let loose even without her here."

"Yeah?" He glances, his expression contorted in disbelief. Skipping the ice, I go right for the soda. I'm not watering it down. If I'm doing this, I'm winning this round. "No ice, huh?"

"Ice is for wimps. I like my soda straight up for the full effect." I rip off another big bite of my corn dog.

His shoulders shoot to his ears. "So you'd be up for a candy bar as well?"

"Fuck yeah. Bring it on."

Laughing, he walks down the snack aisle and grabs one from the box. "Don't you dare say Snickers are for wimps."

It feels good to laugh. "Wasn't going to, but real men eat

the king-size Reese's Cups. Just sayin'." I leave him on the aisle and head for the register.

The blonde smiles as soon as I step up to the counter. She can't be a day over forty, but her clothes skew younger. "Haven't seen you before. You passin' through town?"

"Yep." Brady comes up beside me and shows her his snack supply. "Add his to my bill."

Her eyes widen along with her smile. "Oh." She fluffs her hair. "Hello."

"Hey," he replies, leaning against the counter like some convenience store Romeo.

Not sure what's happening here . . . Actually, I know exactly what's happening, but I don't like it. I tap the card to the reader and grab my stuff. "I'll see you outside." Usually, I make a great wingman. My brothers can attest. I'm not in the mood today to help him get laid, though. I toss the soda after a few sips and lean against the vehicle until Brady comes out.

With Tuesday still on my mind . . . always, I text the private investigator to see if he's found out anything else about her life. He replies a few seconds later: *No. I'll be in contact when I do.*

I appreciate the confidence. Not *if*, but *when* he finds new details and clues.

Always jolly, he's laughing when he pushes through the door, and aims the fob at the vehicle. The locks are released, and I start to get in. "Judge Judy wouldn't approve of you flirting with another woman."

"Don't worry, she's into that kind of thing. Anyway," he says, eyeing me over the windshield. "We've run our course. I made sure she got bored of me." He climbs in on the driver's side.

"Too wild for you, huh?" I open the front passenger door and get in.

"I want to be with someone I can take home to meet my mom. Not someone who wants to role play *as* my mom. Ich." He shakes his head as disgust makes him cringe.

Why does it not surprise me she tried that with him?

"What are you doing, Loch?"

"What?"

With a grin that he always seems to be wearing, he thumbs toward the back seat. "This is my domain up here. Get the fuck back there."

It was all fun and games until Brady called the front his domain. So much for our bonding time. I get out and move to the back. "Take me to the office when we get to the city," I say, not hearing any argument from him.

And just like that, we're back to our pre-Tuesday relationship.

I'D FORGOTTEN about the party until I walked into the office.

Leisa rushes to me and places a sash around my neck that reads "Partner," with a horrid drawing of a holster and a cowboy hat. There's no fighting this embarrassment once the room erupts in a round of applause and laughter. I'm glad Brady isn't here to bear witness to this embarrassing situation.

He refused to hang out after the corn dog conversation, claiming he had cooler friends to hang out with, but I know he's joking. No one is cooler than me.

I chuckle, probably still high off the Reese's Cups I devoured, or maybe I've just discovered my sense of humor again. I wish Tuesday was here to see this, especially since she planned the party.

"Congrats," Leisa says. "We got cake."

Great, more sugar. Bring it on. "Nice touch on the cowboy theme."

"The partner reference made Tuesday laugh since there seems to be a lack of 'attorneys making partner' supplies on the party market. She said you'd lose it. I couldn't tell if she meant laughing or your temper, but this is what she went with." Looking toward the door, she asks, "Where is she?"

"Long story."

Walking through the crowd, I'm shaking hands and getting pats on the back. Even the Reinhold Group execs are here to celebrate. Before we reach the cake, she whispers, "How about the short version?"

"She found out who she is."

"What?" Her shock pulls my attention away from the clients ahead. I stop to look back to where she planted her feet, recognizing the emotions engulfing her face. I've felt it all day without minor distractions keeping it at bay.

She says, "I'm sorry . . . We're happy for her, right?"

"Right. Happy for her." I nod once and then turn to greet the clients. "Thanks for coming to celebrate."

Shaking my hand, Mr. Reinhold says, "Life is good, Loch. Quite the success."

It sure doesn't feel like it with Tuesday gone. In fact, it feels the opposite. "Life is . . . yeah, a real success."

"If it isn't Lochlan Westcott, Esquire," my younger brother's voice booms across the office.

I turn to see both of them walking in. Mr. Reinhold says, "More Westcotts by the looks of it. You've got some competition."

"They're not attorneys, and we learned a long time ago

not to let anyone come between us." It would be unprofessional to share why that rule came about, so I keep it to myself. "Excuse me."

Harbor is first, wrapping his arms around me. "You did it, brother. All your hard work has paid off. Congrats."

"Thanks."

He notices me looking for Lark. "She got called in, or you know she'd be here."

Bottles of champagne are popped, and I hear that food is in the kitchen. Noah asks, "Where's Tuesday?"

I have a feeling that's the running theme tonight. "Long story."

Leisa greets my brothers and offers to get us drinks. Noah steps up. "No way. I'll get them. What are you having?" he asks her with a wink. Always turning on the charm. He doesn't realize she's immune to his antics.

I'm in no mood to party, so I ask Harbor to my office, shutting the door behind us. "The party's great. The office deserves it more than my name being added to the letterhead."

He sits on the couch. "It's okay to let loose and celebrate your achievements, Loch."

"You're the second one to tell me that today."

"Who was the first?"

"Brady."

He chuckles. "My man knows what he's talking about. You should be on top of the world, but you're not, so what's going on?"

Sitting at my desk, I tell him the story and how Tuesday went back to Rhode Island.

Noah eventually comes in and sets down two bottles of water. "Who's the hot new hire?"

"I'm not looking to get sued," I snap.

"Right." He grins, and I already know he's going to walk that line. "I should introduce myself." Then he looks back and forth between us. "What'd I miss?"

"Nothing," Harbor and I say in unison.

Chuckling, he says, "That's believable." He hasn't even taken a seat, and he's already heading for the door again. "I think this room needs something stiffer. If you want bourbon, I'm happy to get it."

"I want it," I say, running my hand through my hair.

"On it." He's already out the door on a mission.

There's an entire office of people celebrating my accomplishment, and I'm in my office, not able to think about anything else but Tuesday. "She's only been gone a few hours, and I'm already a fucking mess."

Harbor says, "You're a mess, but you know what's really happening?"

Looking for that one piece of advice to get me through, I ask, "What?"

"You're in love."

I sigh. "I know that already, and I've told her. Plenty."

"Hear me out." Sounding serious, which is rare for my brothers, he stands and plants his hands on the desk opposite of me. "This isn't about saying the words, Loch. It's deeper than that. I know the feeling. You're lost without her."

Lost.

That's exactly what I am.

Lost. *That's heavy.*

Fuck, I could really use that drink right about now.

Then he says, "I lost years I could have spent with Lark by making a decision for us on my own, instead of talking to her. It's not the same situation, but since you don't know when she'll return, give her the time she needs, but remind her where her heart lives."

Remind her of me.

Harbor almost lost his life once. He doesn't treat things like love or family frivolously. He makes the most of life and gives trusted advice that's not about him, but the wisdom of his experience, so I listen. When he walks to the window, he asks, "What are you going to do?"

Joining him, I let my gaze travel as far as my eyes can see. I refuse to lose her to her old life, not when we're so good together in this one. Feeling a renewed determination, I cross my arms over my chest. "Make sure I get her back."

33

Tuesday

I SORT OF HATE THAT I'm smiling while looking at my things.

Photos.

A dried corsage from a dance.

Clothes that spill over onto the floor of a walk-in closet.

Shoes that must have cost a fortune.

The handbags are a whole other story of their own.

I spy several Hermès, Chanel, Vuitton, and YSL. The last one makes me think of the purse Loch sent to me the first night at the hotel. He spared no expense when he brought me into his life and took care of me the best way he knew how, protecting me from the world.

This isn't about money, though I've been spoiled. No, this goes deeper.

Loch doesn't realize he did more than save me. He brought me back to life by loving me. That's why this world, although my things have me smiling, makes me miss the life I've been living with him even more. I pull my phone from my bag and text: *I miss you.*

Staring at the screen, I will him to see it. Relief washes over me when I see those three dots on the screen. But nothing compares to the joy I feel when I see his message pop up: *I miss you more, baby.*

I hold the phone to my chest as the adrenaline of being here wears off and question why I even came when I have Loch to traverse this with me at home. Especially because the mental gymnastics with my "fiancé" have already worn me down. He speaks in riddles and references things I can't remember. How long can I really pull off this charade?

Add in that my mind can't settle on one thing that has truly gotten me closer to recovering my memories and it feels like an impossible task to achieve. Why do I stay? The money is mine, enough to live a very comfortable life, and safe in my bank account. All I have to do is prove who I am to claim it.

It makes it even more tempting to tell Loch to come get me and make me forget about this day.

But can I?

Can I really move on knowing this world exists, my past life still filling the walls of this room and gifts under the tree? I don't even know my parents anymore. I would love to see them, but are the strings too tenuous to hang on?

I move to the alcove of the window, folding my legs under me and relax in the peace of the view. It's nice to breathe without having someone breathing over me, like that man was. A soft cushion spreads end to end with hidden bookcases on either side. Classics lining the shelves along with a few books by authors I must have treasured based on how many of their titles I own. I breathe it in, this area saying the most about me yet.

Books.

A nook.

And a view.

I haven't read a book since I've been at Loch's, but something about being near my collection is so comforting. I take one of the novels down and flip through the pages of the romance. A quote stands out, reminding me of the fairy tale I was living.

You're where time begins and ends and every moment between.[1]

Why'd I leave Loch? I know the rational answers, but love isn't always logical. So why do I keep trying to make sense of it? He's been every minute of the life I know, and I love him with my soul. Yet I'm sitting here in the middle of another state away from him.

A knock on the door draws me from my thoughts. I've been here for hours, but not heard another person. Until now . . . I stare at it, praying he hasn't come back. After the second rap, I stand and call, "Yes?"

"C?" a woman asks through the closed door.

C?

Not Céline. *Huh*? Who is it now? We must be close enough for her to call me a nickname. I take a step but then stop again. Do I answer it or tell her to go away? Me saying I was tired worked as an excuse with him, but maybe this lady is a new opportunity for information. Nearing dinnertime, I have to leave eventually, so I say,

"One moment." I open the door and peek out. Curls of red hair and eyes that shine bright like fresh-cut grass in the spring greet me.

"It's true," she says, raising her hand with an enthusiastic grin that's too big to contain on her small face. "You're back."

I open the door wider. "I am." I can't stop myself from smiling. If only everyone was this happy to see me. "How did you know?"

"I made Carter swear to me he would tell me the second you arrived. He texted me begrudgingly." Her laughter tinkers in the air in a higher octave. She throws her arms around me before I have a chance to escape. "I'm so happy to see you."

"Carter?" So that's his name. With no justification whatsoever, I can see how it fits.

"Yeah, you know how he gets." She rolls her eyes as she heads straight for the window seat where I had been sitting and tucks her legs under her. Her outfit is similar to mine, but she's in a baggier white button-up over her fitted ankle jeans. It's the colorful scarf around her neck that catches my eyes. The hair and large green eyes contrast the more muted outfit, but someone as pretty as she is with her button nose doesn't need distractions from her natural features.

She says, "I need to know everything. Why did you leave? Where have you been? I need all the adventure details." Energy vibrates from her, but after dealing with Carter, it's nice to be in the mix of her liveliness.

"Actually, I was hoping you could tell me a few things." I sit on the chaise at the end of the bed, thinking she's just the breakthrough I need to solve these mysteries in my life.

Her head tilts as her smile finally settles into something more subtle among friends who casually hang out. "What do you want to know?" she asks. "We've just been here not doing much of anything. Well—" She waves her hands again, waffling them back and forth. "You know how boring it gets around here."

She sort of reminds me of myself. I wonder how close of friends we were and if we formed our habits together. "I'm still working on my site. Not a shocker, but it's finally in the testing stages. Oh," she says, dropping her feet to the floor and sitting forward. "Do you mind being a client for me? I really need someone from the outside to use it so we can find any bugs and fix them."

"Sure." I have no idea what I'm agreeing to. It's been all of two minutes, but I can feel the connection to her, and trust for her. "I don't know your name." I didn't intend to be so soft-spoken, but my worry for how she'll react gets the better of me.

"What?" she asks, her smile growing but not quite reaching her eyes.

"I need to tell you something. Can I trust you?"

"Can you trust me?" She comes to sit beside me as confusion pinches her brow. "What do you mean? You know you can trust me with anything." She looks down at her lap as soft laughter rattles her shoulders. "I never told anyone it was you that caused Joslin and Matt to break up when you made out with him at your sweet sixteen party. Or that you did it only to make Carter jealous. Not a peep left my lips when your parents found the fender of their Rolls dented, and they blamed Blake, who got sent to military school for lying about it since it was his third strike with trouble." My stomach tightens as she continues, "Do I really need to remind you how you cut my ponytail off in second grade?"

I feel sick. "No. Please don't. I sound like a horrible person." I wanted to know my past, but I wasn't prepared for this. Sadly, me and Carter might be more alike than I realized, so dating him makes more sense, quite honestly. And Loch saying I was rude tracks with what I'm hearing now. I sigh. Wow, I was a mean girl.

"What are you talking about, C?"

"I got someone sent to military school because of something I did . . .?"

"You got an asshole who tried to assault me sent away. I don't feel an ounce of sympathy for him. Joslin had been fucking with you and Carter for years. You may have made out with Matt to make Carter realize what he had with you, but Matt and I wouldn't be together now if you hadn't exposed her cheating. I mean, it took him years to really see me as more than his hot friend." Clicking her tongue, she then adds, "But he got there in the end."

Her personality is so magnetic that she's managed to make me feel less guilty for my bad behavior. *Impressive.* "And the haircut?"

"That was just a bitchy move." She laughs. "There's no excusing that, other than we were seven."

How did she manage to make me feel better about the awful stuff I've done in the past? If one thing is apparent from this quick rundown of stories through the years, she's loyal. I angle toward her, and confess, "I really don't know your name."

"Why do you keep saying that?"

"I was attacked in New York City. Mugged, actually. I hit my head and—"

Her hand covers her mouth just as she gasps. Lowering it, she asks, "You really don't remember me?"

"I don't remember anything. I didn't even remember *me.* I still don't. That's why I'm back."

I'm not sure how long she stares at me with eyes wider than I'd think possible, hand back over her mouth, but her silence is not doing us any favors. I shift and then eventually stand, walking back toward the window. Resting my hands on the sill, I finally can't take it any longer. "Please say something."

When she lowers her hand, her mouth remains dropped open. "I don't know what to say, Céline." Looking into the void of the far corner, she takes another moment before turning back, and asking, "You don't remember anything?"

"No."

Jumping up, she rushes me and brings me into an embrace. "I'm so sorry. Are you physically okay?"

I nod, my eyes suddenly tearing. *Why?* Why am I so weak to my emotions? Because this is the welcome wagon I had hoped for. Family. Friends. Finding someone to help me through this. But it's frustrating that I don't even know her name.

She holds me tighter. "It's okay. I'll help you however I can." Stepping back, she asks, "Is that why you were gone so long with no contact?"

"For the past two months, yes. I had a concussion, but I'm doing much better now, except for the memory loss. I woke up in the hospital and didn't even know my own name."

A small gasp is sucked in again as she shakes her head. "That's awful." Taking hold of my hand, she holds it between hers. A smile matching the gentle kindness of her grasp shapes her expression. "I'm Allison. Allison Wyatt. Your best friend since preschool. The other pea in your pod, peas to your carrots, BFFL, ride or die, but let's not die. Okay?"

"I'm trying not to." Laughing with her invigorates me, renewing the strength that had been waning. "Deal. Also, that's a lot of peas going around." I like how easy it is to talk to her. "I'm Tuesday—"

"Tuesday?"

Nodding again, I reply, "I just discovered that my real name is Céline the other day."

"Wow, that's intense. What do you want me to call you?"

I wish I could be Tuesday with her, but I don't know if she'll even want to be a part of my new life. "You can call me C or Céline. Whatever you're used to."

"C will be a hard habit to break." Her welcoming and warm demeanor gives me the reassurance I need to feel safe to stay. "Where did Tuesday come from?" Taking a few steps back, she sits in the chair close to me.

"Apparently, it's the name I gave for my coffee order right before I was mugged outside the shop."

"You never did anything without thought, so I'm curious where that name came from."

I'm eating up the insight she's sharing. "Me too, but I'm curious about everything."

"Oh my God! I just realized you met Carter. How'd that go?" Her expression tightens, cringing, but she still laughs. I think it's nervous laughter. "You didn't know who he was, did you?"

"No."

"I'm sure you put him in a tizzy." Her eyes dawn as they set on me again. "You probably have a lot of questions. Ask me anything."

"I have so many that I almost don't know where to begin."

"If it's not too presumptuous, I could start telling you things." She heads for the door. "How about we get something to drink first, and then I can give you a tour of your house while we chat about everything?"

"I'd love that."

With the doorknob in hand, she says, "I'm just happy to have you back. If you can't remember all the shitty things I've done to you, that's just a bonus."

"Is it as awful as what I've done?" I ask, following her into the hallway.

"Worse. Like I said, at least you had good reasons. I was just a bitch."

"I'm sure you had your reasons as well, just like I did."

"This amnesia thing might work out well for me." Her laughter travels the hall and then she puts a finger to her lips as if I'm the one making all the noise. *Okay, I like her a lot.*

Looking around, she points down the opposite side of the hall from my room, and whispers, "Carter's office is down that way. He started staying here when you disappeared, claiming to need to manage the property in your absence and 'the long commute' was problematic. Even though his family's estate is less than twenty minutes down the road."

"He cheated on me . . ." I grab the railing, not for physical support but because I may not love him now, but I probably did back then. I was marrying him, for Pete's sake, so I must have.

Sympathy floods her complexion, turning it red. "That's why you left?" Dropping her forehead into her palm, she says, "You didn't tell me, but I should have known."

It's such a genuine reaction from a true friend that I'm feeling the same emotions as her. I take a breath and try to wrangle the thoughts it spurs in me. "How would you? I can only imagine the pain I felt, so speaking to anyone about it wouldn't be easy." I cover her hand that she's gripping the railing with. "I don't think it's a loss. My gut tells me he's awful."

She nods. "There's a reason you ran down that aisle and disappeared."

"One of many, it seems."

---

1. Quote from Swear on My Life by S.L. Scott

34

Tuesday

OVER TWO GLASSES of Perrier and now pizza and wine, I've learned more than I had in the seven weeks prior.

I'm an only child.

Graduated at the top of my class from Columbia with a major in business and a minor in fine arts. I would have guessed the opposite.

I work for my family's company in marketing, which gives me peace of mind that I was doing something with my life. The downside is that Carter had been brought on in accounting, apparently by my request. That makes no sense to me because I can't figure out our relationship. It doesn't sound like we had a particularly good one, and he talks about the cheating being within the guidelines. *Really weird.*

In my heart of hearts, cheating is a no-go. Not only can I not handle it, but it feels wrong, hurtful, and disrespectful to your partner.

As I sit here trying to bridge the gap of who I am now and my beliefs to who I was in the past, so many things don't add up to being in love with him. Much less putting him in positions of power in my life. "If I had a job," I start, "why was no one questioning when I wasn't showing up for work?"

"Well, 'showing up for work' is relative to the situation. The company is run out of France."

"France?"

She nods as if she's just shared the juiciest secret. Looking at her eyes, I can't tell if they're more playful from the bonding time or if she just loves to gossip. Either way, I'm here for it. "Yep. Your family owns an olive oil company in France. It's a stunning property that's been in your family for generations, like two-hundred years or something."

France . . . my mind wanders the imagery of the country-side that's popped into my head. "I like it there."

"You *love* it there. You always called it your happy place."

"Why was I living in Rhode Island if my happy place is in France?"

"I'm off." We both turn to see Carter in the foyer. When he sees us sitting in the living room, he adds, "Thought you were going to rest? I knew I shouldn't have texted Allison. Leave it to her to barge in like—"

"Like I'm her best friend?" Allison shoots me a *got him* look, a small smirk playing on her lips. As if she didn't make it clear before that she's not his biggest fan, she's crystal this time. "You're not wrong there."

It's safe to say they mutually dislike each other.

I say, "It's been good to catch up with her again."

He spins the key ring around his finger, his eyes darting to her like she might spill the beans. I have no doubt that if she has beans on him, she's spilling them. "Well, don't wait up."

Staring at him, I reply, "I wasn't planning to since you'll be staying at your place."

The chime of the keys clanging together in his palm breaks the silent standoff between us. His eyes stay fixed on mine, but the humor he thought he had in the situation has gone. "Maybe I should stay."

Whipping around, Allison asks, "No, we're good. Right, Tues—C?"

With both sets of eyes glaring at me, I shift and take another sip of wine. "We clearly have a lot to talk about, Carter. I look forward to that tomorrow, but tonight, I'm spending time with Allison. She's filling me in on everything I missed."

"She'll get you drunk and feed you lies, Céline. You know how she is."

Allison tenses and fists her hands. "You know what—"

"I can think for myself." I step in before a war breaks out.

"Isn't that what got us here?" he barks, the veins in his neck bulging. "I'm already late meeting *the guys*. We'll talk tomorrow." He walks out the door, letting a gush of cold wind and snow rush in.

Chilled, I turn to the fire, holding my hands out to warm them. The flames remind me of Loch's eyes and the way the fire inside him licks at my body when I'm lying naked. He looks at me like I'm his whole universe.

Though Loch comforts me momentarily, a shiver runs up my spine that the guy who just left has probably seen me naked. Ugh. That's a memory I hope I never retrieve.

"He's such an asshole," Allison says. "You really need to toss him to the curb."

"Why haven't I?"

With puffed cheeks, she exhales loudly. "Only you knew why and now you don't know at all."

"Truer words have never been spoken."

I drink more wine and curl my legs beside me. "It's a mystery. That's for sure."

She scoffs. "He's so frustrating. He loves playing mental games—"

"That's exactly what I was thinking earlier. The verbal sparring with him is exhausting." Holding the glass on my leg, I catch the fire reflecting in the crystal. "I'd like to get back to France."

"Me too. We should go."

Laughing, I add, "I meant back to what we were talking about. If France is my happy place, why'd I stay here?"

Her eyes find mine under her laughter. "We've had some killer parties here, for one. They were the most coveted invite in town. That is, until Carter put an end to them. He hated all the attention you got from other guys. He's such a weasel."

She gets up and digs in a cabinet next to the fireplace. "You left once, but Carter got on a plane and brought you back within a week. Only you know what he said to convince you to come back. Another mystery to solve." Pulling out a book, she opens it and then returns to the couch next to me. "Whatever he has on you, it must be bad because you could have any guy you wanted."

Whatever he has on me?

"You think he's extorting me or—"

"Just a hunch since you never seemed that over the moon about him. Sure," she says, shrugging, "you've had good times, but something was always off. I think you two are from a small pool of choices. I'm not judging. I'm in there swimming around, too. We can't just date anyone when our families have so much wealth." Her head wobbles. "Well, we can, but is it worth the hassle of possibly being cut off?"

"Why would we be cut off?"

"You know what I mean. It's just easier to date people splashing around in that same pool as you than to fight to be with someone else. Not saying it's impossible. Look at Matt and me. He's broke. But I love him, so he's worth the fight."

"You had to fight for him?"

Her shoulders roll up and then fall again. "Not really. My mom loves him, but Carter's family is different. I think you were the goal from the moment his family met you."

"That's so romantic," I say, feigning a swoon.

"It's about a suitable match in their eyes, not romance."

I never thought twice about Loch's money in terms of what I could get from him. If we'd met with less, I still would have fallen in love with him.

Holding the photo album, she places her hand on it. "You always dreamed of moving to France, but Carter put an end to that. So is extortion out of the realm of possibility? Not with him,"

Sounds like the end of me. *Till death do us part indeed.*

"But that's just me because I think he's an asshole."

"I left, Allison. I left during the ceremony and didn't go through with it. He cheated on me, but it doesn't sound like it was the only time. So what was different that day other than the obvious and the wedding?"

She sits back, chewing the inside of her cheek. Reaching for her wine again, she finishes it. "When you left, you left me as well. I was left in the dark as to what had happened."

Reaching over, I touch her arm. "I'm sorry."

"It must be hard not remembering, but for what it's worth, I tried my best to make his life a living hell for what he did to you." She stands. "More wine?"

"I think I need it."

She's quick to the kitchen and returns with the bottle we already opened. Refilling our glasses, she says, "I was hurt when you left. We talk about everything, but there was no contact from you, and you never answered your phone."

Her admission draws my attention. "I'm sorry."

An assuring smile is quick to appear. Sitting down next to me again, she taps her glass against mine. "That doesn't matter now that you're back. Anyway, I know what's happened since."

She doesn't, though. Not the full story of me in Manhattan, living a life I could only dream of. She doesn't know the little things that matter, the parts that I protect in my heart from the outside world—how he looks at me like I'm his savior, the kisses he sneaks on my cheek when he thinks I'm sleeping, or how he stopped his life to tend to mine until I was steady on my feet again.

I sip wine and take a gulp, knowing I want to shout about Loch from the rooftops, to speak so freely about my feelings like I do at home . . . *home*.

Loch. "I fell in love," I blurt.

Wine spews from her mouth, causing me to jerk back. "You what?"

I burst out laughing, but it feels so good to speak freely. "Good thing it's white wine on these light-colored couches."

She's dabbing the sides of her mouth with her shirt when she asks, "You're in love?"

"I am." My body reacts—heart thumping in my chest and a smile that gives away the truth. "My whole soul is in love with a man in New York City."

Allison leans forward, her hand touching my forearm. "I've never wanted anything less than true love for you. Céline," she gushes, her shoulders faltering under the weight of a resolved breath. "*Tuesday*. Are you Tuesday with him?"

"Yes. He was in the coffee shop that day before the mugging. We actually talked while waiting for our orders." I leave out the part about being rude to him even though this aligns with who I used to be. I don't want that associated with my relationship with him. I want her to know him like I do. "He saved me, Allison."

"Saved you?" A bated breath is held and then she reaches over to take my hand. "How?"

I let my thoughts return to the many moments I spent with him—seeing Loch standing there at the shelter after I thought I had no other option but to go in. The anger that surged in his eyes when the hotel manager thought I was a call girl . . . the heat that man brings to every one of our sexual encounters. I fan myself, but that doesn't help, so I press my hands to my cheeks, remembering when he tossed me on the bed and then climbed over me, kissing me, bending me over the desk, loving me . . . the words "I love you" falling from his lips as if he'd wanted to say them all along.

I swallow my memories, wanting to hold on to them for as long as I can. "He didn't just give me a place to heal. He truly healed me and my heart, and showed me what real love is."

Squeezing my hand, she says, "I think that's the dreamiest thing I've ever heard." Her eyes are brighter, the joy she feels shining through. The happiness is for me . . . something only a true friend would feel. "Is that where you've been? You've been with him all this time?"

"Since the moment I left the hospital."

She leans forward and steals a piece of pepperoni from a

slice of pizza on her plate that was abandoned a while ago. "Where is he now?"

"He drove me to Rhode Island because I needed to do this alone. But he'll wait as long as it takes me to figure out this part of my life."

"So basically, you're saying he's the perfect man?" She opens the photo album. "Ignore me." She waves me off. "I'll just be here all jealous."

I giggle. "Not to brag, but to totally brag, he's pretty damn perfect."

"Wow, I never thought I'd see you so happy." Bursting out laughing, she adds, "You must have really hit your head."

I join in the joy. She was so unexpected, but it's amazing to have found an ally in her. "I guess it finally knocked some sense into me."

She shifts closer to look at the album, but then her gaze rises to mine. "I could see it the second I saw you again. You carry yourself differently. You even sound different. You're still my best friend, just different. It's your aura, the glow you have shining from the inside. You're not the same girl who got Blake sent to military school."

"Stop it," I say, tapping her with my hand.

"No, for real. He deserved it." Her grin vanishes. "One thing, though. If I noticed how different you are, Carter did too. Be careful, okay?"

35

Tuesday

"This is your family's château," Allison says, pointing at the first photo in the album.

A white stone structure with a dark-tiled roof sits at the crown of a hill keeping watch over acres of groves. History but with such French elegance in the details. "Wow, it's beautiful."

"It really is."

Thinking about the sweet things in the room upstairs—my life in trinkets and fashion—but nothing in that bedroom or down here, for that matter, inspired memories. "I have a wild idea."

"*Oohh*, I love when you get those."

Guess I've had a few in my lifetime. "You said this is my happy place."

"It is. That's why you wanted to get married there."

Setting my glass on the table, I say, "We should go."

"We should totally go to France." *I love her and how she's up for anything.*

I look around the room, realizing this house hasn't done what I hoped it would. "I think that could be my best shot of getting my memory back."

She leans over and hugs me. "Let's do it." I hug her because it feels good to spend time with my friend. She makes me feel less alone. Popping to her feet, she says, "No time like the present. Let's pack."

We run upstairs, vowing to be ready for a flight first thing in the morning. But in the excitement of the moment, I only have one thing on my mind—texting Loch: *I'm going to France.*

My phone rings immediately. "Hello?" I answer, grinning ear to ear.

"France wasn't the agreement, Tuesday. Rhode Island was." *Why must he sound so sexy when he's being overprotective?*

"I have to go, Loch. This may be my last chance to get my memories back. It's all I have left." I walk into my massive closet, thinking this might be my actual happy place by its impressive size.

"What are you talking about?"

Running my hands along the pretty clothes, I reply, "Allison—"

"Who's Allison?"

He exhales slowly, but I answer anyway. "My best friend since preschool. She said the place my family owns in France is my favorite place in the world, and since nothing here brings back memories, I figure my best shot is to go there."

I hear him sigh like it's already been a long day. I wish I were there to ease the muscles in his shoulders and take his mind off the things that trouble him. Wait a minute. *Am I what troubles him?*

"Allison is a woman you just met, *technically*, but you trust her?"

"I do trust her. I'm going with my gut here, Loch. And my parents are there."

"That does change things." A harsh breath travels the line to my ear. "How are you getting there?"

"We haven't booked flights yet. We just know we're leaving first thing in the morning."

"Let me take care of it for you."

"You don't have to do that."

"I do, and I will. I feel . . ." The emotion heard in his deep tone, and then the sudden pause, causes my chest to tighten.

I whisper, "It's okay."

"It's my job to protect you. I *need* to." His voice is so quiet as if the words themselves cause anguish.

"No, your job is to love me, and you excel in that. I'm safe, babe. I don't need you to worry." I imagine he's shaking his head, though he doesn't say anything. "I appreciate your help."

The silence extends, but then he says, "I'm glad you have your friend."

"And tomorrow, I'll have my parents." I wish I was better at containing my emotions, but tomorrow is what today was supposed to be—the day I get my life and family back.

He says, "I'll text you the details at five o'clock in the morning, so you can get some sleep."

"Thank you."

"I love you, Tuesday." How is it possible to miss him after such a short time apart? I do, I miss him, and I adore hearing him call me by that name. *My name.*

"I love you, Loch."

As excited as I am to go to France and see my parents

and the estate, I wish I were climbing in bed with him, making love until the early morning hours, and then sleeping in with him. He's my haven.

When we hang up, I start packing. I don't plan to stay in France long, but I'm also not sure how long it will take to discover my history. Fingers crossed, it's only for a few days, and then I can be back in Loch's arms and his bed. *Our bed. Again.*

I finish packing and then get ready for bed. My phone rings with a video call. I eagerly answer, "Hey."

With a toothbrush in hand and the phone in the other, Allison enters her bathroom wearing a fuzzy pink robe. "How's it going over there?"

"I'm ready for tomorrow, so now I'm getting ready for bed. You?"

"Just finished." I'm treated to glimpses of her bedroom and the boho vibe she's got going on. Sheer fabric is draped over the headboard, and colorful curtains cover the window. She has photos scattered around, but they're too small to get a good look at who's in them through the screen. A colorful lei is looped around the top of a lampshade on the nightstand, and clothes are scattered at the end of the bed with a few piled on the floor in the corner.

"What are you going to tell Carter regarding France?" she asks over the purr of her toothbrush and running water.

"What should I tell him?"

With a mouth full of foamy paste, she ducks out, and says, "Fuck him."

"Fuck you very much, too, Allison," he says, coming into my room.

"What are you doing?" Thank God I'm still dressed, but I know I need to lock my door from now on or, better yet, kick him out of the house entirely. He can work remote from his place.

He comes to me with a drunk grin on his face, and judging by his demeanor, alcohol courses through his veins. He's loose, totally relaxed in his own skin. So unlike how he was earlier when I met him. "How are you, darling?" He grabs me, but I slip out of his hold on my arm and move away from him.

"I'm—"

"Going to France. I heard. I'll go with you." *No. No. No. No. No.*

Allison says, "It's a girls' trip, so go to bed, Carter."

Completely ignoring her, he says, "You ladies can lounge and do what you do best—look pretty for the camera—while I tend to my meetings. It will be good to be back in the office and for the others to see me in person. When do we leave?"

"It's not your decision. It's mine," I add, opening the door and inviting him to get the hell out.

"We'll take a few days and reconnect, Céline." He comes toward me with a smirk on his face. But it's not the sexy ones Loch gives me. It's insincere. Distrusting of me. "Shoot me your itinerary." He leaves, but from the hall, he chimes, "Good night."

As soon as he's gone, I lock the door behind me and then hold the phone up so I can see Allison again. I whisper, "He's not coming with us, so be ready to leave from here at five."

She silently jumps up and down. "It's so espionage-like."

I laugh, not able to keep it down because I feel the same excitement. "We need sleep, though, so I'm turning in. Good night."

"Good night."

I get ready for bed, but it feels impossible to fall asleep with so much on my mind with the anticipation that tomorrow brings. I close my eyes, though, and let my mind drift away to the city where my heart still lives.

———

ALLISON WAS sweet enough to show up early and help me carry my bags to the car this morning. Tiptoeing downstairs, she whispers, "I need coffee."

"We need to get out of here. We'll get it on the plane."

"I made coffee." Carter's voice causes me to scream and almost fall down the stairs. "Holy—"

Allison slips on a step but catches herself by grabbing the railing. "What the hell are you doing?" she gripes. "Trying to give us heart attacks?"

With him standing at the door, I drop my gaze to the suitcase on the floor beside him. *Oh no.* It's too early to concoct a plan, but I still try my hardest. "It's so nice of you to see us off."

"I'm coming," he says, leaving no room to argue. "You can have your girls' trip, but when it's over, I'll be spending time with my fiancée."

"We still need to discuss that—"

"Coffee is in the kitchen, but we should get a move on." He walks out the door, leaving it wide open for the cold to come in. I'm seeing a trend of dramatic exits when it comes to him.

I look back at Allison, who's irritated with pursed lips and anger darkening her usually wide eyes. "I'm not drinking it. I don't trust him," she says.

"What about the trip? What do we do?"

"Do we have a choice?"

I reach the bottom step and look out the door. He's already climbing in the back of a rideshare he must have called. "Doesn't look like it."

We stand there debating what to do for too long. If we don't leave, we're going to miss our flight.

Huffing, I say, "Whatever. We'll just let him work, and we can do our own thing."

She heads outside, and I follow, closing the door behind us. In the SUV, Carter is tucked in the second row, leaving Allison to climb over him to get to the third row. He might have won this battle, but he won't win the war. I won't let him, and I'm taking this trip to set the record straight with him once and for all.

We aren't engaged.

We aren't even friends.

We won't be.

Ever.

I will do everything I can to get him removed from the company if he decides to fight me on this. There's no way I'll live trying to guess what he's capable of when I can choose to live in peace and love with Loch.

My phone vibrates in my back pocket before I climb into the vehicle. When I pull it out, I see Loch has sent an address of where to go once we arrive at the airport. I knew I had nothing to worry about. He always takes care of me.

Less than an hour later, the SUV turns into an entrance to the airport, and Carter says, "This is the private jets." Since I chose to sit next to Allison, he turns around. "Spending this kind of money is ridiculous. The company better not be paying for it."

Searching outside the window for confirmation because I missed the sign he referenced. But I quickly see what he means when I spot a few smaller private jets parked ahead of larger planes, which is confirmation enough to realize that Loch got us our own plane. He spoils me rotten and will get a big thank-you next time I see him.

Apparently, that will be sooner rather than later.

My heart skips a beat when I see him standing on the tarmac and looking as handsome as ever. As soon as the vehicle stops, I open the door and run to him. His grin tells me everything I need to know. *He loves me as much as I love him.*

I'm about to throw myself into his arms when I hear Carter say, "You must be the porter. Our luggage is in the back."

Oh shit. Loch's eyes harden as he looks over my shoulder. When his gaze returns to me, he says, "Let me guess, your boyfriend?"

The devastation of my past decisions drops to the pit of my stomach. "Worse."

I see the wreckage of realization entering his warm eyes and turning them cold. "Don't tell me you're married."

"Engaged."

"Engaged." He grins. "We can handle that."

Carter walks up the stairs and then calls back. "Come on, darling," he says, laying the love stuff on thick. "Let the man do his job." *I hate him.*

With my eyes never leaving Loch, I beg. "I'm so sorry. I'll clear this up as soon as we're on the plane." As much as I want to kiss him, to hug him like I always do, I turn to the plane, still uncertain of Carter's intentions. I know they're bad, but what he's capable of is still an outlier.

Loch catches my hand and kisses it. "Not if it will jeopardize the trip."

"I can't promise that it won't. I don't know what kind of pact I've made with him, but it's ending very soon."

Loch's gaze reaches the early dawn, and he stares into the sunrise in the distance before he turns back to me and winks. "This should be fun."

36

Loch

THIS IS FUN.

This Carter guy is oblivious to who I am. As much as it's tempting to flip into caveman mode and claim Tuesday as mine, it'll be fun to fuck with him.

Am I her friend?

A guy she's dating?

Work for the airline?

He has no fucking clue, and it's glorious to be in the power position.

I've encountered plenty of assholes who think they're smarter and better than I am—from prosecutors to random guys scared to lose their girlfriends when I'm around. I'm not blind. I know I'm an attractive man. *Fuck, look at Tuesday.* The woman is drop-dead gorgeous, and she looks at me like she's the lucky one.

How does that make sense in any universe?

She doesn't see herself clearly, but I do. She's so much more than a pretty face. She's sweet to the point that people will try to take advantage of her. Trusting when she prob-ably shouldn't be after all she's been through. *Smart.* So fucking smart that I know whatever she sets her mind to, she'll achieve. And whether I deserve it or not, she's loving. Openheartedly, she loves me without conditions, taking care of me when she'd have every right to be selfish, considering what's going on in her life right now.

Inside and out, the woman is nothing less than spectacu-lar. And I'm the lucky bastard who gets to be with her.

So the last thing that's going to happen is this jerk-off taking her from me. Fine, I went a little caveman. Staring me down like he can intimidate me is a joke. If he keeps it up, his ego will get his ass kicked. I take another drink of orange juice and glare at him.

Tuesday comes down the short aisle of the jet wearing pajama pants, a T-shirt, and a baggie hoodie. She makes it hard to take my eyes off her even when she buries her body under layers of clothes.

As cute as she looks, there's a reason I've never given her pajamas. Naked is my preference for her when she's in bed with me. Funny that I didn't even notice what she wore when she hopped out of the SUV. I only saw that beautiful mouth of hers smiling for me.

An hour after our reunion, she drops into the seat next to me after sitting with Allison since we took off. I'm happy to have her back. "How are we playing this situation?" I ask, stealing a glimpse of her eyes.

"Truthfully, I'm not sure how I should be playing it. What do you think?"

"Is he useful for knowledge?"

She bends her knees and wraps her arms around her legs, resolve forcing a sigh from her. "I'm afraid so. After chatting with Allison, he has information that I need."

"Like?"

Leaning closer, she looks around to see if we have privacy. Allison is still in the backseat with her legs spread across another while Carter has been keeping his head down for the most part, except for the occasional staring contest he has with me. "You ready for this?"

"If it's about you having sex with anyone else, I'm not."

"It's about him having sex with someone else . . . *on our wedding day*."

My gaze shoots up to look at the fucker. "He did not fuck another girl on your wedding day."

She shrugs. "He did."

"I should go thank him for fucking up the best thing he ever had."

Laughing, she elbows me. "You're ridiculous, you know that?"

I nudge her gently right back. "I actually do know that."

She goes on to say, "I left him at the altar, so that was his karma. But there's more to the story. "

My gaze shoots to her, not giving a damn if he sees me staring at her anymore. She's worth it. "Whoa. Back up. You left him at the altar?"

No remorse is found when a slight grin wriggles onto her face. "So I hear."

I fucking love her. "You naughty girl."

She takes a ragged breath as she wiggles in the chair. "We need to stay focused, and you calling me a naughty or good girl won't help."

"What happens if we don't stay focused?"

A laugh escapes her pretty, pouty lips, and she rolls her eyes. *There's my girl.* "You get laid, and I don't get any answers."

"I'm not seeing the problem with the first part."

Her elbow finds my bicep much harder this time. Fortunately, assface isn't watching. There's no way we don't look like we're fucking. She says, "Be serious, babe."

"Who said I wasn't?" This time, I'm quicker than she is, moving out of her reach, and chuckle. "I'm kidding. Kind of . . ." I lean over again. "What did you tell him about me?"

"Nothing. He doesn't know about us yet."

"We can show him." The plane is loud enough to keep anyone outside of the two of us from hearing, so why hold back? Let's taunt the fucker who's now glaring at us again.

"You're so bad, Loch."

"But so good that you can't resist me."

"No lie told." Her gaze slips across the jet to this guy claiming to be her fiancé. I'm calling bullshit that it was reciprocal. If she loved him, it was in another lifetime, not the one she's living now. So no stakes are being claimed other than mine. She says, "He still doesn't know I have amnesia."

My eyebrows shoot to the top of the aircraft. "How'd you manage to pull that off?"

"We've barely spoken, and when we do, I'm the last topic he seems interested in discussing."

"Could have fooled me by how his eyes are glued to you."

She angles toward me, but I notice she restrains every part of her body from touching me. *Fucking sucks.* She says, "I didn't expect to see you."

I trust her. I have no reason not to. So maybe it was a mistake to come with her. "It's not fair for me to be here, but living without you is the worst."

"I'm glad you came." She rests her hand on my arm, but I see how she glances across the plane at him. That I've put her in a position to walk this precarious line between Carter and me makes me feel like shit. It also angers me because she should never have to do that. "I never in my wildest dreams thought you'd be here. I love that you are because I know the sacrifice you're making."

"It's not a sacrifice. This is where I want to be."

Her hand slips away too soon and lands on her lap. Resting back, she briefly closes her eyes before rolling her head my way. "And I want you here, Loch."

I nod. Her lids hang heavy, and her smile is slight, but she's no less beautiful. "I'll be here as long as you need me. Now get some rest. I have a feeling you'll need your energy once we land."

Closing her eyes, she grins as if the image behind her lids is too good not to. "Don't worry. I'll save some for you."

This woman . . . She's the gift that keeps giving. That's my whole fucking heart right there. "I'll make sure to burn through every last ounce of it."

"Promise?" she whispers, exhaustion seeming to kick in.

"I promise."

"How is he so hot?" Tuesday's voice ribbons through my consciousness, pulling me from sleep.

"I bet the sex is incredible," Allison whispers loud enough for me to hear. "He's so, *mmm*, deliciously big. Big hands. Big, broad shoulders. Big feet." She giggles.

Amusing, but I keep my eyes closed to see how Tuesday responds. She moans, and it goes straight to my pants. "Yep, big everything. If you only knew the half of it."

"If I knew the half of it, I wouldn't be able to walk in the morning. I have to say I'm jealous, girl, but I'm also happy that someone here is having *big* experiences." Allison laughs again.

As entertaining as it is to hear their private conversation about me, I open my eyes, revealing I'm awake. The two of them are quick to point at a photo in the album on Tuesday's lap like they weren't just ogling me. Tuesday asks, "Did I like my job in marketing?"

"Hey," I say, my voice still groggy.

She looks up from the seat across from me. "Hi, sleepyhead. I never knew anyone could sleep so deeply on a flight, but then again, I don't remember either. Looks like you got some needed rest."

"I did." I sit up and stretch my back. "Did you?"

"A little."

Glancing out the window, I ask, "How long until we land?"

"Less than an hour."

I grab a bottle of water from my cup holder and down half. Looking up, I catch Carter's eyes still on me. There's less anger in them than before, but I'm not sure what's changed. I still won't let my guard down with him.

Deciding to stretch my legs, I get up and walk to the back of the plane and then to the front, stopping to look out the emergency door's window. Not sure why I'm relieved that we're over land when we could crash there just as we could in the ocean.

"So you're not the porter?"

I stand and turn, coming toe-to-toe with the enemy. He thinks I can't see who he really is—insecure little rich boy. This coming from being a rich kid myself. Insecure . . . not so much, though. I spent years disproving the people who think I live off handouts. I had an in with the law firm, but I could have gone to work anywhere after graduating top in my class. I've made my own fortune from hard work and solid investments.

This guy ... I'd be shocked if he's worked a full day in his life. He looks weak, and he's definitely spineless.

Crossing my arms over my chest, I reply, "No. I'm not the porter."

"Do you own the jet?"

"I have no need to own a jet, but I paid for the trip."

He glances over his shoulder to the ladies, who are currently looking very nervous that Carter and I are talking. He turns back, and asks, "Why?"

"Because Tu—Céline needed to get to Europe."

"She tells you to jump, and you ask how high?" He chuckles under his breath. "Now I know why she keeps you around."

"You don't know shit." Smirking, I lower my arms to my sides, trying to keep myself from popping him in that smarmy grin of his. "Trust me when I tell you that's not why she keeps me around."

"I've met plenty of guys like you. You meet a pretty girl and suddenly get a little possessive. Surely, you realize that Céline and I are engaged." Reaching over, he flicks the collar of my shirt.

Fuck his engagement to Céline. I jerk my shoulder back and lower my voice. "Touch me again, and you'll lose that fucking hand."

"Okay. Okay," he mocks, throwing his hands up in surrender. "Settle down."

Is he fucking with me? "Don't tell me to settle down. You came over here for a reason. Get to your fucking point, and then move the fuck away from me."

"What's in this for you? You want money? Fine, I'll write you a check, and you can drop us off and be on your merry way, sport."

He's stupid enough to laugh at me.

Though it won't be painless, I'll make it quick.

"I'VE NEVER SEEN anyone go down that fast," I say, still surprised that's all it took. "Out cold with one little hit."

Tuesday glares up at me. "Little?"

I shrug. "It's not like I was using my full strength or anything. It wasn't much more than a tap."

"Loch," she cautions while pressing an ice pack found in the fridge to the right side of his face. *It's not my fault he didn't heed my warning.*

Even so, the last thing I need to be doing is making her feel sorry for the fucker. "I'll wait over here." I sit in the seat I've occupied most of the flight and watch as Carter starts to come to again.

Allison and Tuesday help him to his feet and walk him over to sit across from me. *Why?* I have no fucking idea, but I've already decided that I need to play nice. When he covers her hand over the ice pack and looks at her like she's not my whole world, but his, I restrain the urge to pummel him.

Allison moves the photo album and is quick to sit next to him. She hands the book to Tuesday, who retreats next to me, resting it on her lap. "He said he won't press charges, but there are conditions."

"Why are you speaking for him?"

"I'm not. I'm just relaying his terms."

"I don't give a fuck about his terms and conditions. He needs to learn respect for others." She stares at me like we've never met, like I'm the adversary. I push up and head for the lavatory. I look back and see them talking, intensity exchanged between them. "Fuck."

Before I can shut the door, a hand stops it from closing. "Loch?"

I release the handle. Tuesday slips inside and closes the door behind her and locks it. A good few seconds pass while I wait to hear her side of things, but the words don't come. She slides her hands under my shirt, lifts up on her toes, and kisses me instead.

This isn't how we handle our issues, but when her hand starts undoing my pants, I realize it's not only desire driving her to kiss me like we won't get another chance. It's need.

The rest of the world can wait. We *need* this connection to each other.

As we pull back, our eyes latch onto each other's, our breath hot and heavy in the tight quarters. I cup her face and kiss her gently. When I open my eyes, her lids slowly open, and I say, "Take off your pants."

I move back and lean against the sink, giving her space. Her hair's a mess, eyes wild, and her breathing shallows as she stares into my eyes. But then she unties the drawstring and pulls her thong down with the flannel bottoms. Stepping out of them, she stays in place. Coming closer, I unzip the hoodie and hang it from the handle of a cabinet. Then I lift the bottom of her shirt, taking her in. "Sit here."

She does as she's told, sitting on the small bench under the window. I kneel before her, taking each leg and placing them over my shoulders.

"Loch—"

"Sh." I lick my lips and bend down. I kiss her once and then again, lingering and dragging my teeth lightly over her lips. Peeking up at her, I say, "I'm going to make you feel so good, baby. I promise."

With a short gasp, she sucks in her bottom lip and pins it with her teeth. With my eyes set on her, I dip my tongue out and drag it through her sweetness. She bucks against me, and that's when I know I have her right where I want her. Diving in, I caress her clit with my lips and then give the gentlest of nips with my teeth.

Noise on a plane isn't the issue since she's competing with the engines, but when she can't sit still, I rest a hand on her lower stomach and start fucking her with my tongue.

With her, everything is better, sweeter, wetter. I crave the feel of her wrapped around my erection, but this isn't about me. It's about making her feel better—not just sexually but releasing the tension to tackle what's ahead.

She squirms under my hand as I circle her bud and use my fingers to encourage her orgasm. "Such a good girl," I say, then hum against her. Her body vibrates in response. But when she slides her hands into my hair and pulls, I know she's getting close. I can handle the pain, but her reactions to me, the way everything I do causes a jerk of momentum and a moan escaping—*Fuck*.

Latching onto her pussy with my mouth, I fuck her with my fingers and see my release through until she's coming with me. With my eyes closed, I roll my head to the side, resting on the crook of her thigh. I know the outside world waits for us, but I just need a few more minutes to regain my composure.

Her fingers stroke through my hair until she finally catches her breath. "Did you come?" she asks.

"I don't want to talk about it." I lift to my knees, well aware that I just came like a fucking teenager. I kiss her mouth and then expose her collarbone by moving the shirt aside. I kiss there too, wishing we had more time and room for me to kiss her everywhere.

The softest of laughter rolls through her. "It's okay, you know. It's only natural."

I'm still shocked he didn't come and bang on the door while I was claiming his "fiancée" with my mouth. "Yeah. Yeah."

With an exhale, I stand and help her to her feet. Holding her around the waist, I kiss her again and then the side of her head. "I love you."

"I love you, too," she whispers, clinging to me around my middle. With her head pressed to my chest, she stifles a sob.

What just happened? Rubbing her back, I bend to make eye contact. "What's wrong, baby?"

"I have to marry Carter."

What the fuck?

37

Tuesday

"No FUCKING way will I let that happen." Loch's eyes have darkened, his hold on me tightening. I still don't hold an ounce of fear with him. This man would protect me to the ends of the earth and beyond.

A tear slips from my eye, and I look down to wipe it away. I'm so frustrated because I'm heading to France with the man I love. I deserve to enjoy it. I'm about to see my parents, people I know love and care about me. And hopefully, this trip will lead to my memory returning or at least help me make sense of everything.

I should be happy . . .

But as soon as Loch got up from his seat, Carter dropped the bomb I knew he'd been waiting to detonate since I showed up at the house. *"You will lose everything, Céline. Dump the loser and get back on board with our arrangement."*

What arrangement?

I wanted to handle him myself, never wanting to worry Loch. But this is getting out of hand so quickly. Loch sits down because if he doesn't, he'll be bolting out the door to find Carter. And if death had a stare, he's mastered it. This isn't the slick attorney skilled at hiding his emotions. No, this is a man whose world has been threatened. "Tell me exactly what he said, Tuesday."

"Carter said he wanted to make it official while we're here. That I have to marry him or else."

Caught after the raw pleasure I was seeking and the temporary escape Loch afforded me, I feel exposed in the aftermath of what we just did. I slip my pants back on, hating that Carter stole our moment and that he's still in my head, ruining each and every one after.

Loch pulls me close, holding me around the top of my legs, and asks, "Or else what?" The warmth of his eyes lit with the desire we shared while anger tinges the outer edges.

I'm feeling the same, caught between warring emotions. "He didn't say, but it was assumed that I already knew. I just wish I could remember." It's absurd to walk a line between two lives but have solid footing only on one side. "I hate this. I hate feeling trapped by his threats. Are they empty, or does he really have something on me?"

Standing up, he cups my face. "Doesn't matter. You're not marrying him."

"I'm *not* marrying him. Whatever it is he has over me, I'll find a way out."

"We will. Together."

"He still thinks I'm Céline and cheating on him. I can tell that makes him anxious about everything working out. What do I do?"

"Watch your back and your front." His hands slide to my shoulders, and he lightly massages. "If he'll threaten you into marriage, he's not above hurting you in other ways."

I embrace him again, breathing him in, his strength and belief in me. "I don't think he'd hurt me. He could have done it already if that's what he intended."

With his chin resting on my head, he nods. "Why do you think marriage is his end goal?"

I've had so many thoughts over the past twenty-four hours about this, but the one I keep coming back to is the most obvious, if not the simplest. "I don't think I'm anything more than comfortable. He's used to me."

The pilot comes over the intercom, telling us to take our seats and buckle in. "It's about to get bumpy."

Little did we know, *it already had.*

HIDDEN behind the tall cypress lining the road, the château comes into view surrounded by sleeping olive groves lining the hills and fields. Even though it's winter, the estate is more breathtaking than the photo could ever show.

I bet it's even more incredible in fall when the olives are ripe with leaves and fruit hanging from the branches. I don't know anything about olives, so how do I know that? Hope blooms inside me as I realize that's a memory coming back, and we haven't even been dropped off yet.

We reach the château and climb out. The front door swings open while we unload the suitcases. A woman I recognize as an older version of myself says, "Welcome." My heart stops still in my chest, knowing that's her. That's my mom. The moment she lays eyes on me, she hurries toward me with arms wide open and wraps me in her embrace. "Céline, my beautiful daughter."

My throat thickens as my body caves to her. I'm not sure if it's her perfume or the comfort of the hug, but she's so familiar that I close my eyes to take in every second I share with her.

I have no idea why I expected a French accent, and there are tinges of one heard, like when you spend too much time someplace and adapt to the surroundings.

She leans back and lifts my chin. "How are you?"

My heart beats harder as my eyes water. I want to tell her everything and wish I could be honest and not lie because of Carter. I raise my chin. I have a feeling it's something she taught me. "I'm happy to see you." *So happy.*

"I'm happy to see you, too, darling." She spies Allison and moves to kiss each of her cheeks like an old friend. "So good to see you, dear." I see the moment her eyes find Loch . . . *and then Carter*. She fails to hide the distinctive difference between smiling and not smiling, but she's quick to right her expression.

"This is my friend," I say, "Loch Westcott."

"It's a pleasure to meet you, Mr. Westcott. I'm Sofie Schroder." When she lifts to give her customary greeting, he meets her halfway. "Will you be staying with us as well?"

The brown of his eyes is brighter under the midday winter's sun, an amber coloring them when he replies, "I will. Thank you for having me."

She's as charming as I imagined, but I can't wait to see if it carries when she greets Carter. Where does he stand in my parents' eyes?

My mom says, "Hello," and then turns and starts for the door. That's it. I approve. He won't win with any of us, especially when we stand together. I have hope that whatever he's holding over me can be overcome, especially here where he'll receive no sympathy. She adds, "We should get out of the cold air."

When Carter passes me, effectively cutting me off from

walking with my mom, he leans toward my ear, and whispers, "It's time to play your part." He leaves me standing on the steps, struck by how bold he's become about his demands. I'm not sure what role I'm supposed to play, so the laugh's on him.

"Hey!" Allison gripes when he bumps her out of his way to get inside. "Asshole," she mutters, leaving space behind him before she continues up the steps.

I linger behind, hoping to steal a free moment with Loch before we go inside and continue this charade. Loch takes my bag from me just as a man comes around and tells us he'll take care of the suitcases.

I'm fired up from that encounter with Carter. Patting Loch on the chest, I whisper, "No marriage is ever going to take place."

"No marriage ever?"

His tone catches me off guard. Not sure how he manages to sound shocked, firm, and worried all at the same time, but he does. It's his expression, though—parted lips that make me want to kiss him, lids narrowed, and those little lines at the sides of his eyes that have me reaching up to soothe them—that has me craving his closeness. Then I realize how that sounded. "Not ever. Just *not* to him."

With Loch, warnings of rushing into marriage would be thrown out the window. I'd marry Loch in a heartbeat. There's nothing I wouldn't do for him. There's nothing I wouldn't do to be with him forever. "I love you," I whisper.

"I love you, too." His words cover me, warming me inside and out.

"There appears," my mother starts, causing us to jump apart like teenagers caught making out, "to be a few things to discuss."

My cheeks heat, and I glance at Loch. When my gaze

returns to her, I grin, unable to stop myself as happiness from having both in my life runs through me. I hurry up the steps, taking her by the hands in my excitement. "There's so much I want to share with you."

"I can't wait." Turning to Loch, she asks, "Are you the reason my daughter's glowing?"

My heart skips a beat when I hear him reply, "I sure hope so."

"I'LL NEVER FORGET THAT DAY," my mom says, leaning against my dad with a glass of wine in her hand. "All plans flew out the window when it came to your birth. You even arrived three days early. I was in the middle of my regular weekly hair appointment when my water broke."

A round of laughter lightens the dark-paneled room. I'm already feeling the best I have since leaving Manhattan. It's been a whirlwind twenty-four hours with so many highs and lows. I needed this time with my friend, Loch, and my parents.

After arriving, I finally reunited with my dad. He choked up when he saw me like my mom, which brought tears to my eyes. Their love extends beyond hugs but is felt even now in the downtime.

My grandfather is a harder nut to crack. We hugged, but after, he was staring into my eyes as if he can tell something has changed. *Everything has changed*, but I'll continue to protect my secrets—*for now*.

He went to bed early but said he'd like to spend some time together. I would, too.

Sitting near my dad, Loch leans back in a leather chair. He's too far for my liking since I choose to warm up by the fire. With his eyes set on mine, he asks, "What day of the week was she born?"

"Tuesday. I had my hair appointments at ten in the morning for about two years."

My dad adds, "She was always a little firecracker, keeping us on our feet."

"I can believe that." Loch chuckles. "Tuesday."

I look up, our eyes finding each other's again. "Yes?"

His grin widens. "Isn't it interesting that you were born on a Tuesday? Have any stories to share, Dane?"

"She'd kill me," my dad replies. Looking at me, he says, "I like this guy."

So caught up in their reminiscence that I didn't catch that huge detail until Loch spells it out for me. I stand in declaration. "I was born on a Tuesday."

Allison says, "That explains some things."

Tuesday is such a unique choice, a name that made no sense when I was in the hospital or even after. Now, I love it even more to know it plays a part in my past story and my present. I start for Loch. "I was born on a Tuesday."

It's so tempting to settle in his lap and be a couple without worries and thoughts of how complicated this whole situation is. I'm trying not to care, to just stay in this moment with him.

But right when I reach him, I hear, "What are we talking about?" *Ugh.* My eyes find Carter in the doorway, making me wonder how long he's been standing there. I thought I had more time with the people I care about before we'd have the misfortune of his company again.

The lightheartedness of the room's mood has disappeared with his presence. When no one responds, he says, "Please excuse my fiancée. We're going for a walk before dinner."

Loch says, "It's dark out."

"She's a big girl. I think she'll be okay."

"I *think*," he says, "doesn't work for me."

Before this becomes a bigger scene, one that could end up with Loch in jail, I touch his shoulder. "It's fine. I have some things to say to him as well."

"Don't you think daylight would be a better time for that?"

I appreciate him wanting to protect me, but so much seems to lie in Carter's hands that I don't want to drag this out. I'm ready to end it tonight and focus on the reason I came here. I say, "I won't be long."

I also won't feed Carter's ego and make every conversation into a big deal. He's probably just pissy that we're having fun without him.

I pass through the grand living room, hearing his steps behind me, and cross into a conservatory I saw earlier on a short tour. The rich architecture and art in each room makes it easy to understand why this place makes me happy. Although I never felt like a traditionalist, this house is steeped in history. There's so much more to it than just ornate furnishings. It has a heart that beats and a soul that soothes.

He closes the door behind me and then stands in front of it, giving me no out. "What is wrong with you?" he asks, staring at me.

Does he know? How would he know? *He couldn't.* "What do you mean?" I sit on the arm of a sofa and stare at him.

"What are you trying to do? Ruin everything? I keep my fucks hidden from view, but you decide to parade yours around? That's not the deal we made, Céline." I really dislike how he says my name like it resides in the gutter beneath him. Crossing the room, he stands in front of a large pane of glass. It's too dark to see outside, so I'm thinking he's staring at his reflection. How very Carter of him.

"Refresh my memory on this arrangement."

He side-eyes me over his shoulder. "Memory lapse, huh?"

"I've forgotten the details."

"Obviously." His eyes return to the window. "Céline, you know we didn't begin this with love at the forefront, but we always got along well enough to stick it out. It only made sense considering the families we come from."

"So we keep doing this for the money? That's it?" I look down disappointed in myself for being so shallow before. "To keep it for ourselves?"

This time he turns back, perplexity shaping his face with tight lips and matching eyes. "Are you feeling all right?"

"Fine. Why?"

He stares at me for a good long time, making me more uncomfortable than I usually am in his presence. Searching my eyes, he asks, "What were you doing in New York?"

I get whiplash from the sudden change in conversation. But then Allison's words come back to me, *"He loves playing mental games . . ."* He just took his turn. It's time to make my own move. "How did you know I was in New York?"

A chuckle on the lighter side escapes him, and he briefly rubs his temple. The actions don't match, keeping me on guard with him. "If it was a secret, blame Allison. You know she can't keep her mouth shut."

I laugh to humor him but circle back again. "If we were married, we'd get everything eventually. That's our motives?"

"Motives?" He scoffs. "Interesting choice of words. We

used to say goals. The combination of wealth would be immense."

"Not everything is about money. Love, for instance."

With his hands cupped before him in some kind of imploring anger, he says, "I don't know why you're acting so different. I'm trying to help you."

"What do you want from me, Carter? Surely, it's not just a marriage arrangement for wealth."

Dropping his hands to his sides, he comes closer. "I've tried to protect you, to give you a way out."

"A way out of what? Happiness?"

He closes his eyes and scrubs his fingers over his forehead. When he looks at me again, he asks, "Why must you always fight me every step of the way? We could have a good life together, Céline."

"I'm in love with Loch." I don't move, not an inch. What more can I say or do anyway? *The ball is in his court.*

"You're willing to risk everything . . . for him?"

I take a calming breath, desperate to keep things controlled when he could so easily fly off the handle over this. "Don't you want to be with someone you love?"

"I love you. You used to love me, too." I still wonder, not convinced because he tells me so. The emotion has escaped his tone as well. It's too calculated. "I think we've done enough damage tonight. Maybe things will look better tomorrow."

"I won't stop loving Loch overnight. I don't think I ever could. He means too much to me."

His gaze travels between my eyes as if he'll find the lie he needs to justify his actions. The thing is, he'll find it because the truth is more powerful than his threats.

"More than a half billion dollars means to you?"

"Yes." There's no doubt in my mind that what I have with Loch is more valuable.

Nodding, he takes a deep inhale through his nose and then slowly exhales. "You're a fool." He takes another pregnant pause, staring at me like he's looking at a stranger he doesn't want to meet. "If we're no longer going to be together, then we need to figure out what to tell people. Maybe put out a joint statement?"

"Seems excessive."

"It's as if you've forgotten who you are."

"Maybe. But I've finally discovered who I want to be."

A smile appears as his shoulders ease from the weight of the burden of our relationship lifting from his sharp features. "Hey, we should go on one last ride tomorrow. Like old times? You always did love riding horses early in the morning before the fog lifted. We can go to the lake like we used to. It's not been cold enough to freeze over."

I ride horses?

Continuing, he starts for the door, "I'll draft that statement up to end speculation and bring it with me in the morning. We can post it by lunch."

So this is how things are done these days? Public joint statements for social media? "Sounds good, but what happens after that?"

"We go our separate ways."

38

Loch

"I'M NOT INTO ROLE-PLAY, but damn, get that fine ass over here."

Tuesday bends to adjust her riding boots. When she stands, she runs her hands over her hips. *The tease.* "Not bad if I do say so myself."

Fuck me.

I'm hard, and she's leaving. *Not fair.* "Not bad at all. Sure you won't stay? I have something much more fun to ride." She bursts out laughing. My ego isn't weak. I rub over my dick, and say, "There's nothing funny about this hard-on, baby."

With the doors on the antique wardrobe open, she says, "Who knew I was into riding?" referencing the equestrian outfits hanging neatly inside.

"Are you sure you know how to ride horses?"

"Why would I have all these clothes if I didn't?" She turns to check out her fine ass in the mirror. "I look cute."

"You look more than cute, Tues." I tuck my hands

behind my head and watch as she pulls her low ponytail tight before putting on her helmet. "At least your head is protected."

"I could have used this when I was mugged."

"Speaking of . . ." Looking at me in the reflection of the mirror over the dresser, she says, "I hate to even bring it up, but any news from the investigator?"

"No. Have you checked in with the detective lately?"

She comes to me and sits on the edge of the bed. "I haven't. The past few days have been a whirlwind." Looking toward the window where the sunrise has just broken above the sill, she adds, "I feel discouraged after talking to them, so I've been putting it off, but I should probably call today."

"Maybe the investigator will dig up something new again soon. He only has the one case while the police are backlogged."

I sit up, grab her, and fall with her in my arms. Kissing her through her squeals of laughter, I realize if I ever had a weakness, she's it. I tap her nose, and say, "Don't get discouraged. We're making progress. That's what counts."

"True." Her blue eyes are happy, and even in the dimmer, overcast morning, they're bright for me. "Did you mess up my hair?"

I study her, all of her, and then smirk. "Maybe."

Smacking me on the chest, she pushes off. "What am I going to do with you?"

"I've already made you a good offer for what you can do with me, but if you want to negotiate, I'm open to a counter."

She giggles and returns to the mirror again to adjust her outfit and helmet. "How about this? We'll skip lunch, and I'll let you eat me instead?"

"So fucking naughty." I rub my thumb over my bottom lip, approving of the direction of this negotiation. "It's an attractive proposition. *Very* attractive indeed," I say, eyeing her tight little body. "But what's in it for me?"

Coming over, she leans down. I think she's going in for a kiss, but she detours to my ear, and whispers, "I promise to make it worth your while."

I grab her, about to pull her onto the mattress, but she's just fixed her hair again. Chuckling, I kiss her and then say, "Deal."

"I knew we could come together on this."

"So fucking dirty."

She kisses my cheek and then takes the lobe of my ear between her teeth and nipping. Whispering again, she says, "You like it that way."

"You're not helping this erection. In fact, you're making it harder than ever to deal with."

Innocence shapes her eyes and smile. "I'm sorry. Kind of ..." She laughs. "I really will make it up to you." Tapping me on the nose this time, she says, "I promise."

"I'm holding you to that."

"I hope so." A shadow casts her eyes that held happiness not even a moment prior, and she says, "Can I talk to you about something that's been on my mind?"

"Always."

"Last night, Carter told me how Allison shared that I'd been in New York."

"And that's something you've shared with her?"

"Yes. I've told her almost everything, anything worth sharing. I trusted her." She sighs, looking down at her lap and fidgeting fingers. When she looks at me again, she whispers, "I don't know how to feel about her now. Why would she tell him anything about me when she knows I don't want him to know?"

Dragging my fingers down her back, I rub her spine

along the way. "I don't know. Is it something you feel comfortable talking to her about?"

"I guess I'll have to. It just . . . it sort of feels like a violation of the trust I thought we'd established."

"I can understand that, but before you concern yourself even more, you should address the issue with her directly. Maybe it slipped out accidentally, or there was a misunderstanding."

A small smile returns to her face, and she leans down to kiss me. "You're right, counselor. Instead of overthinking this, I'll just ask her about it." Standing, she says, "I need to go. I'm ready to get this over with." She crosses the room to leave. "I'll see you later, babe."

Just before she closes the door behind her, I call, "Hey?" I'm given that spectacular smile of hers that I'm used to as she leans on the door. "Always remember I love you."

"I could never forget. My heart wouldn't let me. I love you, Loch."

It's still early, barely seven, so when she closes the door, I roll to the side and close my eyes to try for more sleep.

"MORNING."

I set the coffee pot back on the warmer and turn to find Allison sitting at a table where the sun floods in. As she sips from a mug, she reads the magazine open in front of her. I reply, "Good morning." Recalling the conversation with Tuesday earlier, I decide to get a better feel for her friend. *Best* friend is what I've been told. I sit down but direct my gaze out the window. "Pretty day."

"A little chilly but not too bad." Her eyes stay directed through the French doors. "C tells me you're an attorney."

She laughs to herself. "Tuesday. It's going to be hard to make the change."

"She wouldn't be bothered. She understands it's difficult for others." I take a sip of coffee. "Especially when you've known her your whole life."

"Most of it. The years that matter." She closes the fashion magazine and says, "She speaks highly of you." It's not a question I need to address. "Do you mind me asking what your plan is?"

Plan? She wouldn't be a friend if she didn't look out for her. "I don't have a plan. Like her, I'm taking the days as they come right now."

"How do you imagine your future with her? Are you going to ask her to move to New York?"

Chuckling, I look at her. Her eyes with another thousand questions waiting to be asked and her hair like fire in the morning sunlight. Her striking features don't distract from the information she's trying to extract. "My place is hers, but Tuesday will do as she wants. She'll decide where she wants to live, and I'll support that."

"Even if it's not with you in the city?"

I'd hate it. It would gut me five times over. "If it makes her happy."

"She loves you very much. It's good to see her this happy and in love." She spins her mug around in her hands, the ceramic bottom grating against the mottled wood. "We're going to a vineyard in the area for a wine tasting later. Would you like to come?"

Nothing suspicious is seen in her eyes. She seems quite genuine. "Unless you hate wine, of course," she quickly adds.

"No, wine is fine—"

"And it rhymes." She giggles, even snorting a little.

Her quirkiness is entertaining. "I'm in. Thanks for asking."

"Of course. If C—if Tuesday loves you, that's all I need to know. Her mom and dad are also going."

Though I'm not sure if this is my place to ask, it might be a good time to get her take on talking to Carter about Tuesday being in the city. "I—"

"Where is she—"

A ring from my pocket cuts both of us off. I pull it out to see *John - Private Eyes of New York* flash on the screen. "I need to take this. I'll be right back." I answer as I walk outside into the cold for privacy. "What do you have for me, John?"

"Carter Bingham's family cut off his finances two years ago," he replies, all business. "It seems the Bingham boy developed an allergy to work, and his family decided he needed to make his own way."

None of this surprises me. "Connect the dots."

"Céline got him hired on with her family's company, probably the biggest mistake they could have made."

The cold seeps through my sweater, so I start to pace to warm up. "Why?"

"He has full access to the financials. He's been busy moving money around to different accounts for the past two years. I'm assuming they're oblivious to the twenty million in an offshore account in the Bahamas and the ten million collecting interest in Switzerland."

"Fuck." I drop my head, spreading my clenched brow apart. "He's embezzling from her family?"

"To a level that's shocking. They must trust him something good for him to get away with it for this long and no one notice. Or," he says, "they're so dirty rich that they don't miss thirty million from their bank accounts. It's some nice money."

"Sure is."

"You might want to sit down for the next part."

Looking back into the kitchen, I find Allison at the table. Tuesday's mom has joined her with a cup of coffee. They're sharing something funny because the laughter slips through the cracks of the door. "I'm standing. Hit me with it anyway."

"Guess who's listed as her beneficiary."

"Better not be Carter fucking Bingham."

"Bingo," he says. "Sole beneficiary of the entire Schroder fortune."

I look out over the grove, wondering how far they rode this morning. "She would have never agreed to that. Not as Tuesday or Céline. No fucking way."

"He could have forged the signature and paid someone to notarize it. It's easy to get it done for the right price." There's a slight pause before he exhales. "I wouldn't leave them alone, though. No telling what he'd do."

Fuck. "I have to go." I hang up as I rush back inside, startling the women. "Where would they ride?"

Sofie asks, "What are you talking about?"

"Riding horses."

Allison balks. "Who are you talking about?"

My patience thins as the words rush from my throat. "Carter and Tuesday—Céline. Whatever. Where do they go riding when they ride horses on the property?"

Allison's face drains of color, and she stands, the chair left skidding behind her against the rustic floor tiles. "What are you talking about, Loch? She wouldn't go riding."

Alarmed panic infiltrates Sofie's eyes as her hands tremble, the teacup chiming against the small plate. "Not after the accident."

"What accident?" I grip the wood backing of the chair.

Her mom says, "She fell off a horse a few years ago and broke her arm. She's not been on or near one since."

Allison rushes to me. "She's terrified of them." Tears flood her eyes as she rests the back of her wrist to her forehead. With her back to me, she paces across the room. When she turns back, her eyes are wide as if she's seen a ghost. "He knows she doesn't remember."

We hurry through the door and start down the hall. "Are you sure you didn't tell him?" I ask.

"No, why would you ask that? I would never tell him anything."

"He lied. *Fuck.* I knew I should have tried to stop her."

Sofie catches up to us. "Here are the keys to the G-Wagon. They'd ride to the lake. It's not frozen solid yet." She tosses the keys to me and starts to cry. "Go. Go. Go. I'll call the police."

I run like my life depends on it. *Because it does.*

39

AN HOUR EARLIER ...

I'M GOING TO DIE ...

Terrified, I hold on for dear life.

Carter and I make it to the lake on the far side of the largest olive grove, the horse finally slowing down. I may have a wardrobe of riding clothes, but nothing about riding a horse feels natural or safe. Now that we're here, I take a deep breath to calm my rattled nerves and adjust my helmet that's lopsided on my head.

Fortunately, I survived, but I don't think I have it in me to ride back to the château unless this horse knows how to walk instead of running like we're being chased. My heart still races, but with Carter, I won't let him see my fear. "It's beautiful," I say, trying to sound casual like I do this every day. Not sure I'm pulling off my best performance, so I stroke the horse's mane and look out over the lake. The sun rises high enough to reflect off the thin layer of ice that's formed, a soft shine in my eyes.

Adjusting on his saddle, he says, "You always loved riding so much."

"Guess it's been a while because I was a bit nervous." *Bit* being a huge understatement.

"No need to be nervous," he says. "Just like riding a bike, right?"

Not at all, but I reply, "I suppose." I don't know how long I can keep up the pretense. I can't believe I agreed to this. I could have made a million excuses for not riding this morning. This was nothing more than my pride getting in the way. Like somehow, I'm proving to him that I can't be pushed around.

I want this to be over and to be back in bed with Loch.

He pulls a thermos from a leather pouch and fills the lid with piping-hot coffee. The steam billows from the top, reminding me how cold I am and causing me to shiver in response. Leaning over from atop his horse, he hands it to me. "Your jaw is chattering. This should warm you up."

He almost sounds caring. *Almost.* I don't know what to believe anymore. He's completely changed now that we broke it off. Was that all he was waiting for? His freedom from me . . . from Céline? Anger isn't shaping his features this morning. Quite the opposite, in fact. There's an air of lightness surrounding him. He must feel the same relief I do. *Thank God.* "Thanks." I take a sip of coffee, and then to keep us moving in the right direction of our relationship —*the end*—I ask, "Did you write a statement?"

After drinking from the thermos, he shakes his head. "I fell asleep. Hazard of international travel."

"I'm feeling jet-lagged myself." I leave out the part about

Loch keeping me up and active half the night. Instead, I add, "I don't think a statement is necessary."

He takes another drink and then looks beyond the lake. A mixture of emotions flickers through his expression when he turns to look at me. The only two I pick up on are the most familiar on him—anger and irritation. "Were you ever going to tell me you have amnesia?"

My heart stops with a thud in my chest, my wrist weakening and the coffee spilling to the ground. *Run . . .* everything in me chooses flight over fight. But I may have missed my chance.

The horse shifts under me as it tries to find solid ground on the uneven shoreline.

His eyes darken as something more callous sets in, a vacancy of the emotions he frequents. Stone cold, he says, "You don't ride anymore, Céline. Not after falling . . ." He points at the far side of the lake. "Right over there three years back. It's too bad you only suffered a broken arm."

"And why is that?" Do I want the answer to that? Good or bad, yes, I do. I need him to say the words that have been on the tip of his tongue since I returned.

Stroking his horse's neck, he grins in his deviousness. When his gaze slides to me, he says, "You're wild and unpredictable. You ran when I thought you'd stay. Now you claim to have fallen in love with some guy you barely know when you couldn't manage to love me. You're mouthy when you should keep it shut. The worst part is you still think you have a say."

I glance back toward the château. It's too far to get there on foot when he'd be on my heels hunting me down.

I scramble to grab my phone from my bag. When I retrieve it to call Loch, it rings, startling me and causing it to loosen in my hands. My only opportunity to call for help slips through my fingers. Directing the reins, he sidles his horse closer. The crush of my phone under his hooves is heard, and my heart sinks.

The cracking glass elicits a neigh from my horse, who starts stomping his hooves in protest. My fear can probably be sensed a mile away. If only Loch could also sense it. I hold the pommel of the saddle as the wind picks up, adding to an already freezing morning.

I won't confirm anything for him. "What if I leave?"

He chuckles. "When I told you I tried to give you a way out, I meant it. When I said I loved you, I meant it. Maybe it's not the kind of love that plays out in books or movies, but our marriage would have been good enough. Our union would have given us the world. Now . . ." His eyes deviate from me.

"Now what?"

When he redirects his gaze to me, he adds, "Now I have to worry about myself and do what's best for me."

"Seems you were doing that all along."

"You never learn, do you? Sometimes it's just better to keep your mouth shut." He pulls a crop from the other side of his horse and whacks the back of mine. The horse rears up as gravity pulls me off the back.

I scream, unable to hold on, and land on my backside, my head bouncing off the ground. Roaring that softens as distance is put between the horse and me.

Purgatory and hell.

That's where I remain—eyes closed, unable to move my body, my mind drifting off to sleep. *So tired . . .*

The ground rumbles under me as the stomping of footsteps circle my body. The rough tips of unfamiliar fingers scratch the skin of my face as a pulsing breath scented with acid invades my nostrils. "There are only two ways out of this, Céline. You marry me, or you need to disappear for good."

Softness brushes over my cheeks, providing comfort from the cold stripping me of heat. His hand presses over my mouth, and I realize the fabric isn't meant to comfort me but to suffocate me.

I gasp for breath, my eyes going wide as I grapple to save myself. I yank his wrist away and turn my head to the side, sucking in air as fast as I can, hoping it reaches my lungs.

He stands, pressing his boot into my stomach. It's not enough to cut off my breath yet, so I use all my leftover energy to scream as loud as I can. I grab his leg to topple him, but he's too heavy.

Giving me a reprieve, he bends beside me on one knee, resting forward and amused as if my fear is for his entertainment. "You think you can outsmart me? I knew you were lying the minute you arrived in Rhode Island. Why would you knock on your own door? Your monogrammed luggage was nowhere in sight. But you know what the real tell was?" He scoffs, glancing around as if there are witnesses to look out for. "Lochlan Westcott."

Loch.

My heart beats back to life as I choose to stare up at the sky over the man who wants to murder me. The slightest move has my back twinging in pain. I'm not broken, but I won't be able to escape. I also won't let him win.

I won't give him a sound or an ache.

Clouds have burned away, but his face blocks the blue sky I'd rather see. My varied thoughts jumping from my body to my surroundings, from Loch to Carter and then to my fate, I say, "He saved me."

"You've always been so unpredictable, Céline, but in New York, I could finally narrow down your routine to a ten-minute window. Enough time for me to do what I had to do."

"To do what?"

"Unfortunately," he says as if we have all the time in the world. "He was the one thing I couldn't predict. Nobody expects a hero these days."

My eyes veer to meet his. "You tried to have me killed?"

Expecting the ice-cold version that greeted me upon my return, that harsh reality isn't there. Sympathy. Kindness . . . the softer side is unexpected and not right as he tries to hold on to something we once had. This side of him scares me more. "No." He leans in and whispers, "I didn't *try*. I *paid* to have you killed. The idiot just couldn't finish the job."

I was supposed to die that day . . . on a dirty street in the middle of the city, left to die as if nobody would care.

Someone did.

Loch.

He cared about me before he even knew me. I hold that close as a shield to protect me. Carter doesn't realize I'm not the same person who left him at the altar. I'm not even the same person who showed back up in Rhode Island. I'm more, both Céline and Tuesday.

And I now remember everything . . .

The wedding.

The promise he broke when I saw him fucking a bridesmaid . . . a cousin of mine.

The new will that was sent over to sign as if I wouldn't read the fine print.

I remember the threats . . .

An implication of my parents' wrongdoing.

The deal that was struck—marriage to a man I detest.

Going to New York to get help to save them.

It's all coming back and clearer than ever before.

He will not win. He doesn't realize who I've become, and I refuse to go down without a fight.

I think about moving, but I hit my head too hard to take that risk. I'd never be able to outrun him, so I use a different tactic. "The millions you've embezzled, the extortion to marry you, and now I'll add attempted murder to the list."

His features harden as his eyes narrow. "I always did admire your spunk. The thing is . . ." He stands over me, looking down. "You're not making it out of here. At least not alive."

Walking the perimeter, he finds a large rock at the base of a post near an olive tree. Carrying it to the lake, he smashes through the layer of ice. Tears fill my eyes as I start to push up. I'll never get away, but I'll fight trying.

Kicking my leg behind me, I force myself up, but I'm grabbed from behind and dragged screaming toward the water. He says, "They won't find anything until spring . . . whatever remains, that is."

My last move to make, the only chance I have to save myself. I kick and swing, but nothing lands, but I manage enough force to get the words out, "It's locked in a safe."

He stops on the edge of the lake. "What is?" When I don't reply, he drops, bending down to get in my face, and shouts, "What is, Céline?"

"Everything you've done."

We stare at each other, neither blinking, though my lids burn in agony. He finally looks away, but I can tell his mind is spinning, plotting by his narrowed eyes. I take the second to soothe my eyes by closing them. When I open them again, he turns back to me, and says, "You're lying."

"I'm not."

"Why should I believe you?"

"Because either way, you're fucked. You just have to decide whether you want murder added to the charges."

"Fuck!" he shouts louder, kicking the dirt as he walks away. It coats my lips and sprays my eyes before I can close them.

I'm grabbed like a rag doll and shaken. My brain rattles in my head, intensifying the ache. "Tell me where the safe is."

I'm dropped, left on the ground, and I can't help but notice that the sky belies the situation I'm in. Beauty against brutality. "Doesn't matter." I manage a grin, but even that causes pain, like every breath I take. "Also, there's another copy out there for safekeeping."

I laugh, but it hurts, so I roll my head to the side and watch as he mounts his horse again. I'm not left with a slurry of threats or shaken until I release the location of the safe.

I'm just left.

Trying to bide my time while tears roll down my cheeks, my chest aches and my heart beats hard against my ribs as if it won't settle until we're safe in Loch's arms again. The emptiness of being left to writhe in pain is no less daunting to overcome.

Stay awake.

I hadn't noticed the leaves of the olive trees until now. Lifting my hand, I admire the ring wrapping around my finger—the branches, the leaves, the trees in the grove are one and the same.

The ring more than spoke to me that day in Tiffany's. It beckoned my memories. I rest my hand on my chest and just breathe. I won't give in, but the weight of my lids causes my eyes to close. I open them again, but they're heavier this time, and it's harder to focus on the sky and trees, the birds that fly in formation in the distance.

The sound of tires.

The name I chose as my own is called out like a prayer.

"Tuesday." Hands cup my face while my lips are kissed with breath to bring me back to life.

I open my eyes to find the comfort of home staring back at me. If it's wrong to smile, kill me now because there's no resisting this man. I reach up, caressing his face like Loch caresses mine, and whisper, "Couldn't get enough of me, huh?"

He chuckles, but it's riddled with relief. Kissing me, he gently runs his hand under my head. "I was about to ask the same thing."

"I'll never get enough of you. So if I have to play the damsel in distress for my hero to save me, I'll do it."

His laughter rips through him, but I see the way his eyes well with water. I taste the tear that falls in my mouth and reach to wipe the next one away. "I was afraid you wouldn't remember me."

"You're the only one I want to remember."

He dips his head to my shoulder and kisses my neck and that ticklish spot below my ear. The sirens fail to drown him out when he whispers, "I love you."

"I love you, too." My lids grow heavy as the embers of my strength begin to burn out.

"Stay with me, baby. Everything is going to be okay."

The sound of Allison telling the paramedics where we are has me lifting my lids. I'm greeted by the love of my life. I whisper, "I could never leave you, babe."

I'm lifted onto a stretcher and placed in the back of an ambulance. Loch sits next to me, holding my hand. "I'm having déjà vu."

"Can we make this the last time?"

His smile—though struggling through his worries—still brings one to my face. "Deal." As the ambulance travels to the hospital, I give his hand a little squeeze. And when I have his full attention—gorgeous browns, lips that I adore kissing, and his love burning bright in his eyes—I say, "I remember . . ."

"You remember what?"

"Everything."

40

Loch

Two weeks later...

"THERE ARE WORSE PLACES to recover than in France."

Tuesday side-eyes me over a slice of onion tartlet and salad her mom made for lunch. Since being here, her parents have spoiled us with amazing meals, but I'm ready for a hamburger. I know Tuesday is, too, because last night she told me that if I loved her, I'd fly in some Wendy's or Five Guys for her. I add, "Are you ready to go home?"

Her mom side-eyes me this time. "What's the rush?"

"Mom . . ." Tuesday cautions with a smile, reaching over to grab a piece of bread to drag it through their family's seasoned olive oil. After eating a lot over the past few weeks, I see why it's won so many awards and sells well. She says, "It's a quick trip, relatively speaking, between New York and France."

New York. My girl speaks so freely about where she

intends to live as if there was never a doubt in her mind that she'd be with me.

"I was thinking about getting a bigger place. Then you can visit anytime you'd like and stay however long," I say.

Tuesday starts laughing. "Famous last words."

Her mom's knife clangs against the porcelain plate. Dane reaches over to comfort his wife, and says, "We'll be there for the trial now that Carter's been extradited on the embezzlement charges." He rubs his forehead, trying to ease his own concerns. "The district attorney is still considering tax evasion charges—"

"I know you have attorneys and didn't ask for my help, but I am a corporate defense attorney. Taxes aren't my specialty, but we have an in-house attorney who can take the case and a killer legal team supporting him." I've not said anything, unsure how they'd feel about me stepping in on their business. Also, my focus here has been making sure Tuesday gets better. When she's resting or wants time to herself, I've been working but did enough digging on the potential charges that could be brought against them to know we can help make this go away.

He says, "They know Carter managed the accounting, and every transaction he made is logged under his employee code, but I'm worried that the DA is still considering pressing charges. Can't we just pay the taxes owed?"

"It's more complicated. You're victims of Carter Bingham's, not the government. They'll argue that it's your company, which means it's your responsibility. Also, some DAs want to leave their mark on the system."

Sofie asks, "What does that mean?"

"The government wants to make a show of things to discourage others from cheating the system. As an outsider without intimate details, I only have what's been made public to go off of."

With his elbows on the table, Dane cups his hands together on top. "Do you have a professional opinion you're willing to share?"

"Since you have an attorney already, this is not legal advice. It's just my opinion." Tuesday is rapt in the conversation. Reaching over, I hold her hand on the rustic table. "I always recommend settling cases quickly and quietly. It's easy to run up legal fees if you don't get good advice. Or the charges are pressed even if you are. I think you put your best offer on the table. Make a deal and end this before you're buried under millions in legal fees."

Tuesday asks, "What's the best deal they can offer the prosecution?"

"Potential prosecution," I say. "There are no charges yet, which means there's no case to defend. I think you get your lawyer to meet with the DA."

"I have no confidence in him. He was handling our domains and filed the last two trademarks. He's not a tax attorney."

"Let me help. As I said, it won't be me but one of my attorneys, so there will be billable hours, but he's the guy you want to handle this kind of situation. He knows every DA in the Northeast. I can't speak for him, but if it were me, offer back taxes paid with interest and throw Carter in for the misappropriation of funds if he wants to prosecute someone." Silence thickens the air, so to break the tension, I shrug. "Or not. Whatever you want to do."

Getting up, Tuesday comes behind my chair and wraps her arms around me, and then kisses me on the cheek. "I'm sure my parents are as grateful as I am." Pressing her lips to my ear, she whispers, "Sir."

Fuck me.

She plays dirty, knowing full well that I'll never be able to hide the erection she just inspired.

Stretching her arms over her head, she says, "I think I'm going upstairs to rest." Massaging my shoulders, she adds, "Take Loch's advice and get the best lawyer you can. It's not worth going to court if you can settle beforehand."

"I know he's right. I think I'm still shocked that we're in this mess. We've always done business on the up-and-up, so this is tarnishing our name and reputation."

I stand, bringing Tuesday around in front of me. "I understand your concerns. I'll help you clean this up, and eventually, no one will care or remember." Turning around, I take her hand and add, "Rest sounds good."

As soon as we reach the stairs, I say, "How tired are you?"

"Let's find out."

We enter the room, and I kiss her, holding her to me and being gentle, which is how things need to be for now. When we reach the bed, I stop just shy of tumbling onto the mattress with her. Doctor's orders have kept our activities on first or second base while she recovers, but that doesn't mean the orgasms haven't been incredible. They have. But I miss being inside her. "I want to make you feel good. Are you up for that?"

"I'm always up for that." She climbs onto the mattress and lies back. "I have news."

"Oh yeah?" I start on her pants, pulling them down. "What's that?"

"I've been given the go-ahead," she says while I'm kissing her stomach.

I stop once the words sink in. Resting my hand on her hip, I look up to be met with her smiling face, and ask, "*The* go-ahead? Like all the way?"

She giggles, but then she grabs the front of my shirt and pulls me to her. "Yes, sir," she purrs. Kissing me, I lean forward until we're both lying together. Our legs tangle as our tongues dance. Pulling back just enough for eye contact, she whispers, "This time, I want to feel all of you. You think you can handle that request, counselor?"

"Trust me, baby. I can handle it."

DANE STANDS from the couch and comes to where I've been working at a desk in the corner of the library. "Let's take a walk, Loch."

My gaze finds Tuesday, hoping to read her reaction to the sudden invitation first. She shrugs and quirks an eyebrow. She's basically no help, which makes me chuckle. Guess I'm on my own. "All right." I close my laptop and follow him out the front door of the château.

"Since you and my daughter are leaving tomorrow, I thought it would be good to have a quick one-on-one talk," he says, glancing at me from the corners of his eyes.

I've gotten along well with her parents and grandfather. Allison left us last week, needing to return to take care of her business. It's been the five of us since—sharing meals, playing board games, and spending time together. Tuesday's recovery has gone so well, which adds relief in the aftermath of what happened. "Yes, I'd like that."

Pointing into the distance, he asks, "You see that?"

"What?"

"All of it. It's all going to be Céline's one day, just like the house in Rhode Island is hers now."

"That's very generous. I know she loves visiting."

We start walking toward the nearest grove of dormant

trees. "I have a feeling that you're going to be in her life for a long time to come."

Forever.

The only word that comes to mind when thinking of her. Not sure how the future in-laws will react to my plan of moving forward with his daughter, though. I say, "I hope so."

"Companies aren't built on hopes. They're made of hard work, taking calculated risks, and focusing on goals." He stops and approaches a tree to rub a leaf between his fingers. "You understand that as a partner at the law firm."

"I do."

"When you choose somebody to spend your life with, they need to share your vision and dreams, take those risks with you, and work hard to achieve those goals. Marriage isn't built on hope. It's built on substance." He chuckles. "Love. Romance. The beauty of sharing a connection with someone so deep that you can't imagine this life without them." Turning to look me straight in the eyes, he asks, "How do you feel about my daughter?"

"I love her. More than anything."

He studies me and grins. "You've sacrificed work and your own life to be by her side while she recovers. You're a good man, Loch." He shakes my hand. "If you had intentions of moving things forward more . . . well, since you're an attorney, I'll use your language—legally. You have Sofie's and my blessing. What you've done for her and us can never be repaid, but we'd be honored to welcome you into our family one day."

"That means a lot to me. Tuesday changed my life for the better, and I don't want to live a day without her being a part of it."

"I know you'll treat her right, but a word of warning. She can be a firecracker."

"All the better."

ONE BLOCK from the coffee shop where we met . . . that's the location of the hotel where Céline Schroder was staying.

After showing a copy of the police report proving she was mugged and had amnesia, the hotel manager pulled her suitcases from a locked room in the back office. "Our policy only requires us to hold them for ninety days. I told our GM that we should give it a while longer. This felt different since it was everything, not just a jacket or shoes left behind." Then she hands a notebook to Tuesday. "This was found in the safe. We didn't mean to pry, but we had no choice since no one came to claim the belongings. We hoped it would lead us to you."

"You read it?" Tuesday asks, holding it in her hands and looking down at it like she wouldn't have minded if she never saw it again.

"I was going to turn it in to the police."

She says, "They have all the information. I had it in there just in case anything happened to me." Tuesday glances at me. When she turns back to face the manager, she says, "I appreciate you holding my luggage. Also, if it hasn't been already, I'd like to settle the bill."

While Tuesday stays at the front desk tying up loose ends, I carry the suitcases to the Escalade, thinking about how close we were for the month she was staying at the hotel. Just around the corner from each other. Coming to the same place for coffee at least a couple of times a week. We were so close, but it took a bad day, coffee, and a mugging to bring us together.

I never thought I'd find love when I least expected it.

Guess I should have since Harbor is a prime example for proving it's true. I'm sure he didn't expect to meet his other half at a gas station. Now look at him and Lark.

Brady comes around to open the back. "Surprised they still had her luggage."

"Yeah, me too." I'll be curious about what she does with it. It's another life, but it's hers to claim. Do the clothes inside suit Tuesday as much as they do Céline?

She's going through a transition in many ways. Her moving in with me permanently is just one. Picking out a place to call home together is the next. Making her my wife will be the icing on the cake. Lots of changes ahead. Good for both of us.

He loads them into the back. "It's good to have her back."

"I'm chopped liver over here?"

Chuckling, he comes around and pats my back. "Good to have you back, Loch."

"It's good to be back." We take our respective seats inside the SUV. I look to see if she's coming yet. Since she's not, I ask, "How's the love life?" Who knew that was going to be opening a can of worms.

I might have lost track, but I think we're in the middle of a story about his third date in two weeks when Tuesday joins us. Slipping into the back seat with me, she says, "Before I got my memory back, I thought I was just running away from my life. I wasn't. I was fighting back the only way I knew how."

"By going incognito with your name and whereabouts until you could get that into the right hands?"

"To handle it properly and put Carter away for years to come."

"He managed to do that himself." I chuckle. "How far did he think he'd get on that horse?"

"He was probably hoping for anywhere no one knew him."

She leans forward. "Hey, Brady, do you mind waiting a little longer?"

"What's going on?" I ask.

Popping the door open, she says, "Want to take a walk with me?"

How can I resist when she's wearing that sweet smile for me? I can't. I follow her out of the SUV and take her hand. "Where are we going?"

"I thought we would go back to where we first met. I could use a pick-me-up."

I give her a little wink while we walk. "I picked you up all right." I can still make her giggle. It's a glorious sound.

Rounding the corner, I see the coffee shop ahead, and although we've visited it before, this time feels different. I bring her hand to my mouth, kiss the top of it, and then say, "I've been thinking about that day."

"What are you thinking?"

Pulling her off to the side of the sidewalk and under the awning of the shop next door, I bring her against me to hold. And kiss. "It wasn't the accident that brought us together. It was destiny."

With her palms on my chest, she lifts up and kisses me. "That's the most romantic thing I've ever heard." Whether she was Céline or Tuesday, my soul was meant to meet hers that day. "Can I buy you a coffee?" she asks.

"Absolutely, but I promised to be back at the office in an hour."

She laughs, throwing her arms up in surrender. "Hopefully, it won't take long. No more complex orders. I promise. I've had enough complications to last a lifetime." We place our orders and wait in the same spots as we did the first time. "Did you know that we met on a Tuesday?"

"Was it?"

Nodding, she comes around to face me. "We did. Out of all the days, it just happened to be a Tuesday."

I wrap my arms around the small of her back. "Did I ever tell you how much I hate Tuesdays?"

"What?" Offense riddles her eyes.

Kissing her, I wait until she's kissing me right back before adding, "But damn, I love them now."

Five months later

It's been fifteen minutes, but nurses are busy, so I continue waiting with the bouquet of yellow flowers in my hand. Tuesday said freesia are some of her favorite flowers, and they'd be perfect for this occasion.

The same compassion Nurse Belinda showed me and Tuesday when we were at this hospital last fall still rests on her softened features when she comes around the corner and sees me. I say, "Not sure if you remember—"

"Of course, I remember you, Loch," she says with a gentle smile.

"I brought these for you as a thank-you."

As if she has all day to spend talking to me, she holds the flowers under her nose and takes a moment to smell them. "For what?"

"You knew there was something between us before I did."

She lowers the plant, smiling. "Sometimes people don't see what's right in front of their face. In your case, it sounds like you didn't miss a thing. I take it things went well?"

I unbutton my jacket and tuck my hands in my pockets.

"When I showed up at the hospital, I had no idea what I was waiting for. I took a chance when approaching her that day. Best thing I ever did."

"I'm glad for both of you. How is she?"

"Pretty well healed, and she has her memory back. She's happy, and I've never felt this happy in my life. Thank you. She's the best part of my life."

She quirks a grin. "Sounds serious."

"It is. Serious enough to finally ask her to be my wife."

41

Tuesday

IT WASN'T where tall grasses grew near the ocean but where the olive trees bloomed. That's where I discovered my happy place wasn't a place at all. It was a person.

I turn back to see Loch on the deck overlooking the ocean, watching over me. He waves, so I wave back. Though he can't see it, I smile because of him. For him.

Taking one last look, I appreciate what this tiny state means to me. Its natural beauty, the water that glistens under the late spring sun, and my childhood. I liked growing up in Rhode Island, but it's no longer my home. *He is.*

Traipsing through the marram grass blown by the shifting ocean winds, I graze my fingers across the tops of the blades along the sandy path leading me back to the house. To him.

My love.
My heart.

My everything.

He says, "ETA is twenty minutes."

It's just us alone for a short time, so I slide my hands around this incredible man and rest my cheek against him. "We can do a lot in twenty minutes." His laughter rocks his body. I look up just to take in the glorious sight of him.

He taps my nose. "A woman after my own heart."

"I'm after your heart, all right." Lowering my hand, I run my fingers over his growing erection. "And other parts."

"You're so naughty these days." *I never get enough of him.*

I shrug with a smile on my face that feels permanent. "What can I say? No one ever impassioned me like you do."

He checks his watch again. Tossing me over his shoulder, he says, "Eighteen minutes."

I smack his ass in pure delight. "Let's get to it, babe."

Making love to him is equally the sexiest and the most beautifully aching thing I've ever experienced. To feel so full, so complete, only to have the physical connection ripped away is torture. I could lie with him all day, and it wouldn't be long enough.

Unfortunately, it has to be.

At least for today.

He's already returning from the bathroom and pulling his pants back on. "I'll take care of everyone so you can take your time." He kisses me before slipping out of the bedroom of the rental where we've been staying for a long weekend.

Staring out the window, I let my mind trace over the past year of my life. From the wedding to Carter, which should have never gotten that far, to seeing Loch at the coffee shop the first time we met.

Handsome.

Irritable.

Despite the obvious bad mood he was wearing like a

suit, the kindheartedness in his eyes had me feeling flus-
tered. I can't say I've ever felt intimidated . . . no, that's not
the right word for it. Captivated works better. Tongue-tied
even fits. I made a fool of myself to try to relate to him. But I
read him all wrong.

The mood was bad, but the element of humanity that
had never been present in Carter's eyes prior was shining
brightly in Loch's. It was as if a bad day didn't taint his
compassionate heart.

It was a dizzying combination for any woman to witness.
That day, I was blindsided not just by his looks, though he's
still the most gorgeous human I've ever laid eyes on, but the
soul that made it known he was worth making a fool for. Of
course, I screwed it up and fell into a train of griping that no
one would find attractive.

I was rude.

I apologized to not only Loch but also the barista who
helped me before the attack. I may have been engulfed in a
series of traumatic events that day, but I'm not that person
anymore, and I felt bad. Loch told me not to be so hard on
myself. It all worked out how it was supposed to. I agree, but
the Tuesday side of me just wanted to make it right.

That act of purposeful change, selling the house in
Rhode Island and putting my designer wardrobe I wore as
Céline up for auction, gave me the fresh start I wanted. The
money raised from the clothes, shoes, and handbags all
went to the shelter I stood before when I thought I had
nothing.

I had the profit from the house invested in the olive oil
company. My parents gave it to me, but after a settled deal to
pay the taxes with interest, just as Loch had suggested, I
didn't want the company to go under. The Rhode Island
house saved it. It was unoccupied these days anyway. They

called it an investment in our family for generations to come. That I could turn tragedy into something good means the world to me.

The day I turned over the keys, I found the Christmas present from Carter still there—a blank check to my own account. *How thoughtful of him . . .*

The door opens, and Allison peeks in. "Get out of bed, you sex fiend. Everyone's almost here."

I'm fisting the sheet at my neck. "Aren't we past knocking at this point in our relationship?"

"Yeah, we stopped doing that around age six." Her fire-orange curls bounce as she flops onto the end of the bed. Looking at me, she adds, "Do you guys ever get tired of doing it all the time?"

I smirk. "No."

"I figured that would be your answer. I broke up with Matt."

"What?" The shock spins my head. "Why?"

"It took Matt years to see me as someone worthy of his love, but that's when I only had you and Carter as role models. You and Loch made me realize I deserve better than to be treated as a last option simply because I'm still hanging around."

Sitting up, I rub her shoulder. "I'm sorry. You deserve better, though."

She slides off the bed and stands at the foot of it. Dusting down the wrinkles of her dress, she adds, "It's for the best. It feels good to make a fresh start." Two peas in a pod, like always. "I'm a New York girl now, so let the dating begin." Heading for the door, she opens it, then turns back and whispers, "Just a heads-up, Loch's mom and sister are already here."

"Thanks."

As soon as the door closes, I get up. It was fun while it lasted and much needed, but no more lounging allowed. I'm ready to see everyone. I take a quick shower and get ready before heading into the living room.

"Hi," I say as soon as I see Delta.

She immediately cuts from her conversation with Marina and Allison to hug me. "It's so good to see you, Tuesday. Oh, do you want me to call you Céline?"

"I'm good with either, but I'm quite fond of Tuesday. It's like I've been given a do-over. This time, I'm going to get my life right."

Stepping back, she nods. "We've got to take those second chances when the opportunity arises. How are you feeling?"

"Honestly, never better. I give the mugging, concussions, and amnesia zero stars. But the life thereafter has been nothing short of spectacular."

We laugh together as she wraps her arm around mine, including me in the conversation the group was having. Marina and I do a quick hug before she says, "If I'm an adult —and by every standard of society, except in my parents' and brothers' eyes, I am at twenty-one—age doesn't matter when it comes to dating."

I slowly back away from that conversation. Talk about a hot-button issue for not only her parents but her three older brothers. I think I'll leave that one for them to weigh in on. I overhear Allison say, "I don't see the issue."

Quickstepping to the bar we set up earlier on the far end of the island, I pour a glass of champagne my parents sent over for not being able to fly back for the weekend. They've come so many other times over the past few months that I have no right to be upset. They're just missed, is all. The Westcotts will keep me busy, though.

The day gets more boisterous as the rest of the family

arrives from different places—Lark and Harbor from Manhattan. Noah, Port, and Lark's dad arrive from Beacon. The grill is going on the deck, the drinks are flowing, and the laughter fills the air. I love this big, beautiful family. Although mine was more intimate with just the three of us, they make me feel like one of their own.

As the sun sets, Loch taps a spatula against his beer bottle. "Hey, hey. We have an announcement to make."

My heart stops along with my breath. His eyes find me in the crowd, and he smiles, but then it falters, and he says, "Harbor?"

Loch comes to me, taking my hand, and leans down to my ear. "I'm sorry. I should have warned you."

"What's going on?"

As Harbor rushes from inside the house to the outside deck where we're all waiting, Loch turns and caresses my neck. "There's no doubt in my mind that I want to marry you, but I should have given you a heads-up about my brother's announcement. It was arranged five minutes ago. I understand how you could think I was making one of my own."

Latching onto his wrist, I smile. "It's no big deal. Really. Don't worry about it." It's ironic that I ran from my last wedding, and now I'm running toward this one with him as fast as I can. I need to learn patience. I continue, and say, "I'm just feeling the love being with you and your family. My heart just got away from me. It's all good, though."

"I love you." He turns so my back is to his chest. His arms hold me as Harbor calls Lark to join him.

"My beautiful wife," Harbor introduces her with a smile that's a mile wide like we all don't already know who she is. Lark curtsies under a laugh and a roll of her eyes. She waves.

We clap, always the supporters when it comes to family.

He takes her hand and turns to her. "You are the love of my life, so I feel honored to not only be called your husband but the father of your child."

Lark melts against him, her head tucked against the man who stole her heart.

Throwing her arm in the air, Lark says, "We're having a baby."

While her dad and the family circle them, I turn to Loch. "They're having a baby." I laugh at myself as happiness for them washes away any awkwardness I felt about this not being an engagement. "Did you know?"

"Yeah. I should have told you."

"No, you're right. This isn't the time. This is their moment." I hug him. "You're going to be an uncle for the first time."

Kissing me, he then says, "And you an aunt."

I roll my eyes just like Lark. "Charmer."

"It's not the title I'm going for," he replies, reminiscent of a conversation we once had.

While he brushes flyaway strands away from my face, I ask, "What title are you after, then?"

Loch once replied with such confidence that he wanted to be my boyfriend. Even then, the title didn't feel enough for what he had already become in my life. "Husband and father of your children."

It takes me a second and a few blinks to see the determination in his eyes to realize what's happening. But it's spying my parents coming out the large sliding glass door that has me covering my nose and mouth with my hands. Tears spring to my eyes. "You are not . . ."

"I am." Loch lowers to one knee as I hear the *oohs* and *aahs* behind me.

"You had this planned all along?"

He laughs, wiping his hairline with the back of his hand. "You going to let me do this?"

Tears spring to my eyes as I drop my hands, cupping them around his and the box. "I'm nervous. I don't know what to do."

The light roll of laughter behind me has me laughing as well. Loch asks, "How about this? I'll say what comes from my heart and then pop a certain question. You can answer from your heart, we kiss, and then live happily ever after."

Although it's all in jest, he comforts me like he always does, protecting me from the unknown because he knows I'm not that big on surprises anymore. He gets me like no other. "That sounds like a good plan." My nerves have calmed, and I clasp my hands in front of me. "I'm ready."

"Good girl." Damn, he knows how to get my attention. He holds his hand out for me, and I happily take it without hesitation. "I wasn't looking for love that random Tuesday in October, but it found me anyway. From that day on, I was a changed man for the better." He looks down, seeming to get as choked as I am. When his eyes return to mine, he says, "If I've learned anything from what we've been through, it's that we shouldn't wait to start our lives when we know how we feel. We must act in the moment, make the most of every day, and love to our fullest capacity. That's what you are to me, Tuesday. You're love. You're life. And I'd be honored if you'd grant me the privilege of being your husband and you, my wife. I promise to spend my life and after loving you forever. Will you marry me, Tuesday Céline Vivienne Schroder, and make me the happiest man alive?" He nods and peeks to the right. "No offense to my brother."

I nod, the words not coming. He pulls me to sit on his

bent leg and then opens the blue box that makes every girl's heart skip a beat. "Loch," I gasp again.

To pretend I don't know anything about the four C's—color, cut, clarity, and carats—would be a lie. I love diamonds, and this amazing one does not disappoint. Of course, he never did. He whispers, "Is that a yes?"

"Oh my God, yes. Yes. Yes. I love you so much. You didn't need a ring to get me to agree. I can't wait to spend the rest of my life with you." I throw my arms around him and hug him so tight, not willing to ever let him go again.

His arms are around me, holding me just as tight when he gets to his feet with me still hanging around him. When my toes touch the ground again, he slips the ring on my finger. I say, "I can't wait to wife you up."

He chuckles. "Is that the same as taking me off the market?"

I kiss him. "You're most definitely off the market."

As we celebrate all the good news of the day, he steals his fiancée away to take a walk on the beach in the moonlight. As we hold hands, our feet leaving prints in the sand, I no longer dwell on my past. Loch and I may have met under unusual circumstances, but we sure did turn that tragedy into something amazing. "I'm no longer Loch Westcott's unfinished business. Loose ends all tied up."

Scratching the back of his neck, he chuckles, knowing exactly what I'm referencing. "About that." He stops in front of me, still holding my hand. "Can I plead the Fifth since I'm a different person now?"

"No pleading necessary. I'm just teasing anyway, but I did want to tell you something."

"What is it?" he asks, the moonlight shining over us and reflecting in his eyes.

My heart squeezes, and my throat thickens with

emotion. "I can't imagine my life if you'd chosen to return to the office instead of stopping for coffee that day. Thank you for saving me."

Caressing my cheek, he kisses me, and then says, "You got it all wrong, baby. You saved me."

EPILOGUE

Loch

"TWELVE YEARS, serving seven before you're eligible for parole. For the guilty charge of solicitation of murder, fifteen years with no option of parole. The sentences will be consecutive. At the time of parole or the end of your served time, you will be extradited to stand trial in France for premeditated, attempted murder. The court is adjourned."

When the gavel lands, I stand with Tuesday, wrapping my arm around her lower back. "Are you okay?"

I can see her gaze set on Carter as he's led from the courtroom. Even if it doesn't feel like in the moment, knowing he could get out, this is a win with the sentencing. I wouldn't be upset if that fucker rots in his cell either.

His accomplice received a lighter sentence since he didn't follow through with Carter's order. However, her stolen handbag was valued at nine thousand, so he took a plea bargain and gave all the details of the murder for hire plot to lessen the felony charge. He'll serve three years before he's eligible for parole.

"I'm good." She looks into my eyes. "Don't worry. I really am."

I hug her to my side. I see no lie in her eyes. She looks relieved. I am too. All of us are. "It helps when they plea down the charges to speed up the process." We walk out of the courtroom and down the courthouse steps with our parents behind us. I can't help but think how these steps are the ones that led me to her a year ago to the day.

The group stops on the sidewalk, circled together. Tuesday says, "Now we can put this behind us and move forward with our lives. I'm starving. How about lunch before we leave for France?"

No one would blame her for breaking down. She's had a traumatic year that sounds like it was already bad prior to the attack. Her inner strength is one of thousands of reasons I find her so attractive. That's my soon-to-be wife.

The bravest woman I know.

"How do you feel?" Noah asks, messing with his tie in the mirror.

"I'm good."

He turns back. "Damn, dude, do you ever get nervous? I don't think I've ever seen you nervous. That's not normal."

"I get nervous the night before a big trial and before a verdict is read. Marrying Tuesday . . . There's nothing for me to be nervous about." I get up from the couch, the leather screeching under the lifted weight, and look out the window where the ceremony is about to take place.

My youngest brother fucking with his tie for ten minutes has me wondering what's going on with him. "Why are you so nervous?"

"Weddings, if I'm being truthful. A lot of expectations are involved, especially with single women when they're in attendance. Everyone's looking for love at these things. Add in the commitment stuff—bouquet and garter tosses, dances . . . yeah, weddings just aren't my thing."

The door to the library opens, and Harbor joins us. "Lark's better now. I think she's tired, and she's definitely hungry. If we're going to be delayed," he says, "she says she's picking olives off the trees and eating them."

Taking one last look in the mirror, I adjust my tie this time. "We should be on time."

"Okay," he says, heading back to the door while scratching the back of his neck. "I'll be quick, but I think I'll find something to tide her over anyway."

When he opens the door, Allison peeks in. "You guys ready?" Harbor slips by her.

"Perfect timing." I walk with her down the hall with Noah in tow. "You look nice," I say, making small talk with her, and because she does. Allison's become more than Tuesday's best friend. She's hangs out at our place a lot, and as I've gotten to know her, she's become like a little sister to me.

Wonder where my actual little sister is.

Allison replies, "Not too shabby yourself, Westcott."

When we reach the back doors, I turn to her because I've wanted to say a few things for a while and just haven't had the opportunity. Now feels a good time. "You know, I never did thank you."

"For what?" She moves the bouquet to the other hand and then picks lint off her dress.

"From the day we met, you accepted without question."

"C loves you. That's all I needed to know." Turning away from me, she looks outside the French doors and raises her chin. "Let's not do any more sentimental stuff. Crying will mess up my makeup."

I nod because it's been said now anyway. "Deal." The string quartet begins playing, but I add, "I lied."

Her eyes go wide, wider than usual. "About?"

"Not getting sentimental. You're a good friend, Allison. Not only to her but to me. Thank you."

She waves me off as she turns to swipe at her eyes. "Yeah, no problem," she replies through a series of sniffles. "Now cut it out. C deserves the perfect wedding, not a crowd of blubbering guests."

"Good point." I chuckle. "How's she doing?"

"She's . . ." Her gaze lengthens as if recalling a wonderful memory. When she looks at me again, a smile reaches her mouth. "She's the prettiest bride I've ever seen, but it's not just the dress and makeup. It's the glow that shines from inside. She's excited to marry you and called you her Prince Charming."

"I've waited all my life for her." *Fuck.* The sentimentality is strong today.

My dad comes around to shake my hand. "You look good, son. You ready?"

Bringing it in for a hug, there's solid back patting. "So ready."

My mom, who's been quietly waiting her turn, already has tears in her eyes. "It's a happy occasion," I say. "Don't cry, okay?"

She comes closer. "You were such a little mama's boy and always had to be with me when you were little." Harbor's back and I can hear him and Noah cackling behind us. Giving them a look, she shushes them. "You two were no different."

When she turns back to me, I feel the gravity of her

words. Although I'm a grown man and I've been on my own for years, this is a different stage of life. A new adventure that leads me to start my own family. She says, "You were my little buddy. My firstborn. You taught me how to be a mom, Lochlan."

My brothers' laughter has died down by the time a tear slips from her eye. I hug her, holding her, her head barely reaching my shoulder. "It's okay, Mom. I'll always be your son."

"I couldn't have found a better match for you," she says, leaning back. Holding my face in her hands, she smiles. "Tuesday is wonderful."

She is, but it feels good to hear they love her as well. Marina and Lark come from down the hall. Lark leans on Harbor with the back of her hand resting on her mouth. "I appreciate the bread, but at this stage, I need to get going down this aisle, or I'm going to be sick again."

Harbor pulls a flask from the inside pocket of his tuxedo and hands it to her. When our mouths drop open, he's quick to say, "Ginger ale."

Ah. I chuckle.

Marina drags Noah up to the front with her, eyeing Allison. "I think you two should be together. I'm fine being alone." Opening the doors, she starts down the short aisle with ripened olives hanging from the tree branches as a backdrop. The setting sun casts a golden hue over our nuptials. She couldn't have chosen a more beautiful time of day, the golden hour as she calls it, or location.

Allison and Noah have met many times before, but they're stumbling around each other like it's a first date or something. So my mom shoos them out the door to keep it moving before Lark and Harbor join them.

I walk my mom down the aisle, passing Nurse Belinda

seated on the third row next to Brady and right behind my family. Flying Belinda in to attend felt like the right thing to do. She played such a big role in our lives that neither Tuesday nor myself could imagine a ceremony without her being there. I then take my position at the altar.

Since it's only family and very few friends in attendance, we have the wedding party seated so they can enjoy the ceremony as well.

Intimate.

Magical.

And us.

I couldn't ask for more than this stunning scenery.

The music changes, and Tuesday appears at the end of the aisle. She's the most beautiful thing I've ever seen. She always has been.

Wearing a dress that complements her so well, fitting at the top and then flowing over her hips, the softer hue is stunning against her skin, the style befitting the château and surrounding groves. She's gorgeous with her hair up in the back while strands fall gracefully around her face. Flanked by her parents, she meets my eyes, and in that exchange, I see a life full of laughter and light, kids and love. I see a future that I never envisioned having before. *All because of her.*

I'm the luckiest fucking bastard ever.

Our eyes don't leave each other's as she walks to me, handing off her bouquet, and taking my hands. I like that her makeup looks natural, and she looks like herself. "You're so beautiful."

"Thank you," she whispers, a blush creeping across her chest and higher to her cheeks.

We opt to say a few words beyond the traditional vows we've exchanged. Looking into her eyes, I say, "There are no accidents in life, and I have no doubt that destiny had a hand in bringing us together. From the moment we met, you left your mark on every part of my life and opened my eyes to what happiness is. I changed who I am. Not for you but because of you. You taught me what love is and how to love life again. I love you so much, and I promise to be a partner deserving of you." Running the pad of my thumb over her knuckles, I continue, "Céline Vivienne means heavenly life. That's what you've given me. That's what we'll share moving forward as one forever. It's your name and who you are, but you'll always be my Tuesday."

Allison hands her a tissue and then waits as she dabs the corners of each eye before handing it back to her. I never want to see my girl cry, but these tears are filled with joy, marking the beginning of the happiest years of our lives.

She takes a breath and looks me in the eyes. "You once told me that you never saw me coming. I never saw you coming either, Loch Westcott, and then you were my whole life—my savior, my friend, a support, my hero, and now my husband. I don't know in what lifetime I did something so right that I get to spend this one with you, but I'll be grateful every day for this chance. I vow to love you through your worst days and cherish the good ones we share. I love you so much."

All the love in the universe is captured in her eyes, along with the sun, moon, and stars above, as she stares into mine, and then says, "I will never regret that complex coffee order because it gave me the opportunity to meet you. And babe, you did not disappoint."

You just met Harbor Westcott, Loch's brother. Now you can read a sneak peek by turning the page.

YOU MIGHT ALSO ENJOY

Recommendations - Three books I think you'll enjoy reading after *Never Saw You Coming*. All are stand-alones that will make your heart race and fall head over heels in love through these emotional stories.

**Turn the page to read a sample of Swear on My Life

Read in Kindle Unlimited and Listen in Audio

Swear on My Life - You met Harbor in Never Saw You Coming. Now read the captivating and emotional journey that will break and heal your heart.

READ NOW

Forgot to Say Goodbye - You will be on the edge of your seat with your heart on the line as two soul mates fight for the future stolen from them.

READ NOW

We Were Once - When one time isn't enough, comes a

sweep you off your feet second chance romance. Free in Kindle Unlimited.

READ NOW

Published in the United States of America

ISBN: 979-8-9861994-7-4

*Visit my website for warnings. Please note this page contains spoilers.

You are not a drop in the ocean;
you are the entire ocean in a drop.

~ Rumi

PROLOGUE

*N*UMBNESS BEATS *the pain I endured, but I realize the next stage is death.*

I close my eyes, too tired to hold them open any longer. *So tired . . .* I just need to rest to save my energy. My breath stalls in my throat as darkness takes hold. Despite what you hear, there is no light to guide your soul.

There's music.

My breath returns as a melody calls me back. I open my eyes to a cloud-laden sky and trees that bend to the will of the stronger winds. Roots creep over the edge of the cliff above me while a bird sings from a low-hanging branch.

Broken, I lie there, captivated by the brown-feathered bird and its yellow mask keeping me company. I grin, but the pain that has returned is too much to maintain, so I listen for hours, waiting for my date with destiny.

An ambulance shows up instead.

CHAPTER 1

Harbor Westcott

ROOM 156.

Row 14.

Seat 20.

I recognize her the second I see the back of her head. *I should.* I've stared at it enough to memorize every subtle strand of brown and golden blond that weaves through it, even when it's pulled and twisted on top of her head like it is now.

She's a nice reprieve from the memories that haunt me, like sunshine shining through a crack in the blinds and the first warm spring day after a long, dreary winter.

As I walk toward her, this is the first time I've been this close. She's five-three, maybe five-four on a good day, though I would have guessed a little shorter, sizing her up in the auditorium.

Usually, I see her dressed in a pair of faded exercise pants with a baggy T-shirt hanging over her waist. Today, she's looking damn good in the denim cutoffs hanging on the swell of her hips, and the shortened shirt doesn't dare brush against the top of the shorts, leaving the slope of her waist exposed.

Though, I'd always wondered what color her eyes were, I'm now given the privilege as she looks up as if caught in a thought. Green and bright despite the shadows of her dark lashes under the fluorescent lights of the convenience store. Her sneakers have hit the pavement a few times, judging by the scuffs and black asphalt staining the bottoms that leave the slightest of prints on the white linoleum.

I've always thought she might be a runner by how toned her legs are and her chosen wardrobe in the past. I like that they're not sticks and hold strength in muscle.

It's not that I'm *not* a tits man, but I do love a great ass. *Hers has been noted.*

I move down the aisle from her, eyeing the groceries lining the shelves. There's nothing I need here, but her sweet scent and my deep-seated hunger to be near her draws me closer.

What am I doing?

Why am I acting like a fucking idiot?

I see her in class all the time, at least on the days I go. But I've never craved her company, not like I do now. Sure, she caught my eye. Lots of chicks do. She's different though . . . seemingly oblivious to my existence inside—and apparently, outside—the classroom, judging by her lack of awareness of my presence.

My ego isn't fragile.

I like a challenge, but I *love* the taste of victory.

My life's been boring walking a straight line for too long. This woman is just the detour I'm looking for. *At least for a night or two.*

I imagine she has a boyfriend, probably some schmuck

back home, wherever she calls home, who's waiting for her to return after graduation. I'd bet a day's work that doting middle-class parents who saved every penny to send their only daughter to an East Coast university are a part of her story, along with a hand-me-down Subaru with another good fifty-thousand miles before the odometer rolls over for the third time.

Such a charmed life she must lead.

My assumptions don't do her any favors, but I never claimed I wasn't an asshole. I was never good at balancing bad deeds while looking the part of an altar boy. Not like Lucas was. My cousin is probably laughing beyond the grave, watching me act like a nervous pre-teen having a brush with a middle school crush.

He might have laughed, but he'd also know that hitting on girls isn't my usual MO . . . Opportunity usually presents itself and hits on me first. We never had trouble turning the heads of the fairer sex.

My innuendoes aren't subtle. She's either playing hard to get or is wholly consumed by the can of Beans & Franks in her hand. I'll assume the latter and make the effort. "Don't get hurt," I say. Not my best work, but we're in a convenience store, so I'm certain the bar is already pretty fucking low. When I latch my gaze onto the pale-pink hem of her shirt, a flash of skin is given when she moves. But I catch her gaze just in time to see it sliding up my chest until her eyes meet mine.

Tilting her head up, she studies me in silence, making it hard to read her thoughts. *Did I screw up?* Is she going to give me the time of day or a tongue lashing . . . must rid that wicked thought from my mind or start praying she's into that kind of play. I straighten my shoulders, debating if I should grab the requested diet soda and move on.

But then a half-hearted smile graces her lips. "Is that a warning?" She furrows her brow as her eyes narrow in the slightest. "Have we met?"

I shove my hands in my pockets, eyeing the full package. *She's cute. Innocent, like prey that doesn't recognize the danger around her.* Not sure she would stand out in a crowd, but she stood out to me prior, even in an auditorium full of people.

"No."

"Are you sure?"

"I'd remember." I'm too quick with a response. If I'm not careful, I'll show my cards, and I'd rather her reveal her thoughts first.

Her expression eases, soaking in the compliment. "You would, huh?"

"Absolutely. I'd never forget you."

She laughs, the sound ringing in the air. "Very charming." Her gaze slides down my chest and back to the can as if it's much more interesting.

"I try."

Sighing, she does the slightest of eye rolls before I'm on the receiving end of her glare. "I have a feeling you don't have to try at all when it comes to girls."

Not seeming to break through her cooler composure, I finally realize I have no game with this girl.

"It was a warning," I reply with full intention.

"For you?" She holds up the small can with an all-knowing grin and sees right through me. "Or this?"

This girl.

Fuck me.

What was I thinking? I just hit on her in a gas station convenience store in the middle of the day like she'd fall at my feet. *What did I expect, for fuck's sake?*

I'm arrogant enough to believe I'm worthy of her attention, so I keep my eyes on her. "If you're wise."

"What happens if I'm not wise?" Her voice is as steady as her eyes are on me, which are locked in place.

Call me impressed. The girl can stand her ground, but I'm also starting to think she might be into me. "You might get hurt."

Her gaze shifts, lengthening to a back corner of the store before she looks at me again. "Sometimes the pain is worth the risk." Her body fills with attitude, shoulders straightening and chin held high. "Don't you think?"

"Guess it depends on the risk."

Biting her lip, she smiles to herself and looks back down at the can in her hands. "You're probably right, but I'll take my chances."

Rubbing the pad of my thumb across my lower lip, I then say, "Don't say I didn't warn you."

"Don't worry. You won't be held liable for any damage in the aftermath." She starts to leave but turns back a few feet away. "We're talking about the beans, right? Like, this isn't our meet cute?"

This girl. *Fuck*. She's got my full attention and couldn't care less. "I don't know what a meet cute is."

"It's how they meet in the movies."

"Who's *they*?"

"The main characters," she replies like everyone knows what she's talking about.

I'm still staring at her, trying to figure out what the fuck we're going on about when I realize what she means. "You're really into movies, aren't you?"

"I am. It's a nice escape."

"From what?"

"Life."

That has to be one of the most honest answers I've ever been given, and I've never felt more understood before.

With straightforward honesty like that, I'm determined to find out why this fascinating woman needs an escape from life. "I get that." There's a pause as her eyes look into mine, seeming to search for answers to questions she hasn't asked.

The last thing I want to do is pour out my heart under the stench of gas or show that side of myself that I've worked fucking hard to bury. I need to get over it. I need to get on with life.

I say, "Did we ever decide what you wanted to discuss? The frank and beans or how we met?"

"Quite frankly, pun intended," she says, laughing lightly, "I'm not sure." I have a feeling that's the only thing she's ever been uncertain about.

She has me competing with beans, for Christ's sake. I'll do it if it gets me closer to her. "How about we find out? You can eat that alone, or we can discuss the virtuous qualities of canned meat and beans versus our meet cute over something we didn't heat in the microwave. What do you think?"

She takes me in unabashedly, not seeming the least displeased with what she sees, but then says, "I'm good," and walks away.

Damn.

I played this all wrong . . . *I played her all wrong.*

But when she starts back to me like she's on a mission to settle a score, I know I've gotten to her. Guess I played this right, after all. She holds the can up and waggles it in the air. "And who said I'll be eating this alone?" Cocking an eyebrow in challenge, she knows she scored the winning point. The rubber bottoms of her sneakers squeak against the linoleum tiles as she heads to the register.

I cover my wounded heart. Okay, not really, but I fucking hate to lose. Throwing my arms out to the sides, I ask, "So is that a yes?"

Shooting me a glare that buries any chance of redemption I thought I might have, she says, "It's a no."

They say you can't win them all, but my record remained undefeated until now. I look around, glad there are no witnesses.

I grab the soda for Marina, almost forgetting the reason I came in here, and head to the counter.

"Hey, how are ya?" the guy asks my current fixation . . . *Is that what she is?* Am I fixated or fascinated? I might side with fascination more than fixated, which borders on obsession. Though by how I've watched her over the last month in class, obsession might not be far off.

I don't like the way he's staring at her with his smarmy smile after a quick rattle of his fingers across the register keys. He dips down on one elbow and smacks his lips together. "I get off in an hour if you wanna . . ." Clicking his tongue, he continues, "You know. I'll even let you come behind the counter. There's lots of room down here."

What the fuck? I move to her side, staring the fucker in the face. "What'd you say?"

"Mind your own fucking business, kid," he snaps.

Kid? He's what? A few years older than I am? *He's got some fucking nerve.*

As if I'm the one in need of defending, she edges her shoulder in front of mine. "First of all, you must be new here." Can't say I'm not impressed and a lot amused. The girl's got bite.

He replies, "Just started Thursday."

Leaning closer, she says, "Secondly, ever talk to me or any woman like that again, and you'll be looking for work elsewhere. I know TJ doesn't take kindly to creeps working his counter." She slaps her money on the counter. "And for the record, I am his 'fucking business,' and I want my change for the soda and beans." Turning to me, she adds, "You good, babe?"

I chuckle under my breath. "Yeah, all good, sweet cheeks." I lean in for a kiss because I'm a fucker like that, but I'm met with her middle finger pressed to my lips.

Tugging me by the beltloop of my jeans, she pulls me close, our bodies pressed together, and whispers, "Save it for later. When we're alone."

Fuck. I think I'm in love.

The change clangs against the counter, all twenty-three cents of it. She slides it into the palm of her hand, skipping the tip jar, before taking the bean can from the counter and walking to the door.

Just outside, the door closes, and I say, "I take it you're not friends with that guy?"

She bursts out laughing as we clear ourselves away from the entrance. Eyeing me, she grins. "Can't say we are."

I shove my free hand in my pocket and look at her as if I'm seeing someone entirely different than the girl inside the convenience store. "It's too bad you have to deal with shit like that."

"Part of being a girl." She tries to shrug it off like it was nothing. It was something and made me want to punch his fucking face.

Although I have no doubt she can take care of herself, a vulnerability entangled in her strength causes my chest to tighten. "He was out of line," I say, keeping my voice low between us.

"It is what it is." She starts to back away. "Enjoy the soda."

The soda reminds me of Marina, who's sitting in the car waiting on me. I can barely make out her silhouette behind the tinted window, but I'm really hoping she can't make me out at all, or I'll be hearing about this over the dinner table at every major holiday meal and then some.

"Hey," I say just to the beauty in front of me. "I owe you for the soda."

"My treat." Her shoulders pop up and then down before I'm met with her back as she nears the corner of the building.

I don't go after her, but I make a last-ditch effort. "For real, let me give you some money."

Glancing back over her shoulder, she shakes her head. "It's a soda. It's no big deal."

"But . . ."

"Really. It's okay," she replies, stopping under the awning of the sketchy gas station. Even the potent smell of gasoline and oil slicks on the ground don't make her any less pretty.

Stepping out on a limb, I close the gap by half, leaving enough distance for her to make her own decisions. "Okay, no money, but what about dinner sometime?"

The corners of her lips slope just high enough to back her entertainment, but her eyes reveal a gleam of interest in the way they shine for me. My breath gets caught somewhere between telling her she's gorgeous and reminding her to steer clear of the trouble I bring.

"You don't even know my name, and you're asking me out?" There's no offense to her tone or in her stance by how relaxed she appears.

I should probably take the opportunity she's giving me to prove I'm not a total asshole. Holding out my hand, I say, "People who know me call me Harbor. You can do the same."

She comes a little closer, the heat of her proximity reaching me. As she slips her hand against mine, her chest rises as her lips part. "Are we friends now, Harbor?"

Since not one PG image crosses my thoughts, friends aren't what I had in mind. I'm not friends with anyone these days, but she might be worth making an exception. "It depends."

I'm not sure why my directness puts her at ease, but her smile reveals only intrigue. She should probably run, get away from me as fast as she can without giving me a second thought. "Depends on what?"

"What happens next."

She laughs, rocking back on her heels. "I have to go, so I guess we'll leave it to the fates to decide."

While the distance we had just closed widens, I throw my arms out wide. "You're not going to tell me your name?" In a class of almost two-hundred students, her name is one of the few things I've not caught. I was hoping to remedy that.

The afternoon sun shines on her. "Isn't it more fun this way?"

"Fun is subjective." I watch as she turns around, her shoulders rattling with laughter. "But I'll play along." *Helps that I know I'll see her in class.*

Glancing back, she says, "I had no doubt you would."

"Do you ever have doubts?"

"All the time. See you around, Harbor." She gives me a little wave before she disappears around the corner.

I could chase her down and ask for her number, but two rejections from the same girl is enough for one day. I pull my keys from my pocket and spin the ring around my finger. Anyway, she's right. It is more fun this way. Just wait until she sees me on Monday.

I walk to my pride and joy—my Ghibli Modena—and open the car door. I don't have time to get in fully before Marina asks, "What took you so long? I thought I was going to die of thirst while waiting."

"I didn't think you'd notice since your eyes are always glued to that screen."

"Okay, Dad," she says in a deep mocking voice.

Handing over the soda, I look at her, knowing one day, if she hasn't already, she'll face assholes who will treat her like that guy in there. That's not a conversation to have now, but one we need to have soon. "Don't ever go to this station."

She looks up briefly, her eyes looking at the building behind me. "Ew. I wouldn't anyway." *Good.* "I don't even know where we are."

It's true, this isn't my usual store or gas station, but it's close to downtown, so I made the detour. I reach over to ruffle my little sister's hair, but she blocks me. "You're welcome, by the way."

"Thanks," she replies, pushing my hand away. "Long line?"

"Yeah," I lie, knowing firsthand that sixteen-year-old girls can be ruthless when it suits them.

I start the Maserati, acting as casually as I can. We don't even hit the street before she asks, "Did you at least get her number?"

The last thing my sister needs to hear about is how I hit on a woman with great legs, an even better ass, and a mouth I wouldn't mind occupying for a night. *And then got rejected.* "You saw that?"

She's at least polite enough to keep her laughter under wraps . . . *until she can't.*

"Everyone saw it."

"I didn't ask for it." *Not a lie.*

Her phone is now the least interesting thing in the car when she angles toward me. "Why not? It seems a shame to let all that flirting go to waste."

"Eh," I say, "I think I'll leave it to the fates to decide."

"If the fates have their way, you just met your soul mate."

Surprised to hear the seriousness in her tone, I glance over at my sister. "Why do you say that?"

"Because you weren't the only one flirting."

I return my gaze to the drive ahead, but there's no stopping the stupid grin on my face. I'm not sure about anything when it comes to the gorgeous girl I just encountered, but she's got me thinking about her and this main character business.

I may not believe in fate, but I believe in myself. Wonder what it takes to be the hero of her story?

ACKNOWLEDGMENTS

I have the team who worked tirelessly to help me bring this story to life. Thank you so much to these incredible professionals:

Brittni Van, Content Editing, Overbooked Author Services
Jenny Sims, Copy Editing, Editing4Indies
Kristen Johnson, Proofreader
Cover Design: RBA Designs
Cover Design: Mr. Scott
Photographer: Andrew Gleason
Model: Trey Baxter
Back Image: Depositphotos - CMfotoworks
Spine Image: Depositphotos - Exile7
Erin Spencer and One Night Stand Studios for producing the amazing Audiobook. Ava Erickson and Chris Brinkley for narrating.

Thank you to my amazing Rockin' Readers!

Alexis Alexandris-Bernreuter, Alicia Reed, Ami Lukinchuk, Andrea Johnston, Andrea Rott, Andrea Werner, Angela DeMarco, Ann Goubert, Ann Jones, Anna Fay, Anne Milne, Astevia Carrera, Becky Wise, Christina Hawes, Crystal Cordova, Danielle Wormald, Dimaris Rossy, Elizabeth Breese, Erin Morton, Heather Pollack, Jami Birnbaum, Jennifer DeJong, Jennifer Miller, Jennifer Orton, Judy Lattin,

Juli Huber Hall, Kari Hansen, Kasey Mccarthy, Kelli Miller, Kelly Drudy, Kendra Parker, Kristen Johnson, Kristy Odom, Lana Berry, Leticia Teixeira, Lisa Dols, Lissete Aberg, Liz Mondaine, Liz Thompson, Lulu Dumonceaux, Lynn Miller, Lynsey Johnson, MaryLee Huerta, Melissa Corson-Rife, Mirele Dourado Pauly, Nicole Westmoreland, Patricia Rohrs, Paulette Hess, Phuong Richardson, Rebecca Andrýsková, Rebecca Fairest Reviews, Rhonda Ziglar, Roxane Leblanc, Sarah Jones, Stacie Christensen, Stephanie O'Rourke, Teri Ann C., Traci Brannon, Trish Sutherland, Vidhi Mehta, Viorela Ivan Lisaru.

To my friends who are not only peers but also friends. I adore you! Adriana, Andrea, Heather, Kerri, and Lynsey.

My husband and sons, my mom, my sister, and my niece - I love you!

www.ingramcontent.com/pod-product-compliance
Lightning Source LLC
Chambersburg PA
CBHW060217030726
47499CB00004B/1088